Whispered Confessions

KT WOLT

Trigger Warnings

Before you dive in, here's a heads-up for readers who appreciate a little warning before things get intense.

This book contains themes of murder, kidnapping, and drugging, which may be unsettling for some readers. While these elements are part of the story, they aren't the main focus.

At its heart, this is a romantic suspense novel with a strong dose of rom-com energy. It's a mix of high stakes and humor, emotional moments and playful banter, all building toward a well-earned happily ever after.

If you're in the mood for something suspenseful, intense, and unexpectedly funny, you're exactly where you need to be.

Take care of yourself, and happy reading!

ABOUT WHISPERED CONFESSIONS

She's a liar, a temptation, and the one thing I can't walk away from.

Surrounded by blood, lies, and betrayal, I assembled a ruthless crew and destroyed my father's empire to build my own. I'm so close to victory—I can taste it.

Everything's on track... until I meet Allie.

The beauty with whiskey-colored eyes and secrets deeper than the ocean. I know she's trouble. The kind of trouble that ruins men. The kind whose whispered confessions will burn you alive.

From the moment I watched her incapacitate a man in a back alley—while wearing stilettos— she's done nothing but spill lies from her pretty little mouth. She's hiding something big, and I'm going to find out what.

She's a distraction I can't afford.

I need to walk away. I need to focus on making people from my past pay for their crimes. But every time I look at her, I forget how.

She should know better than to dangle temptation in front of someone like me. I love a challenge, and I won't stop until I get what I want.

Author's Note:

Whispered Confessions is romantic suspense meets rom-com and features a brooding alpha billionaire, long-buried secrets, revenge, secret identity, forbidden love, he falls first, and a guaranteed happily ever after (HEA). While it contains a few steamy scenes, suspense, violence, and emotional intensity, it's not an erotic romance. Sex is fade-to-black and occurs later in the story. If you're looking for open-door scenes, this book may not be what you expect—but if you enjoy slow-burning chemistry, secrets, and tension that simmers until the very end, I hope you'll stay for the ride. You won't regret it.

ISBN: 979-8-9988412-1-7

First Edition: January 2026

Published by KT Wolt
https://www.facebook.com/KTWoltAuthor

Chapter One

Logan.

When I learn he's outside, it takes all my willpower to not grab my Beretta, walk to the front gate, and end the life of Victor Hemmington. It would do the world good to eliminate him. He's a parasite, clawing for power by trying to create an alliance between our families through an arranged marriage between my younger sister, Kali, and his son, Aric.

Our family is one of the most powerful on the West Coast, yet we have never put our hands into drug smuggling. Unlike the Hemmington family.

The study smells faintly of leather and cigar smoke, the air heavy with years of quiet arguments and polished control. My mother sits quietly near the fireplace, a book forgotten in her lap, her spine straight and her expression unreadable.

"Victor Hemmington?" my father says to our butler. "Very well, Harold. Please send him in." His deep voice resonates around the study, not even muffled by all the old books lining the walls.

"Why not turn him away, Father? You're playing with fire having any connection with Victor."

"For insight. Keeping your allies close and your enemies closer will keep you ahead."

"Bullshit." I grit my teeth. "The Hemmington family tips the scales with their sick fixation on aligning our families, all so he can expand his territory and grow in power. What has your insight done for us?"

"Logan, watch your tone with your father. He's only trying to explain how to handle situations."

This, of course, is from my mother, who's perched in her favorite red velvet reading chair. Always to my father's rescue. Always standing faithfully by her husband's side, no matter whether she feels he's right.

I turn to her, exasperated. "And what? Watch as Victor convinces Father to approve an arranged marriage between Kali and his disturbed son?"

My father should have laughed in Victor's face and buried him behind the vineyard the first day he presented the idea.

He responds for her. "There will be no arranged marriage between our families. You know that. We've done everything in our power to keep Kali out of this lifestyle and will continue to do so. This has been made clear to Victor."

"Yeah, and after your oh-so-clear message to Victor, his piece-of-shit son still showed up to woo Kali."

My father nods and runs his hand through his salt-and-pepper hair. The disgruntled look in his whiskey-colored eyes is one I have become quite familiar with lately. "Yes, he did. And then what happened, Logan?" He gives me a glare that would terrify most men.

Aggravated, I push my blond hair out of my face. I hate how calm he can be in situations like this. I don't understand why he believes there isn't a threat breathing down our necks.

"What happened, Logan?" he repeats.

I don't answer, only glare in response. A war silently rages inside me. I want to confess the truth to him about Kali's feelings, but I don't know what the outcome would be if he knew.

"Nothing came of it," he says relentlessly. "Kali wasn't wooed by Aric's manipulating ways, and nothing has changed. Victor will tire of the chase and set his sights on someone else for his son to marry."

I shake my head but say nothing. He has no idea how wrong he is. Kali believes there is good in everyone she meets, no matter who it is. Case in point: Aric. He did indeed woo her, and if not for me, who knows what the future would hold for any of us right now? I may have gotten Kali's head on straight, but Aric is another story. He knows damn well he charmed her, and that son of a bitch wants to rip away the lightness Kali brings to our dark world.

But I'm not in charge. My father is. He has the final answer to everything, regardless of my opinions.

Victor strolls into our study as if he built this mansion with his bare hands. "James, it's wonderful to see you again."

Several of Victor's men walk in behind him, causing my nerves to go on high alert. Victor always travels with an entourage, but normally only two or three goons accompany him. Today he brought six, and his son isn't one of them. Our study is quite vast to accommodate larger meetings. Their presence, though. It's suffocating.

Something's not right about this surprise visit.

I watch Victor and my father shake hands, my father visibly taking notice of the other men in the room but not showing a care in the world.

Victor strides across the room to my mother. "It's always a pleasure seeing you, Marion. I swear you're more beautiful every time I see you." He raises her delicate hand and kisses the back of it.

This asshole deserves to be gutted like the pig he is.

His gaze finally meets mine. I'm sure he can feel the hatred pouring out of me.

"Logan, you're growing into quite the young man. I recently learned someone has hacked into my security system." He clasps his hands behind his back. "Perhaps, with your extensive knowledge of computers, you could help me identify the perpetrator."

I sit quietly, not giving him the pleasure of acknowledging his presence or addressing him. No doubt he knows that the person who hacked into his system was me. Victor has always been well guarded, physically and virtually. My primary focus is on my father, and I can only hope he's taking note of the shift in the air too.

"Victor, please sit and tell me what this unexpected visit is all about," my father commands.

"Always ready to talk business. I like that about you." Victor ignores my father's request to take a seat. Instead, he paces, his hands still clasped behind his back. He's dressed in his normal Brunello Cucinelli three-piece suit, which puts my father's Armani suit to shame. "James, I came here to discuss your lovely daughter again. It seems my son Aric has taken quite a liking to Kali."

My father smiles. "I'm sure he has. It's impossible not to fall for my Kali. Unfortunately, she doesn't feel the same way about Aric. It's time to put this matter to bed."

Victor nods and turns, pacing away from my father and toward my mother. Every muscle in my body locks up, ready to charge him if he lays a single finger on her.

Speaking to my father but looking at my mother, he says, "You see, James, I don't believe you've allowed enough time for your daughter to make a clear decision about my son. Surely you know it takes more than a couple of encounters to truly know what you want." He turns on his heel. "I'm here because I have a proposal for you. I would like to bring Kali to Chicago with me for a couple of weeks to allow them the time they need to get acquainted. If Kali's feelings don't change, she will return home, and I'll accept that a marriage isn't in their future."

"Like hell you will." The words are out of my mouth before I can stop them.

My father gives a slight shake of his head, indicating with his brief stare to calm down. "Victor, please explain to me, if your son is so interested in my daughter, why he did not grace us with his presence here today."

A dark chuckle erupts from Victor as he reaches the far wall and stops by the bar with its gleaming bottles of liquor and crystal rocks glasses. "My son is a terribly busy young man and couldn't make this last-minute trip. He's dedicated to his work, a quality I'm sure you'll appreciate once he becomes your son-in-law. Rest assured, he's eager to see Kali again."

"How unfortunate that he couldn't make it. I'm sorry, but I can't allow Kali to leave with you. Perhaps Aric would like to pay another afternoon visit," Father suggests.

Victor's face fills with irritation as he reaches for a bottle of bourbon and pours himself a glass. "I see." He takes a sip of his drink, taking time before he swallows. "Well, I'm sorry to inform you that this isn't a request. Kali *will* be leaving with me tonight. I'll leave it to you to decide how this is going to go. These men here are only a portion of what I brought along in case we had any issues."

The tension in the room magnifies. I find myself teetering with indecision about what to do next. I want nothing more than to slice Victor's throat wide open and watch him lie in a puddle of his own blood, struggling for his last breath. But I wouldn't live long enough to watch him die before his men shot me dead.

"Logan," my father says calmly. "Please fetch that bottle of Double Eagle Very Rare bourbon for Mr. Hemmington and me to enjoy while we go over the details of Kali's trip."

"Ah, making your son do your butler's job. I like that idea. Perhaps I should do the same with Aric."

Unbeknownst to Victor, I won't be getting any of our bourbon for him to sip. Double Eagle Very Rare is a code my father came up with when Victor first started showing up in our lives. My father wants me to take Kali to the Oasis. He has made it quite clear that in no way am I to sway from his wishes once the protocol has been invoked by mention of the bourbon.

And I can't help but hate him for that.

I glance at my mother, who remains frozen in her chair. She knows what Father means. This won't end well for any of us.

I nod and rise from my leather chair. "Mother, please come with me. I don't want to grab the wrong one," I say, secretly pleading for her safety. She needs to come with me if she wants to make it out alive.

"Any bottle will do, Logan. Just do as your father requests."

I want nothing more than to scream at her, to shake her and ask why she wants to sacrifice herself. Why we—Kali and I—will never be enough for her. But I don't need to. She never has and never will leave my father's side.

Even in death.

"All right, Mother."

I take one last look at them. This might be the last time I see either one of them alive.

Kali.

My cell phone has been pinging nonstop for the last twenty minutes. I'm never going to finish this painting if that damn thing doesn't stop. I set down my brush, grab my phone, and flop onto my bed, tossing pillows to the floor. I don't know why my mom insists on twenty different pillows for my bed.

I glance at my notifications. Everyone from Oakmont High is heading over to Monica's house to celebrate the end of high school. Everyone but me.

The sad part is that Monica and I used to be best friends. A few months ago, I went to her house for a party. Her boyfriend Linus grabbed my wrist when I was walking by to dispose of my plate. Before I knew what was happening, he pulled me into his lap, gripped my head tightly, and slammed his lips to mine.

I was shocked. Linus had just stolen my first kiss, and he was my best friend's boyfriend. Monica came into the theater room to find us lip-locked. I pushed off him in a rush, causing myself to land hard on my ass while everyone laughed.

"What the hell, Linus?" Monica screeched. Her face was as red as an apple.

"Hey, don't ask me. Your friend"—he pointed to me—"is the one who kissed me."

My mouth fell open at his lie. What the hell? I attempted to tell Monica the truth, but before I could even get a word in, she screamed at me to get the hell out.

I called Logan to pick me up and begged him not to tell Mom and Dad. He never did, thankfully, but he made me promise to stop hanging out with people who don't respect me.

I turn off my phone and chuck it to the floor among the pillows. Logan was right. Other people are nothing but a distraction, and I need to stay focused on my goals. I return to my painting just as my door bursts open.

I jump. "Cheese and rice, Logan! You about gave me a heart attack." I exhale a large breath, my hand holding my chest.

Logan's long strides quickly eliminate the space between us and I see nothing but anguish in his hazel eyes, which makes my heart stop.

"What's wrong? Did Dad make you mad again?"

"We need to go, Kali. Now," he says firmly. He grabs my hand and pulls me toward the door.

I dig my heels into the plush carpet and rip my hand from his. Logan is never like this with me. His whole body is tense, like he's holding a bomb and it's about to explode.

"Logan, what's going on? Are Mom and Dad all right?"

"Would you stop with the million questions and just listen for once in your life?"

I'm in a state of shock from the way my brother just spoke to me. It doesn't take long for my shock to turn into rage.

"No. I'm not going anywhere until you tell me what the hell is going on," I snap, putting my hands on my hips. "I'm not a little girl anymore. I'm eighteen and don't need my arrogant big brother trying to boss me around."

Without a word, Logan grabs my arm tightly and drags me along. His strength is too much to withstand. As soon as we cross the threshold of my room, I hear glass breaking. My heartbeat kicks up, thumping so hard I think it's about to break out of my chest.

I lunge forward, no longer caring about my annoying brother, and beeline to the staircase. Logan yanks me back to him hard.

"Logan!" I shriek.

He covers my mouth and presses a finger to his lips. He tugs me in the opposite direction toward the back staircase, which is only ever used by our staff.

A thud hits my ears, like something heavy falling to the floor, before Mom's scream slices through the house. We both freeze.

"Mom," I barely choke out in a whisper, tears gathering in my eyes. "Please, Logan, you have to help her."

Logan stands still, and I can see the war going on inside him. Why is helping our mother even a question? I know I stay out of the family business, but this is different. I have no idea what's going on and panic is building inside me at a rapid pace.

Logan's cell pings. He takes it out, taps out a quick reply, and slips it back into his front pocket.

"Who was that? Dad?"

Without responding, Logan grabs my arm again, and we take the last couple of steps down to the main floor into the staff's kitchen. Not one of the household staff is anywhere to be found. Logan unlatches the lock on the small hidden door beneath the stairwell. This was my favorite place to hide as a kid when I could convince Logan to play hide-and-seek with me.

Logan's hands wrap around my face as he leans down. "Kali, I need you to promise me you'll stay in here and not come out—no matter what."

"What's going on? I'm scared."

"I know, but you'll be safe here. I'm going to get Mother and then we can all get the hell out of here. Just stay quiet and don't leave this spot."

I nod and climb through the small opening. It's a good thing I take after my mom's size. Dad's always telling me I'm so tiny that he wants to roll me up and carry me around in his pocket.

"Get Dad too, okay?"

His eyes are vacant, as if what I'm asking is too much, but he nods, shuts the door, and drops the latch, locking me in.

I rummage to the farthest point of the cramped area and lie down, trying to piece together what's going on. Logan, Mom, and Dad were discussing whatever shipment was coming in next, but I didn't know anyone was coming by tonight.

I turn my attention to the ceiling right above me, and the sight that greets me causes a sob to escape. It's been so long since I hid here that I forgot about my painting on the wooden ceiling. I painted it years ago while my family was discussing business. Again. Like they always do.

A strange smell reaches my nose. Smoke begins creeping underneath the door. I don't know what to do—break down the door and try to find where everyone is or stay put like Logan told me to. With the smoke getting thicker, I'm about ready to kick the door open when a loud bang rattles the small locked door that's keeping me hidden. I slap my hand over my mouth to muffle my whimpers. I can hear strange men grunting, the sounds of fists breaking bones heavy in my ears. A gunshot rings out a minute later, and I hear something heavy—a body?—hit the floor before all falls silent again.

I've never wanted a gun until this very moment. Not that I would be a good shooter. I'll never forget the day my dad and Logan convinced me to shoot one of their guns. It was a Colt .45.

The way my dad gazed lovingly down at me after I missed the first five shots, smiling his beautiful smile. He told me he was so proud of me. I never understood why; I only hit the target once. I wish I could go back in time and practice more. Become the daughter who could hit the target every time. I could use that skillset right now.

Tears burn the backs of my eyelids. I cough into my arm, my chest hurting. I pull my shirt up to cover my face from the irritating smoke.

I wonder if I'll ever see my mom and dad again. I wonder if I missed the opportunity to tell Logan I love him one last time. I lie in the smoky darkness, praying that Logan will return with our parents any minute now.

But as time passes, I become less hopeful. I don't know how long I've lain here, but my head pounds and my nose is running.

My eyelids grow heavy. If Logan hasn't returned yet, he probably isn't going to. And that means he couldn't get Mom and Dad in time. Pierced by the realization that my family is dead, I allow the fight to drain out of me and darkness to take over.

My eyes burn badly. I feel I've been walking through the desert for weeks on end. No, not walking. I'm bouncing. My head is throbbing, my throat is dry, and my chest feels tight. Like I've been a lifelong smoker of two packs a day.

What's going on?

I crack my raw eyes open and see nothing but trees. We're in the forest behind our home. Logan's face is covered in something black.

It hits me with as much force as a freight train slamming straight into my chest going a hundred miles per hour. There were strangers in the house. Glass broke. Logan put me in that secret closet, but not before I heard our mother's screams.

"Lo—" I choke before I start into a coughing fit. My chest feels trapped in a vise, and it's tightening.

"Shh, it's all right, Kali. We're almost there."

Logan's voice is strained. I'm tired and every breath I take is a painful wheeze. A light glows behind his shoulder. *What is that? Did Mom turn on all the lights in the house?* I bury my head in his chest and close my eyes, trying to create tears to relieve the dryness.

I must've fallen asleep because the next thing I hear is Logan talking with someone.

"No, you don't get it. Victor had six men with him when he showed. After I hid Kali, there were more than double that number. Maybe triple." Logan's hushed roar echoes through my ears.

"How's that possible? Harold wouldn't have allowed that many guys to pass through the security gate."

"I don't believe Harold is alive to explain what exactly happened."

"Harlow?" I cough, dragging my eyes open to see her. Her long chestnut hair is pulled into a messy bun and she's wearing jeans and a simple T-shirt.

"Hey, baby girl, don't you worry at all. You're going to be all right, okay? Everything is going to be all right." By her tone, I don't know whether she's trying to convince me or herself.

"Mom. Dad," I say as Logan opens the back door of Harlow's truck, which I didn't even notice we were next to. He lays me across the seat. A blanket is tossed over my body. I try to roll to my side to sit up, but my arms are too weak.

"Come on, let's go. I have a medical team waiting for both of you," Harlow says.

"I'll meet you there. I'm going back."

"What? No! That would be suicide, Logan. The house is burning down. We need to get you both safe and treated, then devise a solid plan. I can't lose you too, Logan."

"I'm not negotiating with you. I'm the boss now and it's time to take this asshole out once and for all. Don't stop for any reason. Get straight there and text me when you have an update on Kali's health."

If Logan's in charge now, that can only mean one thing. Dad didn't make it. And if Mom isn't here, she didn't either. The wetness that I've been fighting to achieve easily fills my eyes. If I'm right and they're gone, that means I only have Logan left. If he dies, what reason is left for me to live?

"I'm coming with you," I cry, attempting to sit up.

Logan's hand presses me into the seat before his face appears in front of me. "You can't. I should've gotten you out of there right away like Mother and Father wanted me to. I already messed that up."

"They're gone? They're really gone?"

Logan's hazel eyes well with tears, but not one falls. He leans forward and kisses my forehead before he pushes out of the vehicle.

"Logan, please don't leave me. I can't lose you too." I sob. This whole situation feels so surreal. One moment I was painting and annoyed with my so-called friends, and the next... I can't even go there. I'm not strong enough for this. Not alone.

"Drive as fast as you can, Harlow. I'll be in touch," Logan states in finality before he shuts the door.

An image swims up in my mind's eye: a memory of a day my whole family was in the wildflower field at the Oasis, sun-drenched and laughing. Our lives will never be the same.

Chapter Two

Allie.

I have worked too hard for this to not happen. Every time I take two steps forward, I get knocked back three. But not this time. Not today. I'm tired of getting knocked back.

I abruptly halt in my tracks and get a hard shoulder from a person rushing along the sidewalk. Grumbling, I dip into a side alley and dig out my phone.

Harlow is the only person who can help me. The squeaky wheel and all. She answers within a couple of rings. By the tone of her voice, I can tell she has been dreading my phone call. Good. That alone makes me smile.

"I just need one name. One person I can help." There's honestly no need for formal greetings. She knows exactly what

I need because it's all I have talked about over the past month. "Fletcher is only giving me until the end of the week to get him the name of a family. Otherwise, he's going to donate to some stupid foundation where only pennies of each dollar actually go to the charity. We both know that only puts money into pockets that don't need it."

"Meh. Don't listen to him." She sounds ostentatiously unconcerned. "If you can't find anyone in need of his security system, he isn't going to pull the trigger on whatever tax write-off he wants. He technically has until the end of the year to donate."

I love Harlow. I really do. But sometimes she can be as frustrating as a cat that doesn't know whether it wants to stay in or go out… or in… or out. She introduced me to my boss Fletcher, so she knows damn well he will do exactly what he says. It's taken years to get him to agree to this.

I owe Harlow my life, though, and because of that, I try to bite my tongue. Like I do every single day. When all I want is to withhold her wine and .357 until she succumbs to my requests. "But you know a ton of people who could use this. I don't understand why you won't give me one name. I promise I won't tell anyone who I got the name from."

Harlow and my parents go way back. They helped fund her business when she first took over from her grandparents. She strived to create a place where all are welcome for any kind of assistance they need.

Need a place to lie low? Go to the Oasis. Need stitches and a few bullets pulled out? The Oasis has a full medical team on staff 24/7. You can go there to recover or hide out, all while your enemies could be there at the same time, and no one sweats the load. It's safe. It's neutral ground. And everyone knows if they go against Harlow's strict rules, they will be on the outside looking in.

"Everyone I deal with is loaded to the gills, and you want to talk about putting money in the pockets of people who don't need it."

I sigh loud enough for Harlow to hear it. "What about all those people who were strapped financially, but magically their bill was next to nothing?"

Silence carries over the phone, and I find myself holding my breath. I lean against the old brick building. I'm not against begging, pleading, and laying the guilt trip down thick. Lord knows I've had to do plenty of that over the past seven years.

"I need this, Harlow. I want to help people like you do. I don't understand why it's okay for you to do it, but not me. After your inspirational speech about needing to be fearless in the pursuit of what sets my soul on fire, I thought you would be there to support me."

"I said that to you years ago!"

"I was moved," I reply.

"And I was a few bottles of wine in when I said it. I didn't think you would hang onto it like a witch with her voodoo doll."

"What can I say? You light the fire in my soul."

Harlow mumbles under her breath, "Like a damn barracuda."

"Thank you?" I say, posing it as a question. Hopefully, she can't tell I'm now grinning from ear to ear.

I can feel her exasperation over the phone. Which is good. I'm starting to break her down. Hopefully not too late. Time is ticking to find a family to help, and it's not a question you can spring on strangers. "Excuse me, I know you don't know me and I don't know you, but do you have anyone in your life who hurts you? Abuses you? Perhaps wants you dead? Well, great. I'm the woman for you. And let me tell you, I have just the solution you need."

I'm sure anyone would wonder what madhouse I escaped from. Not that I could blame them one bit, but that doesn't mean I won't do it if it comes down to it.

Social media would be a tremendous help. I could stalk unknowing candidates and see who is living through hell, then try to rope them in. But I'm not allowed to be on any social media, even under my Allie identity. The risk is too great.

Harlow lets out an audible breath as if she might be tired of her little barracuda, as she so politely put it. "It's not a safe job, Allie, and you of all people know what extremes I go through to stay in control of these... businesspeople. I know you want to fight this battle and bring justice to your family's murderer, but you're not to that point yet."

By businesspeople, she means Mafia, cartels, corrupt politicians, secret societies... I could go on. I did enough snooping around while I was living with Harlow to discern that those people are on a whole other level. I also know that most of them are good people inside.

"You know how hard it is for me to sit back and do nothing. I'm tired of sitting on the sidelines. What's it going to take to prove myself?"

"Oh, sweetie, I wish you never had to go through any of this, but you need to be smart. We're making progress. I just heard late last night another two guys have been eliminated. It won't be long until everyone is gone and you can get your life back."

Get my life back. I'm pretty sure I will never have my life back. I might as well have died that night right along with my family. Something like that changes a person's soul. No matter how positive I stay or how hard I work, what will really change when the endgame finally happens?

When I was younger, I never cared or wanted to be involved in my family's business. Even as I got older, I still had no desire. My parents never pushed me into any of their meetings. In fact, reflecting on it, they pushed me away from things like that. But now they're gone and everything has changed. I no longer want to be kept in the dark about anything entailing my family.

A noise comes from behind me. *Did someone just get slapped?* I glance over my shoulder. Nothing.

"You still there?" Harlow asks.

I purse my lips.

"Look," she says. "I need to run. A new family should be here any minute now. I'll give Fletcher a call to extend this nonexistent deadline of yours."

"Yeah, all right," I reply. Maybe Fletcher will agree to Harlow's request in case he needs a place to go one day. One can hope.

"Keep your head up. We'll figure something out. Love you, girl."

"Love you too. Go save the world. I'll just hang out and wash my hair."

I end the call without another word. People can sympathize with you all day long, but no one truly knows what it's like to carry this emptiness in your heart. Time heals nothing. You only learn how to live with it.

I dump my cell into my bag and hear the same noise again. I whip around to see a dark-haired woman falling to the ground with a man standing over her.

Oh, ho, ho, ho.

He picked the wrong day, time, and place to do something like that. This is exactly what I need to blow off some steam. I march deeper into the alley, my black heels clicking loudly on the dirty asphalt below. I watch the man's head snap up. His eyes narrow.

Yeah, buddy, it's time a woman teaches you a lesson or two about hitting a woman half your size.

He snaps at me, "If you're smart, you'll turn that sweet little ass around and mind your own damn business."

Ha. I love when a man thinks he can demand anything from me.

"Oh man." I pout. "That's really too bad. You see, my Glock G43X really wants to come out and play today." I ignore the way my body is shaking. I can only hope he doesn't see it. "But now..." I trail off, letting him assume the worst about how that sentence ends.

For good measure, I lock my shoulders and tap the side of my purse to indicate said gun.

Is it in my purse? Absolutely not. I don't even own a gun. They honestly freak me out. I don't mind shooting them from time to time with Harlow. I mean, I don't have anything against guns. I merely prefer not to carry one around. You never know when it could accidentally go off, shooting a hole in my foot. Or worse, my purse. That beautiful stretch of leather took months to save up for.

His eyes go large. That means he can't tell I'm about ready to pee my panties.

I approach and notice that the woman is younger than I originally thought. She's seventeen, maybe eighteen, by the looks of her. I give a reassuring smile and offer my hand to help her up.

"Come on. Let's get out of here before I get charged with prison time for murdering this pathetic pimp."

She stares at my open hand, my nails painted Barbie pink, and her jaw drops open. She must not be used to women taking charge of their own lives.

Don't let the pencil skirt and blouse fool you, honey. I should invite her to one of the Krav Maga classes Harlow set me up with.

"Th-that's my father," she whispers, an internal battle evident in her demeanor.

I drop my extended hand, taken aback. What father would ever hurt his own child like that?

"That's right, so get lost, lady. This is a family matter." He spits as he speaks. Disgusting. Didn't his mother teach him any manners growing up?

I glare at this soulless man. I can tell just by looking at him that he's made bad choices in his lifetime. The deep wrinkles in his face have aged him and the scars slashed across his cheek don't help matters. But taking his misdeeds out on his daughter isn't going to fly with me.

"That's going to be a hard no," I reply with a glare.

I offer the girl my hand again right at the same moment that the man decides to charge me. I try to sidestep, but in four-inch heels, that is easier said than done. His arms cage around my waist as we fall onto the pavement.

His daughter cries out, but I can't focus on her at the moment.

I have never been more thankful for my Krav Maga classes than I am in this moment. I break my fall, so the impact doesn't affect me as much as it does him. If I have learned one thing in my classes, it's to react quickly. I instantly go for his eyes as he tries to roll on top of me.

He yells out in agony as my nails dig in, causing him to roll to his side. I jump to my feet and away, breathing hard but ready for anything he's got. I just hope I don't have to take these heels off. This alleyway is gross with all the trash lying around.

I keep my eyes locked on the man who holds the worst dad in the world award as he tries to get up. I do what I have learned in my classes. I kick him right in the ribs. Hard. He collapses to the asphalt, coughing roughly from my blow.

I'm about to grab this girl and make a break for it, but the telling sign of a gun cocking from behind me has my legs frozen in place. This situation just went from bad to worse.

The man on the ground doesn't seem to notice we have a guest as he again struggles to get to his feet.

A deep voice booms behind me. "I would highly recommend you don't move another inch." I have no idea if he's talking to me or this guy.

I want nothing more than to turn around, but I find my feet rooted in place at this stranger's command. This is just my luck.

The girl's father gazes up at him blearily, no doubt having trouble seeing. His reaction is the only way I will know what I need to do. Whoever is behind me makes his skin go pale. "Mr. Mc-McCollin, I'm sorry, sir. I didn't know she was with you," the girl's father sputters as he drops to his knees.

Didn't know I was with him? What is he talking about?

The stranger stands close behind me, his minty breath hot on my neck as his voice softens. "Are you all right?"

I suck in a deep breath, trying to calm my racing heart. I turn on wobbly legs to face the new guest.

I've never seen a man so beautiful, so gorgeous, that I've lost my breath. Where a simple response is too much for my brain to comprehend. Until now.

He isn't wearing a suit or covered in gold rings that call out "I'm powerful—bow to me." No, this stranger holds all his power in his icy-blue eyes. He's dressed in dark denim pants, a plain navy shirt that fits snugly around his large tattooed biceps, and black combat boots, topped off with a backward black hat.

His clothes may be casual, but they are made of the finest material. I would know. I used to have a closetful of fine fabrics.

His chiseled jawline and straight nose are so sharp, he should have gone into modeling. Or maybe he is a model? His dark wavy hair shows slightly underneath his cap.

I'm having a hard time deciding whether I should mention my nonexistent Glock or make out with him.

"Who are you?" These are the only words I'm able to get out. His eyes blaze into me as if he can see all my secrets deep within my soul. It sends a shiver throughout my body, but I can't seem to pull my gaze from his. It's as if he has hypnotized me within a matter of seconds.

His lips tip up from one side as if he won a bet. "Why don't you take the girl and get out of here? I will…" He pauses as if choosing his words carefully. "Handle the rest."

His voice sounds better than the sweetest song I have ever heard and he's not even singing. But somehow, it commands compliance. The deepness of it rocks through my body. I've officially lost my mind. How can I find a man who just got done telling me is going to *handle* the situation so sexy?

It doesn't take much common sense to understand the meaning behind that. I must be a total idiot if I am being mesmerized by a man who clearly intends to hurt another individual. Then again, the guy on his knees behind me does have it coming to him.

He cocks his brow, probably wondering why I'm still standing here like an idiot, practically drooling over him.

I turn on my heel, take the girl's hand, and head back to the main road with her in tow. I refuse to look behind me. If I want any of my senses, I have no choice but to not look back. That man is a distraction I can't afford.

We are a block away before I notice the cut on my forearm and feel the road rash on my upper thigh. Great. I hope this heals before the expo this weekend. The last thing I need is Fletcher telling Harlow I'm all marked up.

"What's your name?" I ask the girl. I stop, causing her to do the same.

"Sofia," she whispers.

She continues to stare at the ground. My heart breaks for her. I'm not sure what went down between her and her father just now, but regardless, he had no right to hit her.

"I'm Allie Smith."

Sofia gives a slight nod, still refusing to look at me.

"Are you all right?" I ask gently. Based on the red handprint across her cheek, she took a hard hit.

She sniffles before nodding again.

Maybe this is it. This is the person who I can help. She seems like the perfect candidate. Yeah, so she might not have a home to put Fletcher's security into, but I can figure that out later. I damn sure won't let Fletcher install anything into her father's home. I'll just leave out that minor detail with Fletch and we can go from there. In the meantime, she can stay at the Oasis.

"Listen, Sofia, I can help. I have a friend who has a place you can stay. It's only a couple of hours from here. You would be safe there."

She stands frozen, reminding me of myself after my family was murdered. Lost, confused, hopeless. Not knowing whether life is worth living anymore.

"I can get you set up in a home. One for yourself, with state-of-the-art security that no one could ever breach. No one could threaten to hurt you again."

"Why would you do that? You don't even know me. For all you know, I could've deserved that." Her voice is light as a feather.

I grab her other hand, which has a small heart outline tattooed on her pinky finger. I bend to look into her downcast eyes. "Because I understand. I was in your shoes once. Well, wait, no. Not exactly. My dad was great to me, but he was taken from me. Before he passed, he taught me what it was like to be loved, to be listened to, even when I knew I was driving him batty with my wild stories and artwork."

Sofia lets out a laugh, one I would have missed if I wasn't watching her so closely. She shakes her head. "It's more complicated than that."

"Hey, I'm all ears. I can tell you that no matter what you think you might have done wrong, no father should ever lay his hands on his baby girl."

Her brown eyes rise to meet mine. Despite her evident fear, she's beautiful, with long dark brown hair that seems to flow effortlessly around her face. I bet she has every boy pining after her.

"Thanks for the offer, Miss Allie, but I think I'm going to pass." She squeezes my hands and pulls away, taking a step back.

"Please don't tell me you're going back to your father's home."

If she says yes, I'm going to kidnap her. She would have backed me into a corner with no other reasonable options.

"My father made it clear today where he stands. I have a friend I can stay with." She takes another step back.

I'm running out of time. "Wait, hold on one second." I dig through my purse and pull out my business card. "If you change your mind, please call me. I meant it when I said I could help you. Anything you need."

She takes my card in her small hand. "You work at Shield Tech?"

I'm surprised she's heard of it. When I was her age, my biggest concerns were what movies were playing at the cinema and which trail I was going to hike.

Fletcher's grandfather started Shield Tech decades ago, but Fletch has been able to take it to the next level. Shield Tech is now the largest developer of security for homes and businesses afar. If you have the kind of cash it takes, he can make any place impenetrable.

"Yeah, I've been there for a few years now, and we're looking for a person to help out this year, free of charge."

Sofia nods and slips my card into her pocket. Without another word, she pulls up her hood and turns on her heel, heading down the busy sidewalk.

I let out a rushed breath and lean against the building. At least she took my card. I debate following her, but she's already shaken enough.

I examine the cut across my arm. It's bleeding, but I doubt I will need stitches. I've had worse in Krav Maga class. I should have enough supplies in my first aid box to push the skin back together and clean it up.

I glance at my watch. My Krav Maga class started twenty minutes ago. "Dammit." This is the first time I have missed one.

I turn on my heel, intending to head to my GMC Jimmy, when I slam into a hard body. I let out an "Oomph" as large rough hands wrap around my arms to keep me from falling back. I don't have to look up to know who it is—his minty scent surrounds me.

It's warm and muggy today, but that doesn't stop the chills that run down my body at the realization I never heard him approach. I'm never like that. Well, not anymore. I've made it a habit to be aware of my surroundings. Harlow made sure of that.

"Look at me." His voice is deep and rough. My gaze lifts to meet his on command. I'm guessing he's over six feet tall. I might be short, standing at five feet three inches, but with four-inch heels, I still struggle to meet his eyes.

I wonder what else is large about him.

His eyes are as blue as Peyto Lake, a place my family visited many years ago, but I can see the danger that lurks behind them. The hardness within them. His eyes are the exact reason I should be running the other way, yet I find myself leaning toward him.

"You're bleeding," he says.

I assess the damage to my arm. Why? I have no idea. I already did that, but apparently, I want to do it again.

As soon as I do, he slips his hand under my chin, gently lifting my head to meet his gaze. "Come with me. I can get you patched up."

My face slackens at his offer. He may be the hottest man I have ever seen, and he may have helped me in that alley, but

I know a dangerous man when I see one. "What's your name?" I ask.

"You already know my name."

I shake my head until I recall Sofia's father calling him by his last name. "Mr. McCollin."

"You can call me Gage," he says as his thumb caresses my cheek. The way his touch is lighting my body on fire, I won't be able to stand in the next minute.

"Gage," I whisper, testing his name on my lips. I hate that I love his name. And his touch. And his eyes.

"And you are?"

At the rate my heart is beating, he might as well call me one fry short of a heart attack. "Betty. Betty Jones," I blurt. Why I didn't give him Allie Smith is beyond me. It's not as if that's my real name. But I guess my fifth-grade English teacher's name will have to do.

"Betty Jones," he repeats suspiciously.

It's clear he's questioning my honesty, so I swiftly pile some bullshit on top of the lie before he can process the name.

"Yeah, Betty Jones from Kansas. Never been to Seattle before, but my husband likes to pull out surprise trips all the time. I'm sure I have *tourist* stamped across my face." I glance around, wide-eyed, like I've never seen so many brick buildings in one place. "So here I am, walking around, taking in the sights. That mountain here is something else, don't you think? I'm going to climb it. Not today, of course."

He smiles quizzically, revealing an irresistible pair of dimples.

I gesture at my heels. "These babies aren't met for hiking, let me tell you." I let out a light exhale. "So yeah, I think I—we—will go tomorrow. All depending on the weather. I didn't realize how hot it was going to be here." I look up at the sky as if the clouds must be magical and at any moment a unicorn is going to leap out of one with a rainbow coming out of its ass.

"Where's your husband?"

"Oh, psh, he's not here, obviously. *But* he's right around the corner. I'm surprised he hasn't come hunting for me yet. He's a big—huge—man. Abnormally large. He has so many trophies for wrestling, cage fighting, martial arts... You name it, he's got it. He's the overachiever in our marriage." I laugh and top it off with a wink for good measure.

Gage is still caressing my cheek, his attention completely locked onto me as if I'm the main attraction of a circus show. Now that I think about it, I guess I am.

"I really do need to get going. We still have a ton of things to do today. You know that chocolate factory here?"

His lips curl upward ever so slightly. I hope it means he's buying what I'm selling.

"We're about to head there and then we're off to dinner and—oh! Then we're going to jump on one of those romantic boat cruises where some guy plays a violin, just like they do in Paris. Oh God, Paris. Have you ever been to Paris?"

I put my hand on my chest as if it's my dream location, but in reality, I'm checking to make sure my heart isn't about to give out. When his only response is to arch one of his perfectly manicured eyebrows, I take it as a cue to continue.

"Mmm, I haven't been there either. But I'm going to go one day. With my husband, of course. And our dog. That furball is a mean little sucker, though. Took a bite out of our neighbor's kid just last month like he was taking a bite out of crime. Vicious, even with his heart defect that means he can't travel by plane. So, instead of going to Paris, we brought him here. But once that old furball kicks it, I'm booking our flights the next day." I give a light chuckle before meeting his icy-blue eyes. They remind me of a black hole that wants nothing more than to suck me into its twisted orbit.

After a moment of silence that makes time feel frozen, I can't take it anymore. I ask the one question that I cannot seem to figure out. "Why are you still caressing my face?"

His hand freezes against my cheek, his body going stiff, as if he didn't realize he was doing it. His hand drops away, and I hate that I miss his touch immediately.

What in hell is wrong with me? I don't care that he looks like he just walked out of a *GQ* modeling gig and his touch is like magic. I can't date. I would have to lie about everything since my life is so upside down.

I take a couple of steps back to create some distance between us.

He watches my every move, making me feel like an antelope trapped in a lion's gaze. His scrutiny slowly drops down my body and takes in every detail of me. It's unnerving and causes me to squirm. I lock my shoulders, ready for what might come next.

"You hurt your leg."

Oh. I glance at my leg and can feel the road rash burning my skin. To my surprise, beyond the dirt, there's no sign that my leg is hurt or bleeding. "No it's not."

He raises his eyebrow at my denial. "You're favoring your right leg. You should let me look at it."

I take another step back. Gage tilts his head to the side as he assesses me. "Why are you afraid of me?"

"I'm not. My husband should be here any second."

He takes a step closer. It feels like a game of cat and mouse. "Why do you keep lying to me? What are you hiding?"

"I'm running late." I don't know what it is about this man that has me jumbled up on the inside, but I need to end whatever this is.

He shakes his head. Disappointment crosses his beautiful face, and I can't help but feel guilty.

"Listen, thanks for the help. It was nice meeting you, but I need to head out. Don't want to keep the ole ball and chain waiting." I laugh nervously, turning on my heel.

I'm now heading in the wrong direction, away from my old SUV, but I couldn't bring myself to walk past him. I can feel his eyes burning into my back every step I take. I pray to not fall on my ass; my nerves have gone haywire, and my legs feel wobbly. If I do, he will demand that I allow him to care for me.

The farther I get away from this mystery man, the more I know I made the right choice to take the long way to my Jimmy. He isn't just a normal bystander in this world working a nine-to-five job. No, he's bigger than that. He's a man on top, sitting on his throne without a care in the world.

Watching everyone with a close eye as he controls the strings of every puppet beneath him.

And if Sofia's abusive creep of a dad knows him, I'm betting his throne rests atop dead bodies.

As I get ready to turn the corner, I chance a glance over my shoulder to see if he's still there. His artic-blue eyes drill into me and I inhale deeply before whipping my head back around and turning the corner.

I managed to avoid two outcomes that were destined to be destructive.

And to think that Harlow believes I'm not ready yet.

Chapter Three

Allie.

It's only Tuesday, yet it already feels like the longest week. I drop my purse under my desk and head to the kitchen area for some overdue coffee. Sleep eluded me and I wish I could say it was caused by being banged up yesterday. But that would just be another lie. My restless night consisted of artic-blue eyes, a chiseled jaw, and muscles wrapped in beautiful artwork.

Gage McCollin holds forces within himself that no woman could simply ignore. His self-confidence is untouchable. He looks as if God himself crafted him inch by inch, slowly and with the utmost accuracy. That voice of his sings in the deepest tone and his fresh scent of spring and mint.

Slap a bow on him and he becomes every woman's wish when she blows out her birthday candles.

Unfortunately, I don't celebrate birthdays any longer. I do, however, dream a lot, and I have a feeling Mr. Artic Eyes will be making quite a few appearances in the weeks to come.

Grabbing a caramel coffee pod from the stack—which is three-quarters empty, compared to the full stacks of dark roast and decaf pods flanking it—I fire up the Nespresso machine and brew a cup. Thankfully, the cleaning crew that works for the owner of the building comes in on Wednesdays and will refill our supplies tomorrow night. I head back to my desk and plop down, checking my voicemail first to make sure Sofia didn't call.

A half-dozen voicemails later of nothing but vendors who will be presenting at the International Security Expo this weekend, I put down my phone. I didn't expect Sofia to call so soon, but I needed to make sure.

The intercom buzzes and Fletcher's voice comes across my desk. "Allie, stop by my office. We need to go over preparations for the expo."

I press the button and respond that I will be right there. I'm Fletcher's only employee, as I learned quickly that he doesn't trust many people with his security inventions. Even though my title is assistant, I like to look at myself more as his right-hand woman. Outside of planning the expo, I manage his calls, arrange meetings with his clientele, and handle all the paperwork and logistics. Basically, I do anything and everything that is needed.

I stand and flatten my black skirt. It's one of my favorites because it goes with absolutely every blouse I own. Because of my sleepless night thanks to the person who shall not be named, I only had enough time to pull my hair into a sleek ponytail. I take after my mom and her thick blond hair. I remember complaining to her about how long it would take just to dry. She would always tell me one day I would be grateful.

I'm still waiting for that day to come.

I grab my coffee and notepad and head across the room to Fletcher's office. We are located on the twenty-ninth floor of Transcend Towers. There are only thirty-three floors. From what I've heard, the top four floors consist of offices and a penthouse for the owner of the building, but no one has ever seen those before.

Or the owner.

I give a light knock, enter without waiting for a response, and see Fletcher typing away at his computer. I take a seat across from him and get myself arranged while I wait for him to finish.

His office is beautiful, like the rest of the space that Shield Tech takes up. The floors are made of black galaxy marble that is dusted with silver flakes, making it feel as if you are walking on the stars. The walls are bright white and the furniture is a mixture of black and white with silver accents. The wall to the right has a built-in bar with the finest liquor known to humanity, followed by the door to his own personal bathroom. The back wall is covered with monitors and six different computers. Yes, six computers.

Fletcher is nothing more than a hot computer nerd. Muscular, with long brown hair that normally looks better than my rat's nest. Not only is he hot, he's smart and the best in the business. No one comes close to competing with him.

The wall to the left is my favorite, and it isn't because of the floor-to-ceiling windows, which overlook the Cascades. Though the sight of the mountains alone will take your breath away every single time, Fletcher normally has the shades drawn. Which is exactly how he has them now.

What makes that wall my favorite is the beautiful mirror that stands from floor to ceiling. Every one of his clients questions why Fletcher would want such a large mirror in his office, but only a select few know what the mirror is.

I am one of the few who do, and the only reason is because of Harlow and Fletcher's relationship. They don't call it that, but I do.

They have known each other since childhood, and from what I gathered over a couple of years living with Harlow, Fletcher would make overnight trips out to the Oasis for some "business" that needed to be handled.

They can think they're sneaky all they want, but I know damn well a business meeting doesn't leave you walking out with your hair a mess and your lips swollen. The. Next. Morning.

But that's none of my business. I love them both. Even if Fletcher doesn't even know that Allie isn't my real name.

Back to the mirror. What makes it so amazing is this: Not only is it a double-sided mirror, but there is a safe room hidden behind it, and if you don't place your hand in just the right spot, you'll never find the entrance.

It's one of Fletcher's greatest inventions, in my opinion. The walls are built with steel, and several four-foot-thick cement posts hold up the ceiling in the small room. There isn't much in there except a staircase going up to a small platform. At the top of the platform is a picture of Fletcher's grandfather hanging on the wall. Behind that picture is a safe. The only thing in the safe is a jack-in-the-box toy.

I never laughed so hard in my life when he showed me.

It's brilliant because it's a distraction from what the room really is, which is an exit.

There is a small button underneath the second step—or wait, maybe it's the third step? When you push it, the staircase rises to reveal a hidden stairway underneath that goes downward. Once you reach the fifth step on the hidden stairway going down, the floor above drops back down. That way, in case someone does break in, they won't realize there is a hidden exit.

Being up on the twenty-ninth floor has its disadvantages for escaping unnoticed, but Fletcher put in a secret elevator that the hidden stairway leads to. It will shoot you straight down to the underground parking garage. He even keeps an old crapper Impala down there to get away in. We call it the rusty hoopty.

Some might call him paranoid. I call him smart. Our clientele isn't always the Mary Poppins type.

"Sorry about that, Allie," Fletcher says as he locks his computer to give me his full attention. "I got a call from Harlow last night."

My cheeks heat with embarrassment. "I'm sorry. I didn't ask her to call you. She offered and I should have told her not to bother you."

Fletcher waves his hand, dismissing my explanation. "Have you not been able to find a family to help yet?"

I shake my head. "No. Well, maybe? I just met her last night. Sofia. I stumbled across her in the street. Her dad was hitting her."

It's funny how quickly the irritation crosses his face. He drags his hand through his long brown hair, narrowing his gaze. "Care to tell me what you did when you saw that?"

Absolutely not, but those words don't come out. I know better. Ever since my family was murdered, Harlow went to great extremes to keep me safe and alive. Even though Fletcher and Harlow are five years older than me, they act like overprotective parents at times. "It wasn't a big deal. There was an officer close by and I got him. End of story."

Fletcher leans back in his chair as I keep my face set in stone. If he knew I threatened to take Sofia's dad down with a nonexistent Glock, I might as well pack my bags and head to the Oasis.

"There was an officer present while a grown man hit a child?"

"Yeah, can you believe it? Ha. Well, he had his back turned when it happened, but yeah, he was right there. He came over flashing his badge like some comic book superhero. It was quite the scene. Then BAM! He slammed him to the ground and cuffed him in three minutes flat. It was like being in that show *Cops*. I couldn't get the 'Bad Boys' song out of my head all night."

Fletcher steeples his hands under his chin with a hint of impatience.

I scramble to steer the story closer to reality. "Oh, and she isn't a child. Well, she is, but she's not a little kid. She's older. Maybe seventeen, but I'm not sure. She didn't tell me her age.

Not that I asked her what her age was, but she didn't give it out freely. I gave her my business card to call me so we can start setting everything up, but nothing was on my voicemail this morning, so—"

He puts his hand up, and for that, I gratefully stop. I would have kept blabbering on if he hadn't.

"What happened to your arm?"

I glance at the bandage and shrug. "Burned my arm on the oven last night when I made lasagna."

His eyes narrow as he watches me intently.

I yawn.

"What was the officer's name?"

"Um." I look up at the ceiling as if his name is on the tip of my tongue.

"Or the badge number? Perhaps when he was flashing it around like a superhero you saw it."

"Oh yeah, for sure. It was 347. Wait, no, maybe it was 247." I bite my nail, focusing on the beautiful floor, where I can see the cleaning company missed a spot. A nice-sized dust bunny is snuggled up against his big black desk. They're probably overworked and underpaid.

"The cleaning crew is not overworked or underpaid."

Whoops. Guess I said the last part aloud. I take a play from his book and throw my arm around, dismissing the faux pas, before I reply, "Anyways, yes, it was 227."

"You just said it was 247. Which one was it?"

"Honestly, I have no idea. The sun was reflecting off it. I think that cop takes a lot of pride in his badge and must polish it on the daily. It was impossible to read." I slump back into the chair, feeling as if I just ran a marathon and never made it to the finish line.

"And you're telling me the truth?"

I nod, not trusting myself to open my mouth again. You never know what kind of garbage will come flying out, and quite frankly, we don't have all the time in the world. The expo is four days away.

"Do you have a last name for Sofia?"

Finally back on track. "I don't."

"What about her father's name? Did you get that?"

"Nope, but let me tell you, she's the perfect candidate. I told her all about the program and how we can help."

"Let me get this straight. You're telling me that you found a possible underage girl, you don't know her last name, you don't know where she lives, and you don't even know if she has her own place outside her father's."

"Minor details. What's important is that she's interested."

He pinches the bridge of his nose. "How are we supposed to locate her when we have no idea who or where exactly she is?"

I debate mentioning her father being acquainted with Gage McCollin but quickly toss that idea out. One, it won't go with my story, and two, that probably won't get us any closer to finding out Sofia's last name. "You should stop looking at the glass half empty, Fletch. I have a good feeling about this one. I say we have at least a 50 percent chance she'll call." I watch his face turn a shade of red. "How's your blood pressure, Fletch? Are you feeling all right?"

He shakes his head, mumbling something I can't make out under his breath. He grabs the remote for his wall of computers, turning on the largest screen behind him.

"Have you heard from Antonio's on the menu yet?"

Apparently, we are done talking about Sofia. On to work. "They left a message confirming they'll be ready Saturday. They're requesting a walk-through of the kitchen."

"Great, that's good news. Are they supplying the bartenders?"

"No, Roxanne is."

Fletcher nods as he makes notes on his computer, which I can see on the screen directly behind him.

"Have you decided which new inventions you're presenting?" I ask, wondering if he will bring forward his double-sided mirror safe room. I hope not. I like being one of the elite few privy to it.

"Not the complete list, but I'm working on it. I'm debating showing the—"

He's interrupted by his door opening. The screen goes black behind him instantly.

I whirl around in my seat, wondering who in their right mind would think they could barge in on Fletcher Roxwell. He might be a James Bond nerd, but he's stacked and has little patience for the majority of humankind.

My breath catches in my throat as my eyes hit artic-blue ones that send an electric shock throughout my body.

Crap. How am I going to talk myself out of this one?

Chapter Four

Gage.

I feel as if I walked through this door and into a dream. The mysterious little liar who escaped me last night is perched stiffly in a leather chair before me, clearly as surprised to see me as I am to see her. Her throat flexes as she gulps audibly.

I had my best guy Link run a check on a Betty Jones from Kansas last night, even though I could tell she was lying through that pretty mouth. I was hoping maybe her name was partially right, though she looks nothing like a Betty.

As expected, he only got a handful of potential hits and none of them matched the age or description of this mouthy angel.

Link is the best at what he does. Any background check I need, he can get it to me within the hour. Any security cameras that need to be checked, erased, or turned off, he's on it.

His combat skills are strong, but he prefers to stay incognito most of the time. I trust this man as much as I trust my longtime friend Conner, who is currently trailing right behind me.

Conner Hayes is as loyal as they get. The thick white scar that runs down his temple to his chin causes people to start praying when they see him. But even without any scars, his size alone will have people turning the other way quicker than lighting their ass on fire.

"Gage, what a surprise," Fletcher says, rising from his chair to shake my hand. "What brings you here today?"

It takes every ounce of willpower to peel my eyes off her, but I manage the impossible. Just barely.

Grasping his hand in a mutual firm hold, I give my attention to Fletcher. He's a long-standing ally I met through Harlow several years ago. The man is the leader in security and has done several of my homes and warehouses throughout the world. He's not cheap, but no one can compete with his level.

What I want to understand is how this little vixen and Fletcher know each other. I always thought Fletcher and Harlow had something going on behind the scenes.

"I wanted to discuss the expo's guest list with you, but I see I have interrupted something." I turn my gaze to the frozen beauty in his leather chair.

"Not a problem. We're just finishing up."

I turn back to Fletcher. His eyes move to her and, if I'm not mistaken, turn softer. I find my hand locking into a fist at that gesture. An unexpected move on my part that shocks me.

Fuck. I don't even know her name and she already has me twisted inside. The caveman inside is pounding against my ribcage, begging to be let out.

He says, "Go ahead and call Antonio's to schedule the walk-through. Let them know it needs to be tomorrow. Start going through the guest list to confirm reservations for anyone we haven't heard back from yet. I'll email you a list of the other security firms that need to come in earlier than originally planned to set up their booths. We need to spread them out so everyone isn't arriving at the same time."

The mouthy vixen stays completely silent, only giving a nod. She grabs her notepad and coffee before leaving the room. After the soft click of the door shutting, I swear I can hear her exhale in relief.

She can feel I'm a dangerous man and wants absolutely nothing to do with me. Her refusal to acknowledge me and her quick departure is more than telling of that. I have no doubt she's hiding something behind those whiskey-colored eyes, and the urge to find out what is growing by the second.

She didn't tell Fletcher she met me last night, which is interesting.

Is this her husband or her boss? Though the softness that filtered through his eyes when he looked at her suggests he cares deeply for her, I'm putting my money on the latter. He didn't offer to introduce us as anyone of significance to him. If she were my woman, I would shout it to the world.

One thing is for sure: She's no tourist. Maybe a mistress? I dismiss that thought immediately. I may not know her yet, but my intuition has never steered me wrong. She could never be a mistress. The stark shift in her demeanor since yesterday is telling, and it only intrigues me more. She shouldn't dangle something mysteriously sweet in front of my eyes.

"Please, have a seat," Fletcher says.

I lower into the chair she was just in, while Conner takes the one next to mine. The seat is still warm and her scent surrounds me. A beautiful mixture of cherry blossoms and wildflowers, smelling as beautiful as she looks. I inhale deeply, thinking of her underneath my hardened body, coming undone in pure ecstasy as I rip orgasm after orgasm out of her sinful, tight little body.

Conner clears his throat, pulling me out of the dream I haven't been able to leave since I met her last night. I glance over and see confusion written across his face. I'm never distracted. Ever.

Fletcher pulls up the guest list behind him on a large screen. He wastes no time giving me what I came for. He's intelligent enough to know it's in his best interest to accommodate me in any way necessary.

That's why I like the guy.

I adjust my baseball cap to the backward position and lean forward, placing my elbows on my knees as I scan through the list until I see the name I was expecting to see. "Aric Hemmington. Has he confirmed he's attending?"

"Not exactly. He requested an invite, but he's become a ghost since then."

I nod, resting back in the chair. Aric is known for his games. This is nothing surprising. "Will he come?"

"You got me. Hell if *anyone* knows what Aric's motives are. He's craftier than his old man."

Fletcher's right. Aric is the only son of Victor Hemmington and has shown he is just as hard to nail down as his father is. Victor's defenses have proven to be top-notch and impenetrable. Aric could be the only weak link in Victor's armor... and the only way to get answers about my mother's sudden passing.

I'm not looking to blame anyone but myself for her death. I'm the one who drove her away from our family and into the arms of Victor. I am the reason she went to that cliff. But I will serve justice to everyone involved in her death. Just as I am serving a lifelong sentence of turmoil and guilt.

Confronting Aric is my ticket, but his ability to stay just out of reach is wearing my patience thin. Aric likes to showcase boredom in everything he does, but I can see his front from a mile away. I don't trust that cat. He is a mastermind who has a plan for everything.

"I can have Allie make that her top priority when she is confirming the reservations."

It takes me a second to realize who Fletcher is talking about. It appears Betty Jones does have a name. The thought of Allie talking to Aric makes my blood boil.

He would devour her in two seconds flat, and if anyone is going to do that, it will be me.

"No, I want *you* to handle the guest list. This is too critical."

Fletcher leans back in his chair. "With all due respect, you're in no position to tell me how to operate my business."

"I don't want any danger to come to Allie. Aric's too unpredictable."

My words hit their mark. Fletcher only takes a moment to agree. "I can make some calls, see what I can find out."

My phone buzzes in my pocket. I drag it out to see Link's name on the screen. I can't believe it took him this long to call me about my whereabouts.

I stand. "Do that. I need you to make this your top priority. This may be our only in with Victor."

To Conner, I say, "Update Mr. Roxwell on everything else we have and come up with a plan for this week regarding what you two will need to do. Aric didn't request an invite for no reason at all. He's coming and we need to be prepared."

"You got it, boss," Conner says.

I suppress the flicker of annoyance that passes through me at his words. I wave my phone at Fletcher. "I need to take this call. Make sure to free up some time this evening. I might need to tweak a few things and need you on board."

Fletcher nods.

Link's first call ended, but he's calling me again. I answer and exit the room. The desk across the room remains empty, so I take a few steps off to the side, looking down a hallway, but it's clear as well.

Where did my little vixen disappear to?

"Link, you got anything?" I answer as I walk farther down the hallway, glancing in doorways to try and find her.

"Yeah. Some asshole is at Shield Tech when it was planned for only Conner to go talk to Fletcher." He's pissed. I can hear it in his voice. Link doesn't like it when plans change. He claims it's reckless. He might be like a brother to me, but that doesn't mean I'm going to follow his rules, no matter how much he tries.

"Aw, you miss me already?"

"We had a plan."

"I changed my mind. You should come out as well. I'm meeting with Fletcher tonight. Bring your mystery girl. Conner and I have waited long enough to meet her."

Anytime we get a break from work, he takes off for the night to spend with a woman Conner and I know next to nothing anything about. We can't blame him. One of two things would happen. We would either scare her off *or* she would want to jump our bones. Either way, it's a lose-lose situation for Link.

He ignores my comment. He always does. "I gave you Fletcher's list last week, so explain to me why you needed to see it from Fletcher himself?"

"As soon as you explain why you aren't here right now. This entire time, you've been gunning for Victor as strongly as I have, yet you still haven't come out of your man cave."

"Maybe I should have after you had me run a background check on a Betty Jones last night. You getting distracted, man? What was that even about? Can't find anyone under sixty-five who would put up with your ass?"

"Listen, if you can't handle getting your hands bloody, no judgment here."

"Fuck you," he says.

I chuckle. Link has never batted an eye to killing anyone to date, but it doesn't mean I can't give him some shit. "You're not my type."

I hear him grinding his teeth on the other end of the line. His dentist should thank me for that bill coming down the pipeline.

"You know I have to stay here with all my equipment, you asshole."

I hear the light clicking of heels and head back up the hallway. Leaning forward, I peek around the corner to see my little liar returning to the empty desk, dropping a thick folder on top of it. She glances around nervously, and I know it's because of my presence. I watch her flip her nameplate and push it behind her printer.

No longer interested in firing Link up, I walk out from the hall and head straight for her. Her eyes are downcast. She's unaware of being stalked. She's mumbling unhappily to herself. A smile creeps across my face.

"Let me know if you find anything. I have some other business I need to attend to."

Link grumbles and hangs up. I don't hide the noise of my footsteps, causing her to jump and take notice of my approach. *She thought I was still in Fletcher's office.* My walk is slow and confident. The jig is up.

I slide my phone into my pocket as I reach her desk. Her eyes go wide like those of a startled fawn. I snatch her nameplate, which is poorly hidden, and read it aloud. "Allie Smith."

Her gaze darts to Fletcher's door. She's breathing heavily, her chest rising and falling quickly.

"Easy." I lean against her desk, wishing it wasn't between us. She sinks back into her chair, probably wishing it could swallow her whole and she could vanish in a puff of smoke. *Not this time, sweetheart.*

"No hiking today with the husband?" I ask, taking my time to look at her completely. She is a remarkable sight. Her long blond hair is pulled back. Simple diamond stud earrings, a silky purple blouse that hugs her every curve, and a tight black skirt that rests just above her knees. She's tiny, but her body is toned to perfection. After witnessing her ability to break away from a man twice her size, it's clear she does some type of training.

"I'm filling in for the day. I don't work here."

I remain silent, watching her go to war within herself. Waiting for her to admit that this little charade is over. Silence will always say more than a thousand words and when you give that to someone, they start to panic.

She lets out a defeated breath. "Okay, okay. Betty Jones was my fifth-grade teacher. I don't know why I even lied to you yesterday, but please don't say anything to Fletch—Mr. Roxwell—about last night."

"And why not?"

She glances at his door before leaning in closer. She's completely oblivious that I can now see perfectly down her top and the black lace bra she is wearing underneath. Her voice turns low. "Because he's a real asshole. You know, the typical grade A prick who thinks no woman is at his level. He would be furious if he found out I took down a man last night. He only hired me because of a mutual friend. But hey, I need the money and can handle the heat. Breaks and lunch, ha. What are those? Don't worry, though. I already have a meeting with HR later this week." Her voice drops lower. "Don't tell him I said that either."

From the way Fletcher's eyes went soft when talking to her, I know that's another lie. I also know that Fletcher doesn't have an HR department at Shield Tech. He follows the same tracks as his grandfather, believing that the fewer people involved, the less risk you run of someone stealing your inventions.

Which tells me he must trust this clever beauty without a doubt in his mind to have her as his assistant.

With her leaning in closely, I take the opportunity and wrap my large hand around her wrist, finding her pulse racing. She has a small heart-shaped birthmark on the underside of her wrist.

Her entire body goes stiff at my touch. She's weighing her options. Fight, flight, or freeze.

I give her another choice. "Breathe."

She stays frozen in place for a moment before she takes my advice, dragging in a few deep breaths. After a minute, her pulse slows a bit.

"Good girl," I say.

She licks her lips in the most delicious way. As strongheaded as this woman is, she yearns for a man to take control. Even if it's only in the bedroom.

"Do you have a husband?" It's not the question I should be asking, but the thought of her being underneath another man sends my thoughts into an inferno. She's not wearing a ring, but that doesn't mean anything nowadays.

"No."

"A boyfriend?"

Her pulse is starting to quicken. She glances at my hand wrapped around her tiny wrist and shakes her head.

Good.

"Why were you in that alleyway last night?"

Her eyes narrow to slits, reminding me of an angry kitten. It's adorable. "I was walking by and heard that man hit his daughter. What did you do to him after we left?" She's still whispering. I smile at her reversal tactic. It's admirable, but it isn't going to work. She's hiding in plain sight, and I need to know why.

"You thought you could take on a full-size man by yourself, little lion?"

She defiantly lifts her chin. "I was handling the situation just fine."

And she was. Her skill level is clearly advanced. Anyone could see that. Ricardo, the man I witnessed her drop, could testify to her strength. But Ricardo isn't a real man, and she would be wise not to pull that stunt on just anyone. Not that she would listen to me right now if I told her that. She's on defense and I need to change that.

I look at the bandage job on her arm from the cut she took when they crashed to the ground. "A woman who needs no hero. Are you trying to break every man's heart?"

She snorts. "The only thing breaking would be their fragile egos."

I laugh, clutching my chest with my free hand. "You're surely shattering mine."

My little lion rewards me with a small smile. It's sweeter than any victory I have ever won.

"Not everyone is powerless to your good looks."

I release her and stand at my full height. "So you *do* think I'm good-looking."

She raises an eyebrow at my smug smile. "Yeah, sure. If you're into the whole boy-band aesthetic."

"You're telling me you aren't?"

She shrugs, a smile teasing to be released. I take a step back from her desk and bring my hands to my chest, creating a heart symbol with them, and thump it across my chest. I follow up with a one-eighty turn and point to her.

"Like this?" I ask, smirking.

Allie bursts out laughing at the absurdity and quickly covers her mouth to repress the sound. It's the sweetest laugh I have ever heard. I bounce three steps to the right, then back to the left, pounding my arm into the air.

"Oh my God, you are downright crazy."

I laugh, feeling lighter than I have in a long time. "Hey, now, don't hurt my feelings here. You know that's cool."

"What I do know is Fletcher has cameras out here."

"Well, shit. Now your asshole boss is going to steal my secret moves."

Allie shushes me.

"What? Isn't that what you called Fletcher? An asshole? The typical grade A prick?"

"Stop! He is going to watch this whole feed tonight because he doesn't have a life," she says in a half whisper, half yell.

"Have no worries, my lady. I have a guy who can delete it." I wink.

She shakes her head, her body more relaxed now. "All right, Mr. McCollin, why are you really here?"

"What is your part in the expo this week?"

Confusion crosses her face. She may know some people Fletcher does work for aren't for the faint of heart, but she can't know how bad some of these men truly are. I must be the starting act for her.

"Aligning the vendors and other security firms, confirming the remaining guests on the list, staging the expo." Her angelic voice is soft. I could listen to her talk for hours. Even if it is lies about nonexistent husbands, vicious dogs with heart defects, and asshole bosses.

"Fletcher will be confirming the rest of the guest list now." I hold my hand out and nod to the folder sitting on her desk.

She changes from a sweet kitten to a raging bull in one second flat. No joke. It takes everything I have to not smile at the claws coming out. She doesn't take well to *some* kinds of authority, I see.

"Why, because you're not on his list?" she snaps, her body wound up like a spring.

I should have figured she would have checked the list the second she left the office for my name. I may not be on it, but that's all right. I will be running the show now. "Give me the folder."

"Why is it so important to see a guest list for an expo? What's really going on?" She might be a hot blonde, but she isn't dumb. She knows this isn't normal protocol for Shield Tech's yearly expo. I find her confidence intoxicating and annoying.

"Maybe I just want to see if my old high school buddies are going to be there."

Her eyes narrow to little slits, as if she is trying to burn me alive.

I can't help but let out a small chuckle. She is too damn cute for her own good. "Why did you lie to me last night?" I ask, snatching the folder off the desk since she clearly isn't going to give it up freely.

"Why do you dress like that for business meetings?" she retorts, crossing her arms.

I don't have to wonder why she asks that. I'm sure the clients she is accustomed to come in wearing three-piece suits and dresses that cost thousands. I'm dressed as casually as you can get, more like a street gangster than a member of a boy band. My washed-out jeans and white T-shirt contrast against the dark ink that spreads across both my arms. My favorite black baseball cap—the one my mother gave me right before she decided I was a lost cause—fits snugly against my head.

I choose not to show my power with what I wear, and quite frankly, I don't need to. My name and reputation alone do that. I may have just shown her a side of me that not many people have witnessed. What can I say? I'm young at heart and she's easy on the eyes. My mother had quite an impact on me in my younger years. What I can say is that no one dares to cross me unless they want to meet their maker.

Instead of telling her any of that, I decide to give her some honesty, in the hopes that she will do the same in return. "Because every day I dress like this, I hope my father is rolling over in his grave with disgust."

Her thick lips drop open at my truthfulness. Fletcher's door opens and I turn to both Conner and him approaching us.

"Everything is in order," Conner says.

"Great. Fletcher, we'll be by later tonight to discuss the rest of the changes."

He nods.

I turn to my little lion. "Betty, it's been a pleasure."

She doesn't respond as her face turns beet red. As Conner and I exit, I hear Fletcher ask her why I said Betty. I bite back a chuckle.

Conner doesn't say a word as we take the elevator down, nor when we get into my triple-black R8 Audi and I slam the accelerator. He knows I was off my game and he clocked that beauty as the reason.

Finally, he says it. "I'm taking it the Betty Jones you met last night is the Allie Smith we saw today."

"Why do you think that?"

"Beyond you calling her Betty and the bandage on her arm?"

I remain silent. Conner's as sharp as you get, letting nothing get by him. He knows me better than anyone else.

"She's a distraction." His statement hits me like a cement truck to the chest. And right there is why I sometimes wish he weren't as good as he is.

"No, she just needs to stay safe during this operation. I don't want to see anything happen to her because we're reckless." My hands are turning white from gripping the steering wheel. She *is* a distraction, not that I would ever admit to it. I need to get control of the situation. But how?

"I don't know. From what you said about her taking on Ricardo last night, it seems she can handle herself."

She was handling the situation when I caught sight of what was going on down that alley, but it doesn't mean she can handle someone like Aric—or worse, me.

All I want to do is call Link with her actual fucking name, now that I have it, but after the shit he just gave me on running a check for a Betty Jones, I decide it's best to leave it. For now.

"She's naïve. She isn't a part of our world and it's best to keep it that way."

Now I just need to convince myself of that.

Chapter Five

Allie.

I check my watch to make sure I'm not late for Krav Maga class. I still have ten minutes until it starts, but the locker room is empty. Normally this locker room is packed full of women changing out of their work clothes at the last minute. I fold my skirt and blouse, set them in my locker, and pull on my yoga pants and tank top.

Thanks to Gage's surprise visit, I haven't been able to focus on anything today. And the scariest part? I was grateful to have seen him again. There aren't men out there like Gage McCollin.

He's hot, then cold, making it hard to put a finger on who he really is. One moment he is busting through the doors, demanding attention. The next, he's dancing like an idiot just to make me laugh. And it worked.

I'm sure he could tell I was having a panic attack. How was I supposed to know I was going to see him again? And at my place of employment, of all places. I felt as if I was sinking into quicksand, trying to pull myself out. That the truth would come out about last night and Harlow would be on her way to jump ten feet up my ass.

I tried questioning Fletcher about why Gage was acting as if he was running Shield Tech, and all I got in response was not to worry about it.

This isn't my first time preparing for Shield Tech's annual expo, but it feels as if it is. Fletch has never allowed anyone to make any decisions on this event. And that makes sense. He's the king of security in the country, and this expo is funded by him. Sure, he gets a few hella tax write-offs from it, but regardless, he writes all the checks. He may allow other security firms to fly on his coattails, but they have no say. Not one of them has ever argued with that.

Something is going on and I need to understand what exactly that is.

I plop onto the bench and tie my gym shoes, thinking about Sofia's dad charging me and how I was unable to avoid being brought down because of my heels. At least I was able to escape his hold when we tumbled to the ground. I want nothing more than to tell Riggs, the owner and trainer of Elite Defense. Talk to him about what happened and how I could improve.

But I can't. Harlow is good friends with Riggs, and I can't take the chance of this getting back to her. Life would be so much easier if she didn't know half the population of the country. It wouldn't surprise me to find out she knows the president himself and sets up coffee dates with the First Lady.

I slam my locker shut before heading down the hallway. Before I reach the training room, I can hear chatter and laughter from the other men and women in class.

"Allie," Riggs calls out. I swivel to see him coming out of his office. With his long strides, it takes no time to close the distance. He leans up against the wall and folds his arms across his large chest. He's in black sweats and a tight black T-shirt. I don't think this man has anything else in his wardrobe. But with the way it stretches across his muscles, I wouldn't worry about my clothing choices either.

"You missed class yesterday."

Here we go again...

"Yeah, sorry about that. I came across a little girl on my way here last night. Her kitten was stuck in a tree. Well, it wasn't stuck, but it sure didn't want to come down. She was crying, and I couldn't just walk away. I think this cat was her soulmate, you know what I mean?"

I wait briefly for a reply, but when Riggs's eyebrows burrow together, I elaborate further. "Just picture this: a poor little girl trying to get her kitten home, and no one else around to help her. I had to climb this tree to the top, and I'm talking thirty, maybe even forty feet into the air." I chuckle, letting my eyes drift off as if I am reliving my heroic rescue.

He stands quietly, no doubt digesting my bizarre story. "There was a little girl in the middle of downtown and no one was with her?"

"Yep, but she lived in one of the buildings nearby, so she wasn't far from her parents."

I can see Riggs's mind twisting around the shit idea of a little girl in the city all by herself. Maybe I need to start changing my stories up. No one cares about an adult like they do a child.

"Where is this thirty- or forty-foot tree in downtown?"

Shit. That is a great question, Riggs.

I look at his shoes and bite my nail. "I think it was near the corner of State and Primrose."

"State and Primrose don't connect. They are on opposite sides of the city and run parallel."

"Really, huh?" I laugh. "I guess I was so caught up in the moment of rescuing that jungle cat, I didn't pay much attention." I'm not going to have a thumbnail left with the way I have been going.

Riggs nods and gestures to my bandage. "What happened to your arm?"

"Oh geez, yeah. So, get this. I was climbing down the tree, and the cat tried to jump from my arms. From my arms, Riggs! I couldn't believe it." I shake my head. "I don't know. Maybe the cat doesn't have the same soulmate feelings for the little girl as she has for it. But before that little Puss in Boots could make its leap to certain death, I caught it by the tail, lost my footing, and scraped my arm up against a broken tree branch."

I can tell from his vacant-eyed nod that he's trying to envision the story I've spilled out, no doubt feeling for the cat I dangled from the tree. He loves cats. How a grown, hunky man can love cats over dogs blows me away. But stranger things have happened in this world, I suppose.

He shakes himself. "Wow, okay. I was going to ask for your assistance in class, but it might be better if you heal and take it easy."

"What? No way. I'm fine. This is nothing. What's the game plan?" I say, leaning against the opposite wall in the hallway.

"You sure?"

"Yeah, of course."

"A good friend of mine is here. He's a special guest I told everyone about in last night's class. He's a skilled fighter, and I was hoping since you're one of my strongest students, you could assist in showing everyone some new techniques to go over."

Pride courses through my body. I stand taller and smile wide. "Of course."

We head down the hallway and enter the training room. It's filled with thick black mats in the center and front, while the back half of the room has weightlifting equipment, bikes, treadmills, the whole enchilada. The entire room is covered in mirrors, allowing participants to study their stance.

I'm still working on getting him to invest in a tanning bed. I even got Mimi, his supermodel wife, on board, but once she got pregnant, that went downhill. She's about ready to pop, so I will give it a week or two before I start up my tanning bed riot again.

The women who were missing from the locker room are present, along with the male contingent of the class. They've surrounded what must be the special guest for tonight, forming a crowd of twenty people or so. I notice Tina and Jessica, both wearing brand-new workout gear, both with their hair and makeup done to perfection as if they are planning on going clubbing right afterward. The mirrors reflect the eager faces and create the illusion of an even larger group. The scent of fresh lemons wafts through the air, mingling with faint whiffs of sweat and perfume. The energy in the room is palpable, a mix of anticipation and excitement bouncing off the walls.

"Is this friend of yours famous or something?" I ask Riggs, feeling that I'm missing something big here. Maybe I should have asked who this guest was before agreeing.

A chuckle rumbles out of Riggs. "You can say that. He may not be in showbiz, but very few haven't heard about him."

"Really?" Consternation fills me. Once again, my lack of social media has me out of the loop. "What's his name?"

"Gage McCollin."

As if God himself has decided at that exact moment for the sea to split, everyone breaks away, bringing those familiar artic-blue eyes to land straight on me. And that asshole smiles, equipped with his stupid dimples. Stupid, sexy dimples.

This is so not fair.

Gage slowly makes his way over to Riggs and me as if he is making a grand entrance into a castle to meet the King and Queen of England. Wait, no. I got it all wrong. He's walking as if he *is* the King of England.

Gage is still wearing his black backward hat that has a strange symbol I don't recognize and the white T-shirt from earlier, but he has changed into sweat shorts, showcasing his muscular legs. Tattoos run along his tanned calves. I wonder how much of his body is covered in artwork. Not that I would ever ask him that. I'm not jumping on the groupie wagon. I swallow a whimper at how gorgeous he is.

Gage and Riggs shake hands and greet each other like long-lost brothers. I hate that everyone in the training room holds him in high regard, including the men. His ego is already large enough.

Gage smiles, blinding me with his straight pearly whites. I swear his dimple just winked at me.

I am officially losing it.

"Allie, it's nice to see you again."

"Oh," Riggs says. "I didn't know you knew each other."

"We don't—"

Gage speaks over me. "We do."

Riggs looks between us, appearing even more confused than he was by my rescue mission story. In his defense, I might have already fried his brain in the hallway.

Gage adds handily, "I'm helping out at Shield Tech this week for the upcoming expo."

"Ah yes. You'll be in good hands. Fletch hiring Allie is the best thing he ever did. His expos doubled in size after she took over managing the event."

A smile warms my face. I don't know how true that is—it's not like Fletcher lets me make any of the big decisions—but hey, who am I to argue?

Gage's eyes glisten with amusement. "I have no doubt."

Riggs slaps Gage's shoulder, tells him I will be assisting in the training, then heads over to the crowd of giggling women.

I drop my smile and replace it with a glare. I've come too far to let those bright blue eyes, tattoos, and dimples distract me.

Putting aside that I can't even date anyone without living a life of lies, I know his type. His charming, sexy ways that I'm sure make women lose their ever-loving minds.

He tilts his head. "I'm starting to wonder if you're stalking me now."

I'm sure he's had several women stalk him over the years, and to be honest, I might have signed up for that club. But he won't ever know that.

"In your dreams, dimples." I want to smack myself in the face the second those words leave my mouth.

His smile only grows, showing off his stupid dimples more. "Ah, my dimples are what started you down the path of stalking."

He's teasing me and I want to hate it, but I can't. He has a charm about him that pulls me into his orbit. In another life, one where I didn't have to lie about everything, I would be eating his charm up like a bowl of ice cream covered in sprinkles. "Sorry to burst the arrogant little bubble you are unknowingly living in, but you're the one stalking me."

He laughs and points to his chest. "*Moi?*"

I can't restrain a small smile. I jab him hard in the chest. "Yes, you." I poke him again. "That was my alley you were in last night." I poke again. God, his body is made of iron. "My place of employment." I have to poke him again. It's as satisfying as popping bubble wrap. "And my gym."

"Really? I didn't know you owned this joint." He taps his lips with his index finger. "I knew Riggs was full of shit when he told me this place was his pride and joy."

I shake my head and bite my cheek to withhold laughter. This guy. A man who has eyes filled with danger, a sense of humor that throws you off track, and a smile that would melt your panties right off. "I hear you have some moves to show us. Are you sure you wouldn't feel more comfortable with Tina or Jessica aiding you?"

Gage chuckles, the sound intoxicating. "And miss out on one-on-one time with my new stalker? Not a chance." He winks and heads to the front of the class.

Maybe, just maybe, I can accidentally throat punch him and teach him a real lesson in self-defense.

I drag my legs to where Gage awaits on *his* stage as everyone partners up to practice the art of this supposed prodigy's techniques.

"First, I want to thank you all for coming tonight and letting me host. Riggs has been persistent about getting me to hold a class here for the past six months, and I finally caved. He's filled me in on how incredible you all are, so I hope to not disappoint anyone tonight."

Giggles erupt from the women and the men puff out their chests.

I choose to roll my eyes.

"There are three principles if any of you find yourselves in a tough situation." Gage paces across the mat. "One: Identify the immediate threat. You need to be one step ahead of your attacker. Two: Send a simultaneous counterattack. And three: Fight, fight, fight."

Gage turns toward me, growing serious. "Allie, what would you do if someone tried to choke you?"

"I would kick them in their jewels."

Gage wraps his large hands around my throat. His grip is light, but firm. Instinctively, I wrap my hands around his wrists to balance myself. His hands are warm against my skin. I can smell his signature spring and mint.

"Try it. Try to kick me."

We stand silently, motionless. The room grows eerily quiet. If I were to try to kick him right now, he'd be ready. For this to work, he needs to be distracted.

I take a deep breath and slowly let it out, releasing everything in my mind. I slowly lick my lips and gently bite my lower lip, watching his blue eyes fill with lust as he casts his gaze to my mouth. I swear I hear a faint growl within his chest. I ram my left leg up as fast as I can, but instead of reaching my goal, my knee is greeted with his shin.

Gage smiles brightly and addresses the class while keeping his eyes on me. "That's great. You want to fight. But more importantly... In this second, you want to take control of the situation. I have the control with my hands around your throat. That's your immediate threat."

I drop my hands from his wrists. "I need to go on the defense."

"Exactly. Now, make a hook with each hand and swing your arms over mine. You want to hit me at my weakest point, which is my thumbs. Pull outward, not downward. Then you fight."

I swing my arms around his grip, hooking him, and pull outward, causing his grip to give way. My leg kicks up, forcing Gage's hands downward to block my attack.

I raise my fists and throw three quick punches. An inch closer and I would have made contact. He's lucky I decided to play nice.

I love this feeling. The high I get every time I come to these classes. I put my hands on my hips, my breathing slightly increasing.

Gage stands at his towering height and claps. "That was perfect, Allie. You identified the immediate threat of my hands choking you. You took control by breaking my hands away while delivering a simultaneous attack. Well done."

We stare at each other, smiling. It's obvious that he loves this as much as I do. An outlet to let everything out. To be in the moment with total control. It's hypnotizing. It's powerful. It's everything I crave.

Gage addresses the class. "Now, how do you escape from under someone larger than you?"

As quickly as the words leave his mouth, he grabs my wrist and sweeps his leg under my legs, causing me to fall to the mat. Just as my spine connects with the mat, his other hand wraps around my free hand and pins it beside my head. He sits on top of me, staring with such intensity, I mentally remind myself it isn't real. Gage is more than an experienced street fighter. He's had in-depth training that probably started when he was first able to walk. God help me, this is the sexiest thing since Brad Pitt in *Fight Club*.

"Most people would buck and try to break their arms free. Go ahead, Allie. Show me what you got."

His body is hard and heavy on top of mine. It takes all my willpower to not focus on how he feels against me... or how he would feel inside me.

I take it as a personal challenge and buck while simultaneously lifting my arms from the mat. As soon as one hand gets off the ground, it slams to the mat. I give up the fight quickly, knowing I need to save my energy.

"The problem is that I have a lot of leverage from my angle and gravity is on my side. You would wear yourself out prematurely by fighting. At this moment, I'm not hurting you. I'm not choking you. I am merely showing my power over you."

I can see why Riggs spoke so highly of him. He's a great trainer and that only pisses me off more. No one should be made so perfect. It's not fair to everyone else.

"Allie, here's what we are going to do. I need you to bridge high with your hips and throw your arms low."

"What do you mean throw low? Like a snow angel?"

"Exactly. By bridging high, you're catching me off guard and sending me forward. As soon as that happens, throw low. Once you've done that, you'll need to hug my torso. It will cause me to fall off-balance from your hold. I won't be able to sit up right away, and you need to take advantage of that. In moments like this, you can't afford any hesitation. Then, wrap your arm around mine to trap it and then roll." His eyes sparkle. "We're going to go slowly through each step the first time to show the class. We can increase the speed afterward. You ready?"

I nod. Did it just get twenty degrees hotter in this room?

"Okay, everyone. Your wrists are pinned to the ground." Gage raises my arms an inch off that mat and brings them back down. His serious expression is in place again, but his eyes look devilish, and I love it. I wonder if his lips taste minty.

"Step one. Bridge high, throw low."

I push my hips straight up into the air, while I slam my arms straight down like I'm making a snow angel, causing Gage to fall forward onto his hands.

My face is now level with his torso, and I suddenly wish he would have done this shirtless. But in all reality, I would've just licked him like an ice cream cone, and with so many people watching, it wouldn't have been my best choice.

"Great job. Everyone, as you can see, Allie has caused me to fall forward. Many people have injured themselves when practicing this technique. For the people on top, be aware of what your body is going to do when they throw low. I've seen too many times where people slam into the other person's face below them." He stays in position but pitches his voice a little higher. "Everyone playing the part of the victim, keep your head turned to the side to protect yourself. You don't want to put yourself in more danger than you already are. Immediately after this move is done, you need to do step two and hug your assailant like a tree."

I oblige and wrap my arms tight around him. Every muscle in his body feels like the missing puzzle piece to mine. I soak in his minty fragrance. I think I might be stopping at the store on the way home to grab some mints.

"Now she has me off-balance, making it extremely difficult to sit up. Allie, I need you to wrap my arm with yours, trapping it, and roll to the side."

I do as he says and within seconds, he is off me, and I am on top. I throw a practice elbow to his face and stomach, making it quickly to my feet.

Gage pulls his legs toward his chest and thrusts his body up to jump and land on his feet. My mouth drops open, but I have no time to recover. He wraps his arm around my shoulders, pulling me to his taut body. His touch surprisingly doesn't feel awkward like it does when other men have tried the same thing, and I don't want to think about why that is. Deep down, I know exactly why.

I glance around and see all the women in the class pretty much salivating over Gage and wishing they were me right now.

But then a familiar face shrouded by a hoodie near the doorway takes my full attention.

"Sofia," I call out. I pull away from Gage and head straight toward her. She instantly disappears around the corner, no doubt because all heads turn to her.

Over my shoulder, I find Riggs in the crowd. It isn't hard; the guy could have been a basketball player with his height. "Riggs, have Tina take over," I yell, jogging out of the room.

It may be an excuse to get out from underneath Gage, but he was crossing all my wires, causing me to not be able to think.

With Sofia here, I need to get my head on straight.

Chapter Six

Allie.

To my surprise, Sofia is still standing just around the corner. Even with her hood up, I can see a darkening bruise on her face from the hits she took last night.

"Hey," I say with as much warmth as I can muster while still feeling so much adrenaline. "It's good to see you again. How you hanging in there?"

She glances around nervously and doesn't respond.

"Come on, let's go someplace more private."

I grab her hand and lead her down the hallway toward the locker room but veer into an empty office off to the right. I shut the door and Sofia takes a seat on the couch. I walk across the room and drop into a wide chair that could easily fit two people. "What's going on?" I ask gently.

She's dressed in all black today. Black tennis shoes, black yoga pants, and a black hoodie. Her eyes stay downcast as she rubs her finger across the small heart tattoo on her pinky finger.

I remain silent, knowing she needs to find her grounding. I was once as lost as she feels right now. I think I still am.

"My friend told me I should take up self-defense classes, so I thought I would check this place out."

I nod with sympathy for this brave young girl who has no choice in her current path in life. She should be worried about what day to spend lounging in the sand on Puget Sound or where to shop with her girlfriends. Not how to protect herself from her abusive father.

"I saw an ad for this place on the bus and thought I'd start here. But now I don't know if this is something I can do."

"I get that. Krav Maga training is intense. What makes you unsure?"

"I don't know. I guess the way you were thrown to the mat so quickly. It was scary how fast it happened."

No kidding. I had to remind myself that it wasn't real too. "I didn't start out in Krav Maga either. I watched about fifteen minutes of it and said, nope, not for me, and walked out."

"Really? You did?"

"Uh-huh. I started doing a jujitsu program on a DVD I came across. It taught me basic techniques and helped build my strength."

"I have no idea what that even is," she says, leaning against the couch and dropping her hood. Her bruise is much worse in the light. It takes everything I have not to hug her tight and tell her everything is going to be all right.

But I know she doesn't want pity. I never did.

"I didn't either. Everyone needs to start somewhere and work their way up. I could see strength inside you last night. You have what it takes, I promise you."

She sits quietly, fidgeting with the hem of her sweatshirt.

"How about you come to my place and get that DVD? You can check it out and see if you're comfortable with it. I can drive you to one of your friends' houses afterward."

I'm aware of how bold my suggestion is, but the desperation inside me to help her has me grasping at every possible option. I've never invited anyone—other than my close circle of trust—over to my place. It's better that way for everyone involved. Sofia's different, though. I can feel it.

She remains still for a moment before finally meeting my gaze. "That guy in there you were sparring with. That was Mr. McCollin, wasn't it?"

I was hoping she wouldn't recognize Gage. Then again, after one glance at the *GQ* arctic king, he was burned into my mind as well.

I need to get a better nickname for him. Maybe sweaty meathead. Yeah, that's more suitable.

"It was. I guess he's friends with the owner and came in to host a class. I don't even know him—well, I didn't until yesterday. You don't need to be worried about him."

"I'm not."

Huh. I collapse into the chair, surprised. Given that Gage knows her father, I figured she would've wanted to distance herself from him. I can't help but ask, "You're not?"

"No, not really. I mean, yeah, he has that whole scary vibe about him, but he's never hurt anyone who didn't deserve it. Well, at least as far as I know."

I take that information in like it's liquid gold. All the research I did on him last night came up empty, along with my large glass of wine. "Are you saying you know he *has* hurt people?"

"Yeah, everyone knows someone Gage made disappear." Her tone is very matter-of-fact, without hesitation.

I don't know what to say, and that's saying a lot. I could tell he wasn't a normal guy... far from it. I guess my first question should be—who is he? As much as I want to ask Sofia, she's not the right person.

It's clear that the best choice when it comes to Gage is to walk away. To shut down all thoughts and questions about him. But the way he keeps popping up everywhere is making that a challenging task. Not to mention he's a chiseled piece of artwork from God himself. The bastard.

An uncharacteristically sly smile appears on Sofia's face. "You like him, don't you?"

"What? No. Of course not." When she gives me a deadpan look, I elaborate. "I would rather walk barefoot across a room of LEGO bricks than have to look at his ugly mug again."

I'm blessed with Sofia's smile. It's a beautiful one. "My mom used to step on my LEGO bricks all the time because I never put them away. That was the only time I would hear her cuss, so I intentionally did it all the time."

I smile. "Where's your mom now?"

"She's gone. Died of cancer when I was seven." The sadness that drifts across her face is familiar. I understand the emptiness that lives inside your soul like the disease that took her mother from her.

"I'm sorry. My mom passed away too."

Her eyes widen. "How did she pass?"

I debate exactly what to tell her. The murder of my family was horrible, ruthless, and painful. I'm sure her mother's death was the same, except more drawn out. I need her to believe she can trust me. "You know how I mentioned my dad yesterday? Well, he and my mom were both murdered. I had just turned eighteen when it happened."

"I'm sorry."

"Thank you," I reply, thinking back to the first year after my family's tragic ending and how lost I was. I was just as dead as my family was and angry at God for taking them away from me.

Almost a year later, Harlow decided she'd had enough.

I refused to smile or laugh. I was a wreck until the morning she burst through my bedroom door. She forced me to run with her. Literally forced. She handcuffed her wrist to mine and took off. I was so mad, but then halfway through our run, something loosened inside my chest. It no longer felt like I was being squeezed to death. Each breath was no longer a struggle to take in, maybe because I was *actually* struggling to breathe. It was the first time in a year that I could... breathe.

I found that God never left me. He gave me Harlow as my angel. And now I want to be that angel for Sofia.

"Are you okay?"

I smile. "I am, and I'm so happy we crossed paths again."

"Me too."

A sense of relief flows through me. "What do you say? We can head out and search for that DVD. Maybe grab some dinner on the way... or I could cook for you?"

Sofia tosses her hood over her head and stands. "I'm sorry, I can't."

I stand. "Hey, that's okay. How about this? Do you still have my business card?"

She nods. I take it as a great sign she didn't toss it in the first garbage can she came across.

"I'll find the DVD tonight and bring it with me to Shield Tech tomorrow. You can stop by at any time to get it, or you can call and I'll meet you. Anywhere, anytime. Does that sound good?"

She smiles again. "Thanks, Allie. I appreciate it."

I follow her to the front door and lean against the doorjamb, watching until I can't see her any longer.

The excitement of making such a huge step with her today has me doing a happy dance. I hope my words were enough to sway her.

Class is about to let out. I need to bust out quickly before Gage finishes. I look into the training room to find his eyes locked on mine. I'm pretty sure he witnessed me walking Sofia out and doing a boy-band dance worse than his. I drop my eyes and head to Riggs's office, writing a quick note saying that I was sorry I had to bail. Heading to the locker room, I grab my belongings and change quickly.

As much as I wanted to see what else Gage had to offer in his lessons, and yes, all right, fantasize about his body, I have more important things to do tonight. Finding that damn DVD.

I leave out the side exit in hopes of making a clean getaway. As soon as the door closes behind me, a deep voice comes from off to my right.

"Going somewhere, little lion?"

Shit.

He appears out of the shadows like some dark knight. The sun has dropped into the skyline, calling it a day. I hoist my bag on my shoulder and wait for him to reach me.

"How did you get out here so fast?"

His sexy dimples appear. "Didn't we just cover this in class? You always need to be one step ahead."

"Yeah, of your attacker. So what? Am I your attacker now?"

He shrugs, enjoyment flashing in his eyes. "I think we've already determined you're stalking me."

If he has mastered anything in his life, I would say it's his charming ways that take the gold. If my life had ended up differently all those years ago, I would have sunken into the pleasure of surrendering to his enchanting ways.

"In that case, I'm officially retiring. You can rest assured that I'll no longer be stalking you. Have a nice evening, Mr. McCollin." I turn toward my Jimmy, but my bag is pulled off my shoulder.

"Not so fast," he says, swinging my gym bag onto his shoulder. It looks ridiculous on him with its flower patches. "You can't just retire from stalking. It doesn't work like that."

I put my hands on my hips. *Why do you have to be so much fun?* "Oh, really?"

"Yeah. What kind of stalker retires in two days? You haven't even learned how I like my coffee or what kind of toilet paper I use."

I laugh at the serious tone he is attempting but failing to pull off.

"You know what you need?"

"No, Mr. McCollin, please enlighten me, oh wise one."

"Food. You're getting cranky and ready to throw the towel in after all your hard work in stalking me thus far."

Without missing a beat, he wraps his large hand around mine and tugs me the other way. I feel a million butterflies flutter inside at his simple gesture. His hold is firm, his hands callused.

I should probably stop whatever is going on, but I can't bring myself to do it. It feels too good, too right. Maybe just tonight. I will give myself one night in this man's company and act as if my life is normal and so is his. We can believe that whatever demons chase us in our nightmares no longer exist. For one night, I'm going to let myself feel free again.

We walk a couple of blocks before he pulls me into a restaurant. It's a small Irish pub with tons of woodwork and green shamrock signs hung throughout. It isn't loud, but there's a gentle hum of conversation inside as people enjoy their meals. More than half of the tables are already filled, with patrons savoring hearty dishes and clinking glasses. My stomach growls at the savory aroma of meat and potatoes permeating the air.

I slide onto the bench as Gage does the same across from me, depositing my bag next to him. He's still wearing his sweat shorts but now has a hoodie on. One would think a hoodie would hide his muscular form, but it doesn't.

We place our food and drink orders. He orders the Irish stew with an Irish whiskey and I order a Reuben with a pint of Guinness, which take no time to get.

"Can I have my bag now?" I ask, taking a sip of my beer. I forgot how heavy it is.

"Why? Is there a bomb in this thing or something?" He lifts it like he is checking the weight and has a liable concern. Smartass.

"Has anyone ever told you how annoying you are?"

He leans into the booth, laying his arm lazily across the back. "No, I can't say they have. People know better than to speak to me like that."

"And why's that?"

"Because they know who I am."

His answer is chilling and loaded with so much ammo that I'm not sure how to take it. This is exactly what I have been thinking. He has this hot-cold personality, making it hard to figure out what way is up or down. He has two sides. One is fun-loving and easygoing. The other is dangerous and scary. I suspect not many people see the playful side of Gage.

"I know you make people disappear."

He cocks his head to the side, assessing me in detail. "Does that bother you?"

I stare into his icy-blue eyes and consider his question. I'm sure the majority of people wouldn't hesitate to say yes. But they haven't been through what I have. They haven't seen what evil people will do when greed takes over. How many nights have I dreamed of killing everyone involved who took my family from me? "Are they bad people?"

He takes a drink from his rocks glass and slowly sets it down. His index finger glides along the edge. "You know the answer to your question. Otherwise you wouldn't be sitting across from me."

"Fair enough." I grab my napkin and twist it between my fingers, unable to meet his intense gaze any longer. I take in a sharp breath, trying to steady myself from the anxious energy brewing.

"You don't need to be nervous with me."

Am I nervous? Of course. But not for the reason he thinks. It's more because I feel out of my normal realm, navigating a ship in choppy, unfamiliar waters. "Okay. So, make me not nervous."

He watches me closely. I'm sure he's wondering if I am about to bolt. I grab my drink to calm myself.

His voice drops low. "When I look at you, I know without question I would burn the entire world to ashes and blood would run down every street if anyone were to ever think about hurting you."

I choke on my froth—as in fits of uncontrollable coughing that take over my body. There's nothing sexy about it. I finally get it under control and wipe my wet eyes. His beautiful smile remains intact. "Who in their right mind says something like that?"

"What?" He splays out his fingers innocently. "You asked me to make you not nervous. What else should I have said? You're the attacker here."

His thought process is maddening. "I don't know. Maybe something along the lines of how I have nothing to worry about and you're as harmless as a kitten."

He rears his head back. "A kitten?"

"Yes, a kitten," I reply with a smirk. "Small, fluffy, and utterly incapable of causing harm."

The corner of his lips twitch. "Well little lion, I can't promise you smallness or fluffiness, but I can assure you I'm not a danger to you."

I laugh, feeling some of the tension ease away. "I guess I'll take your word for it. But if I see claws, I'm out of here," I tease. He did just host a class on self-defense. I doubt someone with the wrong intentions would take time out of his day to do that. "So, Mr. McCollin, how about you tell me where you learned to fight like that?"

He takes a sip of his whiskey. "Conner, the guy who came with me to Shield Tech."

I nod. I noticed his massive friend. The guy is kind of hard to miss with his size and that thick white scar across his cheek.

"We met when we were teenagers, both forced into training set forth by our dickhead fathers. If it weren't for him, I probably couldn't have remained grounded in this world. My father ran things with an iron fist, and when I was sent away for training, every part of my normal life was ripped away without notice."

"What kind of training did he send you off to?"

"The kind of training camp no kid should ever go to. Their method was simple—beating the shit out of us every day, forcing us to learn quickly how to fight back. They would keep us up for days on end, giving just enough scraps to keep us alive."

And I just lost my appetite. A glimpse inside his past has my stomach turning over. The fact that he can still have a playful side to him is startling. "How old were you two when you were sent off to this camp?"

"It was my thirteenth birthday present from my father. Conner was still twelve."

"I can't believe there are places like that out there. That's horrible."

"It isn't there any longer. As soon as Conner and I were old enough and had the resources, we killed every trainer and burned the place down."

My jaw drops at how easily he delivers these words. A pang of jealousy slides through that he's able to speak freely about his past instead of hiding it. He takes another sip of his drink as our server arrives with our food. My stomach is in knots, so I pick at my fries to try and calm the sourness.

"Why the obsession with flowers?"

His question makes me smile. I'm not sure if he's trying to get my mind off his story, but I take the olive branch and run with it. "I think it started because my mother was captivated with gardening. I spent a lot of time with her in the vineyards. One year for my birthday I got a package with different seeds in it. It was a mystery package and didn't tell you what kind of flowers were in it, just where and how to grow them. So that's what I did. I shoveled the new soil in, watered them, and waited." I laugh, recalling my frustration. "I was so upset when nothing came up the next day. I had literally spent the entire day picking the right spot, prepping the ground, and carrying a watering jug across the property to give them a fresh drink."

I pop a fry in my mouth and munch away, thinking about the last time all my family spent the day in the wildflower field at the Oasis.

Gage smiles. "I have a tattoo of a flower."

I grin. "Stop it. No you don't."

He laughs. "Okay, I don't. But I'm thinking I need to get one."

"I doubt that would be a wise decision in your line of work. How seriously would a villain take you with flowers tattooed all over your body?"

"It would be worth it."

"Oh yeah, and why's that?" I ask, picking up my Reuben and taking a bite.

"Because then you would become obsessed with me." He grins his devious smile and takes a spoonful of his Irish stew.

I chew my food slowly while I take in his words. Grabbing my heavy-tasting beer, I wash it back before wiping my mouth clean. "I would hate to see the lines you pull when you're on a date."

"Oh, this is a date."

"No it isn't."

He nods, grabbing his whiskey and taking a swig. "It's quite simple. See exhibit A." He points to himself. "Exhibit B." He points to me. "And exhibit C." He points to our food and drinks. "This is most definitely a date. Now I'm trying to figure out how to get to exhibit D."

He leaves it at that and I'm having too much fun not to take the bait. "What's exhibit D?"

"How I can get you to kiss me."

I laugh. This is a man who just stole my bag and left me no choice but to go on this imaginary date. When I picture a perfect first date, this isn't something that would ever cross my mind.

It's better.

As much fun as this is, it can't go anywhere. Including something as innocent as a kiss. The thought that it can't ever be that simple is sobering. I need to change the subject. "Okay, so your father was a complete douche." He smiles at that. "What about your mother?"

His eyes soften. "She's the one I got all my charm from."

"You don't say."

"It's true. Before I went off to that camp, I was a mama's boy through and through. I would follow her around the house. Always helping change a light bulb or fix a broken cupboard. I knew my father was never good enough for her, so I tried to make that up to her. She would always tell me things that a woman I would one day marry would love to have in a man."

I smile at the vision of him as a little boy with his mother. "And what was one thing she taught you for your upcoming role as a husband?"

"How to cook." He gives me a *duh* look.

"Oh, so the rough and tough Gage McCollin knows how to work his way around the kitchen?"

He lights up and it takes a second for me to realize why. I just gave him another compliment. He holds his hand up and points his index finger out. If he's going to do what I think, he can kiss that good-night kiss goodbye.

Wait, he wasn't getting one anyways.

"Let me get this straight, or I'm going to lose count with the rapid speed they're coming in at. Your first compliment was how good-looking I am." He holds out another finger. "The second was something along the lines of dreaming about my dimples."

I roll my eyes as he holds out another finger.

"The third was the meow you let out when you were hugging my torso like a hurricane might blow you away at any second."

"I did no such thing!"

"Oh yes you did. Now don't interrupt me. Okay, where was I? Oh yes." He holds out another finger. "How rough I am." He holds out his thumb. "And you think I'm tough."

"You can't count rough and tough as two different compliments. That's cheating."

"I did and I will. That's five compliments, Allie. You are going to lose your mind when I get that tattoo."

I shake my head and finish my Reuben. Tonight is the most fun I've had in years. "So, master of the kitchen and collector of compliments, what else do you have up your sleeve?"

He grins, a mischievous glint in his eyes. "Well, you already know about my world-class dance moves."

I giggle.

"I could tell you about my incredible driving skills, but I think it's best to leave some mysteries for the second date."

I raise an eyebrow and play along. "And why would you want another date?"

He leans in closer, his voice dropping to a playful whisper. "Because I still haven't figured out what you're hiding from me."

My heart skips a beat, but I quickly recover, giving him a teasing smirk. "And why would you think that?"

Gage shrugs, his eyes twinkling. "Maybe I just have a knack for knowing when someone is hiding something."

I laugh, trying to keep the conversation light. "Well, Mr. Detective, I'm sorry to inform you, but my life is as normal and boring as it gets."

He leans back. "There's nothing boring when it comes to you."

My cheeks heat. "You can't say something like that."

"It's the truth. I've never met a woman who could take down a grown man in high heels. You had me the second you kicked him hard enough to break a couple of ribs. How many men could say they got to go on a date with a mysterious, high-heeled vigilante?"

I toss my head back and laugh harder than I can ever recall that I have. I can't help but love his description of me in the alley.

"I'm serious. You were like a superhero in stilettos. I was half expecting you to pull out a cape and fly off into the sunset."

I shake my head, grinning. "I'm not superhero material, I'm afraid. But I'll take the compliment."

"Trust me, you're more than that." Gage tips back his drink before his icy blues meet my eyes again. "Do you want another drink?"

I don't think I've ever laughed as much as I have. His energy is addictive. Looking at the clock on the wall behind him, I realize how much time has flown by. As much as I don't want this night to end, I know it's time.

"I can't. It's a big week at work with the expo."

Gage nods and waves our server over. He pays the bill and helps me out of the booth. He walks me to the parking lot where my trusty old Jimmy sits. He scrunches his nose but wisely chooses not to comment.

I unlock the door and toss my bag into the passenger seat before turning to him. "Thank you for showing me those techniques. And for dinner."

He rests his hand up against the roof of my Jimmy, leaning toward me. "How about you thank me with a kiss?"

My cheeks warm at his bluntness. I shake my head. "If I kiss you now, it'll only feed my stalker tendencies further."

He nods, smiling. "Good point. I don't want to get a restraining order too quickly. How about a kiss on the cheek then?" He turns his head and taps his cheek. I know I shouldn't, but I can't resist. I rise on my tippy toes to kiss him on the cheek, but he turns at the last moment and our lips crash together.

For a heartbeat, we both freeze, caught by the sudden intensity of the moment. The world around us seems to blur, leaving just the two of us suspended in a bubble of electrifying connection. His lips are warm and surprisingly soft, moving gently against mine as if testing the waters. Tentatively, I respond, my heart pounding in a wild rhythm.

A spark ignites, spreading like wildfire through my body. His hand slips to the small of my back, pulling me closer. I can feel the steady thrum of his heartbeat matching mine. My hands slide up his hard chest, clutching his hoodie as if anchoring myself in this whirlwind of emotion.

Time stretches and bends. I lose myself in the sensation of his kiss, the way his minty Irish whiskey breath mingles with mine. The subtle caress of his fingers along my body. It's a kiss that speaks of desire and promise.

When we finally part, both breathless and dazed, there's a moment of silence where our foreheads rest together, both of us savoring the taste of that kiss.

"Wow," he murmurs, his voice husky and laced with wonder. "That was... something else."

I can only nod, my thoughts a swirling mess as I try to catch my breath. I can't even begin to get my bearings about how right—but ultimately how wrong—this is.

With a soft chuckle, he steps back, his eyes holding a newfound depth. "Guess we just fed those stalker tendencies, huh?"

I laugh, lightly swatting his arm. "Good night, Gage," I whisper as I climb into the driver's seat. He shuts the door and watches me pull away. I glance in the rearview mirror, watching him standing there, a contented smile playing on his lips.

The entire drive home, I can't stop touching my lips.

CHAPTER SEVEN

Allie.

I make it to work fifteen minutes late and drop the jujitsu DVD off with the security guard. He isn't one you can have a couple of words with and be on your day.

After another ten minutes, I make my way to the twenty-ninth floor and check my voicemail. The only message is from Mario, the restaurant manager at Antonio's, confirming he will be at the Onyx building to do a walk-through of the kitchen and serving area at ten this morning.

It's already half past nine and I have yet to check in with Fletcher. There's no way I'm making it to the Onyx on time. Thankfully, I get hold of Mario to push out the meeting time.

I head straight to Fletcher's door, lightly knocking before heading in. Fletcher is standing in front of his wall of monitors, typing on the keyboard in the middle.

"You're late," he states, not bothering to turn around.

He knows it's me, not because he's psychic or anything cool like that. No, he has eyes in the back of his head, not literally. Again, not that cool, but with the hundreds of cameras on this floor, he doesn't miss a thing.

I'm sure he witnessed the hot mess busting through the door. I haven't even had time for a coffee yet this morning, and to me, that's the biggest sin anyone could commit.

"You're never going to believe this. You know how I live out in the middle of nowhere, a good way outside town. Well, right before I walked out, I noticed a gang of raccoons right outside my front door. Right outside, Fletch!" I shake my head as if I still cannot believe it happened. "I could tell that they were all plotting something. You know how you get that strange feeling that something bad is about to happen? Well, I was right about that. Before I could even blink, the ringleader hobbled over with its bent back to my good ole Jimmy and started gnawing on my tire!"

"You don't say," Fletcher replies dryly.

"Yep," I say with a pop. "I ran out of cat food. I think that's why they were plotting in the first place. Luckily, I had a jumbo box of cherry-flavored Pop-Tarts and tossed those to distract them. The ringleader was more difficult, but the second I finally hit it in the head with a Pop-Tart, it realized I was only trying to feed it. In three seconds flat, it snatched it up and ran off like it had just won a gold medal." I laugh, and it even sounds fake to me.

I would never hurt a raccoon in my life. If those cute little masked bandits ever wanted to gnaw my tires off, I would pop a bag of popcorn and watch the show.

"I heard they prefer Reubens and fries."

I jump at Gage's voice and whirl around to find him leaning against the far wall, arms crossed against his wide chest and amusement dancing in his eyes.

He's got the whole street-fighter look going on again, with a black hat, dark gray hoodie, dark jeans, and black boots. Even though his body is covered in clothing, you can still see tattoos on his hands and neck peeking out. His whole look screams bad boy and has my ovaries jumping in joy.

Bitches.

I narrow my eyes as his stupidly beautiful smile grows larger, showcasing his dumb, sexy dimples. I whip back to Fletcher, who's still busy typing away—at what, I don't know. It looks like code. Something Logan would do.

"Anyways," I say in an annoyed tone. "I'm heading to the Onyx to meet with Mario for the walk-through. Hopefully Roxanne will show. She never confirmed."

"I'll join you." Gage comes to stand next to me with his minty smell. It takes every ounce of willpower to not lean in and take a deep whiff like an overeager golden retriever.

"No need, man. You just heard." Fletcher stops and turns to both of us. "Allie clearly lives a life of daily unexpected obstacles. I'm sure she can handle that." The expression on his face is hard to read, but I get the feeling he's being sarcastic about my bandit story. I thought it was good. One of my better ones, at least.

"I'm sure she can, but I'll still accompany her. I need to get an overview of the place anyway. Text me that information when you have it." Gage doesn't wait for a response and walks out of the office.

I turn to Fletcher, my mind blown from the way Gage just ordered Fletcher around. "Are you sure everything's all right?" I probe.

"Everything's fine," he says, dragging his hand through his brown hair. "You know how I get a few days before the expo."

It's surprising that a man leading the security industry can get so stressed. But I guess being the best can add to the pressure of remaining on top. Gage needs to back off and let Fletcher do his thing.

After a quick thought, I suggest, "If you want, I can sneak out through the safe room and leave Gage here twiddling his thumbs. Then he's stuck here at your disposal."

Fletcher laughs and I smile.

"Relax. If plan A does work, we have the rest of the alphabet to figure this out."

Fletcher chuckles again before responding, "Thanks for the vote of confidence. Now get your ass going before Gage gets impatient. He has a lot on his plate right now."

I give Fletcher a salute and head out. Gage walks out of the kitchen area holding two to-go coffee cups and hands me one.

"You look like you could use one."

"Thank you." I peek at his cup. He takes his black.

He lifts a brow.

"Don't mind me. Just keeping up with my stalking tendencies. Toilet paper is where it stops, though."

I see his chest shake as he holds in a laugh. We take the elevator, with only the sound of light elevator music and me slurping my coffee. I'm a little unnerved by the fact that he picked my favorite flavor—caramel—though he did add cream, so at least there's *some* evidence that he's not literally omniscient. When we reach ground level, I turn toward the door that leads to the parking garage where my Jimmy is. Gage's big paw wraps around my hand and he pulls me straight ahead to a shiny black sports car. It's illegally parked outside the front doors.

"Hey, what are you doing?" I say, tugging my hand. It's no use. "You almost made me spill my coffee."

"We're riding together. Get in." He unlocks his car and opens the passenger door.

If I wasn't running behind, I would've argued. But I cannot afford to call Mario and tell him I need another twenty minutes. I zip my lips and slide into the Audi.

His car is beautiful, with an all-black interior and white stitching throughout. A large monitor rests on the dashboard. I always wanted a vehicle with a large screen. His car is spotless, like it just rolled out of the dealership. It's ridiculous. There isn't a speck of dust or even a fingerprint anywhere. I press my thumb onto the passenger-side window, smudging it, and grin. My old Jimmy has seen better days. I can picture him riding in it, looking ready to cry from how it hasn't been cleaned in months. The thought only makes my grin grow wider.

Gage slides into the driver's seat, starts the engine, and propels us out into traffic. A vehicle blares its horn, no doubt because Gage just cut them off.

"What was Sofia doing at Elite last night?"

As the buildings slide by my window, I shrug. "She wanted to know where I get my hair done."

I can feel his eyes burning a hole in the side of my head but refuse to acknowledge it. He might be able to run all over Fletcher, but I will be damned if he does it to me. Last night was amazing. One of the best nights I have had in a very long time. But it's over now and time to get back to the reality of living a life of lies.

His voice grows firmer. "Why was she there, Allie?"

That's it.

I cross my arms and angle my body toward him. "Oh, I'm sorry. Am I supposed to run everything by you now?" I hiss. I don't know why I'm being like this. That's not true. I know why. I want another evening like last night and know I can't have it.

"Careful, little lion."

"No, you better be careful, you… you big macho arrogant dirt-burglar frog!" He is so gorgeous it hurts my eyes and jumbles my thoughts to the point I can't even insult him correctly.

He must have a death wish because his dimples appear. "You think I'm macho?"

"Yeah, as macho as an ant."

He laughs, the asshole. "Considering an ant can carry fifty times its weight, I'll take that as a compliment. What's that, six compliments now?"

"It wasn't a compliment," I huff, facing forward.

We drive in silence for a few minutes before he says, "I just wanted to know if she was okay. It looked like you got to her just in time the other day."

I study his chiseled face and try to detect any manipulation but only find genuineness in his eyes. However, he needs to learn that it's not his business. "She's fine. Well, as fine as she can be. Don't worry. I got it handled."

He nods as if we are on the same page. "That's good. From what I saw, you had control of the situation."

"Are you trying to be sarcastic?" I hate the vulnerability laced in my voice.

"Not at all. I meant what I told you last night. You got charged by a man twice your size, managed to impair his eyesight, and got away from him within seconds. It was impressive."

My mouth opens, ready to issue a rebuttal, but I snap it shut. His response is the last thing I expected. After the day Harlow handcuffed me to herself, I spent the next six years working hard to prove I could handle any situation and help bring justice to my family.

But despite all that hard work, all I hear is *You're not ready yet.*

Gage barely knows me, yet he recognizes my skill set. He said he was impressed, which—after watching him teach part of the class yesterday—feels like a huge compliment. I have no idea what his actual job is, but whatever it is, people seem to bow down to just his presence.

"Thank you."

As we flow through the familiar streets of Seattle, the city's unique blend of modernity and history unfolds before me. The iconic Space Needle is visible from here, its slender form piercing the sky. I can't help but feel a sense of pride for this city that I now call home.

The vibrant energy is palpable: hipsters sipping coffees, families strolling along the sidewalks, cyclists weaving through traffic with effortless ease. I crack the window and breathe in the faint scent of salt mingling with the aroma of freshly brewed coffee—the true Seattle signature.

We arrive just as Mario does. Shaking his hand, he tells Gage it's an honor to work with him. I want to roll my eyes, but technically I'm on the clock and need to keep it professional.

The Onyx is a luxurious building, renowned for hosting an array of high-profile events. It emits an air of sophistication with its sleek, polished surfaces and towering glass windows. This morning, the Onyx stands quiet and still, a serene sanctuary.

Gage keeps his distance while I work with Mario, who inspects the layout in grave detail. I have no idea why. It's the International Security Expo. Nothing wild ever happens.

Like the thought is a light bulb going off above my head, I realize I'm onto something. There must be a group or person coming who's planning to cause trouble. Are Fletcher's top competitors planning something destructive during his expo? Maybe that's why Gage told Fletcher he didn't want me to contact the guests and confirm their reservations. It must be someone who was invited, and they don't want me to get involved.

My question is why allow this person access, then? You can't enter the expo without an invitation. Even if you manage to snag an invitation, your name must also be on the list. I already tried pulling up the guest list on my computer to take a closer look and see if any names stuck out. But Fletcher apparently took orders from Gage, because I came up empty. The file had been removed from the folder I had saved it in.

An hour later, Mario is walking out just as Roxanne is walking in.

"Hey, Allie," she says. Roxanne is tall and slender, with deep green eyes and stunning red hair. "I'm so glad I caught you here. Sorry I didn't return your calls. You know how it gets. My schedule is crammed. Not enough hours in the day."

We shake hands. "Hey, no problem," I say. "I'm glad you could make it."

Her eyes drift over my shoulder and widen.

I can smell spring mint before he ever speaks a word.

"Gage, wow. I didn't expect to see you here," Roxanne says as she drops my hand to tuck her curly red hair behind her ear. She pushes her chest out and gazes at him with lust.

How am I the only person who didn't know who Gage was? Oh, never mind. That's right. I have no life.

"You can call me Mr. McCollin." He reaches out to shake hands with Roxanne.

She giggles. This time I do roll my eyes.

"How's the Red Light running these days?" He's asking about her bar and grill.

She, of course, lights up like a Christmas tree and begins twirling her hair. "It's great, better than great. You should come and have a couple of drinks with me. It's closed until four, but I would be more than happy to give you a personal tour. I'm free right after this."

I tense, waiting to see what he's going to do. She literally just offered herself to him on a platter, right after telling me she was too busy to return my phone calls.

Gage stares at her, his face hard.

I shiver from the intensity of the look he is giving her.

"I think it's best you focus on the job Allie has for you. This is an important event."

"Of course," Roxanne replies, clearly flustered and embarrassed. "I take it you will be attending?"

Gage ignores her. "Allie, let me know if you need anything."

He stalks off and I try. I honestly try not to smile. But I can't help it.

By the time I'm finished, it appears Gage is too. He grabs my hand and leads me out of the Onyx, passing Roxanne on the sidewalk, and opens the passenger door for me.

He races through traffic back toward Transcend Towers as if he is preparing for the Indy 500. He really does have impressive driving skills. I grip my seat belt but can't get the shit-eating grin off my face. This is too much fun and the adrenaline flowing through me is like a drug. I glance at Gage to see him gazing at me. His smile makes him look younger, even carefree.

He whips through traffic with ease, and it doesn't take long before he puts his car in park. Outside my window, a sign made of cut rock declares that we're at Seward Park.

"What are we doing here?"

"I'm starving. They have the best pulled pork." Gage pulls off his hoodie, his black shirt riding up and giving me a view of his hard abs. This man is pure torture. He exits the car before I have a chance to respond and walks around to open my door.

"The best pulled pork you have ever had is in a park?" I ask.

"That's right." He leans in to remove my seat belt. Apparently, I'm not moving quickly enough for him.

"Wait, no. We need to get to Shield Tech. Fletch is already stressed enough as it is."

"Fletcher isn't at the office right now."

"He isn't?"

"Nope, he knows we're getting a bite to eat. Now come on." He takes my hand and lifts me out of the car. "Let's get some food and talk more about how macho you think I am."

I laugh, shaking my head, and walk with him through the park. I've driven by Seward Park a thousand times but never stopped. Now I wish I would have come sooner. I'm immediately struck by the sheer beauty of the natural surroundings. People are spread throughout, some walking or biking, some sitting and talking, others reading.

The birds chirp away like they are performing at the Grand Ole Opry on this warm, sunny day. I take a deep breath, filling my lungs with the scent of fresh pine and earth, embracing our short break. Gage's hand is still interlaced with mine, tugging me along. I like how much he holds my hand.

"Come on, little lion, a man is going to die from starvation if you don't move it along."

I halt in my tracks, releasing his hand and pointing at my heels. "Let me see you speed walk in these babies. On. The. Grass."

Gage peers at my heels as a deliciously dark smile comes across his face.

"Wait, what are you—" I'm cut off as he tosses me over his shoulder. *Tosses me over his shoulder!* Lord, have mercy on my ovaries.

"You really can't get enough of my macho side, can you?"

I shriek as I dangle over him, gripping the back of his T-shirt tightly. "Gage, put me down." I attempt to sound firm but fail miserably. This is too much fun. His ass is incredible from this angle.

"Hold still, little lion. We're on a mission to save humankind."

I laugh, liking the playful Gage. I notice a few smiles directed at us. Gage's muscles flex underneath my body. He carries me as if I am as light as a bird, and it takes me back to last night, when we sparred against each other. His knowledge of fighting came from a dark place. His horrible father, forcing his young son to be beaten every day. I remember his comment about his father when we were at my desk.

Because every day I dress like this, I hope my father is rolling over in his grave with disgust.

As harsh as those words were, I now understand why he feels that way. It's always said you should never speak ill of the deceased. I've never agreed with that. If any human was a horrible person, then they should be remembered for that. By the very actions that they chose to live by.

Gage gently sets me down on my feet at a cute little food cart. It's bright red with a yellow canopy. An older man, probably in his early seventies, smiles largely when he takes notice of Gage.

"I'm going to need two of your best pulled pork sandwiches, some chips, and a couple of bottles of water." Gage's voice drops slightly lower, but I can still hear him. "This beauty is a hard one to impress."

The old man chuckles and quickly makes our sandwiches. He passes the food over to him along with a blanket and smiles over at me. Gage hands him a hundred-dollar bill and jerks his head. I follow over to sit in the long shade cast by a stately magnolia tree. The scent of the white flowers reminds me of the wildflower field at the Oasis.

Wasting no time, Gage unwraps his sandwich and takes a bite so big, almost half the sandwich vanishes. He sighs dramatically as if it's the best thing he has ever eaten. I laugh as I unwrap mine and take a normal-sized bite. The barbeque sauce explodes against my tastebuds, and a moan slips from my lips. It's spicy with a pinch of sweetness.

We eat in silence as I take in the sounds of Canadian geese honking and bumblebees buzzing around us. A large bald eagle soars above us, stealing my breath. It doesn't seem like a place that Gage would come to, but the way he knew exactly where to go, and the old gentleman handing him a blanket, tells me he must come here often.

"Tell me about yourself, Allie Smith. Any siblings?"

I pop a potato chip into my mouth and crunch on it. As much as I don't want to lie to Gage about my past, I have no choice in the matter. The nice thing about lying is that I get to make better endings for my family. "Yes. I have an older brother."

"What does he do?"

I lean back on my hands and stretch my legs out across the soft blanket. I soak in the summer sun's warmth. "He travels the world, helping communities who can't afford modern technology in their schools. What about you? Do you have any brothers or sisters?"

"A younger brother."

"Where is he?"

"Ashton is finishing up in the military."

"He must be very brave to take on a job like that," I reply, cracking my eye open to see he has lain on his side. His hand is fisted underneath his temple with his hat now facing forward to shade against the sun. He looks the most relaxed that I've seen him. "What does that symbol represent on your hat?"

He takes it off. His dark wavy hair is messy, making him look hotter.

I drop down and lie on my side, mimicking his posture as I lean in closer to the unique symbol. Its stark white threads are made up of several different intertwined lines with no beginning or end that I can find.

"It's a Dara knot. It was symbolized by the ancient Celts for inner strength and wisdom during challenging situations."

"I love that." I trace the lines of the knot. "Does it work?"

His artic-blue eyes reach mine as he smiles. It feels like he's stolen my breath right out of my lungs, and I can't help but think about how soft his lips felt against mine.

"Of course it works." He taps his chest where his heart is. "Everything you need is always in here, but you have to decide whether you're going to listen to it."

I laugh softly, not able to understand this gorgeous man in front of me.

Gage clutches his chest. "Are you making fun of my confessions?"

This guy. I throw my head back and laugh hard while he smirks. "No. I just don't understand you. One minute you're all..." I wave my hand in the air trying to figure out the right words. "Ice cream and sandy beaches. The next, you're dark and stormy, ready to burn the world to ashes. It's like you're two different people."

He considers my words—his eyes never leave mine. "I guess I am. I have both my mother and father in me. Even though my father was nothing but scum, I did learn a lot from him. In my line of work, everyone can only see one side of me. They don't know what drives me or what war is battling inside my head. All they see is a formidable opponent."

He wears armor, showing everyone his strength and excellence. I'm starting to wonder if my dark knight is a white knight under his hard shell.

"Where did you get this hat?"

"My mother got it for me."

I smile. His love for his mother is deep. "Does she live close by?"

"She passed away. Suicide. Seven years ago."

My heart plummets into my stomach. He lost his mother at the same time I lost mine. It's something I wouldn't wish on my worst enemy.

"I'm sorry."

"Don't feel sorry for me. I'm the reason she killed herself." Sadness fills Gage's eyes.

He may scare the entire population, but there is absolutely no way his mother killed herself because of him. "You can't say that."

He balances his hat on two fingers. "She gave me this hat the day she decided I was a lost cause. Three months later, I got word she jumped off a cliff."

"Gage."

He slides his hat on and peers at me. "What about your parents? Do they live nearby?"

I want to tell him he can't blame himself for her death, but I can tell he's done with this conversation. He doesn't want to discuss it and that's something I can understand firsthand and respect. I want nothing more than to speak the truth to him. To vent all my anger and frustration. To show him he isn't the only one who lives in the shadows of his deceased loved ones.

Instead, I stick with the story. "They moved to Australia. My mom owns a winery, and my dad owns a retail gun shop."

"Why didn't you go with them?"

"I wanted to... badly. Trust me." I look upward into the blue sky. Not a cloud in sight. "But it didn't work out that way."

Gage nods as if he can see right into my soul. We stare into each other's eyes, feeding off one another. His gaze can be intense. I remind myself not to fidget. He catches every small detail and I can't let him discover that I'm lying.

I move our talk to lighter ground. "What did you want to be when you were little?"

There's no hesitation in his answer. "A superhero."

I can picture an adorable little brown-haired boy with artic eyes running through the house, flashing his dimples, with a red cape flying behind him.

"I wanted to be Rainbow Brite." I smile at the memories of forcing Logan to watch it with me at least a hundred times. "When I realized I couldn't be her, I wanted to be a painter like Bob Ross."

Gage smiles large and says, "Complete with happy little accidents and sending crooked trees to Washington."

I laugh. Gage must have watched him as well. "I used to paint landscapes. My parents would hang every one I painted, even the real bad ones. I remember talking my family into painting a picture of what they loved most, but it couldn't be a person." I made that rule because I was horrible at painting humans. "We all sat in the study that winter night, painting our own little masterpieces. My mom painted a glass of wine, my dad a gun, and my brother a bunch of weird numbers, which I guess was computer code."

"Wait, don't say it. Let me guess. You painted a flower?"

I knock him on the shoulder. "Smartass. And yes, it was, but it wasn't one flower. It was a field of them." I can still remember how happy I was that day. Moments like that were rare. My family worked nonstop and never took the time to stop and smell the roses.

"How did you go from Rainbow Brite and Bob Ross to working at a top security agency and self-defense classes?"

His question is logical enough, but one I can't answer in full.

I drag my finger across the soft blanket, making figure eights. "I don't know. I went through a really hard time in my life. I felt as if I didn't know which way was up. It was like I was lost in a sea with unfamiliar waves crashing into me at every angle. Until one day, I washed ashore with a sense of meaning."

Gage's expression grows distant like he's envisioning it... and maybe empathizing with that younger version of me.

"I started running every day, miles at a time. I would run until I could finally take a deep breath in the drowning sea that lived inside me. In the beginning, it would take me hours to achieve that. As time went on, I didn't have to run as long. So I started self-training, but I quickly realized I didn't have a clue what I was doing. A friend set me up with Riggs once I moved to the city. His Krav Maga class scared the crap out of me when I first saw it." I laugh, remembering how I walked out on Harlow and Riggs showing me what it was all about.

"You seem to have found your footing now."

"Thank you." I twist the cap off my water bottle and take a sip. "When did you and Riggs meet?"

"Not long after my mother died. Every day that passed, I got angrier. I was losing my grounding without her. It wasn't always easy following the ways of the Dara knot. Before my mother left us, she would tell me to take all the hate trying to grow inside my body and beat it out on the punching bags. And that's just what I did. I used it as an outlet for my anger issues, trying to stay true to my core and not become a replica of my father."

My heart sinks with the thoughts of an innocent little boy raised and used in a way no one should be.

"But once she died, I was lost. Conner knew Riggs and that he was opening his own gym. We went one night to check it out and I was hooked. A few months into it, I learned how to control my anger."

"No child should have to go through something like that."

He nods, bringing himself to a sitting position. I follow suit, adjusting my blouse.

"You remind me of my mother and her large heart," he says.

I smile at the bottle of water in my hands, not sure what to say.

"And I think your big heart is why you're wanting to help Sofia."

"I can see the damage her father is doing to her, and I hate that she goes through that," I say. "She told me her mother passed of cancer years ago, and outside of a few friends, she's all alone."

"Her father is involved with some bad men. He works as a drug mule but has been dipping into their profits recently. They're not happy about that, as you can imagine."

"How do you know that?"

His only response is a raised brow.

"I still think I can help her. Fletcher has agreed to donate to one family in need. He's willing to put top security in someone's home, free of charge. I can pick the family since it was my idea, but I hadn't found anyone until I met Sofia. I'm making progress with her, but she's still closed off."

"She's in much deeper than you think. Fletcher's security wouldn't stop them from getting to her."

I stiffen. "What do you mean, stop them from getting to her? Are they planning to use her as leverage to get their money back from her father?"

"Sofia witnessed a man kill her father's best friend, another drug mule who was helping dip into the profits. The prosecution in the murder case is trying to convince Sofia to testify against him in less than two weeks. Until she agrees, they won't provide her with protection."

My lips break apart with a gasp. *That's* why she won't allow me to help her. She doesn't want to drag me into the mess she's in. "Who's the guy they want her to testify against?"

"A very close friend of the Italian Mafia. Domenico Amante. The Mafia sources most of their drugs through Mexico. Ricardo, her father, is the head of operations, and Nico keeps an eye on the operation. You've already placed yourself in danger by trying to help her. The Mafia is searching for the rumored witness who might testify."

"Oh my God." I stand and start to grab everything. "I have to find out where she's at."

Gage grabs my hands, stopping my progress. "Hey, I know you're strong and have a high skill level, but you can't just walk into a den of wolves. I give you my word. I'll take care of this. I already have a plan in place. I'm leaving tonight, out of town, but I'll be back by Saturday—"

"Saturday!" I interrupt. "I can't wait until Saturday to do something." My breathing has turned erratic. My heart pounds through my chest at a rapid rate. "I'm not going to sit around while Sofia is in danger."

Gage releases my hands and cups my face, forcing me to look into his blue eyes. "Calm down and take a deep breath. I wasn't suggesting that."

At his command, I drag in deep shaky breaths.

"Good girl," he says. He leans forward and kisses me gently on the forehead.

"I'll be back by Saturday for the expo, but I'll set up a time beforehand for you, Sofia, and a good friend of mine who has the resources to hide her. You can meet and discuss how to move forward."

"Okay," I say, appreciating the help that he doesn't need to give. His calmness settles my heart. "How will I know when this is happening?"

"I'll let you know." His voice turns firmer. "But I need you to promise me that you trust in what I'm telling you and you're not going to do anything stupid while I'm gone."

I nod in agreement. Gage obviously has connections beyond the normal person, knowing this much about Sofia. I don't know why or even how I can trust Gage as much as I do. But I do. I can feel it in my bones. He might live a mysterious life filled with blood and death, that I am sure of. But I can see the young boy deep down inside him, keeping his core close to his heart like his mother taught him.

"What do you do for work?" I ask, realizing I don't have a clue.

"I'm a superhero," he responds, smiling at me before hoisting me into the air over his shoulder.

"More like a caveman," I reply and feel his chest shake from laughing.

Chapter Eight

Kali.

Gage takes me back to the office and leaves shortly afterward. I race through my list of things to do for the expo, attempting to keep my mind off the danger Sofia's in, knowing I need to trust in Gage's word. One thing great is that Sofia did come by and grab the DVD while I was out. I just wish I could've seen her. I left another card inside the case, this time with my cell phone number on it.

By the time seven o'clock rolls around, I'm spent, and Fletcher is ushering me out of the building. I walk out of the front doors of Transcend Towers and notice a guy standing across the street who appears out of place. He's tall with a large frame and dark hair. He looks scary. He has a magazine in his hands, but he doesn't seem like he's reading it. Could this be one of Ricardo's guys or someone from the Italian Mafia? After what Gage told me, I'm on pins and needles.

Maybe it's all in my head. I wish I could go to Riggs's class tonight. It always grounds me, taking away my anxiety. But that won't be an option for the next few weeks. Mimi went into labor a few hours ago. I haven't heard from either of them yet, but I can't wait to meet their son.

I grab my keys in one hand and fist my pepper spray in the other. Just in case. My mind is somewhere else, jumbled with panic and worry about Mimi's labor and about Sofia. Ten minutes into the drive, just as I'm about to get on the Evergreen Point Floating Bridge, I spot a black SUV a few cars behind me, making all the same turns that I do.

I can't risk leading them to my safe haven in the country, so I deliberately take several right turns, eventually making a full circle to the office. By that time, the SUV is gone, and I gun it all the way home.

I pull into my driveway another twenty-five minutes later, giving a sigh of relief upon arriving at my little home. There isn't much to it. It's a small cottage tucked into a beautiful piece of property. Harlow gave me the money to buy this place. My parents had millions, but I can't spend a dime of it. After all, I'm supposed to be dead.

I pull into my garage and shut the door before exiting my car. I have three deadbolts on every door except the sliding glass door. Even though my home is equipped with the best security from Fletcher, something about a deadbolt still brings me comfort.

My house is pitch black and warm. I love my little sanctuary. But right now, I'm all in my head and need nothing more than to get all these lights turned on. I walk over to my dining room and flip all four switches at once to be greeted by a bulky man sitting at my kitchen table.

I release a bloodcurdling scream and slam my body against the wall.

"It's nice to see you too, sis." My brother leans forward, placing his elbows on my table.

"Cheese and rice, Logan! You scared the crap out of me." I walk over to the table, toss my bag on it, and drop into the seat across from him. I release a breath to calm my heart from slamming against my chest.

He gives a light chuckle. "I see that. Why are you so uneasy?"

"You're sitting in my house in the dark! What did you expect me to do?"

"And turning the lights on wouldn't have freaked you out when you pulled in?"

He has a point. I would've burned rubber getting as far away from this house as possible. I give him the only response I can, which is to bang my head on the table.

"I'm sure you made every screaming goat extremely proud of your performance."

I raise my head and smile at my brother. That fatal night, right before Harlow whisked me away, Logan demanded to go back. I could have lost him that day, and if I had, I honestly don't believe I would've lived much longer. There wouldn't have been any reason to go on. But between Harlow with her damn handcuffs and Logan with his annoying ass, they gave me no choice but to move on and *live*.

I owe them both my life.

"Are you hungry?"

"When am I not? I haven't had a home-cooked meal since the last time I came to see you," he says, leaning back into his chair, slapping his stomach with his hand.

I push myself up and head around the bar into the kitchen. I set the oven to preheat and pull out the lasagna I made a couple of nights ago. "What took you so long to come by again? It feels like forever since I last saw you." I grab a wineglass for me and a rocks glass for Logan.

"Been busy. Got a couple of guys and introduced them to their maker."

"I thought you got everyone who was there that night?" I ask, grabbing Crown Royal for him. It's not the good stuff he prefers, but I'm on a budget.

"I did, but these guys were directly involved with the head snake."

I drop a couple of ice cubes into his drink. "And who's that?"

"No one for you to worry about. We're getting close. It's only a matter of time."

That's always Logan's response when I ask. He keeps me in the dark about who was involved in our parents' murders. The only new people who were coming around the few weeks before our parents were killed were Victor and his son, Aric. But surely Logan would have told me it was Victor if that was the case. We used to get into heated arguments all the time over him not telling me shit, but it would only drive him away.

I miss my brother and love when I do get to see him. I drop the subject for that reason alone.

I pour his whisky and my glass of Moscato wine. I put the lasagna in the oven and return to the table, passing Logan his drink.

"How's your week going, little sister?"

Gage's icy-blue eyes and sexy dimples come to mind. "Riggs had a guest host at Elite Training this week who's a professional fighter, or something like that. He was impressed with my techniques." Although he's not a professional fighter, I don't know what else to say. *Superhero* comes to mind, but I dismiss that right away.

Is it ridiculous to already miss someone you just met? Probably.

"I heard."

"You did?" I struggle to suppress the surprise in my voice.

Logan nods and takes a sip of his drink. "Gage McCollin."

When I sit frozen, staring at him, Logan gives me a look like I might have a concussion. "You know, the same guy who came to your place of employment to meet with Fletcher."

"Well," I reply, smoothing my skirt. "He wasn't wrong. You haven't seen me in action at class for a long time."

"The answer's still no, Kali."

Using my real name is his way of letting me know he's serious.

Could I send anyone *to their maker*, as he so lightly put it? No. I don't even like guns, and the thought of having to kill someone... I couldn't do it. No matter what. Guilt fills me for not being strong enough to get the justice my parents deserve.

"Do you remember the day at the Oasis when you only hit the target one time, but Father was so proud of you?"

I nod. It's one of my favorite memories.

"Do you know why he was so proud of you?"

I don't. It's always confused me, the pride that shone from him when he looked at me. Who would be proud that their daughter couldn't hit a target when their entire empire was built on firearms?

"Because he knew you were better than that. That you were meant for something much larger than anything he could offer. He was proud you couldn't care less about guns or any of our family business. The light you bring wherever you go has no place in the dark shadows that lurk in every corner." He takes a sip of his drink. "He was proud of your heart and the love you find in everything. When he saw you weren't interested in the family business, he made sure you wouldn't be. He made me promise to never let the darkness of this world take your light away. I will honor my promise until my last breath."

Logan's words knock the air from my lungs. I never knew our father felt that way. He never pressured me to be involved in anything regarding the family business, and I never argued. I was content with staying out of the meetings.

But things have changed. He's no longer here to protect me from dark shadows. He's six feet under, next to our mother. Sitting back and doing nothing is saying I don't care. That I don't miss them every single day. That I'm not strong enough to fight for them. "There has to be something I can do."

Logan shakes his head. "You *are* doing something. You're being you, and that's all they ever wanted. This is bigger than some Krav Maga class and way bigger than saving daughters who get knocked around by their fathers or cats stuck in trees."

I scowl. I might be grateful he survived that day, but that doesn't mean he doesn't get on my last damned nerve all the time. He spoke with either Gage or Harlow. They're the only ones with a direct relationship with both Fletcher and Riggs.

I cross my arms across my chest. "For your information, the cat was fifty feet up in that tree. I would like to see you climb a tree that tall in a matter of seconds and catch a ferocious wild animal with claws like a wolverine's." Sure, the story wasn't true, but I need to stay off the topic of Sofia with Logan.

"First off, you told Riggs it was a thirty-, maybe forty-foot tree. I looked at a few local environment databases and no such tree exists off State *or* Primrose."

"And those databases you hack into are probably outdated."

Logan doesn't skip a beat. "And second, if you did climb a tree on a rescue mission, it wasn't some vicious feline with claws like a wolverine. It was probably more like a kitten who was cruelly declawed."

"I did save a cat. That's how I got scratched." I hold up my bandaged arm as proof.

Logan slams back the rest of his drink. He drags his hand through his thick blond hair, which is cropped on the sides and longer on top than I'm used to seeing on him. "Kali, this work... It's too dangerous for you. I can't lose you, not after I have lost everything else. I just can't. I wouldn't be able to live with myself if anything happened to you."

"How do you think I feel? I feel the same about you, and I would rather die by your side fighting for Mom and Dad than wait to hear you're never coming back."

"You wouldn't fight anyone. You'd be too busy trying to find the good in them."

We sit in silence, staring each other down. I refuse to look away or blink first. It may be a little immature, but whatever. I'll superglue my eyelids open if I have to. My clock on the wall ticks in the background and I narrow my eyes to keep them lubed. The struggle is real. The end result is probably the same as throwing sand in my eyes.

Logan widens his eyes and then crosses them while sticking his tongue out and licking his nose.

"Oh my God, you are so gross." I stand and grab his empty glass to get him a refill. Once my back is turned, I blink several times to relieve the dryness.

"I win," Logan crows, laughing.

I toss another ice cube into his glass and fill it three fingers high this time. Maybe it's a good thing that he doesn't come by all the time. The way he slams whisky, I would blow through my savings in no time.

He clears his throat before saying, "What are your thoughts on Gage?"

I wonder where he's going with this. Did Riggs mention he might have noticed the temperature had risen about a thousand degrees during our sparring? I return to my seat at the table, hand him his fresh drink, and shrug. "Not much to say. He knows what he's doing when it comes to fighting."

"What about at Shield Tech?"

I need to reconsider uprooting my life completely so he doesn't have nonstop details flowing in about my interactions. Maybe I can move to Alaska? "He seemed all right." I take a sip of my wine.

Logan, the ass he can be, just stares at me. After the long day I've had, this is the last thing I want to do with my brother.

I aim for everything that gets under my skin about Gage. "He's bossy and won't take no for an answer. He has taken our well-thought-out plan for the expo—and I mean well-thought-out—and tossed it out the window. Poof, we no longer know what the heck we're doing, apparently." I flap my hand around. "He's making Fletch cover the guest list. I always go over the guest list. I don't get why I can't manage calling everyone like I always do. He's nothing more than a hotheaded, egotistical macho man who thinks he's a superhero." I also want to say he's the most beautiful man I've ever seen. That he's sweet, caring, and funny.

Logan's eyebrows shoot up his forehead. "Macho man?"

Does every guy only capture incriminating words when you speak a mouthful? "Yep, that's what I said."

"You like him?"

"Yeah, pretty much." I drag my finger across the rim of my glass. "Did Fletcher tell you I found someone to help out?"

"Nice try."

I tilt my head and project confused innocence. "Huh?"

"Gage is here to work, so let him do his job and don't get in the way. If he doesn't want you doing certain tasks, you need to listen and not ask questions."

It seems my big brother knows exactly why Gage is in town. *Interesting.* "Oh my God." I can't believe I didn't think of this possibility before.

"What?"

"Gage is on your team, isn't he? That's why you're in the area. Gage works for you."

Logan tosses his head back and laughs like I just told the world's funniest joke. His laugh is one of those full-belly ones that is so hard, tears well up in his eyes.

I take a large gulp of wine, annoyed. "Are you done?" I snap.

"Oh God, my stomach hurts now. I'm sorry, that was just too funny."

"And what's so funny about it?"

"That you would think Gage works for me."

Oh.

"Or that he would work for anyone."

I run through all my encounters with Gage and how he has taken control of everything. He took the lead in the alleyway, getting Sofia and me out of there. He took over control at Shield Tech for the expo. And he took over the Krav Maga class as if it was his own. He's literally bulldozed into everyone's lives in a matter of days without hesitation and no one batted an eye. Gage is as mysterious as they come, and I've always been a sucker for a mystery novel. The urge to know every detail about him is scary. He's hijacked my mind, leaving me in uncharted waters.

The buzzer on the oven goes off and I get up. After loading our plates, I sit and ask the same question I always ask before we eat. "What was something good that happened in your day?"

This is an ongoing tradition that our parents started before I can even remember. Every night at dinner, each one of us had to say one good thing that happened during our day. It could be a good thing we did, something good that happened to us, or even something we enjoyed.

"You first," Logan replies around a mouthful of food.

I think about my time with Gage at Seward Park eating lunch. The magnolia tree we sat near was stunning, but he was breathtaking. Our conversation was deep. He shared part of his soul with me, and it's easy to surmise he doesn't do that freely with many. I only wish I could have shared more of my soul with him. Maybe in another lifetime. "I ate the best barbeque pulled pork sandwich in the entire world."

"Really? Where at?"

"You know, I didn't pay attention to the name on the food cart. Some old man sells them at Seward Park."

"No shit."

I nod, taking a bite of the lasagna. "Okay, your turn."

Logan sits quietly for a moment. "Seeing you."

His words make me smile. He says the same thing every time.

After he finishes his plate, he pushes it away. "Tell me about this girl you found to help. You get any more information on her?"

"Not much. Her name's Sofia. I saw her at Elite Training last night by chance and she picked up a DVD Harlow got me on jujitsu this morning. She might be seventeen or eighteen."

His face darkens considerably. "And her father hit her?"

I swallow the warm lasagna. "Yeah, he smacked her pretty good a couple of times, I think. I only saw him do it once, though."

"There was no police officer, was there?"

As much as I want to stick to the story I told Fletcher, I can't with Logan. Where Fletch won't break the law, Logan will hack into anything regardless of the law. He's a wiz on computers and could easily check out my story. Plus, there would be a record of her father's arrest on file that Logan could hack into. But that doesn't mean I can't bend the truth.

"No," I say, stuffing my mouth with as much food as possible. I know what question is coming next.

"How did you get her out of that situation?"

I point to my mouth, telling Logan it's going to be a second. Now that I know he's acquainted with Gage, I'm not sure what to do. If Gage happened to tell him he saw me, I could be caught up in a lie. But if Gage never mentioned it, I could go with an alternative ending—and one that doesn't consist of a nonexistent Glock.

"Her father stormed off after he hit her the last time. Oh!" I say loudly, excited to remember another detail. "Her father's name is Ricardo."

"That's good. Is Fletch planning on helping her with his security system?"

I nod, even though Fletch hasn't confirmed yet. My only hope is that Gage can somehow get me a meeting with his friend and Sofia. He asked me to trust him, and though the number of people I trust can easily be counted on one hand, I feel deep in my bones that Gage will follow through with his promise.

Chapter Nine

Allie.

Yawning, I lock my Jimmy and hustle to the office. After dinner last night, Logan and I watched a movie while he munched some popcorn. He can eat a house down. He didn't watch much of the movie; he worked on his laptop most of the night. He never stops working, just like Dad. I asked him if he would stay the night. I was still worried about the guy I saw outside work yesterday, plus the SUV that might have been trailing me.

Logan agreed but was gone before I woke up. His bed in the guest room was made, and a big fresh pot of coffee was brewed, so I know he stayed until morning. I miss him already.

I get to my desk and check my voicemail, hoping maybe Sofia called, but no such luck. I tell Fletcher I'm heading to the Onyx to meet with the exhibitors who are setting up today, but he shoots me down, saying I am to stay in the building and work on other things.

He doesn't say the order came from Gage, but I have a suspicion it did. I've always handled these tasks every year prior and loved doing it. Instead of arguing like I normally would, I bite my tongue and knock out the work he assigns.

Riggs calls with the news that they welcomed a baby boy late last night. I stop by the hospital after work with a large bouquet of flowers to meet the new little man. He's adorable and I couldn't be happier for them. Jealousy, like usual, flows through me at what Riggs and Mimi have. If my life of lies ever ends, I hope to one day get my happily ever after.

By the time night falls, I'm restless, pacing in my living room. Sofia has been silent. One small glimmer from the day was that the strange man I saw last night was nowhere in sight when I left work, and the same goes for the SUV. Maybe it *was* all in my head.

I've just finished washing the dishes when my cell phone pings. I dry my hands and run over to the couch, where my phone is, and plop down. The number is unknown. I don't give my phone number out, so this might be Sofia.

I open the text and read the message.

Unknown: Are you being a good girl? I don't want to have to strap my cape on and fly in at a moment's notice to make sure.

Gage. His text makes me smile. I lean back into the cushions. He must have gotten my phone number from Fletcher.

Allie: Hmm, it all depends on what you consider good.

I add his contact into my phone before getting another ping.

Superhero: Don't test me, woman. You better be home safe and sound.

A second ticks by and another text comes through.

Superhero: And alone.

My ovaries just exploded.

Allie: But this guy from Krav was just getting ready to show me how to improve my techniques.

I don't know why I'm poking the bear, but the thought of getting him fired up makes me feel better.

My phone rings a second later. I laugh as I answer. "Hello?"

"You better be messing around," Gage says roughly. He could have made millions as a phone sex operator.

I bite my lip. "And why would that be?"

He growls. It's the sexiest thing I have ever heard.

I put some sass into my voice. "You may be able to run over everyone else, but you don't know me."

"If I were there right now, I would bend you over my knee and remind you who I am."

My panties just went up in a cloud of smoke. "You wouldn't."

"You have no idea what I'm capable of, little lion."

The nickname causes butterflies to erupt in my stomach. I lean back into the couch, grinning like a Cheshire cat. "And what exactly are you capable of?"

"Taming little lions, so stop playing around. Are you home alone?"

"Yes, Mr. Bossy Pants."

He grunts his satisfaction. "How did it go at Shield Tech today?"

"Oh, I wasn't aware that you were my new boss."

"Allie." His voice is firm, causing me to laugh.

"It was fine, but for some reason, Fletcher wouldn't let me go to the Onyx to meet the other vendors. You wouldn't happen to know anything about that, would you?"

"Your skills are above that."

His answer awes me. "Okay, you win. You can be my new boss. I want a raise in the form of cheeseburgers and diamonds."

He chuckles into the phone while my smile grows. Knowing I can make him laugh makes me feel like I just stepped out on the moon for the first time. "Any word from your friend on getting Sofia to a safe place?"

"Yes. In fact, I just got off the phone. It's all lined up for tomorrow."

I sit up straight. "Really? Will Sofia be there too?"

"She will be there."

I push to my feet and pace the floor, releasing the energy flowing through me. "Okay, good. Where do I need to be and when?"

"Be at home by six and they'll come to you."

I stop in my tracks. "Wait, at my place?"

"Yes, at your place."

My grip tightens on my phone. "One, I'm not giving you my address, and two, I can't have them coming to my place."

There's a very good reason that Logan, Harlow, and Fletcher are the only ones who know where I live. Staying hidden in plain sight means keeping everything in your personal life on lockdown. Sofia could come, but I have no clue who his friend is, and that's a big risk to take.

"Why is that a problem?" Gage asks, a note of confusion in his voice.

"Because I said it is."

Gage exhales sharply through the phone. "I'm going to need more than that, Allie."

This would all be so much easier if I could just tell him the truth. Tell him who I really am, explain how I can't live a normal life until Logan handles everything. But I can't tell him. As much as I trust him—trust he just earned by following through with his promise—I can't take that chance.

"I'm waiting."

Here we go.

"I'm a germophobe."

"What?" His disbelief is evident.

"Yeah, a germophobe," I repeat. "And I'll tell you, it's bad. The doctors say I'm the worst they've seen. I refused to meet with them in person, even though they swore their clinic was cleaned on the daily. Yeah, right. Can you believe they said that to me?"

I don't wait for an answer before continuing my garbage talk. "They can sing their little 'we're so clean' song all day long, but I know for a fact they're both married and have, like, a basketball team of kids. And do you know what kids are full of? Germs. Horrible, nasty germs."

I love kids. Love. Them. But Gage doesn't know that.

Gage's deep voice fills my ear. "You're not a germophobe, Allie, or you wouldn't have eaten lunch at the food cart... or kissed me."

I prop a hand on my hip. "You're not a kid."

"Neither is my friend."

I can practically hear his smirk through the phone. Damn it. I'm losing ground here. "They probably have kids."

"There are no kids," Gage says firmly before his voice softens. "Allie."

"Yes," I say, breathing hard into the phone. I probably sound like an overweight chihuahua.

"They'll be there tomorrow at six. Be home."

"Okay," I say.

The phone line goes dead.

Later, as I'm getting out of the bath, I notice a text from Gage that melts me on the spot.

Superhero: Sweet dreams, Rainbow Brite.

I'm getting too caught up in Mr. McDreamy—I mean McCollin—for my own good. This isn't going to turn out well.

It doesn't dawn on me until sleep is taking over: How does he know where I live?

Chapter Ten

Allie.

The atmosphere on the eve of the expo is my favorite. The Onyx is a symphony of orchestrated precision and artistry. At least fifty people are running around doing their part for tomorrow's event. The work of every dedicated individual here has culminated in an awe-inspiring masterpiece, each element meticulously crafted and seamlessly integrated. Most of us have been here since before the sun rose from the mountaintops. Bringing all our hard work over the last couple of months to fruition is the ultimate high.

I lean against the bar. In addition to its gleaming marble floors and towering glass windows, the Onyx now features sleek display booths adorned with state-of-the-art security exhibits. I never know how we're going to surpass ourselves from the prior year, but we always do. This year we went with a cream color accented with deep blues and purples. The combo gives off a serenity vibe.

All the security agencies have their own areas set up along the edges of the main ballroom, each of their color schemes flowing perfectly with the main colors. The stage is where we set up Shield Tech's new exhibit. It's at least five times larger than everyone else's, but no one is complaining. Every year we get several hundred requests to be a part of this event. Only twenty are chosen, and they're grateful to be included. People travel from all over the world to see the latest. I learned quickly this business is cutthroat and you must be on your game to stay on top.

What makes Fletcher stand out from every other business is that he is a one-man show. Well, one man and me. He doesn't operate his business with a board where several different people put their ideas together. He doesn't need to. He's that incredible.

"We did good." Fletcher's voice comes from behind me. I turn to see him standing behind the bar, taking everything in.

Sliding onto the sleek black barstool, I nod in agreement. This is one of the rare days I see Fletcher in normal street clothes instead of his usual suits. He's wearing a worn-out Lynyrd Skynyrd T-shirt and blue jeans. His brown hair is pulled back into a man bun.

I was never a fan of man buns until I met Fletcher. Maybe it's his large build that makes it work so well. Like if you were to mix Fabio and James Bond.

"What?" he asks when he catches me staring at him.

"Nothing, just weird seeing you in street clothes. You should do it more often."

He laughs and shakes his head. "If you want to be taken seriously, you should dress the part."

I think about Gage and how that contradicts Fletcher's thought process. Gage dresses as casually as you get, even though his clothing is made of fine material. But I would put money on the bet that Gage doesn't even own a suit. The moment my eyes met his the first time in that alley, I saw the power they held, and I'm sure everyone does.

He must be able to read my mind, because he says, "Gage is different."

"What do you mean?" I ask.

"Gage helped build his father's empire into one of the most ruthless organizations in the world. Once his father died, he dismantled the entire operation and started his own. He could wear sweatpants and everyone would still bow down to him."

I furrow my brows in confusion. *Ruthless?* I think about him hosting the self-defense class and how he wanted to help women and men defend themselves if the worst were to happen. About how he has made me feel safe. About how he lined up a friend of his to get Sofia to a secure place before the trial. How is that ruthless?

"Don't be naïve, Allie. There's a reason everyone listens to his commands."

"If he's such a bad guy, then why are you friends with him?"

Fletcher's green eyes peer into mine. "I don't know if you could call us friends, but I have never respected another man more."

I prop my elbows on the bar top, lost in his words. Does he respect Gage because he's fearful for his life, or does he respect him because Gage is a vigilante under his cloak?

Fletcher knocks his fist into the bar a couple of times. "Why don't you head out early? We're finished for the day."

I glance at my watch. It's just after four in the afternoon. I don't know if Fletcher is aware of my meeting with Sofia tonight, but I choose to keep it to myself. I can't afford for anything to go wrong.

I grab my things and make my way to my Jimmy, my steps faltering when I notice a big black SUV parked across the street. The windows are blacked out, making it impossible to know whether someone is inside. It could be a random SUV, but the chills that run across my skin tell me it might be the same one from the other night.

I pick up the pace, making sure to keep the SUV in sight. I lock my doors as soon as I'm in my vehicle and punch the gas, whipping out of the parking lot like I just robbed a bank.

I check my rearview mirror. The SUV remains parked on the side of the road. I let out a breath. I didn't even realize I was holding it. I'm losing my damn mind. And though that might be true, I still take the long way home to make sure I'm not followed.

By half past five, I'm cleaned up and pacing in my living room. This seems to be my new thing. My home is small, so it doesn't take me long to reach one end before I need to turn back around. The living room has plush, overstuffed furniture arranged around a stone fireplace. The mantel is covered with small trinkets, but no photos. I can't take the risk of anyone stopping over unexpectedly and asking questions.

I turn my television on, hoping it will distract my mind from running a million miles a minute, but the news doesn't do a thing for me. My nerves are going haywire. Someone I don't know is coming to my place and I still can't process that. If it was just Sofia, I would be okay. But it isn't.

If what Fletcher said about Gage is true, then letting one of his friends into my home is a bad decision on my part. I should have asked more questions. I should have refused to meet them at my home. I grab my cell and call Gage to demand answers, but it goes straight to voicemail.

I go over to my purse and grab my pepper spray, dropping it into my pocket. Frantically, I try to identify anything I could use as a weapon if this friend of his decides to make the wrong choice under my roof. *I will protect Sofia with everything I have.*

A sudden knock at the door causes me to jump. My heart beats frantically against my chest. I take a deep breath, trying to calm myself as I wipe my sweaty palms down my leggings. On shaky legs, I walk to the door and look through the peephole.

Shit!

Harlow is here. She's dressed in blue jeans and a white T-shirt. Her chestnut hair is piled on top of her head in a messy bun. I should have known she might be by. She comes to the expo every year, and we normally make a weekend out of it. I have under thirty minutes to get her in and out. She would lose her ever-loving mind if she knew what I was doing.

I unlock the door and open it to see Harlow grinning at me. I can't help it. Even with her incredibly bad timing, it's still great to see her. I hug her tightly.

"I missed you too, barracuda. Now let me in. I brought a bottle of wine." Harlow waltzes in, taking in the small changes I have made to my place since the last time she was here. "Looking good."

"Thanks," I reply. The clock ticks away on the wall. I need to get her out of here before everything goes down, and the seconds are ticking. Literally.

"Listen, Harlow, I wish you would've called me before you came out. I already have plans for tonight and I'm running late already as it is."

Ignoring my plea, Harlow makes her way into my kitchen and opens the drawer where I keep the cork extractor. "Really? I didn't think you would have any plans with the expo going on tomorrow." She takes two glasses out of the cabinet, pouring red wine into each glass.

"Yeah, well, you know me, always on the go." I laugh nervously. "I honestly don't even have time to have a drink with you, but hey, tomorrow after the expo, let's get together and we can drink all the wine in the house."

Harlow carries both glasses over and hands me one while she smiles brightly.

I frown. "Seriously, Harlow. I can't. Not tonight."

I can already envision the shit show that's going to take place in the next twenty minutes. Harlow sits on my couch and swirls the wine beneath her nose, inhaling before taking a sip.

"What's so important tonight that you can't make time for me?" she asks, leaning back.

"I have a date," I blurt, immediately cringing as the words leave my mouth. Harlow knows me well enough to be wise to my bullshit.

Her eyebrow arches high. "Really? You have a date."

I take a large gulp of the bold wine and sink into my favorite reading chair. It's large enough to fit two people, but I sit on the edge, not wanting to get too comfortable.

"Uh-huh."

She takes another sip and her smile widens. "I can't wait to hear everything about him."

Yep, she already knows I'm full of shit. Which, in all fairness, I am, so I'd better make this convincing.

Gage's face comes to the front of my mind, and I know just what I need to do. "Oh, he's a great guy. When you meet him one day, you're going to love him. He's as handsome as can be. Picture this—he's tall with miles of muscles that are wrapped in beautiful artwork. His hair is dark, but his eyes." I pause as his artic blues fill my mind. "His eyes remind me of Peyto Lake. And when he smiles, his dimples appear, and it's the sexiest thing I've ever seen."

She lights up. "Mmm, I've always appreciated a man with devastating dimples. So, where did you meet him?"

"At the Onyx. I was helping set up the bar and he saw me struggling to carry a crateful of liquor bottles and offered to help."

"He works for another security firm? I don't know if Fletcher would like that very much."

"What? No, I would never do that. No, he's, uh... Well, he does..." I bite my thumbnail, trying hard not to burst all my brain vessels. "He's a stunt coordinator."

I am such an idiot.

"A stunt coordinator at an expo for state-of-the-art security exhibition. That's... interesting," Harlow says. Her smile is starting to piss me off.

"Yeah, I thought so too. He's performing tomorrow night. You remember that guy Jackie Chan?" I ask. After she nods, I continue. "He's cooler than that guy! He's going to make it big one day, maybe even in Hollywood."

"Wow," she says, clearly stifling laughter. "Sounds like you made quite the match."

I nod and take another gulp of wine before any more shit comes out of my mouth.

"What is this... one-of-a-kind man's name?"

I debate giving her Gage's name, but I don't want her and Gage crossing paths tomorrow at the expo if she ends up going. That would be a complete disaster. "Um, Kage."

"Hmm. You know, this guy you just met sounds a lot like someone I know."

"Really?" The coyness in her tone is bringing up my guard. Who the hell says a tall, dark, tatted-up stunt coordinator reminds them of anyone? No one, that's who.

She takes another sip of her wine and then smiles so big, I know I'm missing something. Like there's a fucking elephant in this room and I can't even see one of its toenails.

"Gage McCollin."

My mouth falls open. How does she know Gage? And then it hits me like a lightning strike to the chest: Gage told me he has a good friend who has the resources to hide Sofia. "Oh my God, *you're* his good friend."

"Bingo."

I collapse back in my chair, wondering how I didn't put this together before now. There isn't anyone else like Harlow who has the resources to keep someone safe. She shows up just before the allotted time and lets me blab out utter bullshit to try and get her to leave. And she calls *me* a witch!

"I'm such an idiot," I say, setting my wine down and rubbing my hands over my face.

"I thought it was cute, and believe me, you're not alone crushing over a man like Gage McCollin. I'm sure he has plenty of women throwing their panties at him daily."

My embarrassment increasing tenfold, I groan into my hands while Harlow laughs. "I'm not crushing. I just couldn't think of anyone else to describe."

"If you say so..." Harlow says, letting it hang there like the little witch she is.

"Does he know?" I ask, dropping my hands and taking a sip of my wine.

"Does Gage know what, exactly?"

"Does he know who I really am?"

She shakes her head.

Disappointment runs through my body. In a way, I was hoping she would say yes, and that I didn't need to lie to him anymore. I don't want to explore why it bothers me so much with him when I don't have a problem doing it to other people.

"He did learn that we know each other," she amends. "There was no way around that. I told him we met through Fletcher. But that's where I left it." After a moment of silence, she says, "You looked almost sad when I said that."

I nod. There's no way to hide the truth of whatever I'm feeling from Harlow. "You don't trust him, then. That's why you didn't tell him the truth."

"No, not at all. I trust Gage more than most people, but Logan doesn't want to risk anyone finding out that you survived that night, and I agree."

A sense of warmth floods my chest. It feels good, really good that she trusts in Gage. It's a reassurance that he's someone worth believing in.

A light knock sounds at my door. I set my wine down and rush over, peer through the peephole, and hastily unlock the door. "Hey, I'm so glad to see you."

Sofia's dressed in black leggings and an oversized light gray hoodie. She has a large backpack that has probably seen better days, and it's stuffed to the gills. She dumps the bag to the floor and drops her hood. The bruise has lightened in color. She looks around my home, assessing her surroundings.

"Do you want anything to drink?"

She points at Harlow, who's holding her glass of wine. "Yeah, I'll take what she's having."

"Ha, nice try. I'll grab you a water." I open the fridge, grab a bottle, and toss it over to her. "Come take a seat. I want you to meet my very good friend."

She hesitates but follows me over and sits in the chair I was just in.

"Sofia, this is Harlow. Harlow, Sofia."

Harlow's bright smile is welcoming. "Well, aren't you a cute little thing? I need to know how you braided your hair. That's too pretty."

A small smile lifts Sofia's face. "My friend did it. It's called a fishbone braid or something weird like that."

Harlow's nose scrunches up. "Fishbone? Who in their right mind would name a beautiful braid something so gross?"

We both laugh and Sofia starts to relax in the chair. She takes a drink of her water. "Gage told me you were funny."

"Did he also tell you that he can't beat me at the shooting range?"

Sofia shakes her head. "Nope."

"Or that I am the toughest sparring partner he's ever had? Well, up until recently." Harlow's eyes fall to mine. "He seems to be pretty impressed by someone else's skills on the mat lately."

My face grows hot. I try to hide the smile that sweeps across my face. *Gage told Harlow he was impressed by me.*

"She has a crush on Gage," Sofia tells Harlow.

Harlow laughs. "You're seeing that too. I mean, look at her. Her face is as red as a tomato."

"It's because of the wine!" I say.

Both of them laugh harder.

"Yeah, and any time you bring Gage up around her, she gets these little hearts in her eyes." Sofia pokes me.

"Those aren't hearts. Those are glares," I proclaim, but they both know I'm full of it.

"She's completely helpless against his blue eyes and dimples," Harlow says.

I throw my hands up and head to the kitchen to grab myself a water. "You two are out of your mind. I'll be right back."

I head straight to my bathroom and shut the door, hearing their laughter through it. It might be at my expense, but to see Sofia laughing melts my heart. She's going to be all right.

The mirror reflects the truth behind Harlow's statement. My cheeks are flushed cherry red and I can't get this dopey smile off my face.

Harlow and Sofia are both here, just like Gage promised. Sofia came with a bag, which tells me she is planning to go with Harlow to the Oasis.

I don't know how Gage found her and convinced her to come over to my place. I tried my hardest and had no luck. Everyone says he's ruthless and not to be messed with. But everything I see paints a whole other picture. He's a real-life superhero. I have no idea why he's popped up or why he's so involved with the expo. Honestly, I don't care any longer. I'm just grateful he is.

With the expo tomorrow night, I wonder what happens after that. Is he sticking around, or will he disappear as quickly as he appeared in my life? The thought of not seeing him after tomorrow shifts something deep inside me. I push those feelings away. I can't afford to have them.

I splash some water on my face and wash my hands before returning to the living room.

"Do you think they could teach me how to cook?" Sofia asks Harlow. She's leaning forward in her chair, completely enamored.

"Oh God yes. They would love to have you in the kitchen. They tried to get Allie involved, but that girl could burn water back in the day."

Sofia laughs.

"What are you two talking about?" I ask, taking a seat next to Harlow on the couch.

"Harlow was telling me how the Oasis has a full staff of chefs. My mom loved to cook, and she started to teach me, but then the chemo started, so I didn't learn much."

"Be prepared to gain about ten pounds in a week." I grin. "The food is insanely good."

Sofia's whole body emanates hope. "What was your favorite thing about the Oasis?"

I relax on the couch and think about the fun my mom, Harlow, and I had there in my younger years. "Well, the coolest thing I found was the secret passageways."

"No way." Sofia gasps, bringing her attention to Harlow. "There are secret passageways, really?"

"Maybe. You'll have to see if you can find any during your stay."

"What? How am I supposed to find any, if they're secret?"

"Allie did. She even found one I never knew existed."

Sofia turns to me excitedly. "Oh my God, that's so cool. You have to show me that one when we get there tonight."

I stiffen at her assumption. The expo is tomorrow, and I need to be there first thing in the morning. If I went to the Oasis tonight—a couple of hours from here—I could kiss sleep goodbye.

"Oh. You're not going." Sofia deflates, her excitement leaving her body all at once like she wasn't bouncing in the chair just a moment ago.

It makes me feel horrible. Her mother is gone. Her father is horrible. She has no one left to lean on. How am I any better if I don't go?

"If you want me to, I can. The expo Shield Tech's putting on is tomorrow evening." I calculate the time frame. "I would need to leave at about four in the morning to make it back in time for preparations."

Sofia fidgets with the sleeve of her hoodie. "No, it's okay. I understand." Her eyes are cast at her feet.

I look to Harlow, uncertain.

"So what? Am I chopped liver now?" Harlow asks, and Sofia whips her head toward her. "For starters, I am way cooler than Allie could ever be."

"What?" I demand with faux incredulousness. Harlow is right. She *is* one of the coolest people I have ever met. The little witch.

Ignoring me, Harlow continues like she didn't just bash me. "Believe me, Allie here can be a stubborn little ass. Plus, when she doesn't get her beauty sleep, she's the biggest grouch known to humankind. I'm not exaggerating even a little bit. The last thing everyone needs is her ruining the expo because she's cranky and feels everyone else should be as well."

Sofia laughs as I say, "Hey!"

But Harlow, being Harlow, continues like I'm not sitting right next to her. "Plus, my friend Fletcher, who is putting on this expo, has worked so hard over the last year and deserves for the event to go off without a hitch."

"Uh, hello. I worked hard too," I say.

Sofia giggles.

Harlow waves her hand dismissively at me. "What do you say, Sofia? You want to drop this party pooper and head out?"

Sofia's eyes meet mine for a moment before she says, "She's kind of right. You did leave your glass of wine over there half full and grabbed a water."

"Ha! Yes, thank you." Harlow turns to me. "I'm going to freshen up in that six-by-nine box you call a bathroom, then we're heading out."

I shake my head at her exaggeration and look at Sofia, thankful she has a smile back on her face.

She asks, "Can you do me a favor tomorrow?"

"Sure, what do you need?" I ask.

"When you see Gage at the expo, will you tell him I said thank you?" Her eyes glisten and I can tell it's taking everything she has to not allow water to drop onto her cheeks.

"Of course. What am I thanking him for?"

Sofia inspects her nails. "He promised to help my dad with rehab if I go to the Oasis."

My heart swells. If it were up to me, I would have beaten her father bloody and left him to fend for himself in that alley after I watched him hit her. Does that make me the ruthless one? Gage saw what she needed, and that was her father. Sober.

Harlow walks back into the living room, her phone dinging as she does. She reads the text. A dark smile crosses her face, and I can't help but wonder what that message said.

I say my goodbyes to Sofia and promise I will come to the Oasis on Sunday to see her. She bounces out of the house, but Harlow stays as breaking news comes across the television screen, catching our attention.

"Arnold 'the Stunner' Caprese was shot and killed right outside one of his businesses less than an hour ago by what is to be believed a professional hit. Arnold was the leader of the Italian Mafia and was one of the most notorious criminal masterminds of all time. This news comes while a person known to be closely associated with Arnold gets ready for a murder trial taking place in less than a week. No arrests have been made at this time. We'll keep you posted as we learn more information..."

I don't hear what else the reporter says, my mind swirling around her words. The head of the Italian Mafia is dead. Someone shot him. Is that why Gage left town?

I turn to see Harlow's dark smile, the same one she got when she read her text a moment ago.

"The world can breathe easier tonight," she says. She blows me a kiss and walks out the door. I'm locking my deadbolts when my phone dings with an incoming text message.

Superhero: Just finished business. I'll be back tomorrow. Sweet dreams, little lion.

I shut my phone off, choosing not to respond.

I don't know how much sleep I am going to get.

Chapter Eleven

Kali.

The International Security Expo is in full swing and everything is going off without a hitch. I absolutely love it. I was originally scheduled to work behind the scenes tonight, but the bartending and catering staff seemed to have everything under control. Eventually, I got the hint when they kept ushering me away. I tossed in the towel and headed to the bar for a glass of wine.

The main ballroom has ambient lighting that casts a warm glow, highlighting the intricate details of each booth. The subtle hum of electronic devices fills the air.

Mario's catering team, not to be outdone, has transformed a section of the ballroom into a culinary haven. Long, elegantly draped tables hold an array of delectable dishes, each one a work of art in its own right.

I'm wearing a dress Harlow surprised me with a few weeks ago. It's a long black dress with a sexy slit that runs up the right side of my leg, ending just below my hip. The top crosses over one shoulder and exposes the other, showcasing my collarbone, which I've accentuated with a thick band of sparkling pink gems. My high heels are as black as night on top and the bottom soles are a bold pink color that matches the gems perfectly.

It feels like it was made specifically for me. Knowing Harlow, she probably had it custom-made. I sent her a selfie earlier so she could see it. She responded immediately with heart emojis and telling me how beautiful I looked. She was going to be here, but given Sofia's situation, she decided to stay at the Oasis.

My mother would be spilling tears of joy and clapping her hands if she could see me right now. She always wore beautiful dresses like this one.

Roxanne sets a glass of red wine in front of me. I smile and thank her before turning around to face the sea of people. Everyone is dressed in their best, wearing diamonds that sparkle off the lights and fine three-piece suits that probably cost more than my home.

Sipping my wine, I look for Gage, wondering if he's wearing a suit, but come up empty. He never showed this morning, and Fletcher has avoided answering my questions about where he's at. I was going to call him several times but only got as far as pulling his name up. As much as I want to call him, I know I shouldn't. I couldn't offer him anything but lies.

After Gage trampled into Shield Tech and demanded to take over the planning, I find it strange that he's MIA for an event that was so seemingly important to him mere days ago. Why go through all that trouble to not even show?

My mind keeps drifting back to the breaking news last night about Arnold Caprese being killed, and I can't help but believe Gage played a major role in it. I could be completely wrong, but something in my gut tells me I'm not.

Fletcher orders a whiskey and leans up against the bar next to me. "We outdid ourselves again, Allie. Next year we might need to book another venue to hold everyone in."

"Absolutely not. Holding this at the Onyx is a statement within itself."

Roxanne returns with his drink and struts off. He gives it a whiff.

He has worked so hard for this moment, and I couldn't be prouder. I hold my glass out to his, clinking them together. He smiles at my gesture.

"You did it again. Every year only gets better. Congrats," I say. We hold up our drinks in a toast and both take a sip.

"I couldn't have done it without you."

I wave my hand dismissively. "Oh please, we both know you're the one who makes all the decisions."

"But you're the one who brings everything together. I give you a bag of mixed puzzle pieces and you create a masterpiece every time."

"We do make a great team. It's too bad Gage couldn't make it to see the pièce de résistance." I try to hide the disappointment in my voice.

"This sort of thing isn't Gage's MO," Fletcher says, confirming what I was hoping to not be true. That Gage isn't here and won't be.

"It surprises me how much he wanted to be involved. Why come to the Onyx and scope every square inch and then just... not show?"

Fletcher nods as if it makes perfect sense. "I don't think anyone will truly understand Gage and his agenda. He's been a lost soul for so long, I doubt he'll ever find himself again."

My heart tightens. I picture Gage wandering from city to city among the many far-flung homes I imagine he has, doing God knows what. He may claim to be a superhero, but after what happened last night, I'm beginning to wonder if he's the actual villain.

I take another sip of my wine and scan the mingling crowd. Several people are leaning in eagerly at each exhibit, their eyes sparkling with excitement.

The hair on my neck rises as I begin to feel the weight of someone's stare. This time I scan the crowd more slowly, taking a closer look, trying to find who it is.

Fletcher adds in a warm, caring tone, "You look beautiful tonight, Allie."

I smile. He's dressed to the nines with his Armani suit and wingtip Oxford shoes.

"Thanks. You're dashing as well. Too bad Harlow isn't here to see you," I tease.

He fumbles over his words. "It's not like that. We're not..." Fletcher runs his hand through his hair. "Fuck. No, we're just good friends."

I laugh. It isn't an easy task to get Fletcher Roxwell to stumble over his words. "If you say so."

He slams the rest of his drink and sets it down. "Be good. I need to get ready to speak on stage in a few minutes. Let's try not to break too many men's hearts tonight."

I laugh again as he dips to kiss me on the cheek and turns to make his way into the sea of people. I watch him disappear and take another sip of my wine, still feeling someone's eyes on me. I look to my right and see my suspicions were correct.

A gorgeous man in a three-piece suit stands against a pillar in the shadows. His hands are in his pockets. He's well built, with ink-black hair that's short on the sides and messy on top. His eyes are familiar. The bold, deep emerald color shines through the darkness that encases him.

My mind races. How do I know this man? His eyes haven't broken contact with mine. I start to fidget at the intensity of his darkening look. It's almost as if he's staring at a ghost and cannot believe it for himself.

Then it hits me.

I am a ghost to him.

His sharp jawline, his stance, his eyes. I have no doubt who he is, even though it's been seven years since we last saw each other. By the look he's giving me, he knows who I am.

I break eye contact and take a steadying gulp of wine. I slowly set it down and turn on my heel, retreating as quickly as I can while trying not to be noticeable. My heart is pounding in my chest as I round the corner and head straight for the ladies' room. I'll hide there all night if I have to. I can't risk running into him—or *anyone* who might recognize who I really am and realize I'm still alive.

As soon as I reach the door and open it, I almost hit a younger woman whose dress is so tight, I'm surprised she can breathe in it.

"Hey, watch it," she snaps. The restroom is packed with several women fighting over the mirrors to freshen up.

"I'm sorry," I reply, letting the door swing shut and continue farther down the hall. As long as I head away from him, everything will be all right. There are plenty of places to hide out in. The Onyx is huge.

I take a flight of stairs and a couple more turns before I end up in an office full of books and a set of French doors that lead out to a balcony.

I close the office door quietly, slide the lock in place, and rush over to the French doors. I walk into the brisk night and take a large breath, feeling like it is the first breath I could take since realizing who is here tonight.

My hands shake as I lean up against the center of the railing, trying to calm my racing heart. I look up at the star-filled sky, trying to not hyperventilate.

I *always* carry my phone with me, along with my pepper spray. But these dresses don't come with pockets, and I stashed my clutch behind the bar while I was helping Roxanne.

I'm an idiot. The one time I slip up, I am hit with a blast from the past. The first time I met him was years ago, but the memory of that first time feels like it just happened.

I hear the door to the office open and then close, the lock clicking. Footsteps approach me, but I don't turn around. I know it's him who followed me into this room. Why I thought a simple lock could keep someone like Aric out is beyond me.

My brother warned me about Aric all those years ago. I told Logan the next day that I had kissed Aric, and it took an hour to calm him down afterward. He refused to go into detail, but in a nutshell, he told me Aric makes the devil look like a puppy and it would disappoint our parents if I were to consider dating him. But Logan was overreacting about Aric being worse than the devil. I spent a few afternoons with him and he never threatened me in any way.

When Dad asked what I thought about Aric, I made sure to tell him I found him boring. My dad never asked me again.

Goosebumps cover my body. My palms grow sweaty and my heart pumps wildly inside my chest. Aric is the last person I ever expected to see again.

I need to stick with my story and not show any sign of deception. Aric is a man who doesn't just see what is in front of him; he observes it in grave detail. The same way he did all those years ago at my family's estate.

I remember thinking he was shy, but now that I'm older, I understand why he was so quiet. The people in the room who say the least are the people who walk out with the most knowledge. Aric and I met a month before my parents were murdered. A month before the fire that erased most of my home.

Everyone believes Logan and I perished that day. Logan worked hard with Harlow to make that happen. Though the reports on the news said our bodies weren't located in the home, they wrote it off, believing the intensity of the fire had practically cremated everyone who was inside.

I can smell leather and spice. *It's showtime.* I loosen my grip on the balcony railing and slowly turn around to find deep emerald eyes gazing at me. "Why did you follow me?" I barely get the words out.

He studies every single detail, making me feel like I'm on a large dark stage under a bright spotlight, as vulnerable as a newborn baby. "You know why." His voice is much deeper than it was all those years ago.

I take time to study him as well. He was big compared to me back then, but he is even larger now. I suspect that underneath his suit I would be greeted with a toned, muscular, tanned body that has probably seen more hours at a gym in a week than most people see in a year.

This is the moment of truth. The moment for me to prove to Harlow and Logan that I have what it takes to be by their sides in our battle. I can't see Aric being the one behind the death of my parents, but I still don't know who the enemies are. I'll stick to my cover story and prove myself. I lock my shoulders, take a deep breath, and look Aric straight on.

"No, I don't. This is a private office, and you need to leave." My words come out strong and confident, but I'm shaking on the inside.

His sinful lips twitch. "I can't believe it's you." He shakes his head and lets out a sudden laugh. "All these years, I thought you died in that fire, but you didn't."

"I have no idea what you're talking about."

"Tell me, *Kali*, did your parents also survive? What about Logan? Is he here tonight as well?"

I gulp at his ferocity and try to force myself to appear relaxed. "I'm sorry, but you have me mixed up with someone else. My name is Allie Smith."

He ignores me. "I always wondered if that fire story was true. After all, neither of your bodies were recovered. But I must give credit where credit is due. Logan did an extraordinary job covering both of your tracks. It's not often someone can fool me."

I shrug. It takes everything I have to seem casual. "I don't have a brother."

Aric's eyes blaze, his smile one of victory. "How would you know, *Allie*"—he emphasizes my fake name—"that Logan is Kali's brother?"

Shit. He trapped me, making me acknowledge Logan as my brother, when I should have simply stonewalled.

"You need to leave," I respond, taking a step to the side of the balcony.

Aric's smile comes across his face, but it isn't the same smile I remember from all those years ago. This one is filled with darkness and there is nothing friendly about it.

He steps forward as I take another step back. I can't seem to stop my body from retreating until I feel the balcony rail touch my lower back.

Aric places his hands on the railing, caging me in. He leans in, putting his cheek against mine, and inhales deeply.

"Oh, how I have missed your wildflower scent, Kali. You look ravishing tonight."

I want to yell, to scream out, but my lungs are frozen in fear. I take a deep breath, adjusting my bearings. "You're delusional, sir."

Aric pulls back and examines me. "I was supposed to be there that night with my father, but I had a prior engagement and couldn't make it." What appears to be true sadness softens the hard edges of his face. "It's one of my biggest regrets, not being there to protect you."

Heat drains from my cheeks. His father Victor was there the night my parents were killed? Was his father the one who killed my parents? Why wouldn't Logan tell me Victor Fucking Hemmington was there?

"Ah, you didn't know my father was there that night. That's very interesting. Still keeping out of your family's business, I see."

I want to ask him what he knows about that night, what his father told him, but I can't. The one thing Harlow pounded into my head over the years was I had to stick with my story. "I'm sorry, but I have no idea who you are or who you think I am, but I can promise you're mistaken."

Aric wraps his hand around my forearm, bringing it between us as he turns my hand and reveals my heart-shaped birthmark, rubbing his thumb gently across it. "How could you forget your first kiss?" His words are spoken lightly in a whisper.

I suck in a shaky breath, remembering every second of that kiss. I was so young and naïve. Screw this cat and mouse game. I'm fighting a losing battle. There's no way to talk my way out of a unique birthmark. "That wasn't my first kiss and you damn well know it."

"Mmm, but it was. Remember? We erased your first one with ours. I left you that day with hearts dancing in your eyes."

"You manipulated me into kissing you!" I hiss, anger boiling through my veins, lighting me on fire.

He laughs and I want to knock his smile right off his face. "Do you think I could do it again?"

A loud bang shakes the door that leads into the office. I whip my head around and see the doorknob move, but nothing happens.

"Allie, open the door!"

Relief floods my body at the sound of Gage's voice. *He's here!*

"Gage McCollin," Aric remarks in a bored tone. "It looks like my night is full of surprises. Tell me, Kali, have you kissed him yet?"

When I say nothing, he continues. "Well, I would hope not. You haven't even told him your real name. A web of lies wouldn't be the best start to a relationship, now, would it?"

I assert as much hate into my narrowing gaze as possible. "Your time is up, Aric," I spit, barely able to control the rage inside me. I place my hands on his wide chest and push him. He allows me to walk him backward, a wicked smile across his face.

The pounding on the door intensifies. It's only a matter of seconds before the door gets broken down and Aric's game—whatever game he is playing—is over.

"I'll see you soon, Kali," Aric says.

The door bursts open. Gage runs through it straight toward us, his eyes deadly.

I turn to Aric, but he's no longer standing there.

Like he was nothing but a ghost.

Chapter Twelve

Gage.

Watching through the camera feed as Aric follows her is the hardest thing I've ever had to do, but I can't leave until I know exactly where she's heading. The Onyx is a large building, a warren of hallways and rooms.

As soon as she enters the office, I'm out of my chair, seeing red. Aric is going to die by my hands if he hurts her in any way. I don't give a damn that he might be the only way to get answers about my mother. I will find another option.

After the doorjamb splinters open under my blows, I catch a glimpse of him slipping out of sight. It takes me only a few strides to reach Allie. When I step out onto the balcony, Aric has gone up into a cloud of smoke, leaving Allie standing alone. I glance across the courtyard below to see him slinking through the door on the opposite side.

I hit my earpiece to connect with my team. "Conner, he's going through the west wing entrance."

"On it," Conner replies.

"Link, pull up the camera feed in that area. We can't lose him. I'm taking Allie and leaving."

"Get her out of here now. We got the rest," Link responds.

I grab Allie's hand and feel her tremors as I pull her from the office. She doesn't say a word as we walk through the broken doorframe and along the back halls, avoiding the main ballroom. Fletcher's voice reverberates through the building as he gives his speech for the night. If he or anyone else sets sights on her right now, they'll know something is wrong, given how pale she is. We hit one of the back exits, the one nearest my car. I help her into the passenger seat, clicking the seat belt over her.

I slam on the gas and head straight for my place. There's no way I am taking her to her place tonight. Not with Aric in the area.

I'm unspeakably grateful to see her unharmed. Aric Hemmington cannot be trusted. What's alarming is his interest in Allie. The world could be burning down in front of his eyes and that motherfucker would yawn in boredom.

Allie remains quiet the entire ride, not questioning where we're going. I keep glancing over at her, but her eyes remain straight ahead. She might be in shock. Who knows what the fuck Aric said to her.

Twenty minutes later, I pull into the underground garage, and we enter my home. I've never brought a woman here, but Allie is different. She gazes around, her expression neutral, making it hard to read her thoughts.

We step into the living room. It's spacious, with high ceilings that seem to stretch into the darkness above. The ambient lighting highlights the modern art on the walls. The furniture is sleek and comfortable, a blend of contemporary design.

I walk over to the bar and pour us both three fingers of Double Eagle Very Rare, a bourbon I always keep in stock. As I hand her a glass, I can't help but feel a bit anxious. I've never cared about anyone's opinion before. I hope she likes my place and feels at ease here.

She accepts the glass with shaky hands and slams the entire thing back, causing her to go into a coughing fit.

"Easy, little lion." I rub her back until she gets control again.

Her skin is soft, and her dress is the sexiest thing I have ever seen. When I first saw her on the camera feed after she changed, I lost my will to breathe. It took everything to not head straight down to the expo and beat the shit out of every man blatantly lusting over her. The slit up her leg showcasing her toned thigh had every man wishing he was enough to catch her attention. None of them did and I love that.

"Do you want another?" I ask and she nods.

I pour another heavy glass and take her hand, leading her to the master bathroom. I drop her hand, set her drink on the vanity, and jog over to my closet to grab some clothes for her to change into. As much as I would love to peel her dress off her body, I force myself to stay focused.

I walk back into the bathroom and find her still standing in the same spot. I'm going to kill that motherfucker. I set the clothes down on the vanity and place my fingers under her chin, raising her face to meet mine.

"Hey, you're safe now. I got you."

She nods but remains silent.

I walk over and run the water for her to take a bath. She will be the first to use this ungodly large tub. "I'll be right down the hall in my office if you need anything. Take your time and then we can talk."

I turn and reach the doorway when she calls out my name.

"Can you unzip me? I can't reach it." She turns around and lifts her long blond hair off her back, showing her neck. I try to restrain a growl at how gorgeous she is, but I don't know if I'm successful.

I stride over and slowly unzip the back of her dress, revealing the goddess underneath. Her skin is absolute perfection. My desire to kiss every square inch of her body is overwhelming.

I've had to do hard things throughout my life, but this right here takes the prize. If I stay in this room any longer, I won't be able to control myself.

Without a word, I quickly exit the room and head straight for my office. I sit at my desk and call Conner.

"We lost him, boss. That asshole's like a ghost."

Shit. That's the last thing I needed to hear. I grab the bourbon and pour another drink because I left my first one in the kitchen. "Was Link able to find him on the camera feed?"

"He did. By that time, Aric was getting into a black Tahoe. The license plate was covered."

I slam my fist into the wall. I should've jumped the balcony when I had the chance, but the thought of leaving Allie had me halting. I take a couple of deep breaths and slam the bourbon. "All right. Where are you now?"

"I'm still at the expo. Told Fletcher that Allie wasn't feeling well and went home."

"Good. Stay there and keep your eyes open. Aric might try to come back."

I hang up and call Link immediately afterward.

"Did you get her out of there?" he asks immediately.

"I have her here with me. She's shaken, but I don't see any injuries."

"Shit."

"From what I see, she'll be all right. I need a background check on her. Aric's interest in her isn't typical. See if they knew each other back in the day."

"I already pulled it. I'm sending it over now."

"Thanks, man. I don't know what I would do without you."

I hang up and turn my computer on. Just as Link promised, the file drops into my inbox. I open the attachment and stare into the whiskey eyes that have captured me since the day I first saw her.

Allie Rae Smith.

Wasting no time, I read through what Link sent. I stop and reread it. I can't be seeing this right. Her address is wrong. Another issue is her phone number. I swiped it off Fletcher's phone when he wasn't paying attention and have been texting her enough that it's burned into my mind. And her family history is false intel as well. I remember the day at Seward Park when Allie told me she had an older brother and her parents were living in Australia. This report states she doesn't have any siblings and both parents passed away in a car accident.

I lean back into my chair to consider what exactly this means. Either Allie lied to me about her past, or Link sent me a bogus report.

Allie might be able to bullshit the average Joe, but once you get to know her, she's extremely easy to read. Especially when she's lying. I think back to the day she told me about her family; I couldn't detect any deceit. Then again, she did change the subject quickly. It wasn't like I had any reason to suspect she was lying to me. Maybe she didn't want to discuss her parents' deaths because it was too hard for her. But she also told me she had an older brother when this report states she has no siblings at all. Why would she lie about that?

What about Link? What would cause him to lie to me after all these years? I hired him seven years ago because he's one of the best hackers I've ever met.

Hell, he's the one who informed me that my last tech was leaking information on my business. After I beat my last guy to a pulp, I dressed him in cement shoes and dumped his pleading ass into the Pacific Ocean. I offered Link the job the very next day. He can track anyone down I've ever needed, and he's never once let me down. Shit, he's saved my ass countless times, so why would he lie to me now and send a bogus report?

Come to think of it, he has been abnormally concerned with the well-being of Allie, which is out of character for him. Normally, he gets the job done and doesn't ask any questions.

Fuck. I don't want to believe Link is lying to me. He knows exactly what happens to anyone who betrays me—or anyone on the team, for that matter. They take their last breath, and I always guarantee it'll be a painful one.

I call Conner. He answers on the second ring. "Boss? Everything all right?"

"How many times do I have to tell you I'm not your boss?"

He grunts.

"I need you to get a background check on Allie Rae Smith. Anything you can find about her. No matter how insignificant it may seem, I want it."

"I'll call Link and get him on it right now."

"Not Link, just you. This needs to stay between us."

The line goes silent. "What's going on?" he finally asks. It's a fair question.

I decide to be completely honest. If Link is a rat, he needs to know about the risk as well. "Link already sent me her background check, and it's not adding up. Her home address and phone number are incorrect, and it states that she has no siblings and her parents are deceased. The problem with that is she told me her parents live in Australia and she has an older brother."

"Fuck," Conner responds, letting out a large breath.

"Yeah. Link has tomorrow off. He told me he's going to see his girl. I'm going to tail him and find out what exactly he's up to. See what you can get me."

"All right, man, you know I got your back. Let's just hope you're wrong about this."

For the first time in my life, I hope I am wrong, but my gut is telling me I'm not... and Link doesn't have long to live. I send Conner a list of what I know about Allie and lean back in my chair, finishing my drink.

As soon as Allie is out of the bath, I'll do some probing on her family history and find out what the fuck went down between her and Aric. They have some kind of history together, and I'm going to get to the bottom of it.

Chapter Thirteen

Allie.

I remain in the bath until my entire body is a prune and the water is cold. I know what's coming the second I walk out of this bathroom, and I need time to figure out what I'm going to say to Gage.

I don't even know how he knew where I was, but I'm glad he did. He's probably thinking I'm scared of being followed and locked in a room by a strange man. He must think that's why I haven't said more than a few words since he broke through that door.

But what to say about Aric? Telling Gage that Aric and I met years ago would raise more questions about my past, and that isn't an option. I can blow it off like Aric was some typical weirdo and I have no idea who he is. The problem is, I doubt Gage will buy it. If he knows Aric at all, which it appears he does, then he will know better than to believe that bullshit story.

I dry off, release my hair from the makeshift bun I put it in to keep it dry, and brush through my hair with my fingers. Gage left a white T-shirt and sweatpants that are both too large, but they will have to do.

I slip his clothes on and am engulfed with his minty spring scent. I unlock the bathroom door, straining my ears for any sound. Silence. I lay my folded dress on his dresser, grab my now empty glass, and head down the hallway. I'm not a heavy drinker, so the two glasses already have me feeling like I'm floating on air. His home is beautiful and screams how much money he has. The walls are light gray, with a large black accent wall. There aren't any pictures, only beautiful artwork, but that doesn't surprise me. Men like Gage don't live like normal people.

I pass what must be his office, but he isn't in there. I continue along the hallway until I reach the living room to find Gage sitting on a plush black leather couch, holding two drinks in his hands. I enter the room slowly. He looks more stressed than I've ever seen him.

"Hey," I say shyly.

He stands as I make my way over to him. He takes my empty glass, hands me a new glass of bourbon, and gestures for me to take a seat. I shouldn't drink this—I'm already feeling the effects from the first two—but tonight I need some liquid courage. I sit on the far side of the couch and take a sip. It's actually not bad. It has hints of vanilla, toasted oak, and caramel. Gage chooses to sit right next to me, leaving little room between us.

"You okay?" he asks, watching me closely.

"Yeah." I nod. "Thank you for the clothes."

His eyes travel down my body, taking in his fill. "I like you in my clothes."

I bite my bottom lip. He never beats around the bush and I'm finding the confidence he holds sexy.

Gage takes a sip of his bourbon and clears his throat. "I'm sure you don't want to talk about this, but I need to know what exactly happened on that balcony tonight."

"Why didn't you show when you said you would?" I counter, leaning back into the couch to create some distance.

"I was there. You just didn't see me."

A feeling of disappointment bolts through me. *He couldn't come out of wherever he was and say hi?* "You were there because of that guy, weren't you?"

"I've been hunting Aric for years now. I need to know how you know him." Gage leans forward and closes the little distance I've created.

"Why would you think I know him?"

Gage stares hard at me, sending shivers across my body. He glances at my arm—still healing from the alley incident—and takes his free hand to glide his fingers gently across the gooseflesh on my forearm, acknowledging he notices my body's reaction. "Answer the question, Allie," he says, his tone low and deep.

I gulp. This isn't good and I have no idea how to handle this side of Gage. He's intense and demanding. I can only imagine what it must be like to be on his bad side. "Don't tell me what to do," I whisper.

His jaw clenches. "Why are you protecting him?"

I take a large drink of the bourbon before setting it down on the table next to me. "I'm not. Can you please back away from me?"

Gage slams the remaining bourbon before leaning over me and setting his glass next to mine. As soon as he starts to lean back, I go to stand quickly, but I'm not fast enough. Gage wraps his hand around my wrist and pulls me back onto the couch, bringing our faces within an inch of each other.

I feel like I might faint. I should have told him to take me home. It's not like it's a secret where I live anymore.

"Breathe, little lion. I'm not going to hurt you." He releases one of his large hands and readjusts the other, bringing his thumb to my pulse.

I'm certain he's not going to hurt me. He's just going to make sure I can't lie to him. His thumb on my pulse reminds me of that day in Fletcher's office. I've never met a human lie detector before, but it shouldn't be surprising Gage can do that.

"Aric Hemmington isn't a good guy, and I need to understand why he followed you. Now, I'm going to ask you one more time. How do you know him?"

I'm well aware I'm out of options and time. "We met when I was younger."

"How did you two meet?"

"He—he was friends with my brother," I lie. Logan hated Aric just as much as Gage does, if not more.

"I need you to calm down. Your heart rate is beating frantically. Breathe, beautiful. You're safe with me. I promise you."

I give a quick nod and take a few deep breaths, not sure what to do.

"Good girl." He releases my wrist and leans back onto the couch, giving me the space I was asking for. "What's your brother's name?"

I'm grateful that he doesn't have his thumb on my pulse because he would feel it skyrocket again. I keep my face as neutral as possible. "Joe," I lie again, delivering the first name that pops into my head. I suppress a cringe at providing such a basic name. I think the only name I could have done worse with was John Smith.

"And this is the brother who's traveling the world right now?"

"Yeah, my one and only brother."

Gage nods, stands, and walks around to grab his empty glass. "Finish your drink. I'll make us fresh ones."

I grab the glass without hesitation, drinking the last of it before handing it over. He makes his way into the kitchen to refill our drinks. The large windows overlook the city lights. I can't see any stars from his place.

He returns shortly after and hands me my glass before he sits back down on the couch, leaving a few feet between us.

"What did Aric say to you in the office?"

I take a drink of the bourbon, noting this glass doesn't taste as harsh as the last one. Good, the buzz is really starting to kick in. "He wanted to know where my brother was. They lost contact with each other when Joe left the country. I told him I didn't know exactly where he was and that I hadn't heard from him in a while."

Gage sits quietly for a moment, and I almost start in on more details, but with him, less is better. I bite the inside of my cheek to remain silent.

"Thank you for telling me. I'm sorry I scared you. I promise that wasn't my intention. It's just that I've been hunting Aric for so long now that I lost my mind for a second."

"Why have you been looking for him?"

"He has information on someone that I need."

"Who?" I ask.

"The less you know, the better, little lion. How's the bourbon?"

At his remark, I take another swig and look into the glass. "Honestly, it's tasting better with each glass."

Gage laughs, showing off his dimples. "I would hope it tasted just as good on the first glass. This bottle cost five thousand dollars."

"Five grand! Why would you pay that much for a bottle of liquor?"

He shrugs. "Maybe I thought it would impress a certain little lion."

My cheeks warm at his thoughtfulness. "Any twenty-dollar bottle of wine from the grocery store would do for me."

"Duly noted."

It's my turn to laugh. I sink into the couch. Gage is still wearing the same all-black outfit with his signature hat on backward. He's mastered the bad-boy look and it makes my ovaries weep. He looks more relaxed now that we got the topic of Aric over with.

"Sofia asked me to thank you."

"Oh yeah?"

"Yeah, she said you're sending her father to rehab."

"It wasn't a problem," he replies.

Gage's smile is full and so gallant. I want to kiss each of his dimples.

"You looked beautiful tonight at the expo."

I beam. "Thank you. I was hoping... wondering if you were going to wear a tux tonight."

"Were you wondering or hoping?"

I chew on my bottom lip. "Both, but I remember what you said about your dad and how he hated how you dressed, so I guess it was dumb to wonder or hope at all."

"You remember that?"

I nod and take another drink. It's starting to go down like water.

"My father was a businessman. He felt a respectable man should always wear a suit. I never understood why he thought clothing could determine how much power you have."

"People judge others by how they look and what they wear. It's a power play on people beneath them."

"Clothing does nothing in the long term. You can dress the weakest man in the most expensive suit, but at the end of the day, people will only see the lack of competency."

I can't argue. From the very moment I saw him, I knew if he was dressed in rags, I would still sense the power he held. "Maybe most people choose to wear a suit to cover up their self-consciousness."

"Perhaps they do." He takes a drink from his glass, and I do the same. The bourbon is starting to make me lightheaded. We're both leaning back on the couch now, and I feel like a lazy cat on a Sunday afternoon.

"What about your parents? Did they care how you dressed?" Gage asks.

I smile, thinking about my parents. "No, they let me be who I wanted to be. My mom always wore the most beautiful dresses I'd ever seen."

Several memories wash over me of sitting on her bed while she did her hair and makeup. She always took her time getting ready, as if every night she and my father went out was their first date. "She always held herself like a princess. She taught me the importance of being true to yourself no matter what challenges come at you. In stressful situations, she always maintained her composure. And the deep sense of empathy she gave to everyone." I press my hand to my chest at the warmth that fills it. "It wasn't about being nice. She could connect with anyone on a deeper level, leaving everyone she met with a profound impression."

"Sounds like you take after your mother quite a bit."

I could only wish to be half as wonderful as my mother was. Not knowing how to respond, I lift my glass to take another sip but spill some on my shirt.

Wait, not my shirt. Gage's crisp white shirt.

"Shit, I'm so sorry." I try to sit up, but my body is feeling heavier by the second. Maybe today has taken a toll on me after all.

Gage laughs, showing off his beautiful dimples as he leans forward, taking the almost empty glass from my hand and setting it on the table behind him. "Don't worry about it. I have plenty."

I smile back.

"Your mom sounds like an amazing woman."

"She *was* amazing. You have no idea. Her and my father both."

"What are their names?"

"Marion and James," I reply with the truth. Quite frankly, I couldn't care less right now. I'm feeling way too good. "I think that bourbon is worth the five thousand."

Gage smiles. "I think I might have to agree with you."

He takes another sip of his drink, his artic-blue eyes dancing with delight. Not only is this man gorgeous beyond belief, but he's honest. He never hesitates to answer any question I've prodded him with, all while I've sat back and told him lie after lie. I've intentionally set up boundaries in front of everyone I meet because I can't afford to be asked certain questions. Silence is what has kept me safe and alive.

But now with Aric in the picture, how does that change things?

Hearing Gage pound that door down when I was trapped with Aric gave me comfort I hadn't felt in a long time. I need to give Gage at least something for everything he has done for me. The words leave my mouth before I even realize it. "I only met Aric because he was bored."

Gage cocks his head, assessing my words. I, on the other hand, am assessing his look. That pose right there could be his signature money-making pose. If he ever wanted to go into modeling, that is.

"Really? How so?" Gage asks, jarring me from my dreamlike state.

"My dad was talking business, and it was strange to me. My dad never asked me to be involved in his business dealings, but that day he asked me to come to the study."

I let out a light laugh, remembering how stir-crazy I felt that day. But my laugh dies off quickly. I wish I could go back in time and sit in that room like he asked me to. I wouldn't have left his side if I had known what was going to happen a few weeks later.

"I was bored out of my mind, and it was such a beautiful day outside, so I asked if I could take a walk. My dad, being wonderful, was okay with that. Aric followed me because he said he was bored."

"You two only met once?"

I shake my head. "No, we met a couple of times. Aric came over without his dad. But my brother hated him after that first day. I promised my brother that I wouldn't date him, even though I think Aric liked me. Well, I thought he did... until tonight."

Gage watches me closely with his mesmerizing blue eyes. I could get lost in them every day.

"He told you he didn't like you?"

I shake my head and stretch out my limbs. I'm not sure how late I'm going to make it tonight. "No. I was naïve when I was younger, and I've come to understand that he manipulated me to believe that he liked me. Besides, it didn't matter. My brother hated Aric and I guess my parents did too. You know when your brother calls out your middle name, he means business."

His rich laugh brings a smile to my face. "Is that what your brother did?"

I nod, smiling.

"What's your middle name?" he asks.

I don't know why, but I giggle. "You tell me yours first."

"Alexander."

"Gage Alexander McCollin," I say, testing it out. "That's a strong, sexy name."

I can tell he's happy with my response. "Thank you. Now your turn."

"Marie. It was my grandmother's name," I reply with another truth, and it feels good to be truthful with him. If this is our last night together, I'm happy I was at least able to give him a little bit of me. "Am I going to see you again now that the expo is done?"

Gage moves closer. His minty fresh scent is my new favorite smell in the entire world. "Do you want to?"

I nod. "I also want to kiss you again."

Gage's deep laugh prompts me to smile again. When have I ever smiled this much in one night?

"Will you kiss me again?"

He takes a gulp of his drink and sets it on the floor. He cups my face with his large hands. It's a good thing I'm sitting down right now. I doubt my legs could support me. "What if it's the bourbon talking? I wouldn't want to take advantage of you."

I shake my head as much as I can in his warm hands. "I've wanted to kiss you again before tonight."

Gage lets out a rushed breath and presses his forehead against mine. "You are truly breathtaking, little lion."

"Is that a yes?" I ask as he leans back to assess me. I lick my lips, hungry to feel his mouth.

Gage leans in slowly and brushes his lips across mine as my eyes flutter closed at the softness and warmth. I open for him and surrender fully to everything he has to offer. Butterflies erupt inside me like they do when all the wildflowers first come into bloom at the Oasis. His kiss is strong and demanding and I love it.

I wrap my arms around his neck and pull his body to mine. Our bodies become one as we collapse onto the couch.

I feel as if I jumped out of a plane and I'm free-falling into pure bliss. I moan in pleasure and hear him growl in response. My heat blooms below. He's not only skilled in combat; he can also kiss like no other.

He presses his hard body against mine and I arch in response. I can feel every muscle that covers his majestic body, including his hard cock that has me whimpering underneath him.

He deepens the kiss. His hand glides down my side and latches onto my ass, squeezing hard. Another moan rips out of me. It takes everything I have to not start tearing his clothes off.

At this point, if he just grazed my clit, an orgasm would spill out of me instantly.

He breaks our kiss and I whimper, missing the physical contact immediately. After Aric's words today, I wanted to erase our kiss with another kiss from Gage.

He stands to adjust himself before he picks me up bridal-style and carries me down the hallway to his bedroom.

"I'm not ready for that." *I totally am.*

"I know, little lion."

Ugh, he shouldn't be so right!

I lean my head against his hard chest and can hear his heartbeat pumping as hard as mine is. He gently lays me on the bed and covers me with a warm blanket. He leans down, kissing my cheek, before standing. "Sweet dreams, gorgeous." He turns to walk out of the room.

"Gage," I call out before he can leave. He turns, his bright blue eyes meeting mine. "Will you stay with me until I fall asleep?"

His jaw tightens at my request, and I'm not sure how to process that. Nonetheless, he strides over to the bed, kicks off his boots, lifts the covers, and slides in next to me.

I roll over to my side so I'm facing him and snuggle against his chest.

"Thank you," I say, not sure if I'm thanking him for the kiss or the cuddle.

"Anything for you, little lion."

We lie in silence, listening to each other's breathing. My eyelids have grown too heavy, and I can't fight sleep any longer, wrapped in Gage's arms. I hope what I've given Gage will help in locating Aric sooner rather than later, but I honestly don't think so.

"I'm sorry I lied to you about everything. I didn't want to, but I have no choice." My whispered confession lingers in the dark room.

Gage stiffens.

I hurry on. "I should have just told you the truth about Aric when you asked."

He brushes my hair back in such a soothing way that I can no longer keep my eyes open. I'm not sure if I've fallen asleep when Gage asks, "Why does your brother hate Aric?"

"Because I kissed him," I reply, letting sleep take over.

Chapter Fourteen

Gage.

When Allie told me she lied, my heart about gave out. I thought she was going to say she lied about wanting to kiss me.

I may have given her more liquor than she is used to, but it wasn't my intention to take advantage of her. I may be a bad man, but I would never force a woman to do anything she didn't want to do.

I could tell she was lying to me about her brother and Aric. When I realized how much the bourbon was affecting her, I had to offer more.

It paid off.

She went from telling me that Aric was friends with her brother, to how much they hated each other.

Her revealing she had kissed Aric before she drifted off has me seeing red. Her body goes soft in my arms after her whispered words, and I know she's out cold. I relish the moment of her tucked inside my arms and snuggled deep into me. I have never had or wanted a woman to stay the night, yet now I find myself struggling to leave the bed.

I breathe in my scent on her body. It's intoxicating.

I reluctantly unwrap myself from her enticing form and cover her. She looks like an angel asleep in my bed.

I walk out of the room and head to my office. I send Conner the information Allie provided me, hoping it will be enough for him to get a hit.

Allie's words about her mother filter through me and how she referred to her in the past tense.

She was amazing.

Not *is*, but *was*. I don't believe her parents are alive. Her mother for sure, and I'm going to assume her father wouldn't have left her alone after her mother's passing to move to Australia and open a retail gun shop. It's clear she doesn't have much contact with her brother, and I'm 99 percent certain his name isn't Joe Smith. But I asked that question before she started opening up to me. I almost asked her again but didn't want to risk the chance of her catching on to what was happening.

My little lion is all on her own. She hasn't the slightest clue she's swimming in shark-infested waters. I should walk away. She's becoming too much of a distraction, but after that kiss tonight, I'm not sure I'll be able to walk away. She may be too innocent for the world I live in. But she would never be safer anywhere else except beside me.

Right now, I need to understand what role Link is playing in Allie's life—and what his endgame is. At that thought, my cell rings. Link's name flashes across the screen. His ears must have been itching.

"Link."

"Hey, we got a problem. Is Allie still with you?"

It takes all my willpower to not snap at his question, but I manage to reel it in. "She's asleep."

I leave it short and simple. The silence over the line is so strong, it becomes almost deafening. I lean back into my chair and wait for his move.

After a few moments, he seems to get his bearings. "We need to get her out of town. The Italian Mafia has put her name out on the street. With Sofia MIA, they're now after Allie."

My hand tightens at his words. I would slit the throat of anyone who thinks they can speak her name. "How'd they find out Allie was connected to Sofia?"

"Arnold Caprese had a couple of his guys trying to ferret out the witness. When you sent Ricardo to rehab and he disappeared, they noticed."

Air rushes from my lungs. "Fuck." My chest tightens with the thought that I'm the reason Allie's on their radar. I should've killed Arnold the night I first met Allie and taken both her and Sofia to the Oasis. Not that it would have made a difference. You can cut the head off one snake and another one will appear in its place.

"And now that Ricardo's daughter is also MIA, they've put their sights on Allie."

"I'm taking Allie to the Oasis tomorrow. I'll make sure she gets there safely. She apparently already knows Harlow through Fletcher, so I'll push for her to stay there until we can get this sorted out."

"Tomorrow isn't good enough. I can take her there right now. Is she at home?"

I rub my chin. It seems not only does my little lion have past connections with Aric, but she might have current connections with Link. "She doesn't know you, Link. I don't want to scare her more than she already is. Besides, you've told me yourself you don't like to stray from your computers. I'll take her in the morning. She's at my place. No one can get to her here."

"Shit. All right, man. Are you coming straight back? I won't take my planned time off. We need to eliminate this threat right away." Link is desperate and it's oozing out of him. Every second I talk to him, my confidence grows that he's hiding much more than I originally thought. And that is not acceptable.

"I'm only dropping her off and heading straight back. I need to locate Aric before he leaves the area and take care of the Mafia threat. Go ahead and take the next few days off. I don't want to interrupt the time you have planned with your mystery woman. Conner and I can handle this."

Link remains silent; he's all too aware that this isn't my MO. To allay his suspicions, I add, "You know I'm always pushing you to take some time off. Conner and I will keep you updated on what's going on. If we need you, I'll call."

"All right, sounds good. Is there anything else you need me to do tonight?"

"Yeah, try to get the word out that Allie is taking a trip to the East Coast. Florida or something touristy like that. Let's get these guys on a wild goose chase."

"You got it, boss. I'll talk to you in a few days."

I end the call and tug my hand through my hair. The closer I think I'm getting to the answers, the further away I learn I am.

But that's going to end. Allie's secrets will be revealed, and so will Link's. They don't call me ruthless for no reason. Allie will be safe, but Link? He might end up at the bottom of the ocean soon.

Chapter Fifteen

Kali.

When I first wake up, everything is fuzzy from last night. I remember Aric showing up at the expo and Gage coming to my rescue. I recall coming back to Gage's and him questioning me, but after that, I'm drawing a blank.

Well, almost. That kiss we shared has seared into my soul, and I doubt I'll ever forget it or ever have another one that will compare in my lifetime. I can picture myself old, with fully white hair, rocking in my chair on a back deck somewhere, replaying that kiss over and over again.

Gage gives me a vial of liquid, claiming it's good for hangovers. I don't ask questions and shoot it back. The taste is horrible. I might throw it up. But within a few minutes, I'm already feeling better. I take a quick shower, and to my wonderment, I feel whole again.

I need to find out where Gage gets those small brown vials. Harlow would give her right leg to have a supply of them.

Gage must've been a busy man after I fell out last night. When I step out of the shower, one of my summer dresses is hanging off a hook. I dress quickly and go into the bedroom. The bed is made and my suitcase is sitting on top. I open it and almost scream in the joy of seeing my hair dryer.

Having thick hair—blessed as my mom would always tell me—is nothing but a pain in the ass. And if I try to air-dry it, I'm looking at an all-day event. Thirty minutes later, my hair is acceptable and my mascara applied. Lip gloss coats my lips, bruised pink from last night. I try to contain my smile but can't stop the spark I feel inside.

My nose carries me into the kitchen, where Gage stands shirtless. His upper back is covered in black ink, just as I've always pictured it. But better. Across his shoulder blades is a large hawk with its wings spread wide in flight. The wording below is in an unfamiliar language.

"Liking what you see?" Gage asks, his back still to me.

I walk over to a chair, propping against it. "I was just wondering what your tattoo says."

Gage takes the bacon out of the pan, placing it on a plate. "Nothing without effort." He cracks open eggs into the frying pan.

If there's one thing I know about Gage, it's that he's all in on everything he does. From the moment I crossed paths with him, he has collided with all parts of my life without apology, impacting everything like a hurricane.

"My father would shout that at me during his beatings."

A gasp I can't withhold breaks from my lips at his brutal honesty. This is how a little boy went from wanting to be a superhero to a man with blood on his hands. "Why would you get those words tattooed on your body?"

Gage grabs a piece of bacon and walks over to me. I extend my hand to take it, but he pulls the bacon out of my reach, a mischievous smile across his face. I set my hand in my lap. He slowly leans toward me, his eyes burning. "Open up," he commands.

Without a second thought, I do.

He places the bacon on my tongue, and I bite down, the flavor taking over my senses as I moan in gratitude. His eyes flash with desire as he pops the other half into his mouth and walks over to the stove to attend to the eggs.

"I got those words inked into my skin because he was right."

His answer surprises me. "What do you mean?"

He grabs two white plates, filling each with eggs, bacon, avocado slices, and grapes. He sets one of the plates in front of me and leans against the other side of the bar. He stacks eggs, bacon, and avocado on the toast before taking a large bite. Chewing slowly, he watches me closely for a moment before responding. "He told me that to be on top and run the family like he did, I must use every moment to build myself stronger than the devil himself."

"Run the family?" I ask, recalling Fletcher's words about Gage's father's empire and how he dismantled the entire thing. Does that mean he killed his entire family?

Gage takes another large bite before setting his sandwich down and grabbing another piece of bacon off my plate, bringing it to my lips.

I open without being prompted and take a bite. This time the flavor doesn't overwhelm my senses. My mind isn't on the food sitting in front of me. It's on the man standing across from me, slowly revealing his beautifully damaged heart.

"He wanted his eldest son to become more ruthless than he was, and he learned he achieved that many years ago."

I gulp, not liking where this conversation is leaning. I knew his past was filled with darkness, but this morning I'm getting a peek behind the scenes of what's concealed in those artic-blue eyes.

I don't want to ask, but I can't stop the words falling from my lips. "How did he learn?"

He's almost finished with his plate of food, and I've barely touched mine. He's carrying on this conversation like we are merely talking about the weather, but I can see the tension in his taut muscles. "When I put a bullet between his eyes."

My mouth drops open and my heart cries out in pain. I think of my father and all the love he gave me throughout our time together. He never once put his hands on me. He never forced me to be anyone or anything I didn't want to be. He let me be me. He was the exact opposite of Gage's father. My heart breaks.

Gage places the plate into the sink and tells me he's hitting the shower. I watch him walk away as his words simmer. I should feel hate and disgust with him for killing his own father... but I can't. Instead, all I see is a little boy wearing a red cape and having the love beaten out of him every day.

Something no one should ever have to go through. But he did. And as his father pounded *nothing without effort* into him, he took that advice and eliminated the devil himself.

I peer at my plate, not feeling an ounce of hunger. If I don't eat, Gage will hand-feed me every piece. I shovel down the food, trying to get a grasp of my feelings.

As soon as he's out of the shower, he drops his boots with a dull thud to the floor and sinks into the couch beside me.

"I just got off the phone with Harlow. I'm taking you to the Oasis to stay there over the next week."

I don't argue. I already planned to head there today to see Sofia and the time away sounds good right now. I send a text to Fletcher asking if I can have the entire week off, and he responds with a thumbs-up and a thank-you for all my work on the expo.

I don't ask Gage how he got my suitcase filled with my belongings or why Conner is following us in my Jimmy. Honestly, I'm scared I won't like the answer.

We ride in silence the entire way, his hands flexing tight around the steering wheel. He's lost in his thoughts, and as badly as I want to ask what is banging around in that head of his, I don't.

We're only a couple of miles away from the Oasis when he suddenly pulls off the side of the road, the tires crunching against the gravel. Before I can question why he pulled over, he's unbuckling my seat belt and pulling me into his lap. His hands, warm and firm, cup my face, and then his lips collide with mine with a fervor as if he's breathing me in like air. *Like this is the last time he will ever see me.*

I wrap my arms around his neck and pull him in closer, feeling the warmth of his body against mine. If this is the last time I see him, I want to give him everything I have. I feel his growing erection throbbing underneath me and my slick heat pouring out.

The kiss becomes a dance of desperation and desire. I can feel his heart pounding in sync with mine. My entire body trembles with the ecstasy flowing through my veins.

He breaks the kiss and in a deep, rough voice utters, "If you keep doing that, I can't be held accountable for my actions."

Until the words leave his mouth, I didn't realize I was grinding my aching body against his hard cock. My movements stop immediately. He chuckles lightly, nuzzling into my neck and inhaling deeply.

We sit quietly for a moment, while he whispers words in another language. They sound rough and filled with desire, but I choose not to question what they mean.

I doubt I could find the words to explain what is coursing through me.

After a few moments, we get back on the road. I finish the last couple of miles with aching nipples and soaked panties.

To my disappointment, Gage doesn't stay when he drops me off. Conner tosses me the keys to my Jimmy before he and Gage jump into his SUV and take off without another look.

Hurt fills me as I watch Gage drive off, wondering if I will ever see him again. Our kiss only minutes ago felt like something real, but now his quick and cold exit has me confused.

One glance at Harlow and I can tell she's reading everything I'm feeling.

"Come on," she says, putting her arm around me. "Let's grab a glass of wine and get the barracuda back in you."

Harlow and I sit on her back porch, which overlooks the sprawling acreage at the Oasis. This property is vast, with just over two hundred fifty acres of lush green land that stretches as far as the eye can see. Tall evergreens and vibrant wildflowers create a picturesque scene that seems almost surreal.

Over a dozen lodges dot the property, each nestled in its own secluded area, offering a sense of privacy and tranquility. Harlow's grandparents left her this property when they passed, and with the help of my parents, she not only expanded but enhanced her vision of a safe, neutral ground into a beautiful reality. The hot summer air is filled with the sweet scent of blooming flowers and the distant sound of a babbling creek.

"How's Sofia hanging in there?" I ask, sipping on a glass of red wine with frozen grapes floating at the top.

"She's good. Since I introduced her to the chefs, she hasn't left their side. She's making you a surprise lunch right now."

I smile, glad to hear that the fight remains inside her. Gage knew exactly what she needs. Once she learned her father was going into rehab, it appears the heavy world of shit lifted off her small shoulders.

"But I'm not so sure she's on board with up and leaving her life for a new one—if she testifies, they'll put her into the WITSEC program immediately." Harlow picks up one of her guns and starts to dismantle it. Probably to clean it for the millionth time, even though it doesn't look like it needs it.

I lean back into the chair and prop my feet on the empty one beside me. I think back to my first year with Harlow after my parents died and how hard it was for me to accept that I couldn't live the life I once had. Sure, Sofia could choose not to testify and live her days out at the Oasis to remain safe. But what kind of life would she have? She would never be able to live out her dreams, and regret would eventually sink deep into her soul.

I glance over at Harlow and find her watching me.

"I can help her," I say. "I know what it's like to be in her shoes."

Harlow smiles at me sagely. Her long chestnut hair is pulled into a ponytail, and she's dressed in her normal attire, which is ripped blue jeans and a band T-shirt. Today's flavor is Tom Petty.

"You want to tell me about those swollen lips you had when you first arrived?"

I bite my cheek to hold back the smile that wants to crash over my face. I make sure to gather my wits before responding. "I got stung in the lip by a bee."

Harlow's only response is to raise her perfect eyebrows.

My cheeks heat; I'm unable to hide the flush that creeps up my face. I bite my lower lip and glance away, but the warmth of the memory brings a shy smile to my face. "It was... amazing," I admit, my voice barely a whisper.

Harlow's smile grows large. "I can see that just by the look on your face."

I force a smile, hoping she doesn't see through the façade. The truth is, I shouldn't have kissed him again, not with the secrets I'm harboring. It feels like every passionate moment we share brings me closer to the precipice unraveling my carefully constructed life.

When it comes down to it, I have no idea what's going on between me and Gage—or whether I'll ever even see him again. The expo is done and Aric is MIA. Is Gage going to disappear chasing Aric as quickly as he showed up?

I swirl my finger around the stem of the wineglass. "It was sweet and passionate and fiery, all wrapped up like a Christmas present, leaving me chasing my next breath."

"Sounds like something straight out of a romance novel."

"Exactly," I reply and we grin at each other.

There are few people in this world I can trust and Harlow is at the top of my list. She never judges, only shows support. She's the kind of friend who will help you do your hair and teach you how to stitch a bullet hole on yourself while drinking a bottle of red. She's incredible.

"Tell me about the expo."

"Have you heard?"

"That Aric Hemmington was there and followed you into a room? Yes. No one seems to know what happened inside that office."

I exhale and take a swig of my wine. I figured Gage would have filled her in on everything. I go into detail about our brief interaction on the balcony and how he revealed my birthmark, leaving me no choice but to tell the truth. I do hold back on sharing Aric's promise to see me again. I would like to think that was an empty threat, but I'm no longer that naïve girl. If I were to tell Harlow that, I would be stuck at the Oasis for the unforeseeable future. Not that I don't love it here, but I enjoy my new life, my home, and my job.

To my surprise, Harlow doesn't seem to be very upset about Aric discovering me, which honestly has tilted my world on its axis.

"Do you know Aric?" I ask.

Harlow snorts at my question. "Of course I do. Along with his father."

I should have known.

Harlow finishes polishing the outside of her gun, now that it is all reassembled. This woman can never sit still for long. She lays it on the table next to her. The damn thing is shinier than any diamond.

I wonder... If I put my purse in front of her, would she polish the leather and metal on that? Huh. I might need to try that next time.

"Aric may have interesting ways of going about things, but I know he would never hurt you."

"He's manipulative," I counter. "He straight up dogged me out for kissing him all those years ago, and to dig the knife deeper, he told me he left me that day with hearts in my eyes. He's nothing but an arrogant jerkface."

"Oh, I never said he can't be an ass. But don't let him fool you. Aric wanted that kiss more than you did." Amusement dances on her face. "But from what I'm seeing, it sounds like Aric's kiss had nothing on Gage's."

"You got that right." I beam at her. "What do you think about Aric saying he was supposed to be there that night with his father? Do you think Victor killed my parents?"

Harlow leans back in her chair, her eyes grazing the grasslands and mountains, deep in thought. "I know Victor was there that night. When Logan hid you in that closet, he told me at least a dozen and a half men magically appeared."

I sit up straight in my chair, my feet dropping to the ground. This is the most Harlow has ever shared with me about that fateful summer night. I'm not sure why she is now. Maybe I wasn't asking the right questions.

"Were they Victor's men?"

"That's the thing. Logan doesn't think so."

I lean back again. I don't know Victor well. I only met him briefly a couple of times when he came to see my father. He always intimidated me, even though he was never rude in any way. The evil lurking behind his eyes made me shudder. I've been told that Victor is well protected, and if he doesn't want to be seen, he won't be. Much like his son Aric, who's a ghost himself.

I wonder if Gage's endgame to finding Aric is to reach Victor. If Logan puts his sights on Aric instead of Victor, he might have a better chance.

"Does Logan know what happened with Aric and me?"

Harlow nods. "He plans on coming by tomorrow."

I roll my eyes and Harlow laughs. "He's protective, but it's all in good faith."

"Ugh. Promise you won't tell him about the kiss."

Laughing, Harlow makes a gesture of zipping her lips.

Chapter Sixteen

Kali.

Sofia has made the best grilled cheese sandwich I've ever had in my entire life. Outside the three cheeses, the bacon is cooked to perfection, and the avocado and tomatoes take it to a whole other level.

After lunch, I take Sofia to the wildflower field on Harlow's Gator. I turn off the ignition and we walk through the field. My own little slice of Graceland. I'm excited for her to see it.

"Is Gage coming back?" she asks me. "When Harlow told me he was bringing you, I thought he was staying."

I smile as she bends down and picks a daisy. "No, he had a lead on whatever he's doing. I honestly don't think I'm going to see him again."

She throws her head back and laughs like I don't have a clue about anything. Her hair is down, a waterfall of silk.

"Oh, he's coming back. I don't think anyone has ever known the great Gage McCollin to ever be so smitten over a woman before."

My heart kicks up a notch and excited little butterflies break out. I can't resist. I take the bait like the hungry little guppy I am. "Really? He's never been with anyone before?"

"I wouldn't go that far." Sofia snickers.

I roll my eyes. It doesn't take a rocket scientist to deduce that Gage has had his fair share of women throwing themselves at him, but after that kiss, I can't blame one of them.

She relents. "But he's never been known to be serious with anyone. Well, at least not until you."

I shake my head. "That's the thing. We aren't serious. We've never even gone out on a date before." I can't technically count the Irish pub. The only reason that happened was because he was holding my bag hostage. And the lunch at Seward Park was technically a lunch break.

We reach the creek bed and I lay the blanket down for us to perch on. We collapse onto the soft blanket and stretch our legs.

The wildflower field is painted with a kaleidoscope of colors—delicate blue lupines, cheerful yellow-and-white daisies, and the rich scarlet of columbine. I take a deep breath and smell the heady perfume, a blend of sweet floral fragrances that is invigorating and soothing. The field is alive with the buzzing of bees and the thrumming of hummingbirds' wings as they visit the flowers for nectar. The songbirds add their soundtrack to the scene—a cacophony of chirping sparrows, squeaking chickadees, and cooing doves.

Beside me, Sofia blends right in with the tableau with her radiant grin lighting up the space more. She's wearing a pink shirt rolled into a knot on the side along with her signature yoga pants.

"Do you even own a pair of jeans?" I ask, realizing I haven't seen her wear anything else.

She picks a piece of lint off her knee. "Why would I? Wearing leggings is like wearing pajamas all day long and not being judged."

"You make a strong point. I'm just saying, I think summer dresses are more comfortable than any kind of pants. Stretchy or not." I brush off my beautiful lavender cotton dress, which Gage packed for me. I paired it with Harlow's strappy brown sandals once I got here.

"Ugh, please." Sofia scrunches her nose at the thought of having to wear a dress.

"Hey, don't knock it until you try it. Maybe when you start your new life, you can give it a try."

Sofia gulps and picks invisible lint off her black yoga pants. "I don't know if I can do it," she says, shaking her head. "My entire life is in Seattle. If I testify, they'll whisk me away and I won't know where to."

I understand the feelings that are bouncing around inside her. "It's a scary situation. Everyone has a certain level of fear for the unknown."

"It's just not fair. I won't be able to see my friends ever again—or my dad. I won't be able to visit my mom's grave and leave her flowers. I won't see you or Harlow again." Sadness fills her voice and cracks my heart into two.

I empathize with the horrible situation she's in. All because her father made bad choices and her mother passed way too soon. "It's not as bad as you think. It takes a while, but eventually, you'll find your wheels and start moving forward."

Sofia's sharp eyes whip to mine. "Why do you say that as if you live that life too?"

I smile gently. "Because I do."

Her mouth drops open and then promptly closes. "Bullshit."

Now it is my turn to throw my head back and laugh. Sofia sits up cross-legged, facing me. Curiosity pours out of her.

"Can you keep a secret?"

She nods eagerly.

I look out at the wildflowers that surround us and breathe in the beauty that God lays before us every single day. "This is my favorite spot because it's where I had some of my favorite memories with my family." I lower my head and take another deep breath, getting control of my emotions. "After my parents were murdered, I had to go into hiding. My name isn't Allie Smith."

Sofia remains quiet for a moment before saying, "A US marshal told me I would have to change my name too. My mom named me Sofia and I won't give that up." She shakes her head. "I agreed to change my last name if I do testify. I love my father, but this was all because of him."

When I listen to her, it's hard to remember how young she is. She should never have had to choose. "It was hard for me too."

She's rubbing the small tattoo on her pinky finger again. It's simple, just the outline of a heart. "Did you get that tattoo for your mother?"

She peers down at it. "Yeah. I got it last year with a fake ID. My mom had the same one." After a moment, Sofia asks, "Can I ask what your real name is?"

"Kali Marie Keeyes."

Sofia rocks back for a second. I can see her mind twisting around, no doubt trying to place where she's heard my name before. Her hand flies to her mouth. "Oh my God! I remember hearing about you. They said you died in a fire with your parents and brother. Your family members were, like, gazillionaires."

I laugh. Our family was richer than any number of the hundred-dollar bills we stored in the safes.

"Wait, you said your parents died. Does that mean your brother's alive too?"

"You have a sharp mind for the small details. That's a great skill to have."

Sofia's cheeks turn red as she pulls her legs to her chest, hugs them, and rests her chin on top of her knees. "Not always."

"Don't ever doubt yourself. And yes, you're 100 percent right. You'll meet him tomorrow. He's coming by to be the annoying brother he always is."

My heart slams against my chest as I race Logan up the tall mountain to his favorite place at the Oasis, where the crystal-blue Diamond Lake sits at the top like a hidden gem. He's about ten yards in front of me and hasn't even broken into a sweat. Jerk.

"Come on Kali-Allie! You're growing soft on me," he yells, glancing over his shoulder to see my red face.

He laughs and I decide I'm going to shove his punk ass into the lake when we reach it. If I can even reach it. This run used to be nothing to me back in the day. I would run it daily, but after the years passed, I found myself only running to the wildflower field where the creek runs through. Which is all flat ground. Much more my style.

Logan's wearing a T-shirt with the sleeves cut off and a pair of gym shorts. His blond hair is mussed from the run. Every year, I swear he gets larger. Considering most of his work is done on computers, he must spend countless hours in a gym to keep up his physique.

By the time we reach the lake, I'm thinking less about pushing Logan in and more about hurling myself into the cool water.

Logan drops his backpack to the ground, and I'd bet my left leg his laptop and phone are in it. He never goes anywhere without either.

"Still can't be without your electronics, I see."

Logan smiles, reminding me of our father. "There's no rest for the wicked." He heads toward me and I know what's coming.

"Wait," I try to yell, but I'm already laughing too hard to get any words out. He picks me up and tosses me into the lake with little effort. The water surrounds me like an icy fan against my heated skin. I welcome it, choosing to stay underneath for a beat longer.

I break the water's edge, a gasp escaping at the welcome—though shocking—cold, and push my hair back. Logan pops up a moment later a few feet from me, and I splash him immediately. He lunges and I shriek. I dive into the water and propel myself like a torpedo. Logan may beat me in a footrace, but he can't catch me in the water. All those years I spent swimming in the large pond at our parents' home paid off.

I pop up and see Logan more than fifteen feet behind me. "Come on, *Slowgan*, you're getting old on me."

I push myself back so I'm easily floating on top of the cool water, though my skin is now covered in goosebumps. When he reaches me, Logan does the same. We float for a while, basking in the warm sun. The sky only holds a cloud or two.

"You remember the first time you brought me up here?" I ask.

He grunts. "Yeah, I remember having to give you a piggyback ride halfway because you couldn't take one more step."

I grin. Who doesn't want a piggyback ride?

We float for a while, neither of us saying anything, both of us lost in thought. The cold shock after the scorching-hot run has seared my mind clean. My thoughts drift to Gage and his searing kiss. Sofia seems to have decided I'm different from other women, but I'm not sure I agree. Gage has this natural charm that no woman could deny. Top that with artic-blue eyes, dimples, and an eight-pack, and you're as good as gone. But then I was hit with the kindness of his heart. The way he taught the class at Elite Defense ways to defend themselves. The way he helped Sofia and her father.

I think of how Sofia said Gage has made people disappear. I don't know exactly what is entailed in his superhero duties, but I'm not naïve enough to believe that everyone who disappears is sent off to rehab like Ricardo.

Take Arnold Caprese. The head of the Italian Mafia. A ruthless, heartless man who had his goons hunting for Sofia. A man who was no doubt displeased with Domenico Amante having to go to trial because the state has a possible eyewitness. Then the fact that Gage had to up and leave unexpectedly, only for Arnold to be killed the night before Gage returned.

It can't be a coincidence. I believe Gage must have known they were getting close to revealing who the eyewitness was, and to keep Sofia safe, he had to eliminate the head. He turned their world upside down and hoped to throw them off their game long enough for the trial to take off without a hitch and keep Sofia safe.

Does that make Gage the hero or the villain? Does killing someone ruthless and vile make it all right? Or does it make him the same?

If Victor Hemmington is in fact my parents' killer, could I pull the trigger on him?

"What's going on in that head of yours?" Logan asks.

I shield my eyes from the sun, realizing that we have drifted toward the sandy shoreline. "I know Victor was at our house that night."

Logan goes to his feet immediately and grabs my hand, pulling me out of my floating position. "Come on, let's talk about this on the shore. I'm freezing my limbs off."

We trudge through the water, our clothes sticking to us. The blazing summer sun feels good on my skin. I wring out what feels like a gallon of water from my long blond locks. Logan unzips his bag and tosses a towel at me, smacking me in the face with it.

So annoying.

We dry off as much as possible and lay our towels just off the sand in the plush grass. We both sit down on our towels while I wait patiently for Logan to spill.

"Victor was there that night. He showed up unexpectedly, wanting to talk... business. He brought more of his men than usual. After I hid you in that closet, I went back to get Mom." He gulps, holding his emotions in check. I'm not sure if he's doing that for me or himself. "She was already gone by the time I made it back."

I suck in a shaky breath, hating that my brother will probably never get that image out of his head. He took that burden and protected me from it. I grab his hand and squeeze.

"But what's weird is that other men were there too, not only Victor's minions. I had never seen them before, and they were talking in another language I didn't recognize. I don't think they expected Victor and his men to be there."

What does that even mean? "What was the business Victor was there for?" I ask, grasping for anything.

Logan drops his head. I lean forward and put my forehead to his. He's breathing harder than he was when we got to the lake.

"Lo?" I whisper, wishing I could be inside his mind and take away the pain.

He shakes his head before pulling away. He still won't meet my eyes, instead looking at our clasped hands. He stays silent for a long time, and as badly as I want to, I don't say a word. He's kept me safe from the horrors he had to live that day. Much more vivid horrors than I had to endure. I can sit here as long as it takes, giving him whatever time he needs to tell me what exactly happened that night. I've waited seven years... What's a few more minutes?

He lets out a breath. "It was about Aric."

I sit back on my heels. "Aric told me he was supposed to be there that night. He said not going was one of his biggest regrets." The sadness across his face when he said it seemed genuine.

Logan's grip becomes so strong, it hurts my hands. "Don't you ever believe a word that comes out of his mouth." His voice is deep and harsh.

I jerk back, ripping my sore hands from his, just as his phone starts to ring. Logan pushes his hand through his hair.

"Shit, Kali. I'm sorry," he says, grabbing my hands and inspecting them. He's never ignored his phone before, and that surprises me. It rings off. "This entire situation sucks. I just wish our parents were here to help me figure shit out."

My heart breaks to see how vulnerable he truly is under that rough exterior.

His phone starts ringing again. Logan mumbles "Fuck" under his breath. It rings off again. I've never seen him act this way before. He's losing it and I can't have that.

I don't care what it takes, but I will make sure that he doesn't need to worry about me for one more second. "Thank you, Logan."

"For what?"

"For everything. You took all this on by yourself, to keep me from all the hate and ugliness that seeped into our family. You do what you need to do. If you want me to stay at the Oasis, I will. If you want me by your side, I'm there."

Logan shakes his head, letting out a rushed breath. "You're safe for now. Just take the next few days with Sofia and you're good to go home. I got everything under control."

I'm about to ask him what that means when his phone starts going off again. "Maybe you should get that."

Logan searches my eyes like a lost puppy. He nods, releases my hands, stands, and walks over to his bag to dig through it. He answers the phone, glancing over to me briefly before walking off.

Logan has been stressed over the years, but I don't think I have ever seen him like this. Was it caused by my encounter with Aric or the entire situation with Sofia? I will be damned if I'm the reason for any additional stress on him. I lean back on the towel and study him from a distance as he paces. I try to read his expression but can't. He's always had a poker face.

After a couple of minutes, he hangs up, heads over to his bag, and drops his cell into a side pocket. He digs around for a moment before he comes up with another phone and walks over to me, holding it out.

I take it from him, wondering what's going on.

"That's a burner. I already have my number programmed in there. If you ever feel threatened or if there's any kind of emergency, call me. I don't care what time it is. I can promise you I'm closer than you think."

This must stem from Aric finding me. Logan has never offered to give me a phone, much less one with his phone number on it.

"Is everything all right?" I ask, my voice trembling slightly. My heart races and a sense of unease washes over me.

"It will be soon. Let's go." He leans down, grabbing his towel.

I slowly stand and gather my things to return to Harlow's house.

I can only pray that Logan is right. Because I have a feeling everything is about to get worse.

Chapter Seventeen

Gage.

I can't fucking do it. I cannot take one more second of watching them together. My chest hurts like a thousand bullets have pierced my heart.

When I left Allie yesterday, I went straight to Link's location in Seattle. It was the longest couple hours of my life. To my surprise, he was already in the heat of a fierce street battle with a gang of Italian Mafia foot soldiers. The air was thick with the acrid smell of gunpowder, the gunfire echoing off the brick walls of the narrow alley. I almost called off following him when I saw that.

We had already established that he was going to see his mystery woman. Sure, he'd argued at first, but ultimately he'd agreed. But he evidently chose not to. Then when I found him hard at work instead, I couldn't help but have second thoughts.

Is Allie becoming such a strong distraction to me that I'm not seeing things straight?

I decided to stick with my gut instinct and watch his every move. His every kill.

I don't know why he chooses to be behind a computer all day. The man is a machine on the front line.

Then this morning, I checked the surveillance on Link, ready to call it quits and notify Conner that I was wrong. But again, to my surprise, he wasn't at home. He had been on the road for thirty minutes, heading north.

I wasted no time jumping in my Audi and racing toward his flashing red dot on my screen. I had Conner put a tracker on Logan's truck the second things started to not add up. I kept telling myself that as soon as I saw him with his mystery woman, I would spy no longer and let him do his thing.

I caught up and was able to tail him without notice. It wasn't long before we were pulling into the place I was just at yesterday. *Why the fuck is he at the Oasis?* I jumped out of my vehicle and grabbed my binoculars.

I watched him climb out of his blacked-out truck just as Harlow stepped out on the back porch, glancing around nervously. I've never seen Harlow nervous, so the fact that she was looking around for anyone to be watching her at her own home caught me off guard.

But I quickly learned why.

Link wasted no time closing the distance between them. He easily lifted her, slamming her against the back of her cabin. Harlow clawed at his chest as if she couldn't wait another minute. Link lifted her shirt and bra, showcasing her large breasts, and rustled with his belt. He began sucking on her nipples, alternating every few seconds.

I could tell the second he entered Harlow, thrusting hard into her lust-filled body. She threw her head back in pure ecstasy and must have moaned too loudly for his liking because he quickly slapped his hand over her mouth.

I would've never guessed in a million years that Harlow and Link had a side fuck going on. After all, haven't Harlow and Fletcher been fucking for years? I dropped my binoculars into my car and dipped inside, having seen enough. I considered leaving, but now that I was out here again, I wanted to try and get a glimpse of Allie. I traveled to the outskirts of Harlow's property. I couldn't risk anyone seeing me, but I still needed to be close enough to see Allie. I was hoping she'd be in Harlow's home by the way Harlow reacted when she first walked out. And she was.

Time ticked by slowly, but eventually I watched Allie and Link walk out of the cabin together. The smile on her face was telling. *She knows Link. Very well.*

She gave him a playful shove and took off running. He easily caught up to her and they disappeared down the beaten path away from the cabin. I knew exactly where that path led because I have taken the same path to the lake when I've stayed at the Oasis.

And now, watching them run off together, all I see is red—a feeling of rage I haven't felt in many years.

If he's fucking Harlow *and* Allie, I'm not going to be able to restrain my actions. This motherfucker had it coming to him. I think I'd get a pass from Harlow for breaking her strict rules of a neutral ground if I rip her cheating lover limb from limb. She would turn a blind eye.

No one plays me—or Harlow—for a fool and gets away with it.

Familiar with the trails here, I hit the gas on the gravel road that wraps around the Oasis and make it to a high point that will be perfect for scouting. I pop my trunk, take out my Bergara MG Lite bolt-action rifle equipped with a Razor HD LHT scope, and wait.

A short while later, they arrive.

Through the scope, I watch him toss her into the water, and they laugh. *They both fucking laugh.* In fact, Allie is laughing more than I've ever seen her laugh, and the jealousy that swims through my body is unfamiliar... and dangerous.

He swims closer to her, and I watch as they float next to each other. There's a level of comfort between them that looks like it's rooted in a long relationship. Link and Allie have been close for quite a while now.

Is Allie his mystery girl? Or is it Harlow?

Fuck, is it both?

I think about our last kiss—the one on the drive here yesterday, when she was sober. How I couldn't stop myself from one last taste. How I could feel the wetness of her panties through my pants, her nipples hard as ice against my chest. Stopping what was about to go down in the car was the hardest thing I've ever done. Is this why I couldn't put a finger on Allie and her secrets? Has she been playing me this entire time?

They swim back to shore and both dry off. I can't take my eyes off her toned body as she wrings the water from her platinum locks. She's like every man's wet dream. Apparently Link and I have the same dream.

That's not going to work out too well for Link.

They lie on towels that Link provides and go straight into deep conversation. I can't hear what they're saying, but it looks meaningful. My annoyance builds by the second, my finger rubbing against the trigger.

Then my little lion grabs his fucking hands and rests her forehead against his. I thought they were going to kiss. I was two seconds away from pulling the trigger and shooting Link in his fucking skull. But with her forehead pressed against his, I couldn't risk the shot.

That would be too easy of a way out for someone who betrays me, anyways. I grab my earbuds and connect them to my phone so I can watch them through the scope. He ignores my first call and my second. By the time I call again, I decide if he doesn't answer, I *am* shooting him between his eyes.

Finally, as if he can feel my threat, he pulls away from Allie and heads to his bag.

"Boss," he responds low as he glances at Allie and walks off. He doesn't say more, waiting to find out why I'm calling.

"Why haven't you been answering my calls?"

His body goes stiff. "I told you I had plans to meet up with my girl." Link's voice is laced with caution.

"Are you with her now?" I ask. I need to hear it. I've been watching it with my own two eyes, but for some reason, I need to hear him speak his betrayal.

"Yeah, I got here early this afternoon. I stayed back a day to take care of the goons looking for Allie." His voice drops when he says this, and he glances over toward Allie to make sure she can't hear what he is telling me.

Interesting.

"Who's this mystery woman?" I demand. I don't even pretend it's a friendly, curious question. "We've been working with each other long enough to stop holding secrets."

He remains silent and I know why. I've always teased him about his mystery woman, but never pushed as seriously as I am now.

"Why do you ask?" Link challenges.

It takes every ounce of my willpower to not rain havoc down upon him this very second. I take a silent breath in, not wanting to show how pissed off I am right now. "I want to know who's keeping you from work."

Silence again. He's unsure what to do, and in a sick way, I love that I have him fumbling. "You said I could have a few days off."

"Mmm, I did, didn't I." I make it more of a statement than a question. "I guess Conner and I can handle Aric. Enjoy your time with Miss Mystery. Maybe one day you can introduce her to me. We'll touch base when you get back."

"What do you mean, handle Aric?"

I know Link well enough to know he would drop everything and anything to get some one-on-one time with good ole Aric. And now I know why his hate for Aric is so strong. Allie admitted to me she kissed Aric. Today I got to witness Link and Allie play house while Link fucked the landlord behind her back.

"We got him. Conner's taking him to the warehouse off South River Street right now. Don't worry—we can fill you in when you return."

"No, I'm heading your way. Don't do a thing until I get there."

His statement makes me laugh. "You might be confused about your current situation, Link. You're not the one in control. I am." My finger is tight against the trigger; he has no clue how much control I'm actually in.

"Fuck." He runs his hand through his hair. "Yeah, man, I'm sorry. I know you are. Just hearing that we finally got him has my mind twisted. Where did you find him?"

"Still in town. I don't think he realized *I* got Allie out."

He nods in agreement. "That's great." He glances at Allie, who is currently lying out on the towel in her wet running clothes.

She looks beautiful.

"It'll take me a few hours to get there," he says. "Can you guys try and hold off until I get there?"

"Are you sure?" I ask, keeping my tone level and cool.

"Yeah, I can head out right away. She knows how this world works."

I pause as if to consider his request. "If you want. I should be there within the hour," I lie. With the time it will take them to run back to Harlow's cabin, I will have a nice head start. "We'll try and save something for you."

I hang up and watch Link do the same as he heads to Allie, tossing his phone into his bag. He grabs another phone out, a burner no doubt, and hands it to Allie.

I remove my finger from the trigger. Confusion is clear across her face through my scope, and so is the worry that quickly follows. I would give anything to hear whatever bullshit he's giving her. Allie gets up quickly, kisses him on the cheek, and hands her towel to him.

I watch them run back down the same beaten path until I can't see them any longer. I toss my rifle into the trunk and jump into my Audi. As much as I want to head to Harlow's place to make sure he keeps his hands off her, I can't. I need to arrive before he does. The warehouse will need to be set up and waiting for his arrival. I punch the gas and call Conner from my voice assistant option in my car.

He answers after the first ring. "Boss."

"How many times, Conner, do we need to have this conversation? I. Am. Not. Your. Boss."

"At least once more." His loyalty has never wavered.

"I need you to get the warehouse off South River Street ready. I'll be there as soon as I can. We have a special guest joining us tonight."

"On it. Who's the unlucky bastard this time?"

"Link."

Conner's silence stretches across the line for a pregnant moment. "Boss?"

"I just finished trailing him. He went straight to the Oasis, banged Harlow against the back of her cabin within one minute of pulling in, and then spent a lovely afternoon with Allie alone at a lake."

"He's fucking them both?"

I run my hands through my hair, still not fully understanding the entire situation myself. "It fucking seems like it. Allie only kissed him on the cheek, but it was obvious that they know each other well. Did you get anything on her yet?"

"Yeah, but not much. It's like she never existed before a few years ago, and even what's there is limited."

My knuckles are turning white with how tightly I am gripping the steering wheel. I've come across enough background checks in my past to understand what this means. This is exactly why Link gave me a bogus report. He knew it would send off red flags if he sent me her actual background check—a forgery.

Who are you, Allie Marie Smith, and what's your real name?

Chapter Eighteen

Kali.

Saying goodbye to someone you know you will never see again is one of the hardest things I've ever had to do. It isn't until now that I understand exactly what it's like being on both sides of new identities. When I had to give up the life I always knew, it was one of the hardest things. Saying my tearful goodbyes to Sofia is even harder.

Nevertheless, I'm so proud of her for deciding to testify. I want nothing more than to know where she is going afterward and what her future holds, but there's no way around that in the Witness Security Program. I guess I should be grateful she's finally going into WITSEC, but I'm not. After Sofia agreed to testify, Fletcher worked his magic with the US Marshal Service to fund the security outfit for her new home, but even he doesn't know where that's going to be.

Once she's gone, I text Fletcher to thank him and tell him that I'll be back on Monday. Nothing is waiting for me at home, and staying with Harlow has helped my sour mood since Gage went MIA on me. I try calling Logan a couple of times, but he never answers. I find it strange he gave me a phone to call in case of emergency and then not pick up.

Granted, there isn't any emergency, but he doesn't know that. Though come to think of it, I've been at the Oasis all week, which I'm sure he knows, and if I was having a real emergency, he knows Harlow would be in contact.

I haven't heard from Gage since he dropped me off a week ago, and I would be lying if I said that didn't sting a little bit. When I broach the subject with Harlow, she tries to brush it off like it isn't that big of a deal, telling me he has a lot on his plate. I tried calling him after Logan left, but I got his voicemail. I refuse to be the woman who calls him nonstop.

His job is to find Aric and get answers to the questions he never revealed to me. I'm sure he's already bulldozed into some other unexpecting woman's life, turned it upside down, and left her breathless. A woman who doesn't have to lie to him about who she is.

I'm a damn fool.

I wait until late Sunday night before I decide to head home. I'm an hour from the Oasis when my faithful Jimmy starts acting up. I barely get to the side of the deserted road before it dies completely.

Good times.

I try to start it a couple of times, but the engine won't even turn over. I dig into my purse and grab my cell to call Harlow. No signal. I dig deeper and pull out the burner phone that Logan gave me, hoping that one has a signal. Nope.

I glance around the dark surroundings, though I'm not looking for anyone. No, I could only do that if I was in a populated area. I'm surrounded by nothing but woods. So instead, I'm looking for anything that might be hungry. Like a cougar or a bear.

I unlock my door and crack it open to take another look around. The only sounds are crickets. Literally.

I pop my hood and hop out, turning the flashlight on from my cell to see if I notice anything visibly wrong. I come up empty. Not that I'm a mechanic by any means, just hoping to catch one damn break in my lifetime.

I jiggle the cables on the battery, but they're tight. I look for the oil stick but have no clue where that thing is. Even if I did find it, it's not like I have a quart of oil in the back. I scan over the rest, only coming up with dirt and grease. I should have someone clean this thing under the hood. It's gross.

There's a crunching noise close by. My body locks up like a statue instantly. My breathing is deafening, and my heart is pounding hard as if it's trying to break out and run away from me.

Something howls in the woods to my left. I shriek, slam the hood, and run to the driver's door, which is still wide open. I throw myself in, shut the door hard, and press the lock, attempting to catch my breath.

I don't care that I'm going to sit in this Jimmy until tomorrow comes… I'm not stepping another foot outside this vehicle tonight. I assume Fletcher will call Harlow the second I don't make it to work, and then it's only a matter of time before someone comes to my aid.

I rest my head against the headrest.

Just then, a hand clamps over my mouth, dragging me into the back seat. My back slams against a hard chest.

This cannot be happening.

I start fighting with everything I have because I'm surely not going out like this. In this confined space, I don't have many choices for anything I learned in Krav Maga class, but that doesn't mean I don't have any options.

I slam my foot on my attacker's and simultaneously throw a hard elbow into his side. The asshole grunts. I get a short feeling of satisfaction before his hand leaves my mouth and he wraps both his arms tightly around me, trapping my arms against my body. He links his feet around my ankles, locking my legs apart.

That's when I panic. I start bucking wildly in his arms. I'm not making much progress, but I can't give up that easily. This man is built like a brick house, and when I finally tire him out, he's going to regret ever trying to mess with me.

His arms tighten around my chest, making it tougher to breathe. I slam my head back, but he must see that coming because I don't hit anything. I try to lean down so I can bite his arm, but it's pointless. I can't reach. My attempts are getting weaker by the second, and no doubt he can tell.

"Keep writhing your sweet body on mine and we might end up with a change of plans." His voice is low and husky.

I freeze, noticing the hard object beneath my ass—and worse, it's probably not a gun.

His voice, though he spoke low, I recognize. I drag in a large breath and am hit with the scent of leather and spice.

"Aric?" I ask, but I don't need to. He did say he was going to see me again. I just never imagined it would be here, in the back of my Jimmy, in the middle of nowhere.

"Mmm." He nuzzles my neck and inhales deeply.

Goosebumps fly across my frozen body. "Please let me go."

"I don't know. Are you going to be a good girl, or are you going to keep fighting me?"

As much as I would love to keep fighting, my body is tired from my effort. Once I get my strength back, it'll be game on. I need to be smart about this. "I won't try anything."

He chuckles, keeping his arms locked around me. "Such a beautiful liar you are."

I'm on the verge of hyperventilating, even though his arms have relaxed slightly around me. "Aric, please."

"I like it when you beg."

I relax my entire body against his to demonstrate my surrender. We sit quietly for a couple of minutes, my body on top of his. I can feel his heart beating hard against my back. His grip loosens more, and I take the opportunity to slide off his lap, thankful he allows it.

I plaster myself against the door and watch him closely. I know enough to not take my eyes off him, which, strangely, he seems to enjoy. He adjusts himself below, not at all hiding the fact that he's rock-hard, before twisting to face me, his arm resting along the top of my back seat.

"What are you doing here?"

He smiles, his emerald eyes glowing in the dark. I wouldn't be surprised if he told me he was a vampire, given the way he looks right now. "I told you I would see you again soon. I was hoping for another kiss."

I pin him with a hard glare, not wanting to play the sick and twisted games he seems to enjoy. I know damn well he isn't doing all this for another kiss. "And hell will freeze over before that happens again."

His response is to smile, as if what I am saying is a lie. Like he can see into the future. I want nothing more than to knock that cocky smile right off him. I would rather kiss a goat than kiss him ever again.

"Logan is right behind me, and so is Gage. It's only a matter of time before they catch up and take care of you once and for all."

"Is that so?" he asks, amusement jumping in his eyes.

"Yeah, it is. You better get out of here before they show, because I can't promise what's going to happen to you when they do."

"Now you're worried about me?"

What I want to do is smash his head in and gouge his eyes out, but even I'm not reckless enough to try it. Instead, I go for a different method. One I am more accustomed to. Sighing dramatically, I head straight down the rabbit hole.

Here we go again...

"Look, I tried to get them to lay off you. I mean, you were my first kiss. Well, not technically, but you know what I'm saying. Of course I don't want anything bad to happen to you. It's like when you're a little kid and you get your first teddy bear."

He gives me a befuddled look. This is good.

I continue. "You take that damn bear wherever you go, and after time goes by, it starts to get dirty and a seam around the leg starts to unravel. Next thing you know, you're trying to learn how to sew, just to hold on to this dirty, disgustingly dingy bear for only a while longer."

He cocks his head to the side, his lips tipping upward ever so slightly. "Are you saying I'm a teddy bear you can't ever let go?"

I roll my eyes. "No. What I'm saying is that you were an important piece of my life, and I'm trying to sew your leg back on before my brother and Gage show up to tear it clean off."

He sits quietly, watching me closely. He grabs a piece of my hair and starts twirling it around his finger, not concerned about the threat I tossed at him like a hot potato. He's not buying it.

I keep talking, hoping something will come out of my mouth that isn't complete garbage. "All right, fine, that was a bad analogy. Listen, I didn't want to say anything, but I can see there's no bullshitting you." I lock my hands together and take a deep breath, acting as if this is the hardest thing I've ever had to say.

It isn't.

"I don't have long to live," I confess. "I have cancer. It's literally metastasized throughout my entire body. I only have six months. A year if I'm lucky." I peek through my eyelashes to gauge his reaction.

His eyebrows shoot up.

I keep rolling. "Don't worry, I've accepted my death. Honestly, it's been harder on everyone else. That's why I didn't want to tell you. I want you to remember the way I was and not stress. I want to spend the last of my limited time doing things I've always wanted to do but haven't. Like... skydiving. I mean, how cool is that? Jumping out of a perfectly fine plane and hoping to God your parachute works has got to be one hell of an adrenaline rush. But hey, if mine doesn't, no biggie. I'm not going to sweat it."

When he has no comment, I take it as my cue to continue.

"Oh! Or taking one of those donkey rides down the Grand Canyon. One slip of that little donkey's foot and that's all you wrote, my friend. You and that donkey will be waiting at the pearly gates together." I lean forward slightly, dropping my voice for dramatic effect. "Just to be clear, I would *so* let the donkey go through the gates first. It wouldn't be his fault that I paid to take a ride on him down the canyon. He probably hated that job. I know I would. Who would ever want to risk their own life to entertain simple-minded people like me? I wouldn't sign up for that gig, no matter how good the hay was."

I give a light chuckle and smile at a stain on my ceiling right behind Aric, as if I can envision it all so clearly. Letting out a soft sigh, I go for the finish line and hope to God he buys it.

"So yeah, if I survive all that, I plan on going to the beach and maybe volunteering at an elephant rescue. I've always wanted to paint their toenails. I know it's weird, but one cannot simply change one's dreams." I wave my hand in the air. "Anyways. I'll be fine, and I know you will too." I point my finger at him but keep it at a safe distance in case he bites. "But only if you get out of here before Logan and Gage show up. I can't have that on my conscience, Aric. It would kill me inside if I knew anything happened to you because of me."

I pause, a little thunderstruck by the realization that what I just said is true. I don't have beef with this man. Or I didn't, until he pulled this ill-conceived stunt on the side of the damn road. *I just want to go home.* I run my hand over my face. I need to pull myself together. I'm not sure if I want to cry or laugh at my current situation.

He remains silent for so long, I'm about to start squirming. Instead, I bite my thumbnail and focus on my kneecap.

Finally he speaks. "It's funny you bring up Logan and Gage."

He's got my attention now.

"It is?" I whisper, not liking where this is going. Like he's in on a big secret that everyone knows except me.

Story of my life.

"Have you heard from Logan in the past few days?"

He's still playing with my hair, but at this moment, I honestly couldn't care less. I think about the call Logan got when we were at the lake, the one he let ring off twice before he finally picked it up. Whoever called him put him on high alert. Then he gave me a burner. Logan's never given me a way to contact him. His agenda dictated when we would talk or see each other. He always told me it was safer for me to handle it that way.

In delayed answer to Aric's question, I shake my head. Why? I have no idea. I just gave up my only ploy to get Aric to leave.

"Kali, Kali, Kali. Your brother isn't in a good position right now."

"He isn't?"

Aric slowly shakes his head. "It seems he and Gage had a falling out."

I rear back, my head hitting the window. I slap his hand away from my hair and rub the back of my head. "You're bullshitting."

"I would never lie to you, unlike you do to me, my sweet Kali. Although I do love to hear your off-the-wall stories. They can be so... impactful."

I gulp.

His lips lift, smiling in his deviously charming way. "Go ahead. Try to call him."

"I can't. No signal."

He pulls out his phone and taps a few times before he slides it back into his pocket. "It'll work now."

I reach forward and grab the burner phone, which dropped while he dragged me into the back seat. *Asshole.* As he predicted, I have full signal. I tap Logan's number and hit the call button. I have no idea what I'm going to say to Logan to get him to understand the situation I'm currently sitting in, but I will figure out something. I always do.

His phone goes straight to voicemail. I hang up and try again, getting the same outcome.

"Where is he, asshole?" I yell, getting ready to throat punch his ass.

Aric laughs. "He's with Gage, but I'm pretty sure it isn't a slumber party."

My heart rate is picking up by the second. "How can I be sure you're telling the truth?"

Aric reaches into his pocket, pulling his phone out. After a couple of taps, he turns his screen toward me.

It's a picture of Logan. He's wearing the same running clothes he had on before he left the Oasis. I have no clue where he is, but he's in a cell, lying on an old cot. There's a bruise underneath one of his eyes.

My stomach drops with horror. Logan is in danger and hurt. I knew Gage was dangerous, but I never thought he would do anything to my brother. *Shit!* Gage has no idea Logan is my brother. My brother's name is Joe, and according to *me*, he's halfway across the world. "How did you get this picture?"

His smile is sadistic. "One of my guys got it off the camera feed in the building where he's being held, wildflower."

"Don't call me that," I snap, my patience running thin.

"I'm on your side. I'm only trying to help."

"Why would you do that?"

"Because I know you wouldn't survive without your brother after what happened to your parents."

I lose my breath. It's uncanny to hear him say something so piercingly *kind* in this bizarre moment. "Do you know where they're at? If you want to help, then we need to go right now. I can't let anything happen to him."

Aric licks his lips, and his eyes drop to my mouth. "For a price."

I want to pull my hair out. Aric may be the most infuriating man I've ever met. So help me God, if I had a gun right now, I would have it pressed against his temple, and he would be driving me to Logan right this second.

Right after he fixed my Jimmy.

"I'm not kissing you again. What do you really want?"

Aric shrugs like it's no big deal.

"What does that mean?" I ask.

"What does what mean?"

"That shrug." I fling my hand in the air at him. "What the hell does that mean?" My voice rises.

"Nothing. It's just Logan's funeral. But if that's how you want it to play out, I can't argue."

If steam could pour out of me, it would. How someone can sit back and knowingly let someone suffer and die is beyond me, but it's clearly not beyond Aric. "Why should I believe you're going to help me free Logan?"

He sighs. "I already told you. I've never lied to you and never will."

I fold my arms across my chest. "Well, I don't believe you."

He does his stupid shrug again and turns to his phone, tapping away like he doesn't have a care in the world. He leans against the opposite door.

I watch him in disbelief. I may have told him I don't believe him, but the picture of Logan doesn't lie. But is it really Gage who has him?

My phone rings, but it isn't the burner phone.

Aric's gaze still locked on his phone, he says, "I'm sure that's Gage calling to find out why you've been sitting on the side of the road in the middle of nowhere."

"How would he know that?"

"He had Conner put a tracker on your ride and your phone before they took you to the Oasis. Go on, answer it," he says, waving his hand toward my vibrating phone. "But I would be careful. Do you know what alias Logan's using with Gage?"

Logan knows Gage, but I have no idea what story he gave him. Logan did warn me to stay away from Gage. Just as he warned me to stay away from this asshole sitting across from me.

Aric leans forward, grabs my other cell, and places it in my hand. I see Superhero on the screen and feel like the biggest idiot right now. Everyone was right. I'm not cut out for this world.

Wordlessly, Aric tells me to put it on speaker.

"Hello?"

"Where you at?"

I keep my eyes on Aric. Hearing Gage's voice instantly warms me, but I simmer it right back down. I have no idea who the villain is anymore. "I'm heading home. Where are *you*?"

Gage is silent, either because Aric's telling the truth about the tracker or because he doesn't want to say where he's at. I'm well aware my tone isn't coming off the friendliest. Either way, I'm not budging first. Finally, he relents. "I wanted to make sure you made it home safe. Conner wasn't too impressed with your vehicle when he followed us last week."

His concern is strange, considering he hasn't fucking called me once over the past week since he dropped me off like old luggage and left me hot and bothered.

Gage clears his throat. "Harlow told me you left to head home, and I wanted to make sure you didn't break down or anything like that."

Arik's smirk says, "I told you so."

I hate him even more than I did a few minutes ago. "No, I'm fine. Better than fine, actually," I snap. I shouldn't be calling the kettle black. I have done nothing but lie to Gage since we met. But this is different. This is invading my privacy. He had no right.

"Did you stop and get gas or something? I thought Conner filled it up before he dropped it off."

Oh, ho, ho, he's trying hard to get me to tell him what I'm doing. I want nothing more than to light his ass up like Christmas morning, but I'm not giving him the upper hand. "No, I thought I hit an animal and pulled over to check it out, then you called. How do you know I'm parked and not driving?"

He ignores my question. "Are you all right?"

Like you care. "Yep. It's all good. I'm good, the little furball I thought I hit is good. We're all fucking good. Where are you at right now, Gage?" I spit his name from my lips. If he has Logan, I'm killing him myself.

Silence comes over the phone and I glance down to make sure I didn't hang up on him from gripping my phone so hard.

"I'm working."

His simple response has me grinding my teeth. I let out a laugh. "Right, working. Is that what we're calling torturing people now?"

"What's going on, *Allie?*"

The way he says my name with such venom behind it gives me pause. He can't possibly know that isn't my name, but if he does have Logan and has beaten the truth out of him, he might.

Aric is leaning back like he's on vacation and having the best day of his life. I release a defeated breath. If I want confirmation that Gage does in fact have Logan, I need to reel in my bitch act. It isn't easy. "I'm sorry. I'm freaked out right now over the possibility of hurting an animal."

"You want me to come get you?"

"No, I'm all right." I'm pretty sure the devil sitting across from me wouldn't appreciate that too much, but that doesn't mean I can't use Gage to get away from Aric. "But I shouldn't be long. We can meet at my place. I should be home in an hour."

There's no chance I'll get home that soon, but he doesn't need to know that.

Aric's jaw locks.

I grin, enjoying that I just pissed in his Cheerios. My smile doesn't last long.

"I can't," Gage says. "I'm... interrogating a threat that was a little too close to home. We do need to talk, though. Are you working tomorrow?"

The hairs on my arms rise. "What do you mean, too close to home?"

Gage clears his throat. "My IT guy hasn't been as honest with me as I thought. It's nothing for you to worry about. Are you working tomorrow?"

My heart drops out of my chest. Between the picture Aric just showed me and Gage saying his IT guy wasn't being honest with him, I'm certain Aric is telling the truth.

"No," I lie. "I'll be home all day. Just call me first before you head out."

"I will. Get some rest, little lion."

His nickname for me pulls at my heartstrings. I hang up without answering.

Aric wasn't lying.

"Please tell me where he is. Please," I beg. "I can't let anything happen to Logan." The panic in my voice is crystal clear.

Aric slides his phone into his pocket, grabs the one that's still locked in my hand, and tosses it to the front passenger seat. "You know the price."

"Are you kidding me right now? Logan might not have long to live, and you want to suck face?"

When Aric remains quiet, my anger rockets out of me. I lunge across the seat, ready to destroy his beautiful face. He easily grabs my wrists and pushes me backward. I land on my back hard, letting out an "Oof" as Aric settles himself on top of me.

Bringing his face close to mine, he gently blows the hair out of my face. "So violent nowadays."

"Only to jerks like you."

He smiles like this is the most fun he's had in a long time. Actually, I bet it is. "Ticktock, ticktock, wildflower. What's it going to be?"

I scream in frustration. "Eat shit, asshole. You and your pathetic father are nothing but scum, and I can't wait to push the dagger through his chest myself. I'm giving you three seconds to get off me before I make you regret it." My hands curl into fists, but they're currently squashed in between our bodies. I know he can feel it, though.

Aric only continues to smile with his emerald eyes glinting in appreciation of my words, which makes no sense at all. Why he would be happy that I just threatened not only his life but his father's as well?

"You're too adorable for your own good."

I thrust my hips high, trying to toss him forward, just as Gage taught me, but it doesn't work with the tight quarters we're in. Aric has pinned his body to mine, making it impossible to break my arms free from the weight of his body. All I succeeded in doing was bring his face closer to mine. His hot breath fans across my lips as he stares directly into my eyes.

This can all stop if I give him a fucking kiss. Logan has sacrificed so much for me, and I don't even know half of it. Just one kiss and he will help Logan. Problem is, I don't want to kiss his arrogant ass.

"All right, I'll kiss you. But I have conditions."

His eyes burn with victory. "State them."

"For one, not like this. I want us out of the Jimmy and standing. I'm not going to kiss you while you're lying on top of me."

He smirks. "Couldn't control yourself?"

I ignore his comment. "Did you do something to my Jimmy?" The only way my plan's going to work is if my Jimmy is running and I can get away from Aric as quickly as possible.

He smiles ruthlessly.

"I want you to fix it first and then we can kiss outside my Jimmy. But only once."

Aric licks his lips, amusement jumping in his eyes. "You want a fast getaway after."

I don't answer. We lie there across the back bench of my Jimmy, breathing in the same air. I keep my poker face intact and that isn't easy. His gaze is intense.

"Deal," he finally says. He leans up, releasing my hands. The relief I feel is short-lived. This is only step one of escaping him. He unlocks the back door and slides out. I slide my ass across the seat, and instead of following him out of the vehicle, I push myself between the front seats and plop down in the driver's seat.

He chuckles and slams the door shut, walking around the front of the vehicle. I expect him to open the hood to fix whatever he screwed with, but he keeps moving toward my door. My eyes remain trained on him as I slide my hand into my purse, locking my fingers around my favorite weapon. I unlock my door, trying to make him believe I'm not trying to pull a fast one, and hold it open with my leg.

He stops in front of me, glancing at my leg as his eyes slowly travel up my body.

I try to keep the shake from my voice. "You need to fix my Jimmy first."

He grins, but the smile is missing dimples. I mentally slap myself, realizing Gage is now enemy number one on my list and his stupid, sexy dimples don't mean shit.

Aric pulls his phone out and hits a couple of buttons. "Go ahead. It'll start."

I waste no time turning the key that's still in the ignition. It fires right up. "How the hell did you do that with your phone?" *I need that app.*

He smiles and shakes his head. "Now, time to pay the piper, Miss Keeyes."

I release a deep breath and nod in agreement. I stare deep into green eyes that are a burning inferno and slowly lick my lips as seductively as I can manage. His gaze drops to my mouth, exactly where I want it. I bite my lower lip, just as I did for Gage the day we sparred. His lips turn upward in triumph.

Jackpot.

I raise my hand, my finger already on the trigger, and spray him right in the eyes with my pepper spray. Then I kick him as hard as I can in the gut.

His hands cover his face as he is propelled backward, his phone flying from his hand.

I don't wait another second. I slam on the gas and propel forward. The driver's door slams into my knee and I gasp in pain. I check the rearview mirror, but it's so dark, I can't see Aric.

All I can hope is that his phone broke when it flew from his hand and he won't be able to use whatever is on his phone to stop me in my tracks again.

Chapter Nineteen

Kali.

I make it home in record time. It's the last place I want to be, but with a tracker on my vehicle, I don't have a choice. I don't have an inkling of what one might look like, where it might be hidden, or how to remove it. And I can't call Harlow or Fletcher either. My calls and texts could be monitored too.

I hobble into my house. My knee is killing me. I lock the door and set my house alarm. Keeping the lights off, I grab a Ziploc and fill it with ice. Then I grab a bottle of wine and drop onto the couch.

I can't wrap my mind around Aric not disabling my Jimmy again after what I pulled. His phone must have broken when it hit the pavement.

If what Aric said is true, what I don't get is why. Why would Gage track me? I'm not his enemy. He knows where I live and work. Hell, he even knows what gym I go to. It's not like I haven't lived by the same schedule for years.

Maybe he did it because of Sofia? He did warn me that I was on the Mafia's radar for my involvement with Sofia, but then again, Logan gave me his word that I was safe.

My thoughts turn to Logan. What went down between him and Gage? My stomach is sour over not knowing.

Sofia's words drift back to me: *Everyone knows someone Gage made disappear.* Chills skate across my skin. I pray to God I'm not going to become one of those people who knows someone.

By the time the sun starts to rise and the birds begin to sing, I have a solid plan and a couple of hours of sleep. My knee is bruised, but the ice helped reduce the swelling. I shower and put on jeans and a T-shirt. I don't plan on staying at work today, so there's no need to dress up.

Once I get to the office, I'll fill Fletcher in on my brother—a brother he has no clue I have. Then I'm going to convince him to help me track Logan and rescue him. Maybe I can get lucky and Gage will be at his place. Fletcher can be my backup muscle.

I call an Uber to pick me up since Gage believes I'm not working today. I can't take my phone or Jimmy. If he tracks my whereabouts, he'll know I deliberately lied to him. I'm taking control now.

The time the Uber takes to get to my house from the city feels like ages, but once I finally arrive, I take the elevator to the twenty-ninth floor. Relief flows through me at the light on in Fletcher's office.

Everything is going to be okay.

I don't have much time. I have no idea when Gage will show up at my place, but once he realizes I'm not there, he's coming here next. I don't bother stopping at my desk; I barrel straight toward Fletcher's office.

I fling Fletcher's door open, but he is nowhere to be found. *Oh my God, what if Gage already got to Fletcher?* Nothing appears to be out of place, though.

I'm about to leave when the bathroom door opens and he steps out.

He glances at my casual attire. "Are we having casual Mondays now?" But his attention is swiftly taken off me to a beeping noise from one of his computers.

"Fletcher, I don't have a lot of time. I need your help." I follow him over to his computer on his desk. He starts typing quickly, glancing at the screen. "I know you don't know this, but I have a brother and—"

"Allie, shut my office door. Now," he commands, never taking his eyes off the monitor.

I prop my hands on my hips. "Are you even listening to me? I need your help."

Fletcher stops typing and slams his fist onto the desk, causing me to jump. "Dammit, Allie, do what I say and shut my damn door now!"

Fletcher has never yelled at me before. Stress is written all over his face. I sigh, walk over to his office door, and close it. As soon as it shuts, a loud clunk sounds off.

He just activated the vault locks to his office. *Oh. My. God.*

Someone is here and he doesn't want them coming in. Gage? I rush to his desk. My poor little heart is going to be the death of me. I don't know how much more it can handle.

"We've got company," he states, his fingers gliding across the keyboard at a rapid speed.

I walk around his desk to see a group of men, all dressed in black from head to toe. There's no way to know who these men are. Two of them are carrying large black bags. They look heavy, and when one guy drops his bag to the floor and unzips it, I learn why. The bag is loaded with guns. Big guns. The type of guns my dad always loved. The man pulls them out, tossing them to the others like he's passing out candy.

"They don't have a chance getting in here. None of those guns will open this door."

"But that will," Fletcher says.

Another guy is unloading a second bag filled with something I've never seen before. "What is it?"

"A badass safecracker on steroids." When I don't say anything, he adds, "Jam shots, used to blow doors off safes. They use nitroglycerin as the explosive."

I have no idea what any of that means, but I do know one thing. "We have to go, Fletcher. Like, yesterday." I grab his hand and tug him toward the hidden safe room behind the double-sided mirror. I place my hand on the concealed reader and hold my breath. My hand is sweating, and I pray it can be read. Finally, it lights up green underneath my hand. A moment later, the mirror clicks, opening the entryway.

"Go. I'll catch up. Take the rusty hoopty and head straight to the Oasis."

I whip around. Fletcher is back at his computer, typing away. "What are you doing? We need to go *now*."

He shakes his head before his rushed response comes out. "I have to destroy my files. I've worked too hard to let someone steal them."

"Files won't matter if you're dead!" I scream, running over to him. I can understand the fear of losing everything you've worked so hard for, but a bomb coming at you—

And it does, sooner than either of us anticipates.

It rocks the entire building, throwing my body against the back wall. I collapse hard onto the marble floor. I moan in pain, forcing myself to my hands and knees. The wind is knocked out of me, making my first few breaths hard to take in. Debris is scattered everywhere, and smoke hangs heavy throughout his office.

I crawl over to Fletcher. His face is covered in blood, his leg is twisted in a painful position partly underneath his heavy desk, and his eyes are hazy. A sob rips from my chest at the sight of him.

"Fletch, oh my God. Fletch," I cry. I try pulling his desk off his lower half, but it's too heavy.

Gunfire erupts.

I collapse atop his upper body to shield him from the war happening around us.

"Allie."

I quickly lift my head and look at his dull green eyes.

"You need to go," he rasps.

I shake my head violently. "I'm not leaving without you."

"Allie, it's too late. Get to the Oasis and tell Harlow everything. She'll protect you."

Another sob breaks from my lips. I can't wrap my mind around never seeing Fletcher again. His large desk lies on his bottom half, with his mangled leg hanging partially out. Gunfire breaks out again.

Fletcher's voice commanding me to go has me kissing his bloodstained cheek and sprinting to the safe room. I rush through the entryway and shut the door quickly. My hands are shaking so badly, it takes me three attempts to find and push the button on the false staircase that leads to nothing, revealing the hidden steps under it.

The crunching of glass gets my attention. I watch a large figure enter the office through the thick smoke. A huge gun hanging from his bloody hand, he fully emerges from the smoke and his beautiful face comes into view.

I gasp, slapping my hand over my mouth as Gage slowly walks into the office, taking everything in. He's dressed in all black, with his signature hat on backward. His icy-blue eyes find Fletch lying helplessly on the floor. I'm not even sure Fletcher knows what's going on.

Gage scans the room again as Conner appears through the smoke.

"Check the bathroom," he orders.

After a moment, Conner calls out, "Clear."

Gage kneels to Fletcher, checking for a pulse. I hold my breath, hoping he's still alive, but Gage gives no indication in his facial expression.

"She's here. He's hidden her. Find her now. Check the remaining part of this floor and the garage."

Conner nods and leaves the room.

Gage stands to his full height and scans the room once again. His eyes land on me, though I know he's only looking at himself. The double-sided mirror between us is my only safeguard.

The Gage standing before me isn't the Gage who dropped me off at the Oasis a week ago. His artic eyes hold a ravaging blizzard, causing my weak knees to knock together. With the look of pure fury coming from Gage, my body shakes at the thought of what Logan has gone through over the past week.

He slowly walks toward me, and I swallow hard. He's looking right at me as if he really is a superhero and can see through anything.

His gaze slowly lowers. I follow to see the smudgy handprint I left when I unlocked the doorway. He places his hand on top of my handprint, but nothing happens. Fletcher, Harlow, and I are the only ones it'll recognize. It makes no alerts that you don't have access. It simply stands quietly as if it's only a mirror.

But Gage knows better. His head snaps up and his fist connects against the mirror, colliding with it hard. I fall back, the sudden hit scaring me.

I can't tell if he heard my fall, because he stops for a moment. Then his fist slams into it again and again. Blood appears between the mirror and his large fist. He stops abruptly and stalks off, grabs the broken leg of an office chair, and returns with it raised high.

I scurry toward the hidden staircase and fly down the steps, missing several. Thankfully, my grip on the handrail prevents me from tumbling forward. My legs feel as if they're made of wet noodles. My vision is blurred from the tears running down my face.

I reach the bottom step and sprint to the elevator. I barely clock the sound of the ceiling closing above me when I pass the fifth step. I hit the button several times before the door slides open in no hurry. There's only one button inside the elevator; it leads to the underground parking garage, where the rusty hoopty awaits.

I lean my head against the wall, trying to catch my breath as I descend. Elevator music plays softly in the background, and a frenzied laugh bubbles out of my body and then transforms into sobs. Only Fletcher would have stupid elevator music in his escape route. My last image of Fletcher flashes before me and my chest aches. Telling Harlow what happened is going to rip her heart out.

The doors chime cheerfully as they slide open, and I stumble out on shaky limbs. I scan the area. I'm almost certain there's no way Gage has beaten me here, but Conner could be a problem—he left the office shortly after walking in.

I stay along the edge of the dark parking garage and turn the corner. The rusty old car waits like a pot of gold at the end of this messed-up rainbow. I break into a sprint. My body screams in pain from the blast it took, but my adrenaline is pumping too strongly to slow me, and if I don't hurry, I might go into shock.

I run right past the driver's door to the wall it's parked in front of and kick it as hard as I can. The fake concrete easily breaks away, revealing a small box. I grab the keys, just now realizing my hands are covered in Fletcher's blood, and rush to the car door.

With slick fingers, I drop the keys while trying to slide them into the lock. I scramble to grab them just as an arm wraps around my waist and another one covers my mouth.

I kick my legs and swing my arms, screaming as loud as I can, but my voice is muffled by the hand securely in place against my lips.

Conner found me.

Tears stream down my face as I'm hauled farther away from my rusty pot of gold. I'm still frantically swinging every limb I can, but I'm no match against this man. By the time he gets us around the corner, a large black SUV comes into sight.

If I get in that vehicle, I'm as good as dead. Despite my fight, I'm no match. I throw my legs out, my feet hitting the door so he can't open it. He turns us quickly, dropping his hand from my mouth to open the back door.

I let out a bloodcurdling scream before he tosses me in the back seat. I land on my stomach and lunge toward the other door. I grab the handle and push, but nothing happens. The vehicle shifts as he climbs in behind me, and Conner easily flips my body over.

Only it's not Conner.

I'm met with very pissed-off emerald eyes. I start hitting Aric as hard as I can, bucking my hips. It does no good. He subdues me quickly, pinning me to the cool leather seat. His hand disappears into his suit jacket and comes out with a syringe. He lifts it to his mouth. His teeth pull off the cap.

"Oh God no. Please, Aric. Please don't give me whatever's in that. Please don't." I'm terrified now and my chest feels as if it's going to cave in on itself.

My pleas go unheard as he lies on top of me to restrict my movements. The needle pricks the side of my neck and I know I just lost. I feel the liquid flowing into me, and a moment later, my body warms. He watches me closely as my arms and legs begin to relax on their own, despite my internal battle.

Tears leak from my eyes as he leans up, places the cap back on the syringe, and tucks it in his pocket. He reaches behind the seats, probably for a gun to end my life.

Instead, it's a light blanket that he tosses over my body. It's soft, and the urge to snuggle into it is strong, but I can't move from whatever he injected me with.

"My beautiful Kali, you're safe now."

I don't believe the words coming out of his mouth, but the fight has left my body. As the drug takes full effect, my body slowly succumbs to the overwhelming drowsiness, and a crushing sense of defeat settles deep into my heart.

Chapter Twenty

Kali.

My eyes are leaden. Eventually I manage to peel them open. It takes a moment before things come into focus. I'm in an unfamiliar room. The room is elegant, filled with gray, black, and silver tones. It's large from what I can tell, and the bed I'm lying on is as soft as a cloud.

And it smells like leather and spice.

My stomach drops as memories rush in. Fletcher lying in his own blood, bidding me to run. Gage—the man I thought I could trust, my superhero—walking in with no emotional reaction to the state of the office or Fletcher's well-being. And then Aric in his vehicle, his evil eyes glaring at me, clearly enraged about our last encounter.

I attempt to drag my hand under the blanket and across my body to check whether I'm correct in thinking my clothes are missing, but I can't do it. Above me, a leather strap connected to the headboard is looped around one wrist.

With a surge of panic, I roll to my side and sit up, clutching the blanket tightly around me with my free hand. A large window behind the headboard reveals the sprawl of an unfamiliar city skyline. My stomach knots with unease. *Why the hell did he bring me here? And where the hell is here?* I tug at the strap but it only tightens, digging into my skin deeply.

"You're going to hurt yourself doing that."

I freeze. I didn't realize I wasn't alone.

Aric rises from a large wingback chair in the corner and makes his way over to me. He's not in his three-piece suit. A couple of buttons are undone on his white shirt and the sleeves are rolled up, showing off his tattoos.

I press my back against the warm wooden headboard and keep the blanket snug against my naked body. "Why are you restraining me?"

His eyes flash with enjoyment as he stands along the edge of the bed. "For my safety."

I narrow my eyes while he returns my glare with a smile. Asshole.

"I didn't mean to hurt you out on that road." *I totally did.* "I was only trying to scare you." *And hopefully blind you.* "I felt horrible afterward." *Didn't lose a wink of sleep.* "I'm so sorry, Aric." *I'm not.* "How are your eyes?" *I couldn't care less.*

Aric's smile never leaves while I spit bullshit at him. "You've never been a convincing liar, wildflower. But you're cute when you do it."

"Don't call me that."

Aric cocks his head to the side. "I don't believe you're in any position to tell me what to do."

I huff, because I know he's right and he knows he's right and, well... that just isn't right. "Why am I naked?"

His smile returns. "Because you were covered in blood and dirt. We needed to ascertain the extent of your injuries."

I frown. "We?"

"Me and the doctor. Beyond some bruising and dehydration, you're in good shape. He came back again early this morning to give you fluids to help hydrate you and injected a mild pain reliever."

Shit. I've lost a day. "Where the hell are we?"

Aric sits on the edge of the bed near the footboard. "Right outside Chicago."

I take in everything he's told me. It's true that my body doesn't feel as bad as it should. Between my knee from Aric's roadside sabotage, the bomb exploding, and Aric tossing me into the back of the SUV like a sack of potatoes, I feel good, considering.

Good enough to kick his ass the second I convince him to take this strap off me. My stomach sours with the knowledge that he's wasted a day I could have used trying to find Logan. The thought has anger vibrating through my bones.

I glare, hoping to shoot lasers straight through his thick skull. "I have to pee." It's the only obvious reason to get untied promptly.

Aric peers at me, his expression tense. I want to look away but don't allow myself to. Showing any kind of weakness is never a good idea.

"What's between you and Gage?"

His question feels like a curveball. He made fun of me for having hearts in my eyes the day I kissed him on the dock all those years ago, so why does he give a shit about me and Gage? I need to understand why he cares and what his *real* endgame is. I pretend to adjust myself, that the strap around my wrist is bothering me. It's not. I need to give myself time to run through my choices.

I can lie and tell him that Gage and I are a couple. Gage is powerful and maybe that will discourage Aric from whatever plans he has. From what I know of Gage, he's widely feared. I can only hope Aric fears him as well.

Or I can tell him the truth. That I have no idea what's going on with me and Gage. That there might be a good chance he now knows who Logan and I really are. And if Gage has hurt my brother in any way, then Aric can step aside, because I will kill Gage myself.

Neither option stands out as the best choice. I need to get a better feeling of Aric to decide which route will work the best. "That's none of your business."

Aric shakes his head. I'm coming close to telling him to shove it where the sun doesn't shine. I take a deep breath, trying to calm my soul deep within myself.

"Answer the question and I'll let you up to use the bathroom."

I move my legs, so I'm now sitting on the edge of the bed. "I could just pee all over your bed."

He nods as if he isn't concerned in the least. "You could, and I could make you lie in it for the next twenty-four hours. Do you want to do this the hard way or the easy way?"

If looks could kill, he would already be dead, but unfortunately, I don't have that superpower. He's not budging. "Are you genuinely going to help Logan?"

Aric's piercing look tells me I am out of time.

Honesty might be my best play. If I'm going to go up against Gage, I'm going to need a strong ally by my side. "Okay, okay. Look, I don't know what the hell is going on between me and Gage. He ghosted me after he dropped me off at the Oasis. I haven't talked to him since you decided to fucking attack me on the side of the road."

He raises an eyebrow. "I'm assuming you saw him yesterday morning but didn't run to him for help. All while your world was literally blowing up around you. Why is that, Kali?"

He's not wrong. Gage's icy glare through the mirror was enough to keep me heading the opposite way.

"He hurt Fletcher and then told Conner to find me. I didn't know what was going on, and Fletcher t-told me to-to go." A sob rips out of me as I think about my last moments with Fletcher. I pray to God that he's okay. All the blood he was hemorrhaging tells me otherwise. I drop my head as tears cascade down my warm cheeks. This is all my fault. I should've dragged Fletcher into that safe room with me, but I couldn't move his heavy desk off him. I should have found a way.

But then Aric was waiting below. What would he have done to him? Fletch isn't a small guy and can certainly hold his own, but he was gravely injured.

Aric's large hand caresses my back—over the blanket—in a gentle gesture. I have no idea how this man's mind works, but the comfort is weirdly reassuring. The waterworks continue to flow. I can't seem to stop.

It doesn't take long for Aric to let a defeated breath out. "Do you want to save Logan?"

I peek up at him, my vision blurred from my water-welled eyes. I never considered the damsel-in-distress tactic with him, but damn if it didn't work like a charm. Too bad it's not an act on my part. "More than anything," I whisper.

He nods and stands, producing a key from his pocket. He unlocks the strap behind me. I should be ready to kick his ass now that I'm free, but I can't. My wrist drops to the bed. I don't feel any fight left inside me. All I feel is drained.

Aric bends over and picks me up bridal-style. He carries me into the bathroom with the blanket still snug against my body. His bathroom—I guess it's his, anyway—is probably half the size of my entire home and is fitted with gray-and-white marble.

He gently sets me down, and once he's convinced that I can stand on my own, he walks over to the large tub and starts the water. His house may not be warm, but this marble is. Are heated floors even a thing?

"My father knows you're alive."

My head jerks up, meeting his gaze. "You told him?"

He shakes his head, taking a step closer, but remaining a few feet away from me. "Someone showed him a picture of us together the night of the expo. I haven't seen it, but I know we were on the balcony."

I swallow down the lump lodged in my throat. By his grim face, Aric isn't happy that Victor knows I'm alive.

"You have nothing to worry about. I have everything under control." He runs a hand through his dark hair. "Everything you need is on this shelf. Towels are in the cabinet." He points then faces me, assessing my well-being. "Take your time. Get yourself cleaned up and your mind in the game. If we are going to get Logan back, I need you sharp. You have a lot to offer, wildflower, and I need you just as much as you need me right now. Can you do that?"

What does he mean he needs me? I would think I need him more to take on Gage, but he seems to feel differently. I give a slight nod, followed by a sniffle. Aric walks over to me and places both of his hands on my cheeks.

"Good girl," he says, leaning in and kissing my forehead.

I could kick him in the nuts right now, but I would only end up on my ass with this blanket tangled around me. Not to mention I would end up back in bed with the leather strap secured, and I really do need to pee. The water flowing in the tub is pure torture right now.

And what other option do I have? This is where the deck of cards landed, and I need to play the hand I've been dealt. Logan may not be too thrilled with me coming to his rescue with Aric Hemmington in tow, but what else is there?

I decide to take Aric's advice to the fullest. After the most blissful pee I have ever had in my life, I sink into the deep tub and cry my eyes out of tears. Then I pick myself back up.

No one messes with a Keeyes and gets away with it.

After a late lunch, Aric drives us through the bustling downtown area of what turns out to be Evanston. I feel completely lost again. When I got out of the bathtub, I found a beautiful yellow sundress laid out on the bed. It's simple but classy. The material is soft against my skin, and it should be. The price tag on the dress states it was over two thousand dollars. It fits me like a glove. A pair of white strappy sandals with a large flower at the toes fit perfectly. I hope he realizes he's not getting this outfit back.

Once I was ready to face whatever plan he had in store to get Logan back, he blew it out of the water by telling me that we're heading to his father's house here in Chicago first. Because of course he has an ulterior motive. After all, why else would he have dragged me across the country? Gage has Logan. Not Victor, but Gage. My mind spins but I can't figure out why we're going to see his evil father. Victor may know I'm alive, but if Aric has everything under control, why do we have to go there? It can't be anything good.

But I would be stupid to miss this rare invitation. Victor was there the day my parents died. That means Victor knows what happened that night, and I need answers—and preferably a gun, a weapon I have recently considered wanting. Even though Aric gracefully turned down my request for one, he still doesn't know I have had a lot of training in my Krav Maga classes. I might be small, but I can cause a lot of damage in a short time frame.

The road gently curves right as the first view of Lake Michigan's expansive blue waters comes into sight. Aric turns on Lake Shore Boulevard. The homes are all extravagant. After a short moment, the gates leading to what must be Victor's home open.

The driveway is long and lined with beautiful midsize crape myrtle trees, the kind that's so pink it hurts your eyes. They have clusters of bright pink blooms and purple-green foliage. How can someone so evil live here? "How's this getting Logan back?" I ask again.

Aric smiles at me. "My dad knows you're alive now. If I don't bring you to him, he will come for you, and I can promise that wouldn't go over well for either of us."

"But what does this have to do with rescuing Logan?"

Aric is reclined in his black leather seat like he's about to go to his movie premiere. He's dressed in a three-piece suit with a piece of fabric tucked into his outbreast pocket that perfectly matches my dress.

We've only been in the vehicle for five or so minutes before he pulls the vehicle to the mansion's front entrance—wait, *castle* might be a better description of his father's home—and puts the vehicle into park.

He faces me again. "My father is the biggest threat to you right now. We need to eliminate his threat so we can focus on getting you to Logan."

I rear back at the casualness of what he just implied. "If you're suggesting we kill your father, you should've let me bring a gun."

His laugh booms around me in the SUV. "I'm sorry to disappoint you, wildflower, but we'll not be killing my father today. Besides, no one can enter this fortress with a weapon. Me included."

"So how are we going to eliminate the threat?"

"You're going to act like you're in love with me."

Now it's my turn to laugh at the absurdity. "I doubt a man as evil as your father will let love change his mind."

"Not when it's me who you're in love with. You're the only heir left to the Keeyes fortune, and that means you come with a lot of money and power. If you're head over heels for me, he'll want us to marry to strengthen his empire."

"But I'm not the only Keeyes left."

"He doesn't know Logan survived, and I haven't told him any differently. Let's take a walk and I will fill you in."

"But won't your father think it's strange that we show up and not go see him right away?"

Aric's smile grows. "We're early, but believe me. He'll be watching us on the cameras. There isn't any audio, but he'll be able to watch our every *affectionate* move."

Before I have a chance to respond, Aric is out of the SUV and heading to my door. He places his hand inside and I hesitantly take it and step out. He doesn't let go.

We walk around the side of the house and pass a pool that looks like it came straight out of a resort in Mexico.

He bends his head toward me with practiced intimacy. "Did you know that Gage and his father were there the night your parents died?"

His words stop me in my tracks. I stare at him, trying to get a read on whether what he said is true. "That's a lie. I never saw Gage doing business with my family. He never came to the estate."

"Are you sure about that? As I recall, you were never involved in the family business."

I look at the thick green grass and can't help but accept the truth in his words. I never wanted to be. While Logan may have lived for those days, I dreaded them. Who wants to sit around and talk about guns and ammo all day long?

Okay, besides Harlow.

"Do you know who killed my parents?" I ask quietly.

He shakes his head. "If I did, I would have rendered justice for you in a heartbeat. Not going there that night has been the biggest regret of my life." He tugs on my hand to continue down the path.

Does Gage realize who I am? Is that why he overtook my life? Has he been playing me this entire time and laughing behind my back at how naïve I've been? Is that why he has my brother?

It makes me sick to think Gage might have something to do with my parents' deaths. I remind myself that this is Aric I'm talking to. Aric, who—Logan insisted in no uncertain terms after I admitted to the kiss seven years ago—can masterfully manipulate people, myself included, to believe anything he wants.

"What were you doing the night my parents died that kept you from coming?"

"I was saving a lost soul."

"What does that mean?"

Aric is silent for a moment as we walk hand in hand. "Sometimes people unknowingly walk into a lion's den."

"So, what? Now you're claiming you're a saint? A knight who charges to the rescue?"

He shakes his head. "I'm no knight, Kali. My soul has been tainted with too much evil to be pure like yours."

"A pure soul is nothing more than a weak person." My honesty surprises me.

"And that's where you're wrong, wildflower. Your pure soul holds more power than anything in this world. Nothing can touch your innocence in this dark world."

I don't know how to respond, so I choose not to say anything. We cut across the side of the property, the gardens coming into view. I gasp and pull Aric's hand, tugging him quicker toward all the beautiful flowers in front of us. Back in the day, I would have painted this garden a thousand times over.

Aric laughs at my excitement, letting my hand go as I run over to the first batch of purple daylilies and lean in to take the delicate aroma they give off.

"You're performing well, wildflower." Aric reaches me and takes my hand again.

"Acting? No, this isn't acting. This is one of the most beautiful gardens I've seen in a long time. How many people does it take to manage this?" The size is stunning; it would take an army to keep up everything here.

"Twenty total. They work throughout the property."

"Wow. This is amazing," I say.

He pulls me to his chest and gazes at me lustfully. "Not as amazing as you."

"You said there's no audio out here, so you can stop with the bullshit lines," I reply, keeping my smile intact.

"Good point." He leans his head toward mine, and I know what is coming next, but I wasn't prepared. Out of instinct, I lean away from him. He must anticipate that, because he quickly turns me, bending my body before his lips crush against mine.

I don't kiss him back until I realize we need to do this because his father's watching. His tongue nudges my lips until they crack open, and I let him in. His kiss is nothing like I remember from all those years ago... and doesn't hold a candle to Gage's. I wrap my arms around his neck and pull him closer. If getting Victor to believe this act is what it takes to save Logan, so be it. I already messed up once by not kissing Aric. I won't be doing that again.

I picture Gage and how ravishing his kisses were, as if he couldn't go one more second without my lips fused to his. I miss his minty flavor. I miss Gage, and I hate that I do. What kind of person does that make me, knowing what I know now?

Aric pulls his face away from mine, our bodies still bent together like a perfect statue in the middle of a perfect garden. "You taste even better than I remember." I audibly gulp at his confession as he raises us both up to stand. "I told you I'd get you to kiss me again."

His words and smug demeanor piss me off. "Joke's on you. I was imagining Gage." The words leave my mouth before I realized I was going to say them.

His eyes pierce mine. "If only I had known all I needed to do was to hunt your brother down and torture him to get you to like me, I would've beaten Gage to it a long time ago."

I push away and walk farther into the garden. My reality is nothing like a fairy tale. The one man who catches my heart is the villain in my story. I thought I knew who Gage was, but I don't know what to think anymore. If Gage was in fact there during the worst night of my life, that changes everything.

Aric's hand grabs mine. "I'm sorry, joking about torturing your brother was wrong. Please forgive me." He lifts our joined hands and lightly kisses my birthmark.

I nod, impatient with his mind games. We need to get in and out as fast as possible so we can get Victor off my back and focus on getting Logan. "Let's just get this over with."

Aric nods and pulls me toward a cluster of orange tiger lilies. He drops my hand and plucks one. He tucks my hair behind my ear and slides it in, careful not to allow the dark pollen to fall on my dress and stain it. The moment is small but intimate.

He tugs me close to his body, bringing his lips to my ear. "Don't leave my side once we are in the house."

I nod against his face. We head toward the castle of doom. Only now do I notice several armed guards stationed throughout the property. My heart rate kicks up and my nerves dance through my body. I take a deep breath and slowly release it.

He must sense my tension, because he squeezes my hand for reassurance.

This is the biggest show of my life. It's time for Victor to face me. It's time to demand answers about what happened that horrible night.

Victor Hemmington won't know what hit him.

Chapter Twenty-One

Kali.

It's remarkable how one second you can be filled with confidence and the next second you're shaking in your boots. Victor Hemmington is not someone you mess with. Just being in his presence for a few seconds tells me that. The hard creases in his face and his dominant stance show he has no mercy. Taking a deep breath, I remind myself that no one messes with a Keeyes and gets away with it. I stand tall and lock my shoulders.

I grip Aric's hand tighter as we come face-to-face with his father. I peek over at Aric, trying to get a read on how he's feeling, but to my surprise, he looks as cool as a cucumber in the hot summer sun. In fact, he looks bored. Like he has played this game so many times, it's no longer scary to be around this evil man every day.

My heart tightens at the thought of what Aric must have gone through growing up with a father like Victor. Aric is a manipulating asshole, but when you see past the layers, he's nothing like his father. He still has goodness deep inside him. At least I'm hoping I'm reading that right.

"I cannot believe it. Miss Keeyes, back from the dead." Victor approaches us and lifts my free hand to kiss it.

His veiled reference to whatever role he played in bringing me *back from the dead* is disturbing. This is a man who cares about only himself.

"No thanks to you," I hiss. *Damn, I've allowed him to get the better of me within a matter of seconds.*

Aric squeezes my hand, I'm sure to try to calm me down. That only makes me madder.

Victor's eyes light up with amusement. "Son, your stunning kitten has claws. I like it."

I speak up before I lose my courage. "Did you kill my family?"

Victor's hard stare bores into my soul. I won't let this man intimidate me. He could be the very reason my life crumbled underneath me. He's still pinning me with his gaze when he says to his son, "You should have muzzled her before you arrived."

My jaw drops, but Aric shrugs it off like it isn't a big deal. "My wife-to-be has the right to know. The only way for us to have a successful marriage is if she understands what took place."

A successful marriage? What the hell is Aric talking about? I thought we were playing like a young couple falling in love with each other. Not a damn marriage on the horizon.

We all stand there quietly for what feels like days as Victor and Aric stare at one another. This would be the perfect moment for a tornado to drop on us and whisk me away to the Land of Oz.

Eventually, Victor nods. "As usual, your insight behooves you."

Victor turns his attention to me. "I'm sorry about the loss of your parents and brother. I promise I had nothing to do with it. I enjoyed the company of James and Marion. Come, I will tell you what I know."

His sudden graciousness surprises me. Could I have come to his front gate and asked him what happened and he would have just told me? It can't be that easy.

He walks over to the sitting area and waves for us to join him. Aric gives my arm a pull to uproot me as if I am a stubborn weed. Dazed, I follow. Victor's home is as impressive on the inside as it is on the outside, only it mimics Aric's place. Not by looks, but by feeling. The walls are a deep red, probably to remind visitors that his house was built with blood money. I'm sure if I were to see this home for sale, the pictures would capture me. But it's lacking the most important detail a home needs. *Love.* This home is much like Aric's. Cold and lonely.

When I sit on the light tan leather couch next to Aric, my entire body sinks into it. This couch may be nicer than my bed.

Aric's hot hand lands on my bare thigh as he settles in next to me. A moment later, a young lady comes in with a tray of ice water. Her eyes are trained down, both not acknowledging our presence and coming to serve us at the same time.

The water is filled with cucumbers and mint leaves, which tugs at my heart, reminding me of Gage's minty spring scent.

She pours sparkling water into each glass and passes them to us. I thank her because that's what people should do. She stiffens with shock as if I just told her I like to skin kittens and make slippers out of them. She doesn't respond and heads over to pour Victor a glass of water as well. She produces a rocks glass with three fingers' worth of dark liquor and hands it to Victor.

Victor's smile is filled with devilry while the young girl leaves the room as quickly as she entered. He swirls his drink a few times before lifting it to his thin lips and taking a sip. At last he meets my watchful gaze. "You remind me of your mother Marion. She was stunning and could handle any firearm you gave her. Your mother had everyone's attention the second she walked into a room."

Victor speaks of my late mother with nothing but warmth. He liked my mother, causing me to question—why would you kill someone you liked?

"Well, everything except your whiskey-colored eyes. Those are your father's."

The fact that he can remember even the smallest details about my parents has my body on pins and needles. I don't have anything to say in response, so I grab my glass with trembling hands and take a drink of the minty water. Gage's smiling face flashes in my mind.

I'm sitting in a room with possibly my parents' killer, while his son's hand rests on my thigh as if it belongs there. And I can't seem to get Gage, a man who has kidnapped my brother, out of my mind for even a second.

This cannot get more messed up than it already is.

"I could always see why my son was so enamored with you. If only you two could have married sooner, as we all planned. But oh well. Now is better than any time." He plants a smug smile on his face.

Confusion hits. *As we all planned? Who the hell is "we"?* I expect Aric to add to what his father just said, but his bored look is in full motion, watching his finger lazily drawing circles on my thigh.

I clear my throat and find my voice. "What do you mean, *we all planned?*"

Victor's laugh comes off as condescending. "Your parents never told you?"

I shake my head, at a loss.

"We were planning an arranged marriage between you and Aric to combine our families' wealth and power and to expand our territories across half the country."

That can't be possible. There's no way in hell my parents would agree to anything so absurd. Who has arranged marriages nowadays, anyways? "You're lying."

Victor's jawline hardens. "I assure you I'm not. I went there that night to bring you back with me. You were going to stay here for a couple of weeks to get better acquainted with my son. Your father and I were preparing to celebrate the union of our families. Aric told me how smitten you were with him back then. Am I wrong in saying that?"

I gulp. I expect Aric to be wearing the same bored expression, but I'm proven wrong. His deep emerald eyes meet mine, and I can tell he wants to hear what I have to say.

I nod.

Victor reclines in his chair, satisfied with my nonverbal response.

"If everyone was happy about the decision, what happened that night?" I ask. None of this makes sense. If my parents and Victor were celebrating an upcoming wedding, how did my parents end up dead and our home in ashes?

"Frank McCollin happened."

McCollin? As in Gage McCollin? Victor's emerald eyes are set on mine, and as if he can read my thoughts, he says, "Yes, Gage McCollin's father. He and Gage showed up that night right before the celebration was to start."

"What were they there for?"

Victor adjusts his cufflinks. "To take what wasn't theirs."

Gage is loaded, and his father supposedly had an empire. "What would they want that they couldn't have? Guns?"

Instead of Victor answering, Aric does. "You."

My head feels like it is about to explode. I collapse into the couch. If that's the case, then there's no mistake Gage knows—has always known—who I really am. He stormed into my life, taking over every part of it. He played me like a fiddle, and I walked right into his web of lies. I stare at my glass of minty water and wish it were filled with whatever Victor's drinking.

"But now everything is how it was meant to be. Your parents can rest peacefully, knowing you are where they wanted you to be."

I don't respond. Gage chose to lie, and now I learn he was planning on kidnapping me. He's even more dangerous than I imagined. I need to get to Logan fast. I can only hope I'm not too late.

"Now, tell me, Miss Keeyes. How did you and my son reconcile? It must have been frightening to see him after so many years in hiding."

Aric replies, keeping his voice bored and neutral. "I've told you. We saw each other at the expo and spent the next week together. What does it even matter? She loves me and we will be wed by the end of the month."

"I want to hear it from her," Victor replies, his villainous eyes boring into Aric. Aric may have underestimated his father—he's sharper than he thinks. Victor turns to me. "Enlighten an old man."

After all these dropped bombs, I feel off my game. I can tell a story at the drop of a hat, but I can only hope that Aric stayed general with his story so I don't unintentionally mess everything up. Attempting to calm my nerves, I take another drink. I hate minty water now, but my throat feels as dry as a cactus under the hot sun.

I have no idea what Aric has already told him, so I need to tread carefully. If Victor is aware that this is a ruse, it might delay getting to Logan, and I can't have that. Damn Aric for not telling me this before now. He could have easily said, "Here's the story. Stick with it." But he didn't. He pushed me into a lake of piranhas that missed their last meal.

Victor presses, "You *did* reconcile with my son, right?"

The question is understandable. Sure, I can make anything up, but if it doesn't match with Aric's story... All I manage to utter is "Huh?"

Victor readjusts himself in his chair before and leans forward, placing his elbows on his knees to bring himself closer to me. "Are you here of your own free will? Do you love my son as he proclaims you do?"

I can feel my heartbeat in my stomach. Is that even possible? "Yes," I whisper.

Victor's eyes hold mine. I feel like if I look away for just one second, he will know I'm bullshitting him. I don't want to know what happens after that. He motions for me to talk. The pressure is almost too much for me to handle.

Okay, Kali, think! Someone on Victor's payroll snapped pictures of you and Aric on the balcony at the expo. Anyone with eyes could tell it wasn't a heartfelt reunion, and I'm sure they watched Aric jump from the balcony to escape Gage.

"You have me at a loss here, Miss Keeyes. This shouldn't be a hard question to answer. I'm starting to wonder how honest you and my son are being right now. And let me warn you, I don't handle being lied to very well."

Well. Shit. Let's roll back the curtains and let my story be heard.

I clear my throat and unlock my shoulders. I lean against Aric and look into his emerald eyes as if he's my long-lost soulmate. As if he was taken away from me by a sea of darkness, only to return to my light and make everything as it once was.

He returns my smile with his own.

Asshole.

"We first saw each other at the expo. He caught my eye, and even though I didn't recognize him right away, something inside felt like a magnetic pull." I turn back to Victor, my eyes going large. "Have you ever felt something so strong, you would swear that you were being pulled in by a force unknown to humankind, one that you had no choice but to submit to?"

Victor smiles at my analogy. "So you ran into his arms, and it was love rekindled at first sight?"

"No, I ran the other way as fast as I could."

Victor's eyebrows come together and slant inward. He clearly wasn't expecting that.

My smile grows larger. "After all, I can't make it easy for him. No woman with class would chase after a silly boy. I wanted a man and I needed to know if Aric was the man for me. So, I took off to see if he would chase."

I let out a sigh and try to put the biggest hearts into my eyes. "He found me in no time. I was scarfing down sushi and sipping fine champagne. The only problem? I didn't expect how famished I was. I went to town on them. Of course, Aric found me with a mouth full of fish eggs, and instead of running the other way, he handed me a napkin to clean my face."

I glance at Aric and smile brightly at him. He shakes his head, his eyes jumping with amusement. "And that's how he gave me the pet name Red Balls. You know, because he found me with a mouth full of red fish balls. Well, I guess technically they were orange, and they weren't balls—they were eggs—but you catch the drift." I chuckle as if it is the cutest nickname in the world.

Victor has a disgusted look on his face, which brings me immense gratification.

"After he cleaned me up—which, let me tell you, was a job and a half—he took me somewhere much more private. I knew he wanted to kiss me, but for some reason, he wouldn't." I let out a defeated breath. "I couldn't understand why at first, and then it finally dawned on me." I lean toward Victor. "I'm sure my breath wasn't the freshest."

I cock my eyebrow like I'm saying, *You know what I mean, right?* I don't give him a chance to respond. I lean against Aric and continue. "I'm not sure if you've ever eaten an entire tray of *tobiko* in under three minutes, but it doesn't feel too good on your stomach. I literally felt like all those fish eggs decided to hatch inside my tummy and cause havoc for eating them. Which, hey, if I were them, I would have done the same thing if someone ate me."

My hands are trembling so I clasp them together. "Long story short, I started to belch, and your son here"—I unlock my hands and pat his thigh—"was never once rude about what he had to smell, but we did argue about me not accepting a mint." *God, I miss Gage's minty smell.* "He ended up jumping off that balcony, which was great, because I needed the nearest bathroom, like, yesterday." I shake my head ruefully. "And you want to know what happened the very next day?"

Victor doesn't look too sure that he wants to hear the rest, but he nods because, well... he did ask for it.

"He called me."

I leave it at that and say no more. More confusion crosses his hardened face. This is the best day of my life. He trains his attention on his son, but Aric remains silent.

"He called you?" He states it as a question, clearly not understanding why that's so important to my story.

I nod enthusiastically. "Yeah, and you want to know why that was so weird?"

"Because you had a mouth full of fish eggs and your breath stank?" Victor asks dryly.

This is great.

"No, because I never got the chance to give him my phone number. Your son turned into a stalker within minutes of seeing me again and somehow got my number." I smile brightly, resting my head on Aric's large shoulder for a moment. "Do you want to hear about the rest of the week? I can fill you in on how horrible of a kisser Aric is." I laugh lightly. "But don't worry. That won't stop us from getting married."

He shakes his head with such vehemence that I know that I have done my job. He thinks I'm a complete idiot and probably doesn't have the slightest clue about why his son likes me so much, but because I'm a Keeyes, he isn't going to interfere with his plan for world domination.

"Why isn't she wearing the ring yet?" Victor asks Aric, and now it's my turn to look confused. Aric slides his hand into his pocket, pulling out a little black box.

A small gasp escapes my lips. I'm sure to Victor it looks like a gasp of surprise, but in reality, it's a gasp of *What the fuck?*

Aric opens the box and takes out a large diamond ring that almost blinds me on impact. He slides it onto my left ring finger. "Marry me."

He doesn't ask the question like a normal man would. It comes out more as a demand. I remind myself that this is all for show, but by his face, it doesn't feel like one. His hand clasps the back of my head and he pulls me in for another kiss. This time I bite his bottom lip.

I'm going to kick his ass the second we leave this castle of doom. The next hour goes by as slowly as watching paint dry. Victor and Aric talk about business crap that bores me to the core. By the time Aric is ready to leave, I jump off the couch with way too much excitement.

Aric takes my hand as we exit the cold *home* and says, "Come on, I need a drink."

"Why didn't you have a drink at your father's house?"

Aric's gaze slides over to me. "Because nothing good comes from having a drink with the devil. Now let's get your brother back."

Chapter Twenty-Two

Kali.

Instead of heading to Aric's cold, heartless place of residence, he takes us to a helicopter pad, and we lift off quickly. It shouldn't surprise me that he owns a helicopter and pilots it too. I give up asking where exactly we're heading and how we're going to get Logan, because Aric refuses to answer any of my questions.

I tried passing the fake engagement ring back to him, but he only shook his head, telling me to keep it on in case someone is watching us.

Aric maneuvers the helicopter like he does this all the time. Maybe he does. I take in the sun reflecting off the water of Lake Michigan below us. Our trip takes a couple of hours. I have no idea where Logan is, but I surmise that he's close enough to take a helicopter to reach, which is great news.

It isn't until we touch down on a small chunk of land surrounded by deep blue water that I start to question what's going on. A lone house sits on this island, and only a couple of lights are on. The house is modern in every aspect and screams money. It doesn't have the look of a place where someone would torture people to get information out of them.

Is this where Gage is keeping Logan? I thought going into this that Aric would want to use the element of surprise and catch them off guard. But the thundering noise of the blades whooshing above us means there is nothing stealthy about our arrival.

Aric gets out and lifts me down. He takes my hand and we make the trek across the greens to the house. The sun is setting over the water, the light of the day fleeting. Aric enters a code and the lock disengages, allowing us access.

He places his hand on the small of my back to lead me inside. I'm not sure what to expect, but there is no sign of Logan—or anyone, for that matter. The lights turn on automatically, revealing a beautiful interior of whites, blues, and greens. The outer walls are full of windows, giving a view of Lake Michigan that most people could only dream of. The wood floors are light, with rugs placed perfectly throughout the open layout of the beach home.

"Where are we?" I ask as he walks across the room to a minibar.

"My own little oasis on Lake Michigan."

I walk over to the windows and look across the white sands and blue waters. "I didn't know Lake Michigan had white sand."

Aric pours two drinks. "Not on Chicago's side. The eastern side of the lake will remind you of the Caribbean."

I make my way across the room to Aric as he drops a couple of ice cubes into our drinks. "Why are we here? I thought we were going to get Logan."

"We are." Aric hands me a drink and walks past me toward large sliding glass doors.

I follow because I have no other choice if I want answers. We walk out onto an outdoor patio with bright white wicker couches and deep blue pillows scattered across them. If I were here under different circumstances, I would be ecstatic to vacation at a place this beautiful. In contrast, I drop into one of the plush padded seats and mumble under my breath.

Aric sits next to me and takes a long pull from his drink before he relaxes on the couch and closes his eyes.

What.

The.

Fuck.

"Aric."

"Hmm," he replies.

"Where's Logan?"

"I haven't the slightest clue."

My jaw locks. He told me the entire time he knew how to rescue Logan, and it was all a lie. I went through a day of hell at the castle of doom acting like a lovesick puppy all for nothing?

Heat spreads through my chest, igniting a sharp tension in my muscles at the thought of being played. Again. I'm going to prison for the rest of my life because I'm three seconds away from killing him. I take a large drink of whatever shit is in this glass. "You told me you would never lie to me."

"I haven't."

"Bullshit, Aric! You told me you were taking me to Logan, not to your playboy house on an island in the middle of Lake Fucking Michigan." I hate the vulnerability in my voice.

Aric turns toward me, a ghost of a smirk tugging at his mouth. "I left a big trail of breadcrumbs for Gage to find and track us down. I couldn't make it appear like I did it on purpose, so I took you to my sanctuary, a place no one knows about. He will need to develop a plan to get on this island unnoticed and come to your rescue."

He takes a slow drink, letting me digest his words. "He's then going to take you to wherever Logan is, and he will also take me because he needs me just as much to get to my father. The entire reason for him to be involved in the expo was to find me. I'm guessing he'll be making an appearance within three hours."

I open my mouth to respond but snap it closed. How could he possibly know what Gage is going to do before he even does it? This could turn into a complete disaster, two hotheads colliding with one another. It could easily end with one of them dead.

I don't want either of them to die tonight.

All I want is my brother safe and sound. I want to return to my same ole boring routine, where I call Harlow on the daily because I'm losing my mind.

I do what anyone in my current situation would do. I slam my drink and rest my head against the couch, closing my eyes to the mess that's going to be knocking on the door in three hours.

Though *knocking* is probably a bad choice of words. I'm sure the door is going to be kicked, blown, or annihilated in some way without a second thought.

Aric removes my empty glass from my hand and his footsteps head inside. Hopefully, he's refilling it. It may taste like crap, but I'm going to need something strong before this turns into a shit show.

He's gone so long, he must be distilling his own liquor. When he arrives with the decanter in one hand and our glasses in his other, I sit up and grab the drink, ready to tip it back completely. But then I think better of it and only take a small drink. As much as I would love to be a drunken mess when Gage shows up, I can't afford to be. Logan is what's most important right now. I need to be on my game.

"I just got off the phone with Harlow. Fletcher's going to make it."

I whip my head around. "Really? Fletcher's okay?"

He nods, sets everything down on the table in front of us, and turns a knob on the front edge of the table. A fire roars to life across the crystals sunken into the table. It doesn't produce enough heat. It's more for show, but it sends calmness through me anyways.

Fletcher is going to be okay. Relief fills my body. The guilt of not being able to save him has been weighing on me heavily. But Harlow will take good care of him. I can't wait to get back to see him.

Wait a minute.

"You talked to Harlow just now?" I ask as Aric plops down next to me.

He loosens his tie and grabs his glass. "Yep." He says it as if it isn't a big deal. "You need to be focused, and Fletcher's fate has obviously been bothering you."

"Can I call her? It might be better if she can talk to Gage before he shows up."

Aric chuckles. "Are you worried about me, wildflower?"

I snort but don't give him a response. His ego is large enough for this entire country. Since he didn't answer my question, I won't answer his. I can feel his eyes on me, but I'm refusing to talk first. We sit like that for so long, I begin to believe that we're both stubborn enough to not talk until Gage shows up.

But of course, that wouldn't be Aric's style. He loves his games. "I would've married you in a heartbeat back then. I still would."

I turn to find him still staring at me. I don't know if it's the crap-tasting liquor I have been sipping or what, but his comment makes me sad. Sure, he might be a malevolent piece of work, but he also hasn't been dealt the best hand in life. His father is a piece of work, and last I knew, his mother was still missing. "You can't say that, Aric. You don't know me."

"I know enough. I know you have the sweetest soul and that you're funny and strong. That no matter what life throws at you, you somehow dust yourself off and get back up. I know you're tired of hiding and having to lie. I can change that for you, Kali. I can make it so you no longer have to live a life of lies. I can give you whatever you need. I can be the person you can always lean on."

He never breaks eye contact, so I do, choosing to look at my glass. The ring he put on my finger only hours earlier is shining like the North Star.

"I don't have anything left inside to give. My parent's death has stripped me bare and frozen my heart."

"Until Gage."

I close my eyes at hearing him say his name. I don't deny it.

We both take a drink from our glasses. "You're a good man, Aric. I can see past all the hard armor you wear. You deserve someone who can give you their everything. That's just not me." I watch him closely as he takes in my words.

"You're saying there's something better than a belching red-ball woman out there?"

I laugh and he smiles. It isn't a happy smile, but it's an accepting one. "As long as it isn't blue balls, I'm sure you'll be fine."

We grin and the subject is dropped. I'm not sure how much time passes, but I must fall asleep, because the next thing I know, something wakes me. I now have a light blanket laid across me. Aric must have put it on me when I fell asleep. He's moved from the couch we were sharing to a chair across the table, and now he's watching me closely. I rub my eyes and see a glass of water sitting on the table. I grab it and am taking a swig when I see something move just outside of the patio.

Gage appears from the shadows of the night. His familiar icy blues lock onto me and I audibly gulp the last of my drink at the anger radiating out of him. The merciless man who attacked Transcend Towers. The man who showed no care for Fletcher's well-being. He's in all black with his signature hat on backward, looking sexier than ever. He's not slowing and reaches us in a matter of seconds. He steps onto the patio and directs his attention to Aric—right before he hammers his fist into his face.

My glass drops to the ground and shatters. I tumble out of my seat to save Aric from the fury of Gage. The blanket gets wrapped around my legs, causing me to stumble to the ground. I kick my legs, break free of the blanket, and rise frantically to my feet. Was Aric planning on Gage beating the shit out of him? This isn't turning out good.

They're both rolling around on the patio and I'm screaming for them to stop. Conner appears out of nowhere right beside me and shakes his head.

I look over at him wildly. "You have to stop them!"

Conner's response is to laugh as he crosses his arms and watches the show before us. "I think they both need to get some frustrations out."

Aric is holding his own against Gage, but not by much. It makes me sick to my stomach. I can't take watching these two men beat each other. I lunge, ready to stop the show since Conner isn't doing a damn thing, but before I make it three steps, Conner's arms pin both of mine behind me. He wraps his arms around my elbows and pulls me against him.

I hastily step back into Conner before twisting my body down and away from his, freeing one of my arms as I shove him backward with my shoulder. I give it everything I got. He releases his hold and staggers back. His arms reach for me again as I scream, "Don't fucking touch me!" That must catch Gage's attention, because he calls out Conner's name. Conner's arms drop to his sides.

I turn toward Gage. His lip is cut and bleeding down his chin. His eyes look like a wild animal's. He's clearly lost touch with reality.

Aric lies there laughing. Laughing like a damn madman. He looks worse than Gage as he rolls over and spits blood onto the floor. "Those hits taste almost as good as her kiss."

My mouth falls open at these words.

Gage slowly turns to Aric. "What did you just say?" Gage growls, his hand curling into a fist.

"Gage, stop! Please, just stop. What the hell is wrong with you?!" I scream, frustrated at men and their testosterone. Can they not learn how to talk? I hold my breath, hoping like hell he doesn't get sucked in by Aric's words.

Aric smiles up at him and I shake my head.

Gage isn't going to stop. He punches him again, making Aric laugh louder, but thankfully he stops after that. He gets to his feet and heads straight for me. I find myself backstepping, now leaning against Conner, not sure what Gage is going to do next.

He stops when he gets a foot away.

Conner moves around me and walks toward Aric.

"You've been very busy." Gage's voice is low, sending chills up my arms.

"So have you," I respond, my blood pumping hard through my body. "I know you have him. Aric told me everything. If you have hurt so much as a hair on his head, I'll kill you myself."

Gage smiles largely, his dimples making an appearance. I mentally remind myself that I hate him. He almost killed Fletcher and has my brother. He brings his bloody hand to my face and caresses my cheek. The warmth of Aric's blood glides across my face. We stand in silence, both breathing heavily.

"You mind taking your hands off my fiancée?" Aric asks.

My heart officially stops beating. I think he might want to die tonight. I move my hands behind my back and take a step away.

Gage steps forward, tugging my wrist and looking at where the large diamond lies on my finger. His eyes narrow. "Oh, he's going to love this," he mutters under his breath.

I'm lost. *Who's* going to love this? "It-it's n-not what you think. It's not real," I stutter. It's the truth, but I'm also trying to spare Aric's life.

Gage tilts his head to the side, assessing me. "Did you kiss him again?"

Aric and his big stupid mouth. I'm not 100 percent sure whether Gage realizes who I am. It's been a big fucking question mark in my head since Aric came back into my life. If he doesn't, I need to keep it that way until Logan is safe. At the very least. It's not like I can tell Gage the truth about why I'm fake engaged to Aric or why I had to kiss him. I already hate myself enough for what I've done. If Gage doesn't know, he will ask questions. And I can't blow my cover until I know for certain. Especially now, knowing that he and his father were there the night my parents died.

My nonresponse must be enough of an answer for him. He drops my hand and turns to Aric, rapidly closing the distance.

Conner, thankfully, holds out his hand to stop his progress. "You're going to kill him if you go at it again. We need him. Afterward, you can do whatever you want. But don't let him choose for you."

"You should listen to your friend. I think you've hurt enough innocent people lately," I snap, tired of the fighting. Tired of the games. Tired of the lies. Tired of every fucking thing.

Gage turns back to me, rage across his face. "You think Aric's fucking innocent?" His voice is weighty.

"You hurt Fletcher."

Gage laughs as he slowly makes his way to me. I refuse to give him the satisfaction of stepping back. I lock my shoulders, readying myself.

He stops when he is a foot away. "You should know what you're talking about before you start throwing accusations around."

"I saw you." I point to Conner behind him. "And your partner in crime too. I saw you both. I watched you walk in after you blew his office up. You walked right up to Fletcher and barely gave him a second thought." My body is starting to shake badly.

"Who else did you see, little lion?"

I stand there, shaking my head. There was no one else. Whoever the guys were in the lobby on Fletcher's security video never made an appearance when Gage and Conner came in. And then I left through the secret exit—right before I ran into...

My eyes snap to Gage, pieces of the puzzle clicking together. I walk around Gage to face Aric. Gage grips my arm, not allowing me to get any closer to him. Aric is standing now, blood running down his cheek, and his eye is starting to swell.

"It was you? *You* put Fletcher's life in danger?"

Aric spits out a mouthful of blood. "My father's men blew Fletcher's door. I told you my father would stop at nothing to find you. That's why I tried to take you the night before. I was only trying to protect you."

"But you let Fletcher get hurt."

He shrugs like it wasn't a big deal. "You're my only concern, wildflower."

We all fall silent for a minute, and I wonder what else I don't yet fully understand.

"Charming. Let's go. Your present can't wait forever." Gage tugs my arm, turning me away from Aric and leading me off the patio.

He leaves no time to understand what he means by *present* as he hauls me out of the house and straight toward Aric's chopper. I attempt to get into the back seat, but Gage pulls me out and places me in the front. Conner and Aric get into the back, and it shouldn't surprise me that Gage takes the controls and pilots it himself.

Do they all have pilot licenses? Why would a stupid question like that cross my mind?

I find myself hoping this helicopter ride lasts longer than the last. I need to figure out what exactly is going on.

Chapter Twenty-Three

Gage.

I haven't felt this unhinged since my mother left us all those years ago to be with Victor Hemmington. She left her own sons with a monster, only to end up with another monster. I understand why she did it. She thought we were both lost causes, but what she didn't know was I was only playing my father's game, and Ashton was innocent of everything.

I couldn't show any signs of weakness. Not when my father was always watching. Instead, I turned cold to everyone around me... her included. I always expected I'd kill my father, but it wasn't until that one balmy June night that my plan was unexpectedly played out.

I had no plans to kill him that night, but I guess not all plans work out exactly how you think. Like my little lion here—who has barely spoken a word since we left Aric's little paradise.

I knew the trail Aric left when they took off from Victor's home was too convenient. Aric always covers his tracks. Always. He knew I was coming, and he allowed it. That alone is why I walked straight up on them without a second thought. The relief of seeing my little lion resting peacefully against the pillow was a ton of bricks falling from my shoulders. She didn't appear to be harmed. But that didn't mean Aric didn't have a good ass-kicking coming his way.

Conner and I got word that Victor's men were planning to take Allie from her work before it all went down. I wasn't worried at first. I checked the tracker Conner put on her Jimmy the day we brought her to the Oasis, and both it and the one on her phone showed she was still at home. Just as she had told me the night before. Regardless, I wanted to make sure, and I'm glad I did, because when we walked into her home, it was empty.

By the time we made it to Transcend Towers, we were far behind. Conner and I got to Fletcher's floor quickly and unleashed mayhem on Victor's men. Our only saving grace was the idiots who blew Fletcher's office door. It knocked them back hard and they took a while to get their wits. They never had a chance. We put bullets between their eyes before they ever knew what hit them.

I knew Allie was hiding somewhere, and by the time I realized that fucking large mirror was a safe room with an exit, it was already too late.

From where he lay pinned under his desk, Fletcher told me where the elevator led, but all Conner found was a pair of bloody keys next to a rusty old Impala's door. The fear that shot through me was worse than any bullet I have ever taken.

I had no choice other than to turn to Link and ask for his help in finding her. I hated it, but what choice did I have? He was roughed up from our fight but still denying everything. Telling me that he and Harlow have been keeping their relationship secret from everyone and that Allie just happened to be there.

I know what I saw that day, and those two have a close bond. Allie is going to be pissed to find Link with more than a hair on his head out of place, but that's what happens when you continue to lie. I can't afford rats in my close-knit group.

Link was able to find Allie within a couple of hours and confirm it was Aric who took her, not Victor's men. We left Link in a holding cell and took off. To say he was pissed would be the understatement of the year. Link was furious, which only told me there was something between him and my little lion.

By the time we get back to Seattle, it's just after six in the morning. I flew the chopper into Green Bay–Austin Straubel, where I had a private jet waiting. Allie has been fighting fatigue and nodding off and on. She finally fell asleep an hour ago. I pick her up from the leather seat and carry her off the plane. Her sleepy whiskey eyes peer up at me. I doubt she means to show me her underbelly, but she does. It's obvious she feels safe in my arms.

We load into the SUV, but I don't let go of her. With Aric shackled in the back, Conner takes the wheel as my little lion drifts off to sleep. She's exhausted. I lean in, smelling her hair. God, I've missed her so much.

Thirty minutes later, we arrive at the warehouse. As I exit the vehicle, she starts to stir. It doesn't take long for her to find the fight in her, and she demands to walk.

I decide to carry her longer, because I don't want to let her go, but I gently set her down before we enter the warehouse. I grab her hand and pull her through the building. Her body grows stiffer the farther we walk. Her hand squeezes mine harder with each step we take. She can claim to hate me all she wants, but her death grip shows me she doesn't want me to let go. I love that.

The warehouse is full of steel and has no windows. There is nothing comforting in my little lion's eyes as she scans her surroundings. At least the apartments tucked away in this warehouse have a warmer touch, but I can't take her to either one yet.

Conner takes Aric to a holding cell on the first floor, while we climb the stairs to the second floor.

"Are you ready for your present?" I ask, glancing at the ring on her finger. I wanted nothing more than to rip it off her finger, and I will. But I need Link to see it first, so I can gauge his reaction.

My fierce little lion locks her shoulders and nods. Such a brave little vixen. Aric's blood is still dried on the side of her face where I caressed it hours ago. She looks like a warrior. God, I've missed her.

I enter a sixteen-digit code and the door unlatches. I push it open and we enter the larger room that has an open space with a couple of chairs and a table. Tucked in the back corner is a small cell surrounded by bars. I watch as her hands fly to her mouth, gasping at the sight of Link lying on a beaten-down cot behind bars. She rushes forward, crying out to him.

The hurt that crashes through my body, rocking my entire foundation, is worse than I could ever have expected. I knew there was something there... I was just hoping I was wrong.

"Oh my God, oh my God," she cries as Link's head lifts from the cot.

He rushes to her. Jealousy roars through my chest, demanding to let the beast out. I should have killed him right after he located her.

"Shit, Allie, are you okay?" He grabs her face through the bars and checks whether the blood on her cheek is hers.

"Yeah, I'm okay. What has he done to you? Oh God, I am going to kill him and I'm getting us out of here."

Allie is taking note of the bruise underneath his eye. I never tortured Link like I originally planned, but we did get into a fistfight. My ribs are still hurting from his blow. Allie turns her head, and with a look of death, she yells, "You better let him out this second!"

I stay standing at the doorway, my arms crossed against my chest.

Link's eyes widen when they land on the healthy-sized diamond on her left ring finger. And his facial expression doesn't lie. He's just as pissed as I am. "What the fuck is that?" he barks.

Her lips part as color drains from her face. "I... I..." she stutters.

Though I want to knock Link on his ass for speaking to her like that, I force myself not to move. I need to hear what she's going to tell her lover about a ring that didn't come from him.

He grabs her hand to inspect the rock sparkling up at him.

"It's not what you think. It's nothing, I swear." Allie's voice trembles. She shifts uncomfortably, her fingers twitching as if she wants to pull her hand away.

"Oh, now come on, Allie. Let the truth set you free," I say with a smug grin.

She glares at me, and I can only imagine what's going on in that pretty little head of hers. Probably a hundred different ways to kill me.

She's too cute.

Link's eyes narrow. I see the war brewing inside him. "You married Gage? What the hell?!"

He seems to believe the ring on her finger is from me. That's interesting. He knows Aric took her, but he isn't considering that.

She shakes her head frantically. "No, no. It's an engagement ring. I didn't marry anyone."

The fire behind Link's eyes has turned into an inferno. I've witnessed his skills at taking down enemies. If he weren't locked behind those bars right now, he would be charging me at this second. Tonight, I'm getting the answers to whatever the hell is going on between these two.

"The ring didn't come from me, brother," I say.

It doesn't take Link long to figure out who put that ring on her finger.

"Aric," he spits, causing Allie to bow her head and sob. "You got engaged to Aric Fucking Hemmington?" he roars.

I've had enough. It takes me seconds to reach them with my long strides. I'm not going to stand back and watch Link hurt Allie more than she already is. I got what I needed. Confirmation that there's something between them. It won't be hard pulling the details out of Allie. I know her weakness now—Link. I wrap my arm around her waist and pull her away from him, breaking their hands apart.

As soon as Link drops her hand, she whips around and starts hammering her little fists on my chest. She's crying harder, and I regret playing this game with her. If she had just been honest with me, we wouldn't be in this situation to begin with.

"No! Let me go!" She turns her red face toward Link pleadingly.

Link says comfortingly, "He doesn't know anything. Don't you dare say a word. He won't hurt you. You're an innocent."

I stop dead in my tracks as several emotions rip through me. Anger being the front of the matter, anger that he would ever hide anything from me. I've always considered Link a trusted friend. My best guy, maybe even like a brother. Both Conner and I have. I trusted this man with every ounce in me, and he just blatantly confirmed that he's holding information from me. That they both are hiding something.

Right now, I hate how well Link knows me. And he knows without a doubt that I would never, ever hurt Allie. But that doesn't make him safe. His betrayal sinks deep into my bones. "Enjoy your last hours alive," I say, picking Allie up and carrying her screaming, fighting body out of the room.

Conner stands in the hall. I'm not sure how much he heard of what Link had to say, but by his expression, he heard enough. The hurt in his eyes speaks loudly.

My little lion is trying to fight me, but she is weakened by everything that's hit her over the past couple of days. I take her back downstairs to the opposite end of the warehouse from the cell where I'm holding Aric. I enter another code to unlock the door of one of the warehouse apartments.

Once inside, I enable the security system I purchased from Fletcher years ago. Even if she tries to run, she won't get anywhere. She's completely stopped fighting and is gripping my shirt tightly, her face buried in my chest.

The underlying meaning behind what Link said to her had a big impact, and I need to understand why. I set her down on the dark gray couch, and once I'm confident she isn't going to bolt, I head to the kitchen to pour a drink for both of us. We can both use one right now.

The open concept of the apartment is great for keeping my eye on her. I walk into the clean and modern kitchen. It has white countertops, stainless steel appliances, and simple cabinetry. Grabbing a couple of glasses, I pour us each a glass of bourbon. I wish I had wine to offer her.

I debate my next move. I could have Conner put Aric into the same room as Link and see what those two will do. But Link knows there are cameras in the room. He helped install them. He won't say anything in that room that would give me the answers I need.

My eyes find Allie again. She's trying to pull herself together. She's getting ready for battle. I can see it. She's willing to risk everything for Link. My heart tightens painfully.

My phone vibrates in my pocket. I pull it out to see a text.

Conner: What's the next move? Put these two rats together?

I shake my head. We think alike. I want to try another approach with Allie, and now that I know what type of leverage I'm going to use against her, it shouldn't take long to get answers.

Gage: Hold back for now.

I pocket my phone, grab our drinks, and head into the living room. A plush throw blanket is draped across the back of the sofa Allie's sitting on. The small, sleek coffee table made of reclaimed wood that sits in front of her adds a touch of warmth without overwhelming the space.

Though the apartment is a quiet retreat, there's an underlying tension in the air, a feeling that it's merely a temporary escape from the far darker and more sinister sections of the building. The other half of the warehouse holds rooms with heavy doors, cells, and torture chambers—things that seem a world apart from the cozy, subdued comfort of this space.

I hand her the drink and she slams it back in one go. That makes me smile. I sit next to her and take a sip from mine. This bourbon is strong, so the fact that she didn't wince or cough up a lung when she slammed it back tells me a lot about her state of mind. She's refusing to look at me. I give her the time she needs. I can see the brainstorming she's currently doing. The first day I met her, she ran through a bullshit story about a made-up husband and a dog that would attack at any given second. I haven't been that intrigued in years. I can't wait to hear what she has this time. I lean back and place my ankle over my knee. I make it halfway through my drink before she releases a large breath.

"I'm not supposed to tell you who he is."

That's all she says, focusing on her hands as she fidgets with the hem of the yellow summer dress she's wearing. "Link already made that perfectly clear. I don't give a shit what he wants."

Confusion settles across her face. I have no idea why that would confuse her. She gulps.

I wonder if she isn't about to make up a story, but rather tell me the truth.

"He works for the CIA." She turns to face me, her whiskey eyes growing large. "But he's not after you. He's completely fine with everything you do, whatever that is." She clamps her hands together tightly.

She's choosing to tell a story. It's hard not to smile. I drop my propped leg to the floor, get up, and walk over to the dining room. I grab a chair and bring it back to where she's sitting. I push the coffee table away with my foot and place the chair in front of her. I sit on it backward, my arms resting on the top rail.

I want front-row seats to this premier.

"Now, that is very interesting and exactly what I need to know." I finish off my drink and place it on the ground next to me.

Her relieved expression tells me she thinks I'm on board with her story. She nods. "I know. He asked me not to tell anyone." Her eyes grow soft before she says, "But I really wanted to tell you. Badly. I almost did a couple of times, but his boss is a dick and would have him killed if anything got out."

She gives a light laugh and shakes her head as if in disbelief. "I mean, can you imagine working for the CIA and your whole entire job is to catch bad guys, but in all reality, you are working for the bad guys? If you don't stay in line, then BAM, you're done. Toast. *Hasta la vista*, baby. But hey, if that's the life he wants to live, I'm here to support him. That's what friends do." She bites her thumbnail. Her nail polish is chipped.

She's referring to him as a friend. I think back to watching them together at the Oasis. I'm convinced they're much closer than just friends.

"Do you know he has a wife?"

I shake my head and take a trick out of her bag, plastering shock across my face. She eats it right up.

"Yep, and a ton of kids. Like, enough to start a basketball team with. Oh! And she's almost due. She could literally pop out their next little bundle of joy at any moment. What's today's date?" she asks, looking around as if a calendar is going to magically appear.

I can't help but chuckle at her facial expression. She really does have this storytelling thing down. I can tell exactly what she's going for. She's trying to get me to sympathize and let them both go. This woman could sell a box of condoms to a nun.

"August 17th." I rest my chin on top of my arms. She really is the most beautiful woman I've ever seen. I can see why Link and Aric have both fallen for her. Shit, I have too. It goes way beyond her breathless beauty. It's the innocence that sits behind her whiskey eyes. Her enormous heart that only the people she cares most about get a piece of.

She slaps her hands over her mouth. "Cheese and rice! Her due date was three days ago, Gage! Oh no, I need to take him to her right now. Oh God, this is not good." She's shaking her head and starts to rise from the couch, as if that's exactly what she is going to do.

I lean forward in the chair and place my hands on her thighs, gently pushing her back to the couch.

She subsides.

"How did you meet him?" I keep my voice level, not showing my cards.

"Oh." She laughs and stares up at the ceiling. "We went to the same school." The second she says that, she quickly changes it up. "Well, not him and me, but me and his wife... Georgia. When they got married, I was the maid of honor. Georgia was so drunk that night, she accidentally let it slip that he was working for the CIA. We all made a blood pact to never let that information out to anyone. Don't tell him I said that."

"Let me see if I got this right. You knew Link's wife through school, which is how you met him. And he's an undercover CIA agent who also works for me and has somehow found the time in his busy schedule to marry this woman and have a shit ton of kids without me knowing."

She nods. "Yeah, he's good at hiding. Like, the best in the world. I'm pretty sure he has a trophy in his office."

"Answer me this. If he's a happily married man, then why is he so pissed that you're engaged to Aric?"

"I'm not engaged to Aric."

Her words hit me like a sweet melody, but she's still lying. I glare at her ring, raising an eyebrow, the question clear.

She rolls her eyes. "It's fake. Well, I don't think the actual ring is fake, by the weight of it, but the engagement was. As soon as I get... Link... back to Georgia, I'm heading to the nearest pawn shop to sell this baby."

"That doesn't tell me why he's pissed about your engagement."

She bites her damn thumbnail again, bringing my attention to her pouty lips. It takes the strongest skill set I have to resist sealing her lips with mine. I'm seconds away from breaking when she releases her thumb.

"Aric's going to be the godfather of his new baby. I'm godmother to their third child. He's afraid that if Aric and I become a couple and then break up, it will be hard on his children when we're all together. I mean, I can start an argument with anyone, and believe me, I would poke the bear, you know what I mean?"

As much as I would love to keep up this charade, I have to keep moving this forward. Without a word, I reluctantly remove my hands from her knees and stand.

Her breath catches as I make my way toward the door. She stumbles to her feet. "Wait! Where are you going?" Her voice cracks as she takes a hesitant step forward. She's now standing in the middle of the room, her hands tightly woven together.

"I'm going to see Link. I have unfinished business to handle."

She rushes toward me but wisely remains a few feet away. "What the hell does that mean? Are you going to kill him?"

"He lied to me, Allie."

Tears well in her eyes, and I hate that I put them there. I still have no idea why she's so adamant about protecting Link, so I need her to believe that he's going to die if she doesn't give me answers.

"But he can't tell you," she says with a half sob. "Gage, you have to believe me. He can't tell you." She's pleading and it sounds genuine. There's probably truth behind her words, but that doesn't work. It isn't enough.

"Go take a shower and lie down for a bit. I might be a while." I turn and flip open the keypad, ready to put the code in, when she cracks.

"He's my brother," she says, defeat heavy in her voice.

I freeze at her words. Is this just another story? It would make perfect sense—it would explain why they are so protective of each other and why he's pissed at Aric.

"His name is Logan. Logan Michael Keeyes."

My stomach drops. Any doubt I had vanishes. And if he's her brother, that means she's Kali Keeyes.

The girl I was going to kidnap the night her entire life burned to ashes.

Seven years ago.

Gage.

"Victor's already here. This might turn out more in our favor than we anticipated," my father Frank says as we scale the walls of the high barrier encircling a mansion tucked away in the woods.

It isn't going to be easy kidnapping James and Marion Keeyes's only daughter. I've never kidnapped anyone up to this point and hate the prospect of bringing innocents into our fucked-up world, but I have no choice.

My stepbrother Aric Hemmington called early this morning, and normally I would've told him to go fuck himself and hung up, but his words came out rushed. He told me Victor had gotten word of my father's plans to kidnap Kali and that we needed to get to her before he did.

That's the only thing Aric and I have in common. We both hate his father. Victor manipulated my mother into believing he was a good man. She walked away from us to be with him.

I can't say I blame her. My father did turn me into a monster and my younger brother Ashton unknowingly followed faithfully behind me, trusting me to steer him correctly. I need to free her from Victor's clutches and then kill Frank.

Most of my father's men are loyal to him and only him. It won't be as easy as riddling his body with bullets. That will start a war between me and his men. It would set off a domino effect that would leave several dead. They'd do everything in their power to eliminate me. Instead, I'm planning to make my father's death look like an accident. Boating, to be more specific.

But first, I need my mother back, and this is the only opportunity to accomplish that. When my father and I take Kali, we can bargain a trade with Victor. We give him Kali, and in return, we get my mother. This goes completely against my morals. But the thought of my mother in the clutches of Victor Hemmington has warped my mind. Maybe I am more like my father than I realize.

Victor will choose Kali over my mother. He wants this alliance between his syndicate and the Keeyes empire more than anything else in this world. Once Victor accepts Kali, I'll need to find a way to keep her safe.

It's dark. Weapons with silencers are fired, and I don't see but hear two guards drop to the ground. My father's men have killed everyone we have come across so far.

We slip in through a side door and are immediately met with the sounds of a heated conversation nearby. Following the noise, Frank's men file into the room, guns raised. As we turn the corner behind the men, we walk into a room filled with books. Victor is standing with several of his men, who all instantly pull out their guns and aim them at us. Everyone now has a gun trained on their heaving chests.

The barrel of my gun is pointed at Victor. I could do it right now. I wouldn't walk out of here, but at least I could free my mother of the monster. But opening fire would endanger James and his wife—and possibly their kids too if they stumble across us.

"Frank McCollin, what a pleasant surprise," Victor says. "I'm sorry to say my lovely wife didn't accompany me."

"Gentlemen, please," James says. "This is my home and no place for war. I believe we can all put the guns away and figure out what's going on."

I'm positive that the calmness in his voice is an act to regain control. It's ironic. The man who is the head of dealing arms for the majority of this country is the one trying to get everyone to drop them.

My father is the first to lower his gun. Victor nods for his men to do the same.

"Thank you. My son is fetching a bottle of Double Eagle Very Rare." James walks over to the bar nestled in the corner. An elegant woman is seated across the room in a red velvet chair. That must be his wife Marion. "Let's have a drink of this Hearts bourbon while we wait." James pours a glass and hands it to my father. "Frank."

My father takes the drink. He nods for me to search for Kali. The plan is still on. I can only hope my father keeps his rage in check like he promised.

I wait until no one is paying me attention and exit the room. I have no idea what Kali looks like, only that she just turned eighteen. Their son is somewhere in the house fetching bourbon, so I keep an eye out for him.

I tread silently on the fine rugs. I don't know the layout of this house, and that isn't good. We didn't have much time to prepare. It won't be long until shit hits the fan. I open a door.

An empty office. I back out and shut it. I investigate each room but keep coming up empty.

Marion's scream rends the air and rockets me forward. I need to get Kali and get out. I race up a staircase, skipping several steps. The first door I come to on my right is open. The pink walls suggest I've found Kali's room.

The problem is, if I could hear her mother cry out, she probably could too. My gun is ready. I don't plan on hurting her, but I need her immediate cooperation for this to go smoothly.

I enter slowly. A radio plays music at a low volume. A painting sits alone on the stand with multiple paintbrushes on the table next to it. The picture isn't finished, but it's surprisingly superb. It's a colorful bouquet of wildflowers. I drag my finger across the canvas and the paint smears. It's fresh. She's close. I sweep the room.

She's not here. A spike of fear hits me. Could she have made it to the study while I was looking for her? "Fuck." I run back the way I came, just in time to witness Marion fire a shot right at my father, hitting him in the shoulder. Tears soak her cheeks. Her husband's lifeless body lies on the floor with a gunshot wound in his head. He never felt a thing.

My father turns his gun toward Marion. I sprint across the room to stop him. But I'm not faster than the bullet that rips from his Glock and lands straight between her eyes. My body slams into his.

He promised me no one would be hurt. That all he wanted was his wife back. I should've known better than to trust this piece of shit.

Victor is gone. I have no idea where Kali is—or her brother. I stand and pull my father out into the hallway.

"Where's the girl?" he demands.

"She's out back. Conner has her," I lie, leading him to the side entrance, gun raised. "Where's Victor?"

"I don't know."

We exit the mansion. Gunfire emanates from inside. Part of the home is on fire. Fuck! "What the fuck happened when I left that room?"

He shrugs with a disgustingly smug smile.

"Bullshit, Frank. What the fuck happened?"

"You always focus on the wrong thing, son. All that matters is we have Kali and can get your mother. Nothing means shit when you are at war. People die. You need to be a man. I'll be damned if a pussy of a son takes over everything I've built. You have no idea what sacrifices I've made for you."

Fuck my father. No one had to die today. His time has come.

I lead him around to the end of the drive, where Conner is waiting beside the vehicle.

"Conner, where is she?" Frank asks, walking in front of me.

I raise my gun.

Bewilderment crosses Conner's face, but as soon as he sees my gun trained on my father, he erases it. I cock it as Frank freezes in front of me. He slowly turns around.

"Son?"

I hit him between his wide-open, surprised eyes. His body crumples to the grass.

I wish I could have told him everything I wanted to say before I killed him. But it doesn't matter any longer. Too many innocent people have died because of my father. There aren't words to justify destroying another family.

It ends here.

A longing peace glides through my body at the thought. I should have done this years ago.

"Gage," Conner says. I face my lifeless father and tell Conner to take a walk. If the fallout from my decision to shoot him is as bad as I fear it will be, I refuse to have my best friend caught in the crosshairs.

I loosen the tie around my neck. I hate suits. If I make it out, I'll never wear another. I start dragging my father's lifeless body toward the ever-growing inferno. I see a back door and decide to dump Frank's body there. Everyone will assume he was shot by one of Victor's men on his way out.

I'm almost there when Ralph—one of my father's best men—comes barreling out of the door I was heading for. His panicked gaze drops to his fallen leader. He lifts his gun, aiming straight at me. Sweat rolls down his face.

Shit. "Please, Ralph, you have to help me! They shot him. One of Victor's men shot him."

Doubt fills his eyes. The arguments my father and I have had over the years have never been a secret.

I can't allow him time to consider this. "Ralph, now! So help me God, if he dies tonight, it's on you."

That does the trick. He lowers his weapon and runs toward us. I can see the moment in his face when he realizes that Frank's dead. His face pales. "Gage..."

"Help me. We have to get him to a doctor." I start tugging my father's body back toward the vehicle as Conner runs up.

"Gage, he's gone. He's already gone."

I halt. Conner is behind Ralph, his hand on his gun, ready to shoot Ralph if needed. But he knows as much as I do that if I can convince Ralph I didn't kill my father, Ralph will have my back. And if he believes one of Victor's men is to blame, then he will make sure everyone falls in line.

Thankfully, that's exactly what happens. With help from Conner—and a few weeks later, Link, once he joins the team—it only takes me ten months to eliminate every guy on my father's payroll.

Chapter Twenty-Four

Gage.

Back then, my only focus was on my mother. On righting all my wrongs. Once I got her back, I swore I would never disappoint her again for as long as I was breathing.

I'll never forget the last day I saw her. The day she gave me the Dara knot hat. She talked more to me that day than she had over the last year.

And I never said a word.

She didn't care that I didn't speak. She just kept going, showing me the love I didn't deserve. I just sat there, listening. Wishing I could hug her and tell her how much I loved her... but not doing so. Regretting that I didn't get up from that couch and head straight to the devil himself, ending his pathetic life.

The next morning, she was gone, and that's when I realized she was saying goodbye. She had told me to stay strong during challenging times. I should've been sharper, should've grasped the inherent warning in those words, but I didn't.

I've never been a man to walk away from anything before, but the look in Allie's—fuck!—*Kali*'s hurt-filled eyes gut me. She stands there, her hands balled into small fists, looking both defiant and defeated. I'm part of the reason she lost everything. Her parents. Her safety. Her name. I'm the reason she had to hide. I'm the reason her life was destroyed.

I'm also the reason Link's life was shattered.

I turn without another word, punch in the code with fingers that feel like they're made of lead, and walk out the door, leaving her behind. Her voice breaks—shouting and pleading, followed by the desperate thud of her fists pounding against the door that separates us.

This changes everything.

I text Conner to meet me at Link's cell and he promptly responds that he's already there. My steps are hurried as I head upstairs and round the corner to see Conner waiting by the door with questions written all over his face. He's probably wondering if I'm planning on killing Link right now.

I don't keep him waiting. "They're brother and sister. Link's real name is Logan Keeyes."

Shock flashes across Conner's face. He mumbles something incoherent and runs a hand across his short hair. After a moment, he says, "So that must be Kali."

I clear my throat and nod. I'm not surprised that he remembers the name of the girl we were supposed to kidnap seven years ago. Everyone left that house damaged.

"I thought they'd both died." Conner takes another minute to think things through. "That means he was lying to us to protect his sister. He betrayed you—shit, us, for that matter—but I can't say I blame him. I would have done the same."

My chest aches with the knowledge that Link couldn't trust me with the truth, but I respect him for wanting to keep his sister safe. I enter the code and we step inside to find Link pacing. He rushes over to the bars, gripping a bar in each hand.

"If you fucking hurt her, I'll fucking kill you!" he roars, his hands whitening from how tightly he is gripping them.

"We are brothers," I say, waving my hand to encompass all three of us. "Why didn't you tell us, *Logan?*" I drop his real name to make things perfectly clear—I know everything.

His hands loosen and drop to his sides. I now understand his deep concern for Kali. Their obvious connection at the lake. She's the only family he has left, and knowing Link as I do, he will always keep her tucked under his wing.

"Did you hurt her?" he asks, his voice gravelly.

"No, I would never hurt her. You know that."

He drops his head and lets out a breath. I stand patiently, letting him catch his bearings.

Conner, however, doesn't seem as patient. "Why didn't you just tell us? Fuck, man, you know we would have been there for you."

Link tenses. "She's all I have left. I couldn't risk anyone finding out. Victor wanted her bad, and if he found out she was still alive…" He shakes his head as though trying to rid his mind of his next thought. "I couldn't take that chance. Not with her. For years she begged me to let her help bring justice to our family, but I wouldn't let her. She's always trying to find the good in everyone she meets. She doesn't understand the danger that lurks behind people in this line of business. She doesn't know that Victor might be the man who killed our parents."

"He didn't kill your parents," I reply as Conner drops his head.

"What?" Link asks, looking back and forth between us.

"My father killed your parents that night."

Link staggers backward, shaking his head in denial as he drops onto the shitty cot. "No, that can't be right. Victor was there to take Kali and we weren't having it."

"I was there, Link. I killed my father within minutes of him killing both your parents. We erased everything that could have linked us to being there that night and melted into the shadows. Every day since, I've regretted not killing my father the day before."

Link drops his head into his hands, his chest shaking. I step forward and unlock the cell, pushing it open. I'm thankful I only got into a fistfight with him. If I had tortured him… I don't know how we could have repaired that.

Link wipes his face and releases a deep breath. "What happens now?" He stands, walks through the door of his cell, and stops before us.

"First, you need to get it through your head that Kali isn't the only family you have. You have Harlow. You have us. You're like a brother to me." I drop my tone lower. "But if you ever keep anything from me again, you will regret it."

Link nods.

"Conner, give us a minute."

Link waits for Conner to shut the door before speaking. "Did you know your father was going to kill my parents?"

I feel the weight of his question settle in my chest. "No one was supposed to get hurt that night."

A flicker of doubt crosses his face. I feel the need to make him understand, to show him the remorse that is eating at me. "You've known me for a long time, Link. Hell, you even said to Kali I'm not someone who hurts innocents. That's never been who I am."

Link studies me, silent for a long moment, before nodding. "I know."

The guilt tightens in my gut. I've kept him locked in that damn cell while I've tried to figure all this out, and I can tell he feels the weight of it too. The regret is heavy, more than just the fact that I couldn't stop my father, but also what I've done to him since.

"Link, I..." I pause, swallowing down the bitter lump in my throat. "I'm sorry. For what happened that night and for keeping you in this cell."

There's a shift in his expression. Like he's considering my words and weighing them against the anger and hurt he's had to carry. "You don't have to apologize," he says quietly. "I get it. You were trying to protect yourself. You were protecting Kali.

I'm not saying I liked being locked up, but I understand why you did it and I know you're trying to make it right now."

I let out a breath I didn't know I was holding. The tension in my chest loosens just a bit thanks to the fact that he's not holding this against me. It doesn't erase the guilt, but it makes it more bearable. For the first time in days, the weight on my chest feels a little lighter.

"I'll make it right," I promise, my voice steady.

Link nods, the slightest hint of a smile tugging at his lips. "I believe you."

I stand firm, grounded. "I'm going to go tell Kali right now. About my father, about everything. I couldn't do it earlier. I needed a minute."

Link nods in understanding. "I'll come with you."

I shake my head. "No, I need to do this alone, but if there's a chance in hell that your sister could forgive me, I'm taking it, and you're not going to get in the way. She deserves happiness too."

"No, I'm going with you. She's scared and she needs me."

I put my hand up, stopping him as he stares at me. "Go clean yourself up. She doesn't need to see you like this again."

He hesitates for a moment, then agrees. "Fine, but if she doesn't want a thing to do with you, I'm taking her out of here. Alone."

I hate that he's not even sure if she will forgive me. I nod and descend the stairs to the apartment, where I'm absolutely 100 percent positive I have a pissed-off little lion waiting to attack me.

"Gage," Link calls.

I face him.

"I'm sorry. For keeping this from you." He walks with Conner in the opposite direction.

Me too, brother. Me too.

Chapter Twenty-Five

Kali.

After beating down the door for what seems like forever, I collapse against it, the coldness seeping through my entire body. It takes everything I have to not break down and start crying. I'm running off little sleep, and my body is starting to feel it. I need to stay strong for Logan.

I search for another exit but come up empty. There isn't one window in this apartment. It shouldn't be surprising—we're inside a warehouse—but I was hoping for some way to break out of here.

I search for a weapon instead. I yank on a lamp cord, ripping it from the wall. Perfect. The base is made of heavy metal and could give me a good advantage. I unscrew the bulb, tear off the lampshade, and toss them to the side. As soon as Gage comes back, I'm going to give it to him. I wish it was longer so I would have more reach when I swing it, but it will have to do.

I can't figure out how the lights work in this place. There are no switches anywhere. I wait by the door, unsure how long Gage will be. After some time, the lights dim and eventually flick off, submerging me in complete darkness. They must be motion-activated. I lean my body against the wall, not making a move. I want the lights off to catch him by surprise.

Wait, do I?

If I can knock him out and keep the door open, I can escape. I have no idea what the code is for any of these rooms, but I'll figure something out when it comes to the door leading to Logan's cell. We're getting out of here tonight.

I can't decide if I made the right choice by telling Gage the truth. I wanted so badly to tell him, but now that it's out there, I'm not sure how to feel about it. Logan's going to be pissed. But what other choice did I have? I don't know what Gage would have done to Logan if I hadn't said what I did.

But the second he walked out that door, I felt my entire world crashing down on me.

Is Logan aware that Gage and his father were present the night we lost everything? I doubt it. Harlow told me that Logan said there were more men there he didn't recognize as Victor's, and he was right. They weren't. They were Frank's men, and Gage was one of them. He would have tried to kill Gage if he knew that. According to Aric and Victor both, they were there for one thing. Me.

The thought alone of what could have happened all those years ago makes my body shake. I may have just revealed who we both are to our parents' killer.

The door unlatches and I brace myself as it starts to open. I rear back and swing the lamp as hard as I can. It slams into the doorframe. *No! I can't lose this battle.*

I immediately rear back but then the lights come on, blinding me. I don't slow my momentum. I step toward the doorway and put everything I have into my next swing. This one has to count.

With everything I have left in my body, I swing the lamp as hard as I can, but I hit the doorframe again. I want to cry at missing him twice, but I have to stay strong for not only myself but for Logan too. Before I can pull back, Gage steps forward and grabs the base of the lamp. It starts a tug-of-war between us that's shortly lived before he rips my only hope from my hands. I bolt forward, trying to run out the door, but his large arm swings around my waist. He hoists me into the air and kicks the door shut.

The damn door latches shut without issue. Any hope I had leaves me that very second. The lamp crashes to the floor as he carries me into the living room, carefully setting me on my feet. I'm breathing heavily, and it isn't until now that I realize my cheeks are wet from crying.

I have no idea what I'm going to see in Gage's arctic-blue eyes, but what I find there isn't what I expect. I don't see hate or anger. I see regret. I see the man I let into my heart. The only man I could open my heart to is staring at me with remorse.

"Did you do it?" My voice cracks, the question coming out choked with pain. And then I'm screaming. "Did you kill my brother like you killed my parents?"

Shock flashes across his face and for a split second, I see the truth. I want to deny it, to convince myself that Aric was lying, but deep down, I knew. Gage and his father were there that fateful night. My heart clenches. I didn't want to believe it, but the pieces are falling into place and I can't turn away from them anymore.

"Your brother is fine." His voice is steady and he never once breaks eye contact.

I let out a shaky breath of relief, the weight on my chest loosening just enough to let some air back in. *Logan is okay.* That means there is still a chance.

"But you tortured him, didn't you?" He reaches for my hand, but I pull it away. "Answer the question, Gage."

"I didn't torture him. We got into a fight and I put him in that cell. He hasn't even missed a meal since he was in there." He takes a step closer, his stare intense. "People I have tortured look a lot worse than a black eye."

On reflection, outside of needing a shower, Logan didn't look tortured. But still... "You fought him like you fought Aric?"

"No, I only clocked him one good time." When I cross my arms, he continues. "I thought you two were a couple."

My eyebrows knit together as I rear my head back. "What? Why would you think that?"

Gage drags his large hand down his face. "I saw you together at the Oasis, down at the lake." He shakes his head. "I could tell you two were close."

My thoughts turn back to that day. *He was watching me?* "Were you the one who called him?"

"I couldn't watch for one more second."

My lips part. I can understand why he felt that way. "And you didn't know he was my brother." Gage doesn't respond. He doesn't need to.

"Did you kill my parents?"

"No."

"Did your father... Was it him?"

He doesn't flinch. He doesn't hesitate. "Yes."

More tears fall from my eyes, hot and relentless. It feels like a sick joke. I'm in love with the son of the man who killed my parents. It makes me sick to my stomach. I stumble backward as he moves closer until my back is against a wall.

"My mother left my father to be with Victor." His words come out rushed. "We went there that night to take you... as a bargaining chip for my mother." He flips his hat around backward to get closer to my face. "We knew Victor wanted an arranged marriage between you and Aric. My father wanted to use you to get my mother, and I did too."

I feel every word hit me like a blow. He places each of his hands on the wall next to my face and I can feel his urgency, his need for me to understand. "But I promise you, Kali, I would have made sure you stayed safe throughout everything."

He removes his hands from the wall and cradles my face gently, searching me for some sign that I'm hearing him. I want to believe him, but my heart aches too much. I've missed his touch, but I don't know how to forgive him. He pulls me to him, but I shake my head, raising my fists to beat on his chest with the overwhelming rush of emotions that crash over me. A sob tears through me, loud and ragged, as everything starts to ache inside.

"How unfair can life get?" The words spill from my lips in a mix of fury and sorrow. "A man desperate to get his mother back... and in the process, he made mine end up dead."

Gage's face twists in pain. His voice cracks when he responds. "That wasn't the plan. No one was supposed to get hurt that night. I killed my father minutes after he killed your parents." His confession hangs in the air, heavy with guilt. "I swear to you, no one was supposed to die."

I freeze, the world going quiet around us as his words sink in. I stare at him, trying to process everything I've lost, everything I've had to bury inside.

But Gage... He's lost too.

We all lost so much that night. Gage lost not only his father but his mother as well.

"No one was supposed to get hurt that night. God, please believe me," he pleads, pulling me to his chest. I let him this time, feeling the warmth of his embrace.

I cry.

For everyone.

I cry for Logan. For the loss of our parents, the loss of what could have been, the loss of what will never be. I cry for my parents and the greed that surrounded them. For the life they chose to lead, which ultimately spelled their demise. And I cry for Gage. For being the son of a monster. For having to kill his own father, only to learn that his mom killed herself.

My legs feel weak. I'm not sure how long I'll be able to stand. But Gage feels my resolve weakening, and without a word, he picks me up in his arms and carries me down the hallway.

Everything is too much. I lean against him, letting myself take comfort in his presence.

He lays us down in the bedroom, never releasing his hold on me.

I grip his shirt and allow myself to cry against his large chest. I allow the warmth of his arms to give me the solace that I need so much right now. He kisses the top of my head and hugs me tightly, and I take it without a second thought.

None of us chose this life. Not Logan, not me, not Gage, not Conner, not Aric. We were all born into it without a say in the matter. And now we're all left to pick up the pieces of what's been broken.

Gage risked his life to end his heartless father's reign of terror. In that moment, he brought justice for everyone his father hurt, my parents included.

I send a silent *thank you* to Gage's mother for telling him to keep pounding those punching bags, to stay grounded. Through all the evil his father was, she kept the light burning deep within her son. I know she would have been proud of him.

My body is shutting down. I can feel it. The fight has drained me completely, leaving me weak and vulnerable. I snuggle deep into Gage. "Please don't leave." I don't know why I say it, but I do.

"Never," Gage responds.

I fall asleep feeling weak and vulnerable, but I take comfort in the fact that for once, I'm not alone in it.

Chapter Twenty-Six

Gage.

I sense the second Kali lets go and falls into a deep sleep. My strong, brave little lion. I love watching her sleep. Her body has completely relaxed against mine. Her grip has lightened on my shirt, but her head is nuzzled deep against my chest. I feel like a king with my arms wrapped around her. Ever since the first day I laid eyes on her in that dirty back alley, facing off against Ricardo without hesitation, I knew she was different.

Link may think she's not strong enough to stand by our sides, but I would have to disagree. He didn't get to see her when Victor's men blew Fletcher's office. I guess technically I didn't get to see her either, but that's exactly my point.

She has more loyalty than most people I have met... in any capacity. When she's cornered, instead of breaking down and crying, she tells off-the-wall stories that suck you in before you even know what's going on.

The next thing you know, she's gone, and you're standing there like a damn idiot. I should know. She pulled that shit on me the first day I met her.

I pull my arm from underneath her and unwillingly climb out of bed. Since we are lying on top of the comforter, I place a blanket across her body and kiss her temple. I pick up her left hand and slowly pull Aric's ring off her finger.

As tempted as I am to stay with her, my work isn't done yet.

Five minutes later, I enter Aric's cell. He is leaning against the far wall, sitting on the cot, staring right back at me. He could be on vacation in the Hamptons; he's completely relaxed. He smiles largely at me. That only pisses me off. Conner's most recent visit went unappreciated, I see. A tray of food sits off to the side, untouched.

I unlock the cell door and grab a chair. I swing it around so I'm sitting in front of him with nothing between us. I place my elbows on my knees and stare at my stepbrother. He raises a brow, clearly surprised by this. He needs to understand I have no fear of him.

"How's Kali?" he asks.

His simple question makes me want to curl my hands into fists. When I was younger, I would have already been out of this chair and Aric would be black, blue, and bleeding. If there's one thing my piece-of-shit father taught me, it's how to wield cold, calculated patience. And I have plenty.

"She's certainly not worried about you," I respond, tossing the ring over to him.

Aric catches it and holds it, apparently deep in thought. "She really is something special. Different. Like the first breath of fresh air in the morning light."

A growl rumbles through my chest at his words about my little lion. I feel like I'm sitting on the edge of a cliff, about to say fuck it and beat the shit out of him again for even thinking about her.

"How'd you do it?" he asks.

I'm not sure I follow. "Do what?"

He exhales a deep breath. "How'd you make her fall in love with you?"

I lean back into my chair, surprised by his question and even more surprised by my answer. "I have no idea." I bulldozed into her life. Into every part of it. She's like a drug. You take one hit and before you know it, she's all you can ever think about. I want to ask him if she said she loved me, but I refuse to go there with him.

"If you ever hurt her, I'll kill you," he says, his face etched in stone. He means every word, and it widens my smile. It seems she can bring any bad boy to his knees.

I nod as the door opens and Conner walks in. He points at the camera in the corner of the cell and winks.

Aric's smirk pulls at the corners of his lips as he watches Conner enter the cell and lean against the bars with that typical lazy confidence of his. Conner is a big man, bigger than both of us. The thick scar cutting down his face only intensifies his size. Aric is probably assuming that Conner is here for backup, but he would be wrong. Conner is here because he knew and loved my mother deeply. He wants the same answers I do on why my mother killed herself all those years ago.

Jealousy lingers in my chest, though I try to keep it buried. Both men spent more time with my mother than I did near the end of her life. Conner was a constant at our house, and my father never cared when he would help my mother out.

My voice comes out as raw as I'm feeling. "Why did my mother kill herself?" Was it because of Victor? Or was it because of me and how much I disappointed her? It's hard to say which would be worse.

Aric sits quietly. He's assessing me, his gaze studying me with unsettling intensity, like he's trying to read me in ways I don't want him to.

"Why do you care?" His tone is casual, but there's a bite underneath it. He leans forward as if testing me. "Angela told me about you and your brother. How Frank infused evil deep into your lost souls. She confessed that she couldn't bear to watch you sink any further into the hell you were heading for."

His words cut deep, because I know he speaks the truth. That's exactly what I wanted my mother to see. Frank took the training of his heir very seriously and would beat my mother if I or my brother went soft from her love.

There was no room in Frank's heart for love. When my mother and father first got together, she had no idea what kind of man he truly was. He wore a mask in front of her, a wolf hiding in sheep's clothing. Frank impregnated her within the first month and she had me nine months later. Then he knew he had her locked down. He no longer had to play his games and hide the devil inside.

It didn't take me long to figure out how to keep my mother off his radar. I put on the act of a lifetime every time she came to me. I closed myself off, not allowing her to see she owned my heart.

"The only way to beat the devil is by playing the devil's game better," I say. I know damn well he plays the same game with his father, using the bored act all the time.

Aric's expression fills with understanding. "I made sure she was never hurt when she was there."

I feel anger rising inside me. "Never hurt? She jumped off a fucking cliff and killed herself. Where were you that night?" I roar, standing so quickly that the chair clatters against the bars.

"I was with her," Aric responds with boredom in his voice.

I lunge at him, grabbing his shirt and pulling him up so we are standing face-to-face. "Did you push her? Did you walk her to that fucking cliff and push her off?" My grip tightens with every word that spits out of me.

"I saved her that night like you should've done."

A bitter laugh leaves me. "Saved her? Saved her! By killing her?" I twist his body and slam him hard into the wall.

Unfazed, he replies, "She might have died that night, but she was also reborn."

I press my forearm into his throat, restricting his airflow. "What the fuck does that mean?"

Aric laughs and chokes out his answer. "She's living the life she should've always lived."

"At the bottom of the sea?" I snarl.

"No, in Ireland," he responds.

I pause. I glare into his eyes, and he meets mine full force. If this is some sick, twisted game he's playing with me, he will be begging for death by the time I finish with him. A hand comes around my bicep, and Conner pulls my arm off Aric's throat. I allow it.

Aric drops to his knees and drags in deep, ragged breaths. I almost killed him and I didn't even realize it. "You have ten seconds to start talking, Aric. I'm not playing your games."

Aric, being the dick he is, takes all of ten seconds to gather himself before he straightens. "She's alive and well. She resides in Ireland and recently started dating again."

I stagger back a couple of steps as if his words have physically struck me. "That can't be true."

Aric nods. "Just like Kali doesn't deserve this lifestyle, neither does your mother. Well, I guess *our* mother, since she's still technically my stepmom."

His jab about being family doesn't affect me. "Prove it."

"Do you have my phone?" Aric asks.

Conner nods and leaves to retrieve it.

I don't take my eyes off Aric. If he's lied to me about this, I will draw out his death slowly and painfully.

Conner appears and hands me Aric's phone. I wonder if this small electronic device could possibly hold proof that my mother is alive. He'd better hope it does.

He leans forward, taking it out of my hand and unlocking it. He taps the screen a few times and flips it back toward me. I reach out and take it, my hands shaking from the truth in front of me.

My mother Angela smiles as she leans against a man I've never seen before. Time has greeted her, but not in a bad way. She looks as beautiful as the last time I saw her. Her auburn hair is longer than it was. The bright smile on her heart-shaped face is one I have missed so much.

I peer at Aric, who's leaning against the back wall. "Who's the guy?"

"Cillian Fitzpatrick. I've already done a complete background check. They live in Wexford County. He owns a pub and brews beer. He was married once before but lost his first wife to cancer. He has two grown sons he raised on his own and hasn't dated much until he met Angela. He was arrested one time back when he was nineteen for getting into a fight with his first wife's boyfriend at the time."

My jaw unclenches, thankful that Aric's kept a close eye on her when it wasn't his responsibility to do so. It's a cold reminder of another way I failed my mother. "What does she do?"

"She does the paperwork for both of his businesses. They live a normal life. Safe and happy."

I nod, feeling grateful. "Does she know I killed Frank?"

Aric shakes his head. "She has no clue Frank is dead, only that she doesn't need to worry about watching her back."

I can't stop staring at my mother's smile in the photo, one I haven't seen in many years. The knowledge that she is truly happy penetrates my limbs with warmth.

I right the chair, sit down, and run my hand down my face as Aric walks over to the cot and drops onto it. "*That's* why you weren't there with Victor the night we went to take Kali."

Aric brings a knee up and rests his elbow on it. "It was the only way I could get my father far enough away to fake her death and get her out."

I nod in understanding. "Why did you call me and tell me what Victor's plan was? Why did I need to be there?"

He grabs the water bottle from the food tray he's been ignoring and takes a drink. "Because I didn't trust my father's men with Kali. I knew you wouldn't let anything happen to her. Your mother might've told me what your father was trying to turn you into, but she also told me she could see the mask you wore in front of her."

Relief floods my body. She knew that everything I did, I did for show.

"Now I need your help," Aric says, dragging my attention to this cell.

Aric has never needed much help from anyone, so my curiosity rises. As much as I want to tell him to fuck off and never deal with him again, I can't. He was right when he said he did what I should've done years ago. I should have gotten my mother out. He did it, though, and for that, I owe him.

"What do you need?"

"At some point soon, I need your help dismantling my father's empire."

Chapter Twenty-Seven

Kali.

I wake slowly, not sure what time it is. There are no windows in this room—or clocks, for that matter. I roll over to find the other side of the bed empty.

I flip my legs over the bed in a rush. A piece of paper floats to the ground below. I lean down and grab it.

You and Logan are safe. Your phone is on the charger. Take a shower. There are clean clothes in the dresser for you. Come out when you're ready. Beer bitch in full effect.

G.

Beer bitch in full effect? I have no idea what he means, but I release a grateful breath and make my way to the bathroom. I shower and brush my teeth with the brand-new toothbrush I find on the vanity.

Wrapping a towel around my body, I head to the dresser. After pulling every drawer open to only find Gage's clothes, I roll my eyes but can't stop the smile. I dress quickly and unplug my phone. Now that I finally have my phone again, I don't waste time. Unlocking it, I pull up Harlow's number.

"You about gave me a heart attack!" Harlow exclaims as soon as she picks up.

A smile tugs at my lips just from hearing her voice. It's a small comfort in a world that's felt upside down for too long. "How's Fletcher doing?" I ask, trying to ignore the knot in my stomach.

"He's in good spirits. He has a long road ahead of him with therapy, but he'll get through it."

I collapse on the edge of the bed. "Thank God," I whisper, the weight of my guilt pressing down on me. "I didn't want to leave him, Harlow. Please believe me. His desk was too heavy and he was telling me to run."

"Hey, it's okay," she responds gently. "We all understand what happened. Fletcher's tough. He's going to be okay. But what about you? How are you holding up?"

I release a breath, thankful she understands, but it doesn't diminish the guilt I still feel. "What do you know?"

"I just spoke with Gage a little while ago," Harlow says softly. "He told me you were pretty upset last night."

I lean back into the pillows, staring at the white ceiling. "I was. It was a lot to take in. So much more than I was ready for."

Her voice softens further. "Do you need me to come get you?"

"No, I'm okay." I hesitate for a second, trying to figure out how to express what I'm wrestling with. "I just don't know...

I don't know how my parents would feel about me being with Gage, knowing his father was the one who killed them."

There's a long pause on the other end of the line before Harlow speaks again. "Kali, don't do this to yourself. Your mother... she would be happy for you. She'd be cheering you on. Gage is a good man. Your parents might not be here physically, but I promise you, they are with you spiritually and they want you to have happiness. They *are* proud of you and Logan."

Her words hit deeper than I expected. Given how close Harlow and my mother were, I trust her. "Thank you, Harlow. For everything you've always been to me."

"You don't ever have to thank me for that," she says with a soft laugh. "I love you like a sister. Always."

A genuine smile tugs at my lips as the tension in my chest loosens. "I love you too. Is Fletcher near you? I need to talk to him about everything that happened."

"He's asleep, but I can have him call you as soon as he wakes up."

"Okay, yeah. Thank you."

There's a pause, then Harlow adds, "Kali, you deserve your happily ever after too. Don't let what Gage's father did destroy what you two have. Don't let that shadow ruin what could be a beautiful life together."

My throat tightens. I swallow roughly. "I won't."

"Good," she responds firmly. "Now get that barracuda back in you and start enjoying your life. There's nothing holding you back anymore."

When the call ends, I sit in silence, water pricking at the edges of my eyes. She's right. I don't have to hide anymore. There will be no more lies, no more pretending to be someone I'm not. I can finally be me again.

I pocket my phone. I slowly turn the door handle, opening the bedroom door. Food sizzles in a nearby pan as I make my way down the hallway, my stomach growling at the heavenly smell.

I expect to find Gage in the kitchen, but I don't. What I find is even better. Logan stands at the stove. The kitchen is filled with the comforting scent of simmering chicken and herbs.

"Logan," I say.

He turns, his face lighting up. He sets down the wooden spoon. We walk into each other's arms and hug tightly.

He must have showered, because he has fresh clothes on and smells much better than he did earlier. He pulls me away, his hands on my shoulders. He's not tense like he normally is. He looks relaxed and happy.

I take in the greenish-yellow bruise under his eye. "Are you okay?"

He smiles genuinely. "This looks worse than it is. You should ask to see Gage's ribs." When I gasp in surprise, Logan chuckles. "I wanted to thank you."

"For what?"

"For being strong. For being brave. For not listening to your idiotic brother when he told you not to say a word."

I laugh. "You can be a pain in the ass sometimes."

We grin at each other and pull in for another hug.

"All right, enough! Link, we're ready for another beer," Gage hollers from the living room.

We pull apart as Gage walks into the kitchen.

Logan gives me a rueful smile. "I'm now the beer bitch for the foreseeable future."

"Does that mean you're my beer bitch too?"

Gage wraps his arm around my shoulder. "You're damn straight it does. We're going to need three beers." Gage takes my hand and leads me to the living room.

My ears perk up at his response for three beers. Does this mean Aric is here too? When I raise my eyes from our interlocked fingers, I see Conner drinking the last of his beer and the sting of disappointment hits me. What have they done to Aric? That's when I notice the ring is missing from my finger.

"What is it?" Gage asks, taking notice of the panic growing inside me.

"Where's Aric?"

Gage tilts his head to the side. He's probably assuming I'm asking for other reasons.

I clarify quickly. "You can't hurt him, Gage. He helped me. He took me to Chicago to keep me from his father's clutches. And he knew you were coming for us. He planned it. He wanted to get me back to my brother and—"

Gage places his finger over my lips, silencing me. "I know. He's in the other apartment getting cleaned up. We'll meet with him afterward."

This warehouse is much larger than I thought. Gage drops his finger and grabs my hand, leading me into the living room. There's a boxing match on.

"What the fuck? No one's been good since Ronny Jax retired early," Conner mumbles at the television and it makes me smile. I wonder if he was ever a boxer.

Logan appears with four beers and passes one over to Conner, who is sitting on a loveseat. Gage and I take ours and sit on the other couch next to each other. He places an arm around my shoulder and pulls me to him. The warmth from his body and his minty scent surround me.

I glance nervously at Logan, not sure how he's going to handle Gage's arm around me, but he smiles and turns his attention to the boxing match. Here we all sit together, drinking beers and forgetting every horrible that has ever happened to us.

All except Aric. I don't see Aric as the type of guy who watches boxing or even drinks beer, but I'm sure it would be better than sitting alone. I'm not sure how to bring up letting Aric come over now, but I have to do something.

"Where's the other apartment? I need to check on Aric."

Gage turns to face me. "I'll have Conner bring him here." Once a commercial hits, Gage asks Conner to get Aric. Conner, a man of few words, grunts and leaves a moment later.

During the commercial break, Logan heads to the kitchen to work on dinner.

Gage and I are alone on the couch together. His hat faces forward and he's sexy as ever. I ask, "Logan's beer bitch punishment is for lying to you?" His dimples are making my ovaries weep. I bring the beer to my lips to settle the heat below.

Gage says, "It was either that or kill him."

I choke on my beer, not sure he's bullshitting.

He takes a long pull from the bottle and makes a dramatic "Ah" sound before saying, "But this option tastes much better." He takes in my shocked face and adds, "What? Too soon?"

I laugh. "Yes! Way too soon." He's in such a great mood, it's contagious, and it makes me want to soak up his mojo. "You're happy."

He nods. "I got my little lion back."

I grin. I love my nickname.

"Are you ready for your present?" Gage asks.

I stiffen at his question. The last time he asked me that, his gift was my brother locked in a cell with nothing but a disgusting old cot and a toilet in the corner.

"This one is an actual present." He leans over the arm of the couch and reveals a bag that must have been hidden beside him on the floor.

My interest piqued, I hand my beer off to him and grab the bag. I peer inside and pull out a mystery gift wrapped in white tissue. I tear away the tissue and open the box to see a beautiful necklace. The pendant is silver with small diamonds, a symbol identical to the one on Gage's hat. A Dara knot. It's simple and exactly my style.

He takes the necklace and puts it around my neck. His smile grows as he looks at the Dara knot displayed on my chest.

"Do you remember what the Dara knot represents?" he asks.

I nod, trying to keep my tears at bay.

He smiles, his damned sexy dimples making an appearance. I hate how sexy this man is. I have a feeling the pepper spray I've always held onto over the years is going to come into play a lot more when women flock to him.

"The Dara knot... Everything it means... That's exactly what you did for me. I called upon the ancient Celts to give me the inner strength I needed, and they delivered you."

Gage leans in and kisses me gently, stealing my breath and giving me his. The warmth of his lips ignites a spark deep inside me, a fire that spreads throughout my chest and settles in my stomach like butterflies. His minty spring scent envelops me as I lose myself in the sweetness of the moment. I melt like butter in his arms, the softness of his touch grounding me while the electricity between us makes everything else fade away. For the first time in seven years, I feel at peace, as if the world stopped spinning just for this moment, leaving only the feel of his heartbeat against mine. Steady and sure. Every part of me hums with the tenderness of the kiss, as if time itself has slowed to savor this perfect moment.

He pulls away and licks his lips before handing me my beer. He slings his arm around my shoulders, tugging me to him.

The front door beeps, then opens. Aric walks in with Conner and scans the room. Relief shines in his eyes when they land on me.

True to Gage's word, Aric is clean, apparently unharmed apart from the beating he took from Gage on the island... and wearing clothes that are not his. I bite the inside of my cheek to hide my grin. I don't think I have ever seen him in street clothes, and I doubt anyone else has either. He was probably born wearing a three-piece suit. He looks much younger in sweatpants and a T-shirt.

"Beer bitch, we need one for Aric," Gage yells as Conner takes his original seat near the TV.

Aric scrunches his nose at the beer offering and doesn't say anything. He sits next to me on the sectional. He checks out my outfit, which consists of Gage's clothes that are way too big and the new necklace around my neck. "Wildflower," he says with a smile.

That catches Gage's attention because he turns toward Aric and his grip tightens around my shoulders. "Back it on up, brother. I would hate to put you back in a cell."

Aric rolls his eyes. "Better stay on top of your game, because the second you slip up, I'm going to be right there, waiting for my Red Balls."

Now it's Gage's turn to scrunch his nose. I stifle a laugh at the memory of Victor's face when I told him that story and the absolute disgust written all over it.

Logan comes in, handing a beer to Aric and bringing another one to Conner. He settles in to watch the rest of the match. There's still tension between them.

One of the boxers throws an uppercut, knocking the other fighter to the mat.

"Fuck yes!" Aric grunts at the same time as Logan and Conner groan like they're in extreme pain.

I would have never guessed in a million years that this was how things would turn out. All of us together, getting along. Well, for the most part. For the first time since my parents were murdered, I consider painting again. I have missed it so much.

We finish watching the match then eat some amazing chicken tortellini—thanks to Logan's mad cooking skills—and I feel more relaxed than I have in a long time.

It reminds me of the nights Logan would come to my place and I would cook for him. I had no idea that he could cook this well. I assumed he didn't know how. Moving forward, though, Logan will be doing most of the cooking.

After dinner, I hang with Logan and Conner in the living room, watching more boxing matches. Aric and Gage remain at the table, discussing their next moves. Aric couldn't finish the first beer Logan gave him, so after Gage gave him crap and called him a pussy, he grabbed a bottle of dark liquor and poured him a drink. The bottle now has a nice-sized dent in it.

"Is it over now?" I ask Logan.

His eyes lift from his cell phone to me. "Are you tired of being Allie Smith?"

I nod. "Are you tired of being Link?"

He shakes his head and I laugh, hitting him playfully on the shoulder. He smiles, but his attention is on his phone, his fingers dancing across the screen.

"Who are you messaging?"

"Harlow. She was asking when we're heading to the Oasis."

I lean in to look at his phone, but he pulls it out of my view. I can't tell whether he did it intentionally. "Is Fletcher awake?"

Logan rolls his eyes.

I frown at his response. Logan and Fletcher would hit it off as great friends, the computer nerds they are. Regardless, an eye roll as a response to how someone is doing after a bomb went off is harsh.

Logan remains fixed on his phone, so I lift off the couch and head to the dining room. I attempt to sit next to Gage at the table, but he isn't having that. He wraps his arm around my waist and pulls me onto his lap.

Aric's gaze sharpens, but he chooses not to say anything.

"What plans have you two figured out?" I ask, wrapping my arm around Gage's wide shoulders.

Aric's eyebrows lift in surprise. "Since when have you been involved in the family business?"

I like that he said *family*. "Since I was blindsided. Listen, I can bring a lot of value to our team. What should we call ourselves? *The A-Team*? Oh! How about the *Aconitum* Gang?"

"What the hell is *Aconitum*?" Aric asks.

It makes me grin that I know something he doesn't. "It's one of the most poisonous flowers in the world. Some people call it wolfsbane, but I like *Aconitum* better. A few drops of juice from the beautiful flower's roots and you are guaranteed quick heart failure and cardiac muscle paralysis." I smile largely, looking between both men.

"God, you're sexy as fuck," Gage says.

Aric mutters, "Damn straight."

I lean in to kiss Gage on the cheek, but his fingers catch my chin and guide my lips to his. I drag my hand across his chest, feeling his taut muscles underneath his shirt. I could get lost in his kiss for the rest of my life.

Aric wastes no time clearing his throat as we pull apart.

"So, what do you say? I can so make a tea with *Aconitum* drops in it for Victor to drink."

Aric shakes his head.

Gage laughs. "Not this time, little lion."

I put on my pouty face and huff out a breath, crossing my arms. "I'm not going to be Sideline Sally any longer."

Gage's dimples are on full display. "It's not our fight."

I bite my thumb, trying to understand how Victor isn't our fight. *Any* person has a reason to take down Victor.

Gage pulls my nail from between my lips as Aric adds, "Angela's alive and well."

"Who?" I ask, turning my attention to Aric.

"My stepmother Angela. Gage's mom."

How can this even be possible? My heart rate spikes at what this means for Gage.

"The night I was supposed to be with my father at your home, I stayed back to fake her death and help her escape from Victor."

I remember Aric's words when I asked him what he was doing that night: *I was saving a lost soul.*

There's a softness in Gage's eyes I haven't seen before. It's as if he can breathe for the first time in forever. My arms break out in gooseflesh at the sheer depth of what this moment means to him. He spent years believing his mother's death was his fault. This is truly a miracle—a second chance for him and his mother.

"When are we going to see her? Oh my God, this is going to be amazing! You might even have siblings you don't know about! You're right. Screw Victor. Aric can take care of that. We need to start planning. We have to start packing. Does she live in Washington?"

His large arm wraps around my neck, and he pulls me into a deep kiss, stopping my words, but answering in his own way. He's just as happy about this as I am. We pull apart and stare at one another. It's the feeling of the phoenix rising above the ashes.

"Where does she live?" I ask again, needing more details.

He shakes his head. Apparently he decides to dump a bucket of ice-cold water on the burning ashes before the phoenix can even rise, because he says, "I'm not going to see her."

I rear back, shocked by his response.

Aric gets up from the table, giving us the privacy we need.

"I don't understand," I splutter. "Why wouldn't you want to see her again?"

He takes his hat off and turns it around, his finger tracing the lines of the Dara knot. "Just because I killed my father doesn't excuse what I did to her for all those years. I ignored her. I intentionally made her feel like she meant nothing to me."

"You were doing it to protect her."

"That still doesn't make it right, Kali. She's started a new life, one without me, and from what I can tell, she's happy. The last thing I want to do is bring anything bad into her life."

"She would never look at you like that. She cares about you, Gage. She loves you. That's exactly why she gave you that hat with the symbol. She wanted you to break through, conquer the evil, shine like she knew you always would... and then go find her!"

His eyes won't meet mine, but I refuse to let him ruin a future with his mother in it. I place my hand on top of his, stopping him from tracing the outline. "Look at me. Please."

I hold my breath as he slowly raises his artic-blue eyes to mine. He seems to be at a crossroads, not knowing which way to go.

I'm going to make this real easy for him.

"I would give anything to have my mother or father back, even if only for a day. This doesn't happen, Gage. People don't get second chances like this, and you would be a fool to turn it down. I may not know your mother, but I know you." I place my hand on his chest atop his fast-beating heart. "I know the heart you carry inside was loved and nurtured by your mother. And I know that seeing her son again would be one of the best things to ever happen to her."

He swallows. I give him time to process my words. I understand his fears. I would probably have similar ones if I walked in his shoes. Just the fact that he's afraid of disrupting her life shows how much he loves her.

He slowly places his hat back on before smiling at me with those damn dimples of his. "Before you start packing... We have some unfinished business to attend to."

In one fluid motion, Gage picks me up, tosses me over his shoulder, and carries me down the hallway to the bedroom.

Gage McCollin might wear a coat of armor around him, making the cruelest men fear him, but underneath all that steel is a man worthy of the greatest love.

He kicks the bedroom door closed and tosses me on the bed. I bounce on the mattress as a laugh breaks from my lips. Gage tugs his shirt off, killing my laugh. I lick my suddenly dry lips. This man is built like a dream, his body covered in hard muscles. He's a masterpiece.

He slowly crawls onto the bed between my parted legs and settles his body on top of mine. His hot breath fans across my face.

He murmurs, "I love you, Kali Marie Keeyes."

His whispered confessions have my heart soaring.

I place my hands on his bare chest and slide them up before wrapping my arms around his neck. "I love you too, Gage Alexander McCollin."

He grins like he's won the lottery. "Say it again."

My cheeks heat at his burning need to hear me say it again. "I love you, Gage Alexander McCollin."

His lips capture mine as we take each other to another world, one that only holds him and me.

Epilogue

Kali.

We enter the pub, a ding sounding above the door, alerting the staff to our arrival. The place is more packed than either of us anticipated. Gage tugs my hand and we head to a small table in the corner that overlooks the cute village.

His hand is wrapped tightly around mine as if I'm giving him the strength to be here. It took a couple of weeks to work out the plans to come here, and I couldn't be prouder of him.

He helps me take off my coat and drapes it over a chair. As we sit down, a young server walks up to our table and sets down a bucket of peanuts, along with menus. "Welcome to Cillian's Pub. What can I get you two started with?" she asks.

Gage orders an Irish whiskey. I debate ordering a Guinness—it would be the same drink order from our first date. At the thought of how heavy the beer was, though, I decide on a glass of sangria. She bounces away.

Gage turns his hat so it's facing forward. I'm not sure if he's trying to hide his face or stand out. I don't see his mom or her boyfriend anywhere. Aric told us what day and time to come here. I almost couldn't get Gage to leave the hotel.

"Are you feeling better now that we're here?" I ask, taking a peanut and breaking it open.

His beautiful dimples appear. He plucks the peanut I just dug out of the shell and pops it into his mouth. Laughing, I toss the shell at him and grab another one.

"I just hope I'm making the right choice by coming here."

"Your mother will want to see you. She will be proud of who you are today."

Gage dressed casually today, wearing a hoodie and dark jeans. He debated whether he should wear the hat. I knocked him upside his stubborn head and walked out the door when he asked me what I thought he should do.

The server returns with our drinks. I doubt we will be ordering any food on this visit, but hopefully we will next time, because it smells delicious.

"I don't know if you should have worn that."

I glance at my outfit. The weather is much cooler here, so I have a cute pale pink cashmere sweater hanging off one of my shoulders. The necklace Gage bought me rests right above the slanted hem. "Why? What's wrong with it?"

"I'm barely containing myself over here with your collarbone on display."

My face flushes with heat at the memory of his love bites last night all over my body. "You are insatiable, Mr. McCollin."

"As are you, Mrs. McCollin."

If it were up to Gage, we would already be married. I've had to stay strong in resisting his charming ways and make him wait to tie the knot. He hasn't made it easy, and he knows I'm close to caving in.

Gage and I have been staying in between our homes in Seattle. We've been considering buying a new home, one we can call ours, but have yet to find one that feels just right. Time is ticking, though. I plan on starting my own wildflower garden next spring and would like to be settled before then.

We haven't been able to find information on Sofia. Logan hacked into a few systems but couldn't locate anything. Gage was able to make headway with an inside informant. He wouldn't give details of her whereabouts but told us that she is checked upon frequently and is doing well.

Maybe God will one day let us cross paths again.

The bubbly young server returns to check on us. We haven't even touched our drinks yet. I hold my sangria up for a toast.

Gage's attention locks onto something outside the window and I follow his line of sight to see a couple walking across the street toward the pub. They're both laughing as the man twirls the woman around before kissing her. The moment is intimate. Watching them feels as if I'm infringing on their special moment, but I can't pull my eyes away. He releases her, grabbing her hand and turning her toward the pub. She's beautiful, with long auburn hair and crystal clear artic-blue eyes. This must be Angela.

I grab Gage's hand as they walk inside. The person who must be Cillian leans in and gives Angela a light kiss before helping her out of her red coat and walking behind the bar. Angela sits and Cillian hands her a water. Our young server approaches her and excitedly tells her something, though I can't hear what. Her eyes dance with amusement as she listens on.

Gage's eyes grow soft. He's happy seeing her happy. A smile tugs at his lips. He grabs my hand and says, "Thank you."

"It was all you. I just gave the nudge you needed." I smile as he raises our interlocked hands and kisses mine.

I twist in my chair. Angela's gaping at Gage. She slowly stands, her hand clutching her chest. At the change in her, Cillian looks over to see Gage and me. She takes a small step toward us as Gage stands. She no longer hesitates and runs straight into his arms, crying tears of joy at seeing her son again after too many years.

I cover my mouth, trying to keep my sobs low as they embrace each other. It's one of the most beautiful moments I've ever witnessed, and it makes me miss my mom.

Cillian appears beside Angela as they pull apart and she wipes her cheeks. "Cillian, this is Gage. My oldest son."

Cillian smiles widely and reaches out his hand to shake Gage's. "It's an honor to finally meet you." Cillian's reaction shows that Angela has spoken only highly of Gage over the years.

Gage's tense body is now completely relaxed. His worries and concerns have melted away. "Thank you for looking after my mother."

Angela's smiling face turns to mine as Gage pulls me to his side. "Mom, I want you to meet my wife, Kali."

Angela squeals as I ram my elbow into his ribs. "It's not official yet" is all I can get out before Angela pulls me in for a tight hug, her tears flowing again. She pulls away, holding my shoulders. "Oh my, you are so beautiful, Kali." Her smile widens. "Finally, I have a daughter!" She tugs me in for a hug, both of us laughing now.

"Come, come. Let's all sit. We have much to catch up on." Angela takes my hand and pulls us to a corner table, much larger than the one we were seated at.

My heart hasn't felt this full in a long time.

Angela, who insists I call her Mom, has been an angel to me. We spend a couple of days shopping, cooking, and talking. She loves to garden as well. She reminds me a lot of my mother, minus the wine obsession. I can't help but wonder if my mom sent her to me. It feels like she did.

I've made up my mind. When we arrive at the hotel, I'm telling Gage I want to move here, to Ireland. It just feels right, like this place has woven itself into my soul. I don't think I could walk away from it. Washington will always be there for visits, but this... this is where we belong.

Tonight, it's only Gage and me. He bought me a stunning white summer dress that rests just above my knees. I argued that September is *not* the time of the year to be wearing a summer dress in Ireland, but he doesn't seem to care. He bought me a wool coat to keep me warm.

We have a perfect dinner at a gastropub and walk along the waterside. The rhythmic sound of the waves lapping against the shore only confirms my decision to stay.

We make our way back to the car. I thought we were heading to the hotel, but Gage pulls up to a business with a large sign. Ink Studio. I shoot a wordless question at him, but he gets out of the car before I can ask. We enter the building to a buzzing noise, almost like a swarm of bees.

"You're getting a tattoo?" I ask.

"I told you I had to."

"What? When?" This man has completely lost his mind.

"At dinner." He says it like I should know exactly what he's talking about. Heck, I can barely remember what I had for breakfast this morning.

A tall younger woman with curly black hair comes out from behind a curtain. "Mr. McCollin?" she asks and holds her hand out.

He nods and they shake hands.

She turns toward me, her smile growing. "You must be his little lion."

My cheeks warm and I bite my lip. *He told her I was his little lion. Gah!* I hold my hand out. "Kali." We shake hands and walk into the back room. She hands him a piece of paper and starts setting up.

Gage crooks his finger for me to come over to him. He hands me the paper, which holds an exquisite, complicated Dara knot entwined with wildflowers.

"You've left me no choice. After this is inked onto my chest, you won't be able to deny my marriage proposal any longer. Let the obsession begin."

I toss my head back and laugh, now understanding. "You've missed your stalker?"

We grin at each other. The tattoo takes a couple of hours, and after it's covered and he's dressed, we head out.

We pull into the hotel and walk into the lobby, hand in hand, my nerves starting to flow through me. I hope he says yes to living here, because I'm not taking no for an answer. But instead of heading to the elevators, Gage pulls me off to the side. He takes my long coat off and lays it across a chair near us, then grabs my hands. "Little lion." He squeezes my hands. "Before I met you, I was lost and didn't even realize it. Then you came along with your off-the-wall stories that had me standing there like a hypnotized idiot. You've challenged me every day and still do without hesitation. I love that about you. I can't forget about your make-believe husband, and I think that story was you internally telling me how perfect I am for you."

I laugh at his thought process. "Is that so?"

He releases my hands and cups my cheeks. "It most certainly is. I'm a huge and strong man," he says, puffing out his chest, causing me to giggle. "I may not have trophies sitting at home for wrestling, cage fighting, or martial arts, but I can guarantee you that this superhero can kick anyone's ass."

His charm is in full effect right now and his eyes are dancing with delight. "You've made me complete, and I can never thank you enough for giving me the strength to see my mother again. Marry me, little lion, right here, right now, and make me the happiest man in the world." His blue eyes smolder with heat and love.

All I want is to throw my arms wide and scream yes to this incredible man, but I can't. I pull back from him, instantly missing his warm touch on my cheeks. I take a deep breath. "Gage, I can't do it right now. I can't marry you without my brother and Harlow and Fletcher and even Aric. There aren't many people in this world who I keep close, but I need every single one of them there when I do."

His stunning smile is on show. "Is that all?"

I nod, confused that he's taking my rejection so easily.

He walks us over to a set of double doors and swings them open. Light spills into a grand ballroom, where everyone I love waits—dressed to the nines—like a dream sprung to life. Gilded trim gleams along the tall windows, and opulent chandeliers glitter overhead across richly colored walls.

Harlow's standing with a man I've never seen before. A date maybe? I'll be asking her about this new mystery man as soon as possible. Fletcher is on the other side of Harlow. Although he's a bit disheveled, he looks good, considering what he has been through. He doesn't seem to have a care in the world that Harlow brought someone along. That's strange.

Logan and Conner are standing next to Gage's younger brother Ashton, who I just met for the first time last night. Logan has a red mark under one eye and looks pissed when I first see him, but he softens when he catches sight of me. Cillian, Angela, and Aric are off to the side, along with Cillian's sons.

"Surprise!" they all shout.

I burst into tears.

"Oh shit! Babe, I'm sorry. I didn't mean to make you cry," Gage says, engulfing me in his arms.

I shake my head and beat on his hard chest. "Why do you have to be so damn perfect?"

His chest vibrates with laughter. "Because you deserve nothing less. Marry me, Kali."

I pull away, sure that my mascara has run down my cheeks, but I couldn't care less. "Yes! Yes, I will marry you!"

He pulls me into his arms, lifting me effortlessly, and for a moment I feel the weight of everything we've overcome. His warmth wraps around me, the safety of his embrace I have always felt. Our lips meet in a kiss and it holds everything. It's tender and full of promises.

Seven years ago, I lost almost everything. I never imagined I could have something like this again. Something as real and beautiful as the family I have now. They may not be blood, but I would fight for them until my last breath and I thank God for giving me this.

The End

Acknowledgements

When I was younger, I loved writing short stories and plays that my brothers and I would act out. Six years ago, a psychic asked me, "Why did you stop writing?" That question stuck with me. Two years later, I finished my first novel. (It's not this one—but maybe one day it will make its way into the world.)

It took another two years of Kali living rent-free in my mind before I gave in and started writing her story. She was relentless—funny, fierce, and full of life. I couldn't keep telling her no. I admired her strength, her humor, and the way she held onto hope, even when life gave her every reason to let go.

And then came Gage. He showed up and made it very clear that Kali was his—not Aric's—and there was no arguing with that. (He wouldn't let me even if I tried.)

This has been a long journey, full of doubt and learning and growth. Reaching this point feels like crossing a finish line I wasn't sure I'd ever see. And I couldn't have done it alone.

To James, my husband: You're my very own bad boy with a soft heart and I'm blessed to know you. You've been my anchor. Thank you for listening to me talk endlessly about this book and never once falling asleep on me. A glazed-over look? Occasionally. But not once did I catch you nodding off. Well done, popiah.

To Jeannie, my favorite beta reader: Thank you for taking the time to read my words even when your world was upside down. Your feedback didn't just help—it gave me the courage to share this story with others.

To Jessie Campbell, my editor: You are magic. Your attention to detail, your patience, and your above-and-beyond commitment have taught me so much. I would truly be lost without you.

To my family by blood and by love: Thank you for believing in me even before I believed in myself. I love you all more than words can say.

And to you, the reader holding this book in your hands: Thank you. Thank you for taking a chance on a new author. Every page you turn, every story you dive into... it means the world to me. Reviews are a powerful way to support authors, especially those just starting out. If this story resonated with you, I'd love to hear your thoughts.

XO

Sneak Peek

—

Forgotten Confessions

Chapter One

Logan.

Adrenaline hits different when you're somewhere you're not supposed to be, a place you were never meant to return to. A place you are no longer welcome. The excitement of being there causes your heart to pump harder in your chest. You can feel it throughout your entire body. The tingle, the exhilaration. Knowing what's to come before it even happens. Before anyone else. It's better than any drug in this world.

Three distinctive beeps sound in my earbuds as my screen turns from red to green.

Jackpot.

I waste no time slamming my laptop shut and yanking out the earbuds. A glance at my watch confirms it. Under ten minutes to breach the security system. Nine minutes and forty-four seconds, to be exact. Far too easy, and that only pisses me off. Sure, I've been doing this since I was a kid, honing my skills over the years, but this place? It should be locked down tighter than Fort Knox.

After all, what it holds is far more precious than gold.

I've been scoping the layout for three days now. The day after my sister cleared my name and got me released—the same day I learned my yearslong quest for justice was finally over—I couldn't think about anything else but coming here. Still, I took my time, refreshing my memory, watching the rhythm, and learning the current schedule. A schedule I will be adjusting immediately.

I rise from the porch steps, sling my bag over my shoulder, slowly turn the doorknob, and enter the sleeping home.

The sweet scent of vanilla greets me, and I welcome it. Breathing in deeply, I engulf myself in the familiarity, salivating for another taste. I set my bag beside the old couch and the many memories it holds, quietly slipping through the darkened rooms.

Everything is the same. The chocolate-colored furniture. The wood flooring. The stainless steel appliances. The deep blue paint on the walls. Nothing has changed, yet everything has. I may have been banned from coming back here, but the way my heart thumps against my chest, I know this is where I belong. Where I have always belonged.

And this time around, I'm not taking no for an answer. You don't get this gut-wrenching feeling when something feels so right, only to walk away. No, you claim it. There is no other option.

I already know what I'm walking into when I reach the last door at the end of the hallway. I have spent more time preparing myself for this exact moment than anything else. It's critical that I stay in complete control and not lose my temper. A rage has lived in my body for so long, I can't remember what it was like to feel any differently.

I cross the threshold, my eyesight already adjusted to the darkness. The knot in my stomach finally loosens. My muscles relax. I wasn't right, but I wasn't wrong either. This I can work with.

I stay in the shadows along the outer walls of the bedroom, not making a noise. I round the room, stopping beside the plush bed where the jackass lies. Knocked out cold, still recovering. His long hair is tied back into a man bun. The way he's sprawled across the pillows as if he's king of this castle ignites a fire in me. It would only take a single spark to detonate.

Only *I* will be her king.

Since the explosion, he's been on morphine while he sleeps. I know from hacking into his medical records that this is his last night on an IV, which makes this much easier for me. I remove the syringe from my pocket and push the drug through his IV. This is one show he will not be interrupting.

I step back and turn my attention to the real prize. A five-foot-five live wire that will put you six feet under if you're not careful. She's lying on her side, facing the back of a couch that sits near the foot of the bed.

A couch that was never in this room before. The fact that she's sleeping on a couch instead of being in bed with *him* shows the luck we all have tonight. Luck they aren't even aware of.

Her chestnut hair is fanned across the pillow, her beauty stealing my breath.

I stand over her, watching her eyelids twitch from the dream she's having. I wonder if she's dreaming about me. About the life we once lived—five years of fierce love and blind faith, back when we felt invincible to danger and were full of hope. Back when nothing could come between us. The sex was out of this world and our love was unbreakable.

Until it wasn't.

It's been seven years since it all fell apart, but sometimes it still feels like yesterday.

We fought every second of every damn day until it finally broke us. My entire world had exploded around me, and she refused to wait. Not more than a month later, she was already in bed with another man. A man she told me was her best friend and nothing more. The same man who is sleeping in the bed we used to share.

After all our late-night confessions to each other... I guess she's forgotten them all. I think it's a great time to remind her. I can't wait to walk down memory lane with this wildcat.

I see the handgun grip peeking out underneath her pillow. I drag out her .357, careful not to wake her, and slide it under the couch. She always has two weapons on her, so I know I'm missing one. But what fun would it be if I took both from her?

She's wearing a royal blue T-shirt and dark gray boy shorts. She's kicked the blanket off her, showcasing her toned athletic legs. Legs that I loved when they were wrapped tightly around my torso and I was buried deep inside her. I could stare at her sleeping body all night long, but even I know she will eventually stir from her beauty sleep and feel that something is off. The sun is going to rise soon, and when it does, it will change everything for her.

She rolls onto her back, letting out a soft sigh. I don't wait another second. I quickly snatch her wrists and hold them tightly with one of my hands as I slap my other gloved hand over her mouth. I lie on top of her, pinning her body beneath mine.

She doesn't disappoint. She's the most intoxicating woman I've ever met. She bucks wildly underneath me, trying to break her hands free. Her sleepy eyes are unfocused and confused, probably wondering how someone could've broken into her home without the alarm going off.

I guess her boy toy isn't as good at security as she thinks he is.

She bites down hard on my gloved hand, a move I was anticipating, but it does no good. The leather protects my skin from her kitten bite.

I lean against her fighting body. Pulling in her vanilla scent, I drag the tip of my nose along her neck, reach her earlobe, and place a small kiss under it. A growl rips out of her chest, and I can't stop my chuckle at how cute she is.

It must be the sound of my laugh that halts her fight. "Logan?" Her voice comes out muffled under my hand, but I know she said my name. It's the only name that should come from her sweet lips.

"Have you missed me, wildcat?" I whisper softly in her ear, adjusting my grip on her wrists.

"What the fuck? Get off me, you asshole." Her words come out muffled again, but I can catch her drift.

This is great.

She begins to fight again as I adjust my position on top of her. I smile at her reddened face. Her hair is disheveled, and she looks hot as hell. God, how I've missed her—even though I know I shouldn't.

I give her a disappointed "Tsk" and shake my head, then remove my hand from her mouth. "Careful. We wouldn't want to wake your boy toy over there."

As if just remembering she has a man sleeping in her bed, a bed that used to be ours, she quickly looks over. From the couch, she can't see much.

I decide in this moment I'm going to burn that bed come morning rise.

"If you hurt him, I'm going to cut your balls off and shove them so far down your—"

I crush my mouth against hers, silencing her worthless threats. I lose myself in the sweetness of her kiss, cool and sharp like spearmint.

She stiffens at first but quickly gives in, melting into me. This only fuels me further. I deepen our kiss and release her wrists. She slowly glides her hands to my shoulders, then caresses my arms, taking her time. Her touch is soft and familiar, awakening memories of the love we once shared. For a moment, it feels like time has rewound, erasing the pain of our past. Her warmth is a solace I have never stopped yearning for. A reminder that she was and still is everything I have ever wanted. A soft moan escapes her mouth. I press my body closer to hers, letting her know she has the same effect on me.

I run my gloved fingers down her side until I reach the hem of her T-shirt. Wanting to feel her skin against mine, I break our kiss and bring my hand to my mouth, biting the glove and pulling it off my hand. She leans up, capturing my lips again. I grab her hip bone and squeeze gently. My bare hand is running underneath her shirt when I feel a warm, sharp piece of metal press against my neck.

Ah, there it is. I almost forgot. The beauty's second weapon.

I smile, breaking our kiss and resting my forehead against hers, both of us breathing heavily. I push myself onto my elbows, the knife remaining tightly against the side of my throat. "I didn't know you're into knife play."

"I'm about to learn all about it if you don't get the fuck off me."

"Really? I would love to be your first." I lean into the blade. The pressure breaks my skin. A couple drops of blood drip onto her chin and neck.

We lock eyes, challenging each other to make the next move. If her dream is to slit my throat while I lie on top of her, then so be it. Without Harlow, I have nothing. I feel adrift, searching for direction. Looking for a place to belong. If she believes I belong in hell next to the devil, then who am I to argue with that?

She releases the knife, drops it to the floor, and pushes against my chest. I reluctantly sit up, trying but failing to hide my smile as she gets to her feet quickly. She didn't kill me. That has to mean something.

She races over to see if Fletch is hurt in any way. Fucker. She checks his fluids and feels his head—for what, I don't know. A fever? I think the guy has bigger concerns than a fever. I lean forward, grab the gun I slid under her couch, and pop open the chamber. It's fully loaded. *That's my girl.*

I give the chamber a spin and lock it into place. That finally gets her attention off Fletch and where it needs to be. I stand, adjusting myself without a hint of shame for what she made my body feel, and walk toward her.

"What did you do to him? Why isn't he waking up?"

I glance at good ole Fletcher boy, lying there helplessly. I can't stop the smile that creeps across my face. Karma's a bitch and when you fuck with another man's woman, life can take a sudden turn in the wrong direction.

Everyone believes hate is the strongest feeling. They are all wrong. Love is much stronger, making even the sanest person feel crazy.

"Your precious boy toy is fine. Don't worry your pretty little head." I spin the revolver around my finger before stopping it. The barrel now points at me. "I can't believe you still use this old gun." It was gifted to her by her grandparents. I engraved our initials into the grip many years ago.

She narrows her eyes and moves to take the gun from my outreached hand. She doesn't respond, but she doesn't need to.